STEPHEN J. CANNELL
THE DEVIL'S WORKSHOP

Also by Stephen J. Cannell

THE PLAN
FINAL VICTIM
KING CON
RIDING THE SNAKE

Coming Soon in Hardcover

THE TIN COLLECTORS

STEPHEN J. CANNELL

THE DEVIL'S WORKSHOP

HarperTorch
An Imprint of HarperCollinsPublishers

HARPERTORCH
An Imprint of HarperCollins*Publishers*
10 East 53rd Street
New York, New York 10022-5299

Copyright © 1999 by Stephen J. Cannell
Excerpt from *The Tin Collectors* copyright © 2001 by Stephen J. Cannell
ISBN: 0-380-73221-1

First HarperTorch paperback printing: November 2000
First William Morrow hardcover printing: September 1999

HarperCollins®, HarperTorch™, and ♦™ are trademarks of HarperCollins Publishers Inc.

Printed in the United States of America

Visit HarperTorch on the World Wide Web at
www.harpercollins.com

OPM 10 9 8 7 6 5 4 3 2 1

This is for
Leonard F. Hill

Acknowledgments

Heartfelt thanks to my loyal team of supporters, without whom I would be lost: My assistant (sometimes boss) for twenty-two years, Grace Curcio. She caught the first draft with all of my dyslexic misspellings and turned my hieroglyphics into English text in less than eight hours each day, a huge stenographic feat. Kristina Oster inputted the countless revisions and gave valuable creative suggestions. Wayne S. Williams, my friend and noodge, who annoyed me with millions of his suggestions, because most of them turned out to be right. Jo Swerling, who must have reread this novel at least ten times for continuity. It's a wonder he's not in a padded room somewhere, quoting some of Fannon Kincaid's long biblical speeches. My agents and friends, Eric Simonoff and Mort Janklow, who have given me sage career advice and helped with difficult choices. My supporters at William Morrow, who have become more than my publishers but my friends—most notably, my editor, Paul Bresnick (he bought my first novel and has been a valuable "ear" and work-mate ever since). Bill Wright has been incredibly supportive; Michael Murphy has added life and energy to all of our efforts; Sharyn Rosenblum has been there all the way, along with Paul's assistant, Ben Schafer. Thanks to Linda Stormes and Denis Farina for getting the books out, and to Marly Rusoff for her energy and hours of work on my behalf. Thanks to my supervising copyeditor, Bruce Giffords, who checks my facts and keeps me honest, and to Richard Aquan, who designs beautiful jackets.

In researching this novel, there were two major players: Dr.

Peter Heseltine, M.D., who was my scientific advisor and turned me on to Prions. Peter was there for my panicked phone calls; when I didn't have the next scientific beat, he told me how to fix it.

Dave Watson (regional director of the U.S. National Transportation Safety Board) gave me wonderful insight into the rail system; he told me about the White Train and its frightening cargo and, like Peter, was always available for questions along the way.

Without all of you, I would still be digging dirt in Chapter Two.

Finally, thanks to my wife, Marcia, who gives me the love and provides the safety that allows me to try this kind of work in the first place. Thirty-five years of my insanity and she's still there, on the other side of the bed each morning. . . . Go figure.

Science marches on blindly, without regard to the real welfare of the human race, or to any other standard, obedient only to the psychological needs of the scientists, and of the government officials and corporation executives who provide the funds for research.

—TED KACZYNSKI

Where God built a church, there the devil would also build a chapel. . . .

—MARTIN LUTHER KING, JR.

PROLOGUE

[1 9 9 5]

THE END

The tall Marine Captain stood next to his beautiful wife, looking into the open grave. His dress uniform with its brass buttons twinkled in the bright Southern California sunshine. One row of colorful Desert Storm combat ribbons was arranged on his chest directly under his Jump Wings. His Silver Star was a testament to his courage, his gallantry under fire.

The Minister was talking about the inevitability of death. ". . . God has his plan for all of us," he said.

The Marine never took his eyes off the damp hole in the ground, never looked up, never engaged the sympathetic stares of the others. Tall and handsome, he seemed every inch the hero, except for one thing . . . he couldn't stop crying. His shoulders slumped and quivered, his neck and chest heaved in powerful grief.

When the Minister was finished he motioned the young Captain to step forward to give the eulogy for his daughter, but Cris Cunningham could not move. He stood with his eyes down, sobbing uncontrollably.

"This is very hard," the Minister finally said, sympathetically. "We certainly all understand."

They were about to lower little Kennidi Cunningham into the ground. Her misshapen, tumorous body was at last hidden from the hateful stares of curious strangers; department store rubbernecks who would move away in horror when they saw her . . . distance shielding them from possible infection, while providing a second look at the sickness that had mangled her.

The Marine raised his tear-soaked eyes to the small, flower-draped casket, which contained his four-and-a-half-year-old daughter. The huge chrome hoist squatted ominously over the hole, a futuristic spider about to deposit its valuable mahogany cocoon.

Since Captain Cunningham could not stop crying, his father, Richard, finally stepped forward and took his place. He was tall, like his boy, and wore a look of deep concern. His eyes fluttered from his weeping son back to his granddaughter's coffin. "Little Kennidi tried," her grandfather said softly. "She fought with all her soul. But some things, as Father Macmillan has said, are just in God's hands from the start. Some things can't be changed. We will never forget her or her courage." Then he reached forward and took a white carnation off the casket, moved over, and handed it to his son's wife, Laura, who, like her husband, had not looked up. Her eyes, like his, were fixed on the hole that was about to receive their only child.

Both knew they would never have another.

The funeral reception was at Richard Cunningham's Pasadena mansion. It was a Spanish-style house on three beautiful land-scaped acres near the arroyo that ran south from the foothills.

The guests pulled up to the house and got out of their cars, wearing dark clothes and grim expressions. In the entry, the family had put the best picture they had of Kennidi up on an easel. She had been only eighteen months old when it was taken, but already you could see the misshapen swelling. The later photographs were all unacceptable.

The picture of Kennidi showed that she'd had her father Cris's intense blue eyes and blond hair, but that was where the resemblance stopped. The hemangioma tumors that had started growing in her almost from birth were already redesigning her smile and bulging her forehead, eventually numbering in the hundreds. Noncancerous growths made of tangled blood vessels, they grew in her eyelids and mouth and in clusters down her throat and spine. They distorted her speech, and in the end made it impossible for her to walk.

It was then, when she could no longer move, that Cris Cunningham, the Gulf War hero, the courageous Marine, had disappointed everyone.

He started drinking.

The doctors at Bethesda Naval Hospital had tried to explain Kennidi's horrible condition, but they could not be absolutely truthful, so they finally said that sometimes this sort of thing just happens. They said there was no explanation of why Kennidi had been born with this congenital sickness. They looked at the terror-stricken parents and mumbled meaningless platitudes. "Sometimes bad things happen to good people," they said, or "God has his own divine plan for each of us."

The doctors reduced the growths they could get at with laser surgery, shrinking some of them, but, in the end, Kennidi Cunningham could not withstand the ravages of the tumorous disease that was sweeping through her. The losing struggle went on for almost three years. The constant treatments provided only temporary relief, while Kennidi always seemed to be getting weaker and smaller. When she was four and a half, she finally died. It happened during abdominal surgery to relieve a blockage in her intestines.

Of course, the doctors at Bethesda knew it had not been God's divine plan that had killed her. They had already seen more than twenty similar cases.

Her own father had delivered the ghastly death sentence.

The guests filed past the touched-up photo of Kennidi and signed the book, leaving little messages of consolation next to their names. They wandered down to the pool, where a string quartet played softly. They stood quietly holding glasses of wine or punch, their too loud whispers pitting the sweet sad music like sand blown against a window.

By then, everybody knew the story, mostly because of the press coverage about the lawsuit the Cunningham family had filed against the U.S. Government.

None of that seemed to matter now.

Cris Cunningham stayed upstairs in his old bedroom while the mourners arrived. He knew, like the doctors at Bethesda, what had really happened to his daughter. After Kennidi's death four days ago, Cris had collapsed. His grip had finally been pulled loose by the endless tug of events.

Cris now sat on the bed, in the room where he had grown up. This place had been his first safe haven. He tried once more to find himself, sitting in the room where all of his values had once been formed, but his recollections were now skewed in the shifting dimension of Kennidi's death.

He had enjoyed victory after victory here: Scholastic All-American, UCLA quarterback, Rose Bowl MVP. He had dragged all the trophies back to this place and examined each honor carefully, searching for hidden meaning. He had been on such a frantic quest for achievement; he had never spent much time looking inward. Now he was *afraid* to look. Afraid of what was missing.

Even in high school, he'd begun to thrive on the adulation of others. He had tried to sort the meaning, looking for what his father called "the true elevating factors." Now the photographs and trophies from his "Golden Boy" youth mocked him from the shelves of his room and made him feel even more lost and alone than before.

Self-pity was not an emotion that suited Cris, and yet after Kennidi's death it engulfed him, filled his stomach with bile and his mind with confusion.

His father knocked on the door and entered, uninvited. Richard Cunningham had been Cris's inspiration growing up; a college All-American end at Michigan and a self-made millionaire. Cris had desperately wanted to please him and follow in his footsteps, until Kennidi got sick. After that, everything changed.

"Cris, you should come down. It's rude not to at least say hello," his father said. "Laura's down there handling it all by herself. You should go be with her."

"I killed her, Dad," Cris said softly. "I killed Kennidi. Nothing's going to change that. I can't face it. I can't."

"You didn't kill her. That's crazy," Richard said, his voice betraying the sharp new edge of impatience with his son. "If anything killed her it was the pyridostigmine bromide, or the insect repellent, the P.B.-Deet. It wasn't you; the lawsuit will eventually prove it. The new doctors say that . . ." He stopped because he could see he had lost his son's attention.

Cris was looking out the window now, at the old oak tree. He had often lain in his bed in this room looking at the gnarled, twisted limbs and leaves of the ancient oak, turning them into fanciful designs: a dog's head, a map of Alaska. Now he saw nothing but an old tree.

Richard didn't know what to do for his son. Cris's pain was so obvious and so potentially destructive that his father was both angered and paralyzed by it, as if any false move might send Cris crashing down into a cavern of emptiness from which he would not return.

Richard kept hoping Laura would find a way to help. She and Cris had dated since high school. She knew him better than anyone, but Richard had noticed that she seemed to look at her husband now with something close to hatred. Cris's drinking was getting steadily worse. His son, whom he had pushed to greatness, who had been a hero, first on the football field and then the battlefield, had now chosen the coward's way out. He had chosen self-doubt, self-pity, and alcohol.

"Cris, please. . . . Come downstairs."

Cris looked up at his father and finally nodded.

As it turned out, it would have been better had he stayed in his room. Cris got drunk, and while the combo played "Memories," he fell into the pool.

When they fished him out, his drenched uniform clung to him. It was easy to see he had lost quite a bit of weight.

Again upstairs in his room, Cris sat on his bed and cried. His father looked at him from the door, not sure what to do. "Son, you've got to get ahold of yourself. Kennidi's gone. She wouldn't want this. You've got to make a new start," Richard said.

When Cris looked up at him, Richard saw such hopelessness in his son's vacant stare that he was momentarily stunned by it.

"It's *all* gone. This whole thing is over, Dad," Cris said, as he waved a wet sleeve at his trophies. His voice was a monotone of despair. "I can't start over. It's in me. I'm poisoned by it. There's nothing left." The next thing he said chilled his father with its finality. "It's the end," the Golden Boy whispered.

Part One

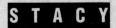

STACY

[1 9 9 9]

Chapter 1

ANYTHING'S FAIR IN A QUAL

Wendell Kinney reached out and squeezed Stacy Richardson's hand for luck. "Just remember, take your time," he said. "It doesn't hurt to platform your answers. There's no time limit, but Courtney always likes to be done by lunchtime, so if we can be out of there by noon that'll help. Ninety-eight percent on your Written is impressive, so this should be easy. And don't worry about Art, I'll keep him on his chain."

It was eight A.M., Tuesday, and they were in the third-floor hall of the old Science Building at the University of Southern California, just outside of Dr. Courtney Smith's office. Stacy Richardson was about to take her qualifying oral exam for her doctorate in microbiology. She'd been existing on less than two hours' sleep a night all through her last review week; probably a mistake, because she needed to be fresh for the "Quals," but the backbreaking job of reviewing four years of complicated microbiology was mind-boggling.

She'd been on the phone late last night for an hour with her husband, Max, who was in Fort Detrick, Maryland. He'd talked her down off her narrow, anxious ledge, getting her back on the ground with sure-handed reason. He reminded her of her academic track record. Throughout her three and a half years of doctoral study, she had carried a 3.9 cumulative G.P.A. He promised her she'd be fine. There had been a moment during the conversation when she'd sensed from his voice that something was very wrong and had asked him about it.

After a long reflective pause he'd said, "This isn't anything like I'd expected. I don't think I belong here, and they sure as hell don't want me." He'd refused to say anything more, because he didn't want to distract her with his problems on the eve of the Quals. Her orals were the last hurdle and would determine whether Stacy would end up with a Ph.D. after her name.

Dr. Max Richardson was head of the Microbiology Department at USC. She had met him in her first post-grad semester. He ran an open lab on viruses and she had listened to his lectures, marveling at the intricacies of his scientific mind and the strong masculine shape of his personality, and okay, his body too. Their romance caused a furor in the department. Dating students was definitely not allowed. Before it became a full-fledged disaster they'd gotten married, legitimizing it, and everything had died down.

Six months after the wedding, Max's federal research grant came through. He'd been working in a new field of microbiology, evaluating killer proteins called "Prions." Max's research had won him a six-month sabbatical to study at the Army Medical Facility at Fort Detrick, Maryland, with Dr. Dexter DeMille, the leading U.S. microbiologist on Prion research.

They'd discussed the bad timing. With Stacy just months from her orals, Max had not wanted to be away, especially since Art Hickman, his mortal enemy in the department, was also on the Advisory Panel, which would be evaluating her. Max and Art had both been up for Department Chair. Max had gotten the job, and Art had been backbiting him ever since. In the end, Stacy and Max

had both decided that the chance to work with Dr. DeMille at Fort
Detrick was such an incredible opportunity for Max that he should
take it. Stacy said she would just study her brains out so that Art
Hickman would not be able to fault her performance.

Wendell Kinney was also on her panel. He was a rumpled old
Microbiology Department lion and a great friend to both Max
and her.

"Remember," Wendell said, bringing her thoughts back, "anything's fair in a Qual. These guys can and will ask you about
everything. Courtney Smith loves her Sterilization and Disinfection
discipline, so she's bound to ask you something on that. And Art
Hickman will drill you on his damned arachnids."

"I wish he'd stayed in the bush with those fucking spiders,"
Stacy said, letting out a sigh that blew a wisp of her long, honey-
blond hair up in the air in front of her. She grabbed the strand and
tucked it behind her ear.

It didn't help that just about everybody felt that Stacy Richardson was drop-dead beautiful. Immediately after she enrolled in the
doctorate program, Art Hickman had tried to become her mentor.
He said he wanted to take her under his wing, but it was soon
apparent it wasn't his wing he wanted her under. She had efficiently dodged him. Art had taken it okay until she'd fallen in love
with and married his departmental rival. He'd been lobbing gre-
nades ever since.

The door opened and Dr. Courtney Smith was standing in the
threshold of her office. There was always at least one woman on
the Advisory Panel when another woman was up for her doctorate.
Choosing Courtney's office for the orals was another extension of
that political agenda.

Courtney Smith was a mannish, Janet Reno–sized biologist who
wore pant suits that were always several sizes too small, as if she
was desperately trying to convince herself she was still a twelve
when she had long ago moved into the "generous" sizes. The
shoulders in her boxy suit were padded to try to give the impres-

sion of a waist, also a lost horizon. She was holding a sheaf of folders against her ample chest.

"Today's the day," Dr. Smith smiled, showing a grayish row of tombstone-shaped teeth.

"Yep. Hope I'm up to it," Stacy nervously replied, as she followed Dr. Smith into the small office.

Stacy had given up wearing skirts and dresses in favor of blue jeans and sweatshirts in an effort to disguise her figure. It was hard to be taken seriously while tenured department morons like Art Hickman referred to her as Max's "Hood Angel."

For her qualifying orals, she had chosen to wear loose flannel slacks, which did nothing for her, and a T-shirt under a blue blazer. She had her hair pinned up with a brown plastic clip and wore no makeup.

She looked fantastic.

The office was small and stuffy. It was April, but the Santa Anas had been blowing a hot wind across the L.A. basin, driving the temperature up into the mid-eighties.

Courtney motioned to the window. "They never have the air-conditioning on this time of year and that window got painted shut around the turn of the century, so I called maintenance to bring us a fan. They should be here any minute."

"It's okay. It's fine, Dr. Smith," Stacy said, her heart jack-hammering, her hands flapping around her like small bony sparrows. She told herself to calm down. After all, she'd been having breakfasts with the entire panel at least once a week, all through the year. She knew them all well.

It was the practice for doctorate students to get as close to their advisors as possible. The faculty viewed this exercise as an attempt to make friends, so students could come to them with study problems, but any post-grad would tell you the real reason from the students' perspective was to psych out the advisor's pet projects or pet peeves. Hopefully one could discern what might be asked on the oral.

Now Art Hickman appeared in the doorway, pushing his new swivel chair. He was heavy-set, and his blow-dried, combed-over blond hair tented a patch of open scalp. A sharp, clipped mustache seemed a misplayed note in a symphony of fleshy curves. "Am I the last?" he said, then turned to Stacy, grinning wolfishly. "Well, Mrs. Richardson, are we ready?" Using her married name was a slap not lost on any of them. Art glanced in Courtney's office. "Where's H.R.?" he asked, referring to Dr. Horace Rosenthal.

"Here," a voice caroled from down the hall, and then Dr. Rosenthal appeared, a large, worn briefcase in hand. He was tall and slender and always wore bow ties. He was "Mr. Plant Virus." Rosenthal could talk for hours on vegetable diseases, soil antigens, and whatnot. Stacy had read all his published papers, searching for his pet theories.

"Stacy. Big day," Horace said, smiling. He had ivory-white skin. Blue veins roadmapped under a papery complexion that suggested he rarely got outside. His bow tie this morning was a cherry-red number with, of all things, a pattern of tiny clocks on it. *Who was it that said, "Nobody ever takes a man in a bow tie seriously,"* Stacy thought nervously.

"Let's get going," Courtney said. "Horace, you can drag that extra chair over from the window."

Rosenthal grabbed the oversized upholstered chair and tugged it around like a rusted gun battery to face the room. Stacy was offered a metal student's chair, but she elected to remain standing. Wendell Kinney winked at her and kicked the door shut.

"Okay," Art Hickman said. "To begin with, 'snaps' on a great Written. You really aced that puppy." He liked to try to sound hip, using the vernacular of his students. "But, as you know, the qualifying orals are intended to be a much wider-ranging set of questions. What we're trying to determine is, not your technical or book expertise, but more how you will deal with the broader, less defined concepts of microbiology."

"I understand," she said.

"Any of us might interrupt you at a given point in your answer and ask for definitions or elaborations of your thoughts, or perhaps even redirect you. Don't view that as criticism. We are only searching the corners of your knowledge," he continued.

"Yes, Doctor, I understand."

"It'd be nice if we could be finished by lunch. I hate sending out," Dr. Courtney Smith said.

Wendell Kinney shot Stacy a slight smile. *He sure called that one,* she thought. If she passed her Quals she would only have her doctorate thesis left, and most of them had already read sections of that emerging document entitled "Neurotransmission in Rhabdovirus Infection of Raccoon Species." It promised to be an exceptional piece of student science.

"So, let's get started," Wendell Kinney said, cheerfully.

Here we go, Stacy thought, crossing her fingers behind her back.

"I'd like you to explain the possible relationship of herpes viruses to multiple sclerosis," Dr. Hickman began, brushing his fingers across his neat little mustache.

"Yes," Stacy said, clearing her throat to buy a few seconds.

"Take your time, Stacy. You don't have to rush your answers," Wendell reminded her.

"Yes, thank you, Doctor. . . . According to a recent study, seventy percent of the patients with the most common form of MS showed signs of active infection with human herpes virus six."

"*A* study, Mrs. Richardson?" Art Hickman interrupted. "What study? The study of California muffler mechanics? Let's be specific."

"Uh, the . . . the finding was reported in the December issue of *Nature and Medicine,* and was conducted at the University of Minnesota. . . . And uh . . . Research Associates funded it, a government bio-research funding bank. The study was annotated by—"

"That's okay," he cut her off. "Just don't use generalities. Go on." He was still stroking his bullshit mustache.

"Yes, Doctor." She continued, "Representational differences

were used to search for pathogens in multiple sclerosis brain tissue . . .''

Joanne Richardson almost hit the University policeman as she pulled her car into the Science Campus lot, parking her red Toyota sloppily across two spaces.

The cop moved to the passenger window of her car and glared in angrily. Joanne was gathering up her purse and had her head down as he rapped on the window.

''Hey! You almost ran me down!'' he growled through the glass. When she looked up, he could see that she was crying. Tears were streaming, running her mascara, leaving black clown smudges.

''Where's the Science Building?'' Joanne sobbed, rolling down the window.

''You almost hit me,'' the University cop said, his anger coasting to an awkward stop as he looked at the pretty twenty-year-old.

''Where is it? I have to get there, now.''

He finally relented. ''The new Science Building or the old Science Building?''

''I don't know, she didn't say.''

''You looking for classrooms or faculty?''

''Faculty,'' she said, choking back a sob.

''First, center this vehicle inside the lines, then go along this walk, past Sprague Hall, turn left at the statue of Tommy Trojan. It's three buildings down, on the left, a big brick job.''

She reparked the car, quickly got out, and ran up the street. It only took her a few minutes to find the building. She ran up the steps into an entry that was filled with glass cases. Some contained faculty awards, some had student projects. Years of Lysol had turned the light gray linoleum floor yellow. There was a reception desk in front of the elevators, where an Assistant Professor sat grading papers, guarding the entrance like a soccer goalie.

"I need Dr. Courtney Smith's office," Joanne said, out of breath.

The Assistant Professor looked up at the tear-streaked face across from him. "Third floor, but I'm sorry, you can't go up there. She's giving orals."

"I've got to talk to my sister-in-law, Stacy Richardson. It's important."

"You can't break into her Quals. You'll just have to wait down here."

"For how long?" Joanne asked, her voice cracking pitifully.

"Could be three or four hours, maybe longer."

"I can't wait." She turned, and forgoing the elevators, ran around him and up the stairs.

The Assistant Professor dropped the paper he was grading and bolted after her.

Joanne got to the third floor and ran down the corridor. None of the offices had names on them, just numbers. She started to look for a directory board, but the man finally caught up with her and grabbed her arm.

"I need to talk to Stacy. She's in Dr. Smith's office," Joanne repeated.

"I told you, you can't talk to her. She's taking orals."

"It's an emergency!" Joanne paused to catch her breath. "Her husband just committed suicide!"

Dr. Horace Rosenthal had abandoned his beloved plant viruses to ask a question on HIV infection. "Give us an identification of the chemokine receptor expressed in brain-derived cells and T-cells as a new co-receptor for HIV infection."

"We have isolated HIV-1 variants that infect brain-derived CK4 positive cells . . ." Stacy began, as there was a knock at the door.

"We're in Quals!" Dr. Smith bellowed at the door. "Go on, Stacy."

"Those cells are resistant to both macrophage M-tropic and T-cell line . . ."

Again, there was a pounding at the door.

"Goddammit," Courtney Smith said, coming up out of her chair, charging the door like an NFL lineman, and yanking it open. "I said we're in Quals!"

"This is an emergency," the Assistant Professor said, pointing to the tear-stained girl beside him. "She needs to talk to Ms. Richardson."

Joanne moved into the office. She had stopped crying, but when she looked at Stacy, she choked slightly. "Max is dead," she blurted.

"What?" Stacy said, her voice too loud.

"He's dead. I just got the call. They couldn't reach you, so they called me."

"How?" Stacy's mind was jumbled. Already a wave of nausea had hit the pit of her stomach.

"They . . . the doctor said he shot himself."

"He what . . . ?" Stacy's mind was reeling. She looked over at Wendell Kinney, who had his bushy leonine head in his hands. Then she happened to glance at Art Hickman, who had a total lack of expression on his face, as if his conflicting emotions over this news allowed him no reaction. His hands, she noticed, were spread in front of him, pushing against the desk, almost as if he were trying to get away.

"Suicide?" Stacy said, and now she started to feel a mixture of emotions too complex to even describe. There was fear and disbelief, terror, anger . . . loss. Then came the tears.

Joanne moved to her and put her arms around her sister-in-law. They stood there in the room full of microbiology professors and held on to each other.

"Are you sure? You're sure it was . . . real . . . not some horrible practical . . ." Stacy couldn't finish.

"I called back. I talked to a Colonel Laurence Chittick at Fort

Detrick. He said . . . Max went into the backyard late last night. He sat on a kitchen chair and stuck a shotgun in his mouth and . . ." Now it was Joanne who couldn't finish.

Wendell Kinney got to his feet. He put an arm around Stacy. "Obviously," he said to the other doctors in the room, "we're postponing this exam."

They all nodded. Their faces were anguished. Except for Art, everybody had loved Max Richardson.

"Let's go to my office," Wendell said, and he led the two women out of Dr. Smith's office and down the hall.

It was four o'clock in the afternoon, and they were back in Max and Stacy's apartment on Alameda Boulevard, just off the University campus. It was a small, cluttered flat in a bad section of Los Angeles. USC was located in a high-crime area and living off campus was a calculated risk. The walls of the apartment were decorated with the modern art that Max liked to collect: Chagall and Picasso prints that only cost forty dollars apiece, but which Max had put in expensive frames to give the illusion of the real thing. He once told her if he ever won the Nobel he would blow a hundred grand and buy a small original. Their two offices were a testament to their different personalities. Max's was in the spare bedroom and was pin neat. Stacy had taken over the pantry and it looked like ground zero at a paper-shredding factory.

Everywhere she glanced she could see her dead husband . . . hear his voice or remember some funny, endearing moment. Augie, the Raccoon, sat in ceramic goofiness on a living-room shelf. Augie was a truly monstrous piece of pottery that Max had bought for her when she was pissed off about a paper she'd been assigned to write on new rabies strains in raccoons. "It's stupid science," she'd told him. Augie was up on his hindquarters, his little ceramic paws outstretched, as if he were soliciting a hug. Max bought him at a student's garage sale and named him Augie, after the Rabies Augmentation Study in Ohio and Pennsylvania, which was the jumping-off point for her paper. He had placed Augie on her desk one evening and said, "You're saving this adorable little guy with your 'stupid science.' Don't give up on the masked rodent."

She had gotten an A on the paper, which had speculated on the viability of using targeted bait to deliver different antivirus liquids into different species of raccoons in the wild. Her paper was published in *Animal Science Magazine*. "Whoopee," she'd said sarcastically, when she got the magazine's acceptance letter and a check for five hundred dollars. But she'd been ashamed of herself and embarrassed that Max had been so right. No science was stupid science if it pushed back a new boundary or asked a new question. All of it had value if it added to the information pool.

"He didn't commit suicide," Stacy said three or four times in the last hour, hanging on to it, as if that one possible inaccuracy would make the whole thing a lie.

"But they said he shot—"

"I don't give a shit what they said, Joanne," she interrupted, "he didn't commit suicide. I talked to him last night till almost one A.M. He was not fucking depressed!" Anger was now taking center stage inside her. Her lover and mentor had been snatched from her at some godforsaken military lab in Maryland, and that fact was now untenable and totally unacceptable.

Wendell sat in the living room, looking at the two distraught women. Joanne was still tearing up, but Stacy, after crying for an hour, had given in to her natural instinct, which was to come out swinging. She had replaced the tears with anger and a stubborn, iron-willed determination. Wendell wasn't an expert on grieving, but he knew that the first stage was denial. This insistence on Stacy's part that Max had not committed suicide sounded like a form of denial to him, but he wasn't quite sure how to deal with it.

"Look, Stace," he said softly, "I think we need to consider—"

"You were his friend, Wendell," she interrupted, her eyes glinting anger. "Do you honestly believe he blew his head off with a shotgun? Do you? It's bullshit!" She shook her head. "Maybe it wasn't even him." She looked at Joanne. "I mean, if his head was blown off, maybe they just think it was him, but it was somebody else."

"Stacy, I think the doctors at Fort Detrick wouldn't make that kind of mistake," Wendell said.

"Max told me last night that he didn't belong there. He said, 'I don't think they want me either.'" She looked up at Wendell.

"That could mean anything. Maybe they didn't accept some of his science. Or maybe he was just having a bad day."

"Bad day? Yeah, sure, that's gotta be it," she said, biting the words off one at a time.

She stood and moved into her bedroom, past the wall-mounted punching bag. Max had painted a frown face on the bag, and on each stitched section he had written a word: INFERENCE—CONCLUSION—ILLATION—JUDGMENT, the four pillars of deductive reason. When Max was stumped on some science problem, he'd stand in front of the bag and fire away. He had been on the boxing team at Stanford and could really get the bag going in a steady rhythm, his athletic body shining with sweat, while working on some brain-stumping hypothesis.

Stacy started throwing things in an overnight case, not even choosing outfits. It was just the act of packing, the feeling of doing something, that she needed.

Joanne and Wendell stood at the door, watching her flurry of activity.

"You're going to Fort Detrick?" Wendell asked.

"Yes," she said through clenched teeth, her emotions still coming in waves. Her anger could, in a matter of seconds, recede and be overtaken by grief so overpowering that it almost buckled her. She was trying desperately not to give in to it. Max was gone. A fact that was impossible for her to fully grasp. He had been her soul mate, her perfect fit. She would never replace him.

"You're going to go back there and accuse those people of misidentifying the body?" Wendell asked. His voice was gentle, sympathetic. "You think that's a good idea?"

"Wendell, someone has to claim Max's body. Someone has to bring him back for burial. That's my job. I'm his wife," she challenged. "And while I'm at it, I'm gonna ask a few bloody goddamn questions about why a guy who had no history of depression, no overriding negative perceptions on either his life or career, after just two months at fucking Fort Detrick, suddenly goes out into his backyard, sits on a kitchen chair, and . . . Oh God. . . ." She shuddered like a spaniel coming out of the water. She shook herself, throwing her hair back, then bit her lip and held on until the moment passed. Then she straightened her shoulders. "Well, I don't buy it!" She slammed her suitcase shut without remembering to put in her toiletries.

"I'm going with you," Joanne said.

"I can do it, honey . . . really."

"He was my big brother. I wanna go with you. I *need* to go with you."

"I'll book us a flight."

"This is not smart," Wendell said. "The doctors at the Fort can make arrangements to ship Max back here."

"I'm sure they can," Stacy said, spitting the words out like fruit seeds, "but I'm not going to give 'em the chance."

She moved into the pantry, booted up her computer, used her search engine to get to "Airlines," then to "Travel Schedules." She found a nine-P.M. Delta flight that arrived at five A.M. at Dulles Airport in Virginia, which was forty miles from Fort Detrick. She accessed reservations, booked two seats for that evening, typed in her credit card number, and downloaded her confirmation. Then she went into the bathroom, closed the door, sat on the toilet, and stared at herself in the mirror.

She looked drawn and frightened. She studied her eyes and mouth. The reflection didn't look like her. It was a new mask, as if her face had melted, then stretched and dried differently in the heat from this disaster. When the anger left her, she felt the hopeless grief. "Max . . . Max," she said, wailing at her reflection, "why did you leave me?"

Wendell knocked on the door and called to her.

"You okay?"

"I'm fine," she choked out bravely.

Why do people do that? she wondered. *A stupid question followed by a lie.*

Ten minutes later, she steeled herself again, then got up off the toilet and moved back into the bedroom, looking at her watch, then at Joanne.

"We'd better hurry if we're going to get all the way to your house, get you packed and back to the airport by eight."

Joanne got up off the bed and they all left the bedroom. Stacy was the last to exit, and she paused for a minute in front of the punching bag. She could picture Max in his pajama bottoms in front of the bag, smiling. *"If I hit this thing hard enough everything seems to make sense,"* he had once told her. So Stacy put down her suitcase and faced the bag. "I'm gonna go kick us some ass, baby," she whispered to his memory. Then she hit the bag as hard as she could.

Chapter 2

A COMMUNITY OF EXCELLENCE

The cab turned off Military Road, past a huge monument sign
that read:

FORT DETRICK

A COMMUNITY OF EXCELLENCE

The letters were electrified, and the monument sat on a manicured
front lawn by the stone-pillared main gate like a misplaced theater
marquee. Three flags whipped in a cold April breeze. The American flag stood tallest in the middle; next to it the flag of Fort
Detrick and the state flag of Maryland. The main post sat on four
hundred acres at the corner of a twelve-hundred-acre government
site. The taxi stopped at the gate while a uniformed Marine M.P.
with a white helmet and webbed pistol belt told them that Colonel
Chittick was officed in Building 810, one block east of Doughton
Drive. He handed the driver a map and let them pass.

The buildings that made up the old section of the Fort were
four-story dark brick structures that had been originally built in the

late forties. They were blocky and rectangular with no design significance. Over the years as the Fort expanded, a startling variety
of architectural styles had surfaced: boxy stucco buildings from the
fifties, concrete tilt-ups popular in the sixties, followed lately by
the steel and glass of the eighties and nineties. Fort Detrick was a
huge, grassy, campus-like facility with thousands of personnel,
both military and civilian. Max had told her that most of the Fort
had been demilitarized in the seventies, when President Nixon had
shut down the U.S. bio-weapons program. The Army still main-
tained a defense bio-research facility that was under strict military
controls. There were officers, both men and women, in every uniform of the U.S. Armed Services moving briskly along the cement
walkways. There were an equal number of people in white lab
coats.

The taxi pulled up in front of Building 810, which was one of
the old brick-faced structures. Joanne and Stacy got their bags out
of the trunk.

"Thanks," Stacy said, paying the driver, who promptly drove
off. She was surprisingly calm, in what she had come to realize
was one of her "disconnect" stages. During a disconnect, her mind
could deal with Max's death as an abstract fact, as something that
had simply happened: *Max is gone. I loved Max. He was my reason
for being. I'll deal with it. I'm functioning.* In this state, these were
just thoughts, not devastating downdrafts that threatened to blow
her against untenable realities. During her disconnects, she was
strangely detached from all of it. Then, just as suddenly, her mind
would swell with anguish and those same concepts would threaten
to drive her to her knees.

She suspected her disconnects were part of the protective mech-
anism built deep in her psyche that allowed her to deal with only
so much grief at one interval. Then she would click into abstract
mode, where, for a few minutes or an hour, she was able to break
out of the black and get a few breaths of air before she would be
pulled down again.

After the cab drove off, the two of them stood uncertainly in front of Building 810. Now that she was here, looking at the huge military medical facility, her idea that she would go kick ass and find out why Max was dead seemed foolish, if not impossible. Somehow, in her mind, when she had envisioned Fort Detrick, she'd made it small and insignificant, like the wooden fort in *F-Troop*. The real Fort Detrick was a huge, menacing facility, with monument signs and flags, full of dedicated, bustling professionals. More than a fort, it seemed a fortress.

"So, let's go talk to this guy," Stacy finally said, gathering her resolve as she and Joanne picked up their overnight bags and moved past the monument sign that read:

BUILDING 810

HEADQUARTERS AND ADMINISTRATION

FORT DETRICK

Colonel Chittick's office was on the fourth floor in the corner, and was a large, square room with wood floors, rectangular windows, and a huge desk. His assistant, an Army Captain with red hair and a mustache, showed them into the empty office. On the walls were pictures of different units that Colonel Chittick had been assigned to. In the shots, the men were arranged in rows like football teams. Under each picture were the unit designations. Stacy was looking at one, labeled:

5TH MEDICAL BATTALION

SAN MARCOS, PHILIPPINES, 1968

She was wondering which of the hundred or so men in the shot was Colonel Chittick, when the door opened and a surprisingly handsome fifty-year-old man in an Army Colonel's uniform entered the office. He had silver-gray hair, a square jaw, and beautiful rows of even, white teeth. On his lapels were the winged medical insignias. He was a recruiting poster doctor, she thought, who now wore an appropriate look of troubled sympathy and grief.

"Mrs. Richardson? I'm Colonel Chittick, and I'm so sorry to meet you under these tragic conditions," he said softly, shaking her hand.

"Thank you," she said, and then motioned toward Joanne. "This is Max's sister, Joanne."

The Colonel shook her hand, then nodded his head, a silent genuflection to their grief. "May I offer you a seat?" he said, and led them to the sofa on the far side of the room, which sat under a huge framed Medical Battalion flag.

The Colonel chose an adjoining chair. "I really didn't know your husband at all," he began gently. "He was working with Dr. DeMille over in USAMRIID—that's the U.S. Army Medical Research Institute of Infectious Diseases. It houses the largest biocontainment lab in the U.S.," he said with a tinge of pride, as if Stacy had no understanding of Max's work. "I understood that your husband was a wonderful, dedicated scientist." He paused before heading into uncertain, potentially dangerous terrain. "I guess sometimes a high-powered mind like his can possess a strange mix of both brilliance and tortured emotions." His voice was slick and cold: Vaseline on ice.

"I'm sorry, what?" Stacy asked, her chin coming up, thrusting forward.

"What I meant was, a genius as complex and gifted as your husband probably found it difficult to live with both his huge intellect and his complicated inner thoughts."

"I thought you just said you didn't know him," Stacy challenged.

"Well, I didn't. I . . . what I meant was, often this is the case. With superior intellect there is sometimes also emotional instability."

"Well, if you didn't know him, Colonel, why don't you keep

those opinions to yourself. Max was very squared-away. He was not some geek scientist, lost in the intellectual ozone.''

"All I meant . . ." He stopped and nodded. "I'm sorry, I take your point."

He was now obviously humoring her. Stacy Richardson was beginning to take a giant dislike to Colonel Laurence Chittick.

They all sat looking at each other, searching for the right thing to say next. Stacy had an uncontrollable urge to get away. "We're here to make arrangements to take Max's body back to California," she said.

Colonel Chittick subtly replaced his expression of gentle concern with a look of mild consternation.

"Is that a problem?" Stacy asked.

"Well, no . . . It's just . . . you mean his remains, I think?"

"I mean his body," she corrected.

"You know, of course, he was cremated?"

"He was *what*?" She looked at Colonel Chittick, her mouth slightly ajar, staring in abject disbelief.

"He was cremated yesterday."

"Who gave you permission to cremate him?" Her voice was ringing against the white walls in the large office.

"He did."

"*He* did?"

"It was in his medical folder, under 'death requests.' Everybody stationed here, both civilian as well as military personnel, fills one out."

"Colonel, he did not want to be cremated. I know, because we discussed it. He bought several plots next to his mom and dad at Forest Lawn when they both died. He wanted the whole family to be buried there, with them."

"He must have changed his mind."

"What the hell's going on here?" she suddenly said, rising off the sofa.

.   "Maybe you need to tell *me,* Mrs. Richardson."

Stacy turned to Joanne, who was sitting up straight, her knees tight together, hands folded in her lap like a good girl waiting outside the principal's office. "Joanne, did your brother want to be cremated?"

"No. Like you said, we bought all the graves side by side, next to Mom and Dad. There's six of them."

Colonel Chittick got up from the occasional chair and moved around to his desk, opened a folder, rummaged in it for a second, found a sheet of paper, and handed it to Stacy. "Here's his death request sheet."

"It's not signed, Colonel," she said, looking at it.

"It wasn't the last page of the medical form. I have that here, with his signature." He again rummaged around for a paper and found it, holding it out to her.

Stacy didn't take it. She was reading the death request sheet. "Under 'Religion' you list seven denominations, and there's just a check next to Catholic. 'Have you had any of the following diseases?' Check, check, check. These are just check marks. Anybody could have filled this out, put this sheet in there."

"And now you're making some sort of accusation?" Colonel Chittick no longer looked like Ward Baxter. Now his skin was stretched tight across his jaw, his eyes were piercing and dangerous.

"Colonel Chittick, my husband did not commit suicide. He had no suicidal tendencies."

"I don't know that you're in a position to judge that, Mrs. Richardson."

"And you *are?* Some guy with a buncha fruit salad on his coat, who never even met him?"

Colonel Chittick moved away from his desk and stood directly before her. Although he towered over Stacy, she held her ground. "You are forcing me to take this into areas I would rather not go."

"Help yourself. If you've got something, let's hear it!"

"Your husband seemed to some of the people he was working with here to have an overly volatile personality. He was subject to huge mood swings."

"That's absurd."

Chittick moved back to the desk, pulled a few official forms out of the folder, and handed them to her. "These are, for want of a better term, colleague complaints, filed by his co-workers here. There were even some suggestions that Max was a possible substance abuser."

"Go fuck yourself!" Stacy said.

Colonel Chittick was unprepared for this. Finally, he recovered and said, "That would seem to bring this interview to a close."

"Substance abuse? Of course we'll never know, because you burned up his body!"

"We complied with your husband's stated requests."

"I don't know what happened here, Colonel, but my husband didn't commit suicide. He didn't use drugs! He wasn't depressed, and he never asked you to cremate him! I think this is some kind of giant cover-up, and I'm gonna find out why!"

"Of course, you're welcome to pursue any legal avenue of redress you find worthwhile. And now . . . I have his ashes, if you'd like to take them, or we can send them to any address you leave with my secretary."

Joanne started crying softly on the sofa. Stacy became aware of her sobbing and turned to her. "It's okay, honey. Let's just get out of here." She helped her sister-in-law off the sofa, and they moved to the door.

"Mrs. Richardson," Colonel Chittick said.

Stacy turned and glowered at him.

"It is very hard to lose a loved one." The recruiting poster guy was back. "Anger is the shadow that always follows death, and it is not uncommon for people to have an urge to strike back."

"Colonel, you haven't seen anything yet," she promised.

Chapter 3

DR. DUC

They were standing in front of Building 810 with their luggage, a cold wind whipping the hems of their dresses. Joanne was still sobbing and Stacy still burning mad.

"That fucking guy . . . who does he think he is?" she said. "A drug user? Max with mood swings? He was the steadiest guy on the planet. He ran the microbiology program at USC. He got that job because he was calm and organized, as well as brilliant. He wasn't some X-over-Y geek head case."

Joanne continued to cry and made no response. Her shoulders were down, her chin on her chest.

"Honey," Stacy said firmly, "I know you're torn up. So am I. But these people are lying. They're lying about Max, and if they're lying, the next question is 'Why?' And why did they burn his body? Were they trying to destroy evidence? What the hell happened here?"

Joanne looked up, tears still wet on her cheeks. Stacy reached into her purse, pulled a fresh tissue out of a travel pack, and handed it to her sister-in-law. "I want to find out what's going on, and I

may need your help, but you can't help me if you don't pull yourself together.''

Joanne wiped her eyes, sniffed, then blew. ''How are you going
to find out what went on? They're not going to tell you anything,''
she said.

''I don't know how Army docs are, but I know how civilian
medical people think. It's standard procedure on a suicide to do
an autopsy. I suppose the same holds true on a military base. If I
ask Colonel Chittick for a copy of the autopsy, I'll probably just
get ten pages of creative writing. So, I'm going to get Max's autopsy report myself.''

''And they're just going to give it to you?''

''Let's go find out.''

They went into the Base Information Center and got the Fort
Detrick phone book. They took it to one of the long wooden tables
at the far end of the room and sat there under the stare of a grand-
motherly civilian volunteer in a brown wool suit.

''What are we looking for?'' Joanne asked.

''Just a minute,'' Stacy said, as she paged through the book
index. ''Under 'Scientific Disciplines,' we have Microbiology,
Aerobiology—that's wind, or insects usually. If this is a defense
facility, I wonder why they're screwing around with that?'' She
shook her head in confusion, and kept going. ''Then we have Im-
munology, Biotechnology . . . Chemical, Industrial. Nothing there.
Next section is Plant Sciences and Entomology. Forget that.
Here we go . . . 'Medical and Veterinary Sciences.' That's in
USAMRIID. Okay, could be there,'' she said, and flipped to that
section in the book.

''What?'' Joanne asked.

But Stacy was scanning, muttering department names as she
went. ''Biometrics, Clinical Investigations, Bacteriology, Diagnos-
tic Systems, Virology, and, bingo, *Pathology*. Page 212.'' She

flipped the book to page 212 and started looking. Then she stabbed
the page with her index finger. "We're headed to Building 1666,
Experimental Pathology, Labs A through H, first floor."

They moved out of the building, still carrying their overnight
bags and the Information Center map of the base. They headed
toward Building 1666 along the manicured walkways.

Fort Detrick was beautiful in late April, with flowerbeds bloom-
ing spring colors. There were elm trees lining the streets and old
Civil War cannons. It was a twenty-minute walk across the Fort
on the strangely named Ditto Avenue. They were chilled by the
brisk weather, but they found the building on the corner of Potter
Street and Randall Drive. It was a huge gray concrete-and-steel
structure, an eighties or nineties addition. The sign out front read:

SCIENCE BUILDING 1666

USAMRIID

They stood in front of it and looked at the imposing architecture.

"What now?" Joanne asked. Her voice seemed small, blown
away in the brisk wind. "What do you want me to do?"

"If I get stopped or it gets goofy, start flirting, distract somebody."

She smiled reproachfully. "Flirting. At last, a job I'm qualified
for."

The building's lobby was large, with a tile floor and a huge
personnel directory along one wall. A half-dozen more flags hung
from pole stands. What they stood for Stacy didn't know, and
couldn't care less. She looked at the directory board.

"What're we looking for?" Joanne asked.

"A secure pathology lab where they would most likely do an
autopsy. They usually keep the paperwork in the O.R. till the body
is released in case they need to check for other possibilities. I'm
hoping it's still there. If they were hiding something I think they'd

do it here, and not take Max to a regular county morgue. They have a secure primate bio-operating room and lab in the basement. That's where I'd do it. Let's start there and work our way up."

"You sure you know what you're doing?"

"If I knew what I was doing I would have talked Max out of coming to this godforsaken base." Then she turned away and walked to the staircase.

The door leading downstairs was open, so they walked into the basement. The smell that greeted their noses was one Stacy was very familiar with, but Joanne wrinkled her nose in disgust. "Yuck."

The smell was a common toxic lab smell caused by the occasional broken bottle of chemicals and preserving fluids. Over it all was the stringent reek of formaldehyde. A man in a Naval Captain's uniform was approaching. He hesitated as they passed.

"Excuse me," he said.

Stacy and Joanne turned.

"You don't have a pass. You can't be down here without a pass."

"I'm from Colonel Chittick's office. I'm looking for the on-duty pathologist."

"You'd better go back and get your pass, first," he said.

Now Joanne looked at him and put her hand to her mouth, "I'm feeling sort of green," she said, batting long lashes. "These smells down here . . ."

"She's our new computer programmer. I was just showing her around. Would you mind taking her out? I'll only be a second. Wait for me outside, hon."

Concerned, the Naval Captain looked at Stacy.

"Please," Stacy added, smiling helplessly. "I haven't got time to go all the way back to the fourth floor of Building 810 and get that damn pass off my overcoat. The Colonel is on a tear this morning."

Her mention of the right floor and building seemed to ease the Captain's concerns. He took Joanne's arm and led her to a door in the center of the hall and then out.

As soon as they left, Stacy was off, down the hall. She approached a desk with a nurse in a civilian smock.

"Who's got the duty down here this morning?"

"Dr. Duc," the nurse said.

"I'm sorry, who?"

"Dr. Martin Duc. And he's heard all the jokes. He's Vietnamese, good guy."

"Which way?"

"Down that corridor, to the right. Through the second set of swinging doors."

"Thanks."

She was gone again, moving fast, bustling now like all the other people at Fort Detrick. Her leather-soled shoes beat a rhythm on the basement linoleum. She passed a medical closet, put on the brakes, backed up, and opened the closet door.

Inside were mops, pails, and cleaning solvents. Then she saw what she had been hoping for: Folded neatly on a shelf were green medical smocks. She put one on, pulled the tie around her slender waist, and grabbed a hair cap off the shelf, pulling it over her head. Then she saw a clipboard for ordering detergents and cleaning fluids. She took it. *Why does a clipboard instantly make you a person in authority?* she wondered.

She reentered the corridor and went down the hall, found the double swinging doors, and went into the lab area. She passed a woman rolling a medical tray full of instruments.

"Looking for Doc Duc," she said breezily.

"Lab B. He's doing a chimp post-mortem."

"Thanks." She pushed into Lab B and saw a tall Asian man in scrubs working over a metal drainage table with a chain-mail autopsy glove on his left hand and a rubber surgical glove on his right. He had a small, dead female chimpanzee opened, with a Y-cut from her sternum to her crotch. He was weighing organs as Stacy came into the lab.

"Who are you?" he said, glancing up.

"Dr. Courtney Smith," she lied. "I'm doing the integrated pathology report on Max Richardson for Colonel Chittick's office, and we didn't get our final copy of the organ recital."

"It was inter-officed over there yesterday."

"Well, it didn't get there," she said, "and our Chief Medical Officer is throwing one of his passive-aggressive fits. I'm taking the heat. If you could get a copy of it for me quick, it would *really* help."

"I've got to get this post-mortem done. And I'll need to see your authorization."

She moved over to him, ignoring the last remark, and looked down at the dead female chimp. The insides of the baby primate were tumorous and devastating. She decided to throw some medicine at him for bonding. "What are those?" she asked, pointing. "They look like clusters of hemangioma tumors."

"Pretty good," he smiled. "Most people think they're just fatty growths."

"She looks too young to have that many," Stacy said. "Is this second-generation infestation?"

"Yep," he said. "We're testing pyridostigmine bromide with some of the Gulf War insect repellent we used. I think, by mistake, there was a bad chemical cocktail over there. The father of this baby chimp is a carrier and seems fine, but his little girl here really got hammered. It resembles a condition we're studying in children of Gulf War vets." He turned off the lamp and peeled off his gloves. "I guess I can get that report for you before I do the brain. I gotta get the rubber apron anyway. The cerebral cut is gonna be a mess." He moved to a file cabinet and pulled it open.

"Richardson . . . Richardson . . ." He rifled through folders.

"Here we go . . . You're in luck. Autopsy is still down here and I have an extra in the folder, so I won't need to make you wait for a copy." He handed it over.

"Thanks a heap," she said, and took the ten-page report.

She was out the door before Dr. Duc turned the light back on over the table.

They were in Unit Six of the Lakeview Motel, which was a quarter of a mile from Lake Frederick with no view of water. While Joanne watched the end of the five o'clock news, Stacy went through Max's autopsy.

His blood work was normal, no trace of drugs, stimulants, or depressants. She paged slowly through, reading everything.

The shotgun had obliterated the palatoglossal arch at the back of Max's throat. The pattern of buckshot had traveled up, taking with it his entire brain stem, blowing a hole out the back of his head the size of an open hand.

She choked back tears as she read.

The big surprise came on page six.

"I don't believe it," Stacy said softly as she finished reading. "The sons-of-bitches actually murdered him."

Chapter 4

CRAZY ACE

Stacy had been unable to sleep. Her mind was crowded with thoughts about the autopsy report and memories of Max. At six A.M. she finally gave up pounding her pillow and snuck quietly into the bathroom, so as not to awaken Joanne in the other bed. She showered, blow-dried her hair, and did a repair job on her sleep-deprived face. She was back in the bedroom sitting in the small, uncomfortable wooden chair next to the desk trying to plan her next move when the phone rang, partially waking her sister-in-law. Stacy got the call on the second ring.

"It's Wendell," her old friend said.

She told him just a minute and pulled the phone as far across the room as she could, then took the receiver the rest of the way into the bathroom and closed the door so as not to disturb Joanne.

"Some guy at Fort Detrick has been calling. They left a message at Max's University office and Ruth at the Chancellor's office picked it up."

"Colonel Chittick?"

"Bingo," Wendell said.

"That's the asshole who tried to tell me Max killed himself because he was using drugs. And, can you believe this? They cremated the body without my permission." She had decided not to tell Wendell what she'd found in the autopsy report. She wasn't sure yet what she wanted to do about it, and she didn't want Wendell, sweet as he was, to start laying down conditions.

"They want to see you," he went on. "According to Ruth, the Colonel was very apologetic about your meeting yesterday, said he thought you might have left angry."

"How perceptive."

"You want his number?" he asked.

Stacy was hurt that Wendell hadn't commented on the bullshit drug abuse accusation or the illegal burning of Max's body.

"Okay, lemme get a pencil." Stacy laid down the receiver, scooted out into the bedroom, picked up the motel pad and pen, then moved back, closing the bathroom door.

After Wendell gave her the number, he asked, "Are you guys okay? I'm worried about you."

"We're as okay as we can be." Then she told him she loved him and rang off. She dialed and sat on the bathroom floor as Colonel Chittick's office answered.

"Army Medical Battalion, Colonel Chittick's office," the voice said.

Stacy pictured the red-haired Army Captain from yesterday. "This is Mrs. Richardson. I understand Colonel Chittick is trying to get in touch with me. . . ."

"Oh, thank God you called, ma'am," the fresh-faced Captain said. "The Colonel was wondering if he could arrange an appointment with you at your earliest convenience to better define his remarks of yesterday."

"It's okay. I understood him perfectly."

"I think it would really be worth your while to see him as soon as possible," the Captain persisted.

"How's an hour from now," she suggested, anger suddenly flaring, drawing her closer to this inevitable conflict.

"We can send a car if you like."

"That's okay. I can get there," Stacy said, and hung up without saying good-bye.

She shook Joanne awake, and her sister-in-law propped herself up on her elbow and looked at Stacy through tangled hair.

"We really shook 'em up, kid. They want to talk to me again, try and put a better face on it."

"Geeze, you aren't going back there?"

"You bet your ass," Stacy said. "If they have caller I.D. they could probably trace the call I just made and find this motel. Remember that Holiday Inn, right out of Frederick? We passed it coming in."

"I'll find it."

"Check in there, and if I don't call you or show up in four hours, call Wendell. Drop the whole package on him."

"You sure you should do this?"

"Yeah. I'm going to leave you the autopsy report. Hide it somewhere."

"Won't you need it?"

"Believe me, they know what it says."

Stacy took another cab to the Fort. When she got to the main gate on Military Road, the M.P. was already expecting her. "Mrs. Richardson?" he said, after she identified herself. "The Admiral was wondering if you would meet him over in Area B, Building 1425."

"Who?" she asked.

"The Base Commander, Rear Admiral James G. Zoll." His awe for the man was unmistakable. "Building 1425 is the Company A, First SATCOM Battalion Headquarters," he continued.

"Communications?" she asked, surprising him with that; her father had been career military and she had a good grasp of the lingo.

"Yes ma'am. He's working there this morning. It's not on the regular part of the base. You go through the gate, take a right on Potter Road." He had a map and was showing the cab driver. "Go along Frontage Road for about two miles. You'll see the satellite uplinks out by the duck pond. It's the big windowless building right next to B-14, the Antenna Farm." Then he politely touched the brim of his white helmet.

"Okay, let's go," she said to the driver.

He drove past the main gate, made the right, and headed along Frontage Road. They left the base area and low buildings behind and drove along a narrowing, rutted road, across hilly green farmland. There were miles of perimeter fencing where the road skirted the edge of the base. The fence was ten feet high with ugly razor wire on top. She noticed a few places where the rusty razor loops had been knocked down and were being replaced with shiny new wire. After going for about two miles, they could see the satellite uplinks by a pond, and beyond that, half a dozen hundred-foot-tall radio antennas beside a huge, windowless building, as described. They neared the building, and she could see two officers standing in front, smoking cigarettes, waiting for her. As the cab pulled up they flipped the butts away and opened the door. Both were Naval Captains.

"Mrs. Richardson, I'm Captain Wilcox," the older one said. "This is Captain Carpenter."

They both gave her touch-of-the-visor greetings as she climbed out of the cab.

"Why don't you wait for me," she said to the cab driver, beginning to feel slightly cut off. But Captain Carpenter had already pulled a wad of twenties out of his pocket and was paying the driver.

"We'll arrange to get you back," he said, waving the driver

off. Before she could protest, the taxi was rolling and Captain Wilcox had his hand on her arm, leading her firmly away from the departing cab.

"Get your hands off me, please," she commanded.

He immediately released his grip and nodded. "Sorry ma'am, right this way."

They led her up a few stone steps and into a lobby that was surprisingly barren. Several wooden desks were pushed against the wall. The flag of First SATCOM Battalion was on a standard next to the American flag. End of decorating theme. Everything else was gray cement and white walls.

"I'd like to use the ladies' room," Stacy said. She had left in such a hurry she had not disposed of the three complimentary cups of motel coffee she'd consumed.

"Right this way, ma'am." They led her through a door and down an overlit corridor. One or two corridor doors she passed had small windows in them, and she could see telecommunications and satellite TV rooms that connected Fort Detrick with bases all over the world. Finally she was led through a door that was marked "SATELLITE UPLINK SITUATION ROOM" into a huge, high-ceilinged area the size of half a basketball court. In the center was a wooden table. Around the table were six wooden chairs. Otherwise, the room was completely empty.

"Where is the bathroom, please?" she repeated.

"If you'll wait, I'll tell the skipper you're here," Naval Captain Wilcox said, and then he and Captain Carpenter left her alone in the huge, windowless space.

Aside from a nervous and growing need to piss, she was beginning to feel vaguely frightened and alone. She fought a round of nausea and fear. "Don't leave me, Maxie," she said softly to the spirit of her dead husband.

She didn't know how long the bastards kept her waiting because the battery in her watch was running down and the drugstore timepiece was slowing badly. If the wait was supposed to intimidate

her and make her pliable, it had just the opposite effect. She was
spitting mad when the door finally opened and a large, lumbering
man walked into the room wearing a Rear Admiral's two stars. He
had gold wings pinned on his tan Class C uniform and under the
wings were at least six rows of combat and campaign ribbons,
along with four or five C.I.B. decorations, which Stacy knew from
being an Army brat were Combat Infantryman Badges. The C.I.B.s
indicated that he had been under fire in several ground combat
zones, which she thought was unusual for a Naval officer. Wardrobe aside, Rear Admiral James G. Zoll was a huge John Wayne–
sized man with grizzled forearms and a raptoresque jawline. He
moved into the room, flanked by his two pet Captains and trailed
by Army Colonel Laurence Chittick. He stopped a few strides from
Stacy and looked down at her. She came to about his breastbone.
Colonel Chittick moved forward and made the introductions.

"Admiral James G. Zoll, this is Max Richardson's widow, Stacy
Richardson."

The Admiral put out his hand, and, after a second's hesitation,
she shook it.

"Shall we sit?" Admiral Zoll said.

"You kept me waiting for almost forty minutes. I'd like to use
the facilities," she said.

"I have a limited amount of time," the Admiral replied. "If you
could wait, I would appreciate it." He sat, indicating the meeting
had begun.

Stacy also sat at the table. She found herself flanked by the two
Captains. Admiral Zoll and Colonel Chittick were directly across
the rectangular wood table from her.

"To begin with, I've been briefed on your meeting with Colonel
Chittick yesterday and I regret, very deeply, some of what was
said." His voice was gravelly and deep, a commanding voice used
to giving orders and getting its own way.

"That's nice of you," Stacy said, coolly.

"I know you are distraught, and I know you think something

strange happened regarding the cremation, or even the death of your husband. However, it is an incontrovertible fact that your husband stated on his medical form that he desired cremation in the event of death. It is also a fact that he shot himself with a shotgun that he purchased in town, two weeks ago, at the Rod and Gun sporting goods store, and picked up after the waiting period last Tuesday. The Provost Marshal here on the base has all of the documentation dealing with his purchase of the weapon, along with two boxes of twelve-gauge, double-aught shotgun shells.''

"So then, just what part of yesterday's meeting with Colonel Chittick is it that you're regretting so deeply?'' Stacy said, holding his steady gaze.

Admiral Zoll was accustomed to being in charge. He didn't have much use for cheeky repartee, and she could see him bristle slightly at her remark. "I do not believe that your husband was using drugs,'' Admiral Zoll said in his sandpaper voice.

"Oh, that. Well, of course that was bullshit.''

"I am also not accustomed to hearing women use truck-stop language.''

"And I'm not accustomed to having people accuse my husband of being a junkie or being told he was depressed and moody. To remind you, Admiral, he was the Dean of the USC Microbiology Department. An honor not usually given to moody, unstable people. Colonel Chittick said that several of his colleagues had written complaints about Max's behavior. I'd like to see those complaints and talk to the people who wrote them.''

"For what purpose?'' Admiral Zoll asked, taking a deep breath and then letting it out slowly.

"Let's suppose, Admiral, that you had just blown your head off sitting in a kitchen chair in your backyard.''

"That is not something I'll ever have to worry about.''

"Neither did Max. But let us suppose it happened to you anyway, surprising your wife, who knows you'd never solve your problems that way. Then let's suppose that, despite all those fancy decorations you so proudly wear on your chest, and despite a career of military excellence, some unnamed people who claimed to have worked with you suggest that you were irrational, with wild mood swings. That you were depressed and, of all things, a drug user. Wouldn't you expect somebody who loved you, your wife for instance, to come forward and demand that your memory be correctly preserved? And if you say no, then you're a goddamn liar."

She watched a line of red climb Admiral Zoll's neck and spread across his face. He didn't look at Colonel Chittick, or the two Naval Captains. His eyes were locked on Stacy. "You might do well, young lady, to curtail your attitude. I do not appreciate it, and it gets you nowhere."

"Well, Admiral, since I'm not in the military and not under your command, I'll adjust my attitude to fit *my* feelings, not yours. And right now, I'm one very mad widow who couldn't give less of a shit how you feel about it."

"And just what do you want us to do?" he said, containing his rage at some cost to his military posture.

"I want you to admit that he didn't commit suicide, because he didn't."

"And you can prove it?"

"Beyond a shadow . . . no, make that beyond a scintilla of a doubt."

"I see. And just how would you do that?"

"You don't want to know, and I would very much like to use the bathroom," she said, starting to rise.

"You sit right where you are, Mrs. Richardson! I want to know what the hell you're talking about."

One of the Captains put a hand on her shoulder and pushed her gently back down into her chair. She glowered at him, then turned back to the Admiral.

"I'm saying that he didn't commit suicide and I can prove it!"

"How are you going to prove it?" the Admiral asked.

"I need to use the bathroom."

"You're not going anywhere until we get this sorted out."

"You mean you are refusing to let me go to the bathroom?" she asked, the disbelief and sarcasm heavy in her tone.

"How are you going to prove something that isn't true?" Admiral Zoll repeated.

"I read Max's autopsy report."

Admiral Zoll shot a questioning look at Colonel Chittick, who shrugged.

Zoll nodded at the two Captains and Colonel Chittick. They all got up from the table and moved out of the room, leaving the Admiral and Stacy alone.

"I must use the facilities."

"How did you get a copy of the autopsy report?"

"None of your business, but I've got it."

"So what? It says he shot himself in the head. End of story."

"It's not the end. It's the beginning. The end of the story makes no damn sense at all."

The door opened and Captain Wilcox had a cellphone in his hand; he motioned to Admiral Zoll, who got up and moved out of the huge room. Again, Stacy was alone. She was cursing herself that she hadn't used the bathroom before she left. She had been so angry she had flown out the door when the cab arrived. Now all she could think about was urinating. She needed to keep her mind off that and on her adversaries, so she got out of her chair and, while she was alone in the room, she removed her panties and quickly squatted by her chair. Hiding as best she could behind the table, she urinated on the floor, then moved the table over to cover it.

Ten or fifteen more minutes passed. She estimated that she had been at Fort Detrick for almost an hour, maybe an hour and a half. With no windows and a broken watch, it was impossible to judge.

Then the door opened and Admiral Zoll, the two Captains, and Colonel Chittick returned to the room and again sat down. All of them unwittingly placed their shiny shoes under the table in Stacy's urine, which had puddled there.

"Okay," the Admiral said, "we just verified that somebody probably snuck into our primate lab and stole a classified document. I'm sure you found it very interesting, but you'd need advanced medical training to understand the intricacies of an M.E.'s death report. You undoubtedly misunderstood what you were reading. It is military property and we demand it back."

"Your own autopsy says that the shotgun blast obliterated the palatoglossal arch and moved upward, destroying everything from the soft palate uvula to the sphenoid sinus. Those two membranes, by the way, are in the back of the mouth roughly at the veli palatine muscle."

Admiral Zoll now looked at the two Captains, who had their eyes on Stacy.

"I can read a medical report," she clarified. "I'm less than two weeks from my doctorate in microbiology at USC." Admiral Zoll and the other officers now traded surprised looks.

"If that's what it says, then okay, that's what it says," Admiral Zoll replied.

"What it also says is, the pattern of buckshot continued up, expanding and destroying everything in its path, including the brain stem. The exact word the report used was 'obliterated' the brain stem. Then the pattern passed into the cerebellum, exiting out the back of his head near the crown."

"Where is this going?" Admiral Zoll asked.

"The autopsy also stated that in the middle region of the left lung, in the anterior region, and in the basal quadrant of the right lung, he had substantial quantities of aspirated blood."

The Admiral looked over at Colonel Chittick. Zoll wasn't a doctor, Colonel Chittick was.

"He inhaled blood before he died, sir," Colonel Chittick clarified, but already he could see where she was going and was getting pale.

"So what?" Zoll snorted. "So he blew his head off and inhaled the blood from the wound before he died. What the hell does that prove?"

"Can't happen," she said. "It's a medical impossibility. What I think happened was somebody beat him up, for what reason I don't know yet, maybe to find out what he knew. During this beating, he inhaled the blood that was in his mouth. At this point, he was still alive. *Then* somebody shot him in the mouth to hide the extensive damage the beating caused. Because Max knew something he shouldn't have, they needed him dead to get him out of the way."

"Of course that's ridiculous, and I don't see why it couldn't happen my way," the Admiral said.

"Sir," Colonel Chittick said, but the Admiral held up his hand for silence, glaring at Stacy.

"The brain stem was gone, Admiral, obliterated." She continued, "The brain stem controls the breathing reflex. Without it, he *couldn't* inhale. It is impossible that blood was inhaled into his lungs *after* he was shot. It had to happen before . . . making your whole theory on Max's death a lie."

There was a long silence in the room.

Now there was something new in Admiral Zoll's eyes. The killer look that had once defined him as a pilot in Vietnam. He flew Intruders off the deck of the *Kitty Hawk*. One afternoon in '72, seven Chinese MiGs jumped him. Young Lieutenant James Zoll became an ace in less than three minutes, splashing five MiGs in the ocean before flying his mortally wounded Intruder at a sixth, ejecting scant moments before impact. He'd been fished out of the drink two hours later. His fellow pilots and shipmates had done something that almost never happened; they changed his call sign from "Hacksaw" to "Crazy Ace." It had followed him throughout his career, and after he reached Admiral, it had been his nickname, behind his back.

"Just what are you suggesting?" Admiral Zoll asked, after taking several moments to consider.

"I'm suggesting he was murdered," Stacy replied, holding his gaze across the wooden table. "And I think you know why."

Then his manner changed abruptly. "Just who the fuck do you think you're talking to?" he said, rising out of his chair and leaning across the table at her.

"I guess, under the right circumstances, even an Admiral will use a little truck-stop language," she said.

"You have the fucking audacity to sit there and say somebody on this base murdered your husband. Okay, so you can read an autopsy finding, big deal. But you can't say without a shadow of a doubt what happened. It's just your opinion. You can't say your husband was murdered!"

"Yes, Admiral, I can! And unless you're planning on doing the same thing to me that you did to him, which would really be tough for the police in this county to swallow, then you've got yourself a giant-sized problem, 'cause I'm gonna keep digging until I find out what got Max killed."

Admiral Zoll looked at her almost as if he couldn't believe what he was hearing. "You have a remarkable imagination, honey," he said.

"I'm not your honey." She had lost all sense of caution, and her anger over what had happened to Max was spilling over everything. But the anger was at least therapeutic. For the first time in two days, she felt the knot in her stomach unclench.

"You have no idea what kind of problems we can make for you," he hissed.

"You got it backwards, Admiral. It's *me* promising to make problems for *you*."

"We fund that fucking university where you were about to get your doctorate. This program at Fort Detrick gives millions a year in research grants. Why do you think we picked the head of the USC Microbiology Department to come here? If you pursue this, you will never get your doctorate. I personally guarantee it!"

"I personally don't give a shit," she said, washing out four years of exhaustive study with one cathartic sentence.

Finally, Admiral Zoll pushed back from the table. Something splashed up on his sock. "What the fuck is under here?" he said, reaching down under the table and feeling the puddle of moisture.

"I wouldn't put my hands in that," Stacy said mildly.

Admiral Zoll pulled up his wet hand. Realization dawned, and his face went red with anger. He got out of his chair, shook the urine off his fingers and both of his wet shoes, then, holding his hand away from his side, walked across the floor, his rubber soles squishing as he went. Colonel Chittick and the two pet Captains followed.

They closed the door and again she was alone.

Stacy sat in the empty room. Nobody came back. She tried the door, but it was locked. She realized that anger had induced her to badly overplay her hand.

Roughly another two hours went by, and she sat there, looking at the blank, windowless walls in the huge concrete room. In her mind, she played out some ghastly fantasies. Would they just kill her anyway? The Provost Marshal could be in on it. What if they rigged it to look as if she were despondent over Max's death and had taken her own life? Would they use some bio-weapon on her and say she had wandered into a "hot" lab? Would they arrange a traffic accident? She had no way of knowing. There was nothing she could do but wait. Exhausted, she lay down on the table and finally got an hour of deep REM sleep.

She awoke with somebody shaking her shoulder. She sat up abruptly and found herself looking at a middle-aged woman in civilian clothes.

"There's a car waiting for you out front," the woman said. Then she led Stacy out of the room.

They walked down the hall and out into the darkening afternoon. It was after four. She estimated she had been there for over six hours.

The car was a brown military sedan with a uniformed woman driver. Stacy got in the back seat and the car took her out the same way she had come. It passed through the front gate and parked at the curb outside on Military Avenue. Then the female Corporal behind the wheel handed Stacy an envelope and, once Stacy was out of the sedan, drove back inside the Fort.

Stacy stood on the curb with the flapping flags of Fort Detrick behind her. She opened the sealed envelope.

The message was typed on plain paper. "Be very careful," it said. "The distance between courage and stupidity is exactly nine millimeters."

The note was unsigned.

Chapter 5

SPRING RIDGE

They took Exit 56 from Maryland I-70 East. It was ten the next morning and Stacy was driving a Mitsubishi from Budget Rent-A-Car. Joanne was slumped in the seat beside her. They pulled up to the Information Center at the Spring Ridge housing development, which was just inside a massive brick wall, with the name of the tract in foot-high brass letters. The guard at the gate had the key ready. He handed an envelope to Stacy and told her how to get to the house that Max had rented.

They drove through the beautiful development that Max had described to Stacy on the phone after he had rented the house from an Army Major who had been transferred.

The house was at the top of Kettler Road, a two-story with Colonial pillars, a brick front, and slate-gray roof. There were trimmed lawns and flowerbeds. A fresh coat of black paint glistened on the front door. Stacy opened the envelope and took out the key, then she and Joanne moved up the driveway to the house. She wasn't sure what she was looking for, but was somehow being drawn to the place where Max had died. She also wanted to try to

find a way to say good-bye, but was having trouble getting closure
and now wished she had taken Max's ashes from the shitbird Colonel. . . . At least she'd have an urn to look at and hold.

Joanne had stopped crying and was now in some kind of
zombie-like trance. She had been frantic when Stacy had been two
hours overdue. She had called Wendell and faxed him the autopsy.
They had just about decided to call the Frederick police when
Stacy walked into the room at the Holiday Inn. The next morning,
they'd rented a car at the desk, thrown their bags in the trunk, and,
after a call to the Spring Ridge development, headed up there.

Stacy unlocked the large wooden door, which groaned loudly
on cold hinges as it swung open to beckon them in and, at the
same time, warn them away.

They entered a large, sunny entry hall lit from above by a sky-
light. Stacy looked at the mail on the front table. Most were flyers
or bills for the long-gone Major. Then she moved slowly through
the house.

She went into the bedroom and looked at Max's clothes. His
suitcases were on the top shelf of the closet, but she couldn't bring
herself to do the mundane task of packing his things. What would
she do with them, anyway? Should she keep his old clothes to
remember him? She decided to put off the decision.

She checked the bathroom. She saw his toothbrush, his razor,
and his pillbox of vitamins. She looked at all of Max's orphaned
objects and fought the tears.

Then Stacy moved into the den. There, on his desk, was his
computer. She wondered what he had been working on when he
died, so she sat down and booted up, staring at the glowing screen.
Instead of displaying a dialog box for Max's password, the words
"preparing to run Windows 98 for the first time" were eerily
crawling across the bottom of the screen. "The bastards swept his
computer," she said to Joanne, who was now standing beside her,
looking down at the screen.

"We'd better get going," Joanne said dully. "The plane takes off in an hour and forty minutes."

Stacy was staring at the computer. "Max, where did you put it?" she said, softly.

"Put what?"

"He always backed up everything. He was fanatical about it. There's gotta be a back-up disk somewhere with all his important documents and research on it."

"Oh," Joanne said, without interest.

She tried all of the obvious places: the shelf, the briefcases, the desk. Stacy opened a drawer and brushed several CD jewel boxes with her hand. One was a restoration CD, used to restore a system to its original state. Stacy's eyes narrowed . . . *This is how they erased all the documents on Max's computer! Still, there would be a back-up. Maybe under the drawers, taped there,* she thought. She pulled out all the drawers and felt under them, feeling goofy as she did, like a spy in a James Bond movie. She checked the bedroom, the kitchen, and the den. Nothing.

Stacy finally stood in the middle of the living room with her hands on her hips, looking around in frustration.

"We've gotta go," Joanne repeated.

"Okay," Stacy agreed, then she moved toward the back deck, opened the sliding glass door, and walked out into the back-yard.

"What're you doing?" Joanne asked, trailing along behind her.

"I don't know. I . . . I just . . ." She was moving in circles, looking down, trying to see where it had happened. Finally, she saw a spot where the grass looked darker. Stacy moved to it, squatted down, and put her palm on the ground. The grass was stiff and hard with Max's dried blood.

"Oh Christ," she said, as a sob caught in her throat. "Why did they do it? Why . . . Oh Max, why?" She held her hand on his dried blood as if touching that spot could somehow bring her closer to him. She was reaching out to him through the patch of blood-dried ground, desperately trying to touch him one more time, but only feeling the stiff grass against her palm. The tears would not stop. She cried until the water blurred her vision.

Finally, Joanne pulled her up. "I know, baby," her sister-in-law said. "I know . . . I know . . ." Joanne held Stacy's head against her shoulder. "Let's go home."

"We've gotta do something," Stacy murmured. "We've gotta. We've just gotta!"

They barely made the Delta flight. Four and a half hours later they landed at LAX. Wendell Kinney met the plane, and they moved with their carry-on luggage out to the parking lot and his four-year-old green Ford station wagon. Once they had cleared the airport and were on the Harbor Freeway, heading back toward USC, Wendell looked over at Stacy. "I think you really shook 'em with that autopsy," he said.

"They killed him."

"Maybe," Wendell said, running a hand through his thick gray hair. "What you're suggesting certainly fits the findings of the autopsy, but there could be other reasons for the aspirated blood, so let's not jump to conclusions."

"What other reasons?"

"He could have gotten into a fight in a bar or someplace. Maybe a car accident where he cut his mouth, aspirated the blood, and then an hour later, in a fit of depression or something, killed himself."

"Bullshit. I talked to him at one A.M. the night it happened. He was *not* in a fit of depression. He didn't wreck his car. Stop saying that!"

"Well, I'm just saying . . ."

"Bullshit," she repeated. "Lemme tell you something else. His computer was erased. It was right back to the way it was the day it came out of the box. I bet somebody downloaded all the data files and erased them off his hard drive. There isn't even any of his personal wallpaper left, and I know he kept photos of me and his family on there."

"Not a good sign," Wendell said, nodding.

"Those guys at Fort Detrick are up to something, something really terrible. Max became a problem, so they fixed it."

"Something terrible? Like what? It's one of the leading medical facilities on the East Coast."

"Prions," she said, spitting the word out. "You know what they're all about? Proteins. Not viruses, or chemicals. They're the perfect bio-weapon, because they're not alive. You can't kill them with fire or cold. They don't die like Ebola or AIDS, and they adapt themselves to body chemistry, so your immune system doesn't even know they're there, doesn't even fight them. Max said they were the deadliest, most terrifying killer agents on the planet. He told me on the phone about two weeks ago that he thought Dexter DeMille might be developing the first Prion bio-weapon."

"Dr. DeMille is a great man, a Nobel Prize winner. . . . He wouldn't do that. There's no bio-weapons program at Fort Detrick, or anywhere else in the U.S. It was all shut down by Presidential decree. All they're doing at Fort Detrick is researching, so if a bio-weapon is ever used by terrorists against the U.S., we'll be able to quickly produce the anti-toxins to combat it. We've been out of the strategic bio-weapons program since the Nonproliferation Treaty of 1972."

"You really believe that, Wendell?" He didn't answer, changing lanes instead to get around a school bus. "A hundred nations signed that treaty," she said, "and we know now that at least a dozen of them continued to actively develop bio-weapons afterward, including Russia, Iraq, Iran, Israel, Great Britain, Egypt, and who knows who else. With all this illegal science taking place, some of it by enemy nations, you really think the CIA and the Pentagon didn't know about it? And if they did, you can bet they found a way to keep our bio-weapons program operating.''

Wendell Kinney was quiet for almost a minute. "What did you say to those people back at Fort Detrick?" he finally said, changing the subject.

"I told them I thought Max found out something, became a problem, and was disposed of."

"Ugggh," Wendell groaned.

"Well, why not call it like it is?"

"Because since you left town, your Quals have been postponed indefinitely," he said. "The Microbiology Department is putting your doctorate under review."

"Somebody made a call," she said, shaking her head in disgust. "Wendell, how much money is quietly given to universities all across this country by the Pentagon for biological research?"

"You don't wanna know."

"Does USC have some kind of covert arrangement with those pricks at Fort Detrick?"

"Not as far as I know," he said. "After all, Max was the one who ran the program. He was a humanist. I don't think he would have agreed to use government funds to develop illegal research that could be turned against people."

"You're damn right he wouldn't!" she said hotly. *Yet he went to Fort Detrick to study Prions with Dexter DeMille, who had been criticized in the past for questionable science that could have military applications.*

Both of them were privately exploring these same thoughts, but neither wanted to express them.

"What about the secret rooms discovered at Fort Detrick in the eighties?" Stacy continued. "That was well after the end of our bio-weapons program. Those rooms were loaded with sarin and different strains of anthrax."

"R and D," he said.

"Research and Development of what?"

"Anti-toxins."

"There was enough shit in there to kill the entire population of the world two or three times over. They faced Congressional oversight hearings on that. The program was censored. Who are they kidding? They were manufacturing and stockpiling that stuff. And what about those mosquito tests by the CIA, where they dropped female mosquitoes with dengue fever and yellow fever on Carver Village, that black town in the Florida swamps, where thirteen people died? The government ended up paying millions in damages to shut the story down. What about airborne bacteria dropped on San Francisco and the subway tests in New York in the midseventies to late eighties? The government has already admitted to all that. Innocent U.S. citizens died, so the CIA assholes at Fort Detrick could study aerobiology."

"Look, Stacy, I'm not saying that our program is without horrible ethical lapses, or that there aren't some rogue scientists, or military and CIA people who are devoted to staying in this field at all costs. But our government is not knowingly pursuing this course of strategic weaponry," he said hotly.

"Okay," she said, "okay. It's just . . ." And she fell silent.

"Just what?"

"I wish I knew what Max was working on, what was on his computer. You know how he was, how he wrote everything down, kept duplicate files. If he was killed because of something he knew, then a copy exists somewhere, believe me. What they erased off his hard drive wasn't the only record of his research."

"I'm afraid we'll never know," Wendell said.

They arrived back at Max and Stacy's apartment, and Joanne took her bag out of the trunk and put it in her VW. She was still too quiet, off someplace else, and had said almost nothing all the way back from the airport. Before she got into her car, she held Stacy's hand. "Stace," she said, "I'm afraid. I don't think you should mess with this."

"I know you don't," Stacy said, and she gave her sister-in-law a kiss on the cheek, then watched her drive away.

After Wendell left, she went up to her apartment, unlocked the door, and dropped her bag in the living room. She looked at the sad little three-room flat that had once been such a happy love nest. Now all she saw was how small it was, how tired and thread-bare the sofa looked, the stains on the worn carpet. She moved into her pantry office, slumped down and looked at her computer. She turned it on to check her e-mail . . .

There it was! "Dearest Stacy," it began, "all is not well at Fort Detrick, so I want you to read this attached file, then hide it in a safe place."

Sometime after they talked two nights ago, and before he died, Max had e-mailed her. On the computer screen before her were Max's letter and his attached research files. The e-mail contained everything he suspected was happening at a secret facility at Fort Detrick, called the Devil's Workshop. Max's notes discussed Dexter DeMille and Pale Horse Prions, and described the horrible human experiments that were about to take place inside an old prison at Vanishing Lake, Texas.

Part Two

VANISHING LAKE

Chapter 6

GUINEA PIGS

They were housed in separate cells on the old death row unit, which was located in the windowless center pod at Vanishing Lake Military Prison. The fortress-style structure was oppressive, and underlit. It had been built in the fifties and had long ago outlived its design as a penal institution. The prison sat on the east side of a picturesque crater lake, almost directly across from a small fishing village, high in the Black Hills of East Texas. The cells, like most of the old prison, were built out of gray concrete blocks. The tiers were old-fashioned narrow rows of windowless rooms stacked one above the other with no center atrium. The two men had only been there for a few days and, although just forty feet separated their cells, Troy Lee Williams and Sylvester Swift had never laid eyes on one another.

"You listening to me down there?" Troy Lee called out in exasperation. "I wanta know what the fuck they're doin' back there on that fuckin' wall. All that hammerin' an' shit's drivin' me nuts."

Sylvester Swift said nothing.

Troy Lee Williams was redheaded and skinny. His too-white skin was covered with an assortment of tattoos. Across his shoulder blades, in two-inch-high block letters, was "MOTHERFUCKER." The rest of his body read like the back wall of a skid-row liquor store. Troy Lee was a sixth-grade drop-out who had chosen the Army over a civilian jail, but had ended up in a cell anyway after raping, then killing a waitress while he was on a weekend pass in Rosemont, California. He'd been court-martialed and had barely escaped a firing squad. Troy Lee had no friends, because he was a diagnosed schizophrenic, and when he was hearing voices, he spooked the shit out of everybody.

"Hey, dickwad! I'm talkin' ta you!" Troy Lee shouted again.

"Shut the fuck up," Sylvester Swift said, his deep bass voice coming out of the cell, two down and one across on the narrow tier.

Sylvester Swift had been doing natural life at Leavenworth for attacking two soldiers in the enlisted men's mess at Fort Dennis with a stolen kitchen knife. The unprovoked assault had been over the theft of some candy bars taken out of Sylvester's footlocker. Both soldiers had died before they made it to the base hospital.

Williams and Swift were the only two prisoners incarcerated at Vanishing Lake Prison. The outdated Texas penal facility had been shut down a year ago, and then given by the state to the Science Department at Sam Houston University, which rented it to Fort Detrick.

Three days ago Troy Lee Williams and Sylvester Swift had been secretly transferred there.

"... Then after, nobody tells me shit. This bushy-haired fuck asks me if I'm a goddamn Jew. Me, he asks *me,* if I'm some ethnic mistake. Fuckin' pissed me off. . . . Hey, answer me, will ya? I'm talkin' ta you!"

Sylvester Swift tried to ignore him. He was also wondering why he'd been transferred all the way here from Leavenworth Prison. He too was worried about the sound of electric drills and saws coming from behind the steel door. One of the M.P. guards had told him the old gas chamber was back there.

Sylvester thought the last ten days had been weird, from the thorough two-day medical exam he'd been given at Leavenworth, to the flight in the unmarked military C-141 Starlifter. He'd been cuffed and seated with two armed guards, neither of whom had any rank or unit designation on his uniform.

They had sat in the back of the huge cargo plane, amid cartons of medical supplies, and flown nonstop all the way to a military landing strip south of Waco, Texas. Then they switched planes, getting into a light amphibious Caribou. They took off again and flew into the mountains. Staying low under the radar, they flew through canyons, eventually making a water landing on a crater lake. As Sylvester got out of the plane, the mountainous wooded beauty of the place struck him. Tall Pines rimmed a clear blue lake, which was almost five miles in diameter, marred only by a huge, gray concrete block prison that loomed at the water's edge like a Transylvanian castle.

After Sylvester was admitted to Vanishing Lake Prison, they examined him thoroughly again, collecting blood and skin scrapings. It was then that he met the strange, skinny doctor with the bushy hair who examined Sylvester's ebony body, looking for physical defects. The plantation-style inspection pissed him off. The skinny man wore no military uniform; instead, he was in a lab coat over civilian clothes. He had piercing green eyes, and Sylvester judged him to be about forty-six or -eight.

The man didn't give his name, but asked Sylvester the same questions they had asked him numerous times at Leavenworth. Did he have any family or friends? If so, would he please list them? Did he know his genealogical history?

"I got nobody," he had growled impatiently, pouring out racial hatred with his best street-corner eye fuck.

Dr. Dexter DeMille looked at the clipboard in his hand containing Sylvester Swift's entire service and medical record. "Your file says you've been incarcerated at Leavenworth for three years, without any personal visits. Do you really have no friends, Sylvester?''

"Got no friends," Sylvester growled. "Want no motherfuckin' friends. Jus' do shit my own self.''

After his check-in at Vanishing Lake Prison, Sylvester had been led in chains across the empty compound. He was taken to the fifth tier of the center pod. As he walked down the corridor in the old death house, he heard the loud voice of Troy Lee Williams for the first time. Sylvester was locked in his cell and had been forced to endure Troy Lee's babble and the sounds of constant construction in the nearby gas chamber ever since.

The drill stopped whining and a hammer started banging at the end of the corridor behind the steel door. "Whatta you suppose them fucks is building in there?'' Troy Lee said.

Dr. Dexter DeMille knew he was on the verge of a historic, strategic military breakthrough. Despite this sense of impending victory, his nightmares had intensified. They had been throwback dreams about his work with Carleton Gajdusek in New Guinea in the early seventies. The dreams were always in black and white. He and Carl would be brutally killing the aboriginal women instead of heroically saving them. Then in the dream he was hacking their heads open like pineapples and emptying their liquefied cerebral tissue onto the dusty ground, watching their brains splatter in the dirt. Every night for a month, he had been waking up in terror, his body drenched with sweat. He was convinced the dreams were ominous warnings from his subconscious.

When he thought of those two men, recently transferred onto the center block, God help him, his mind did a strange emotional pirouette. Thoughts of guilt about their fate were immediately followed by an overpowering thrill of impending discovery.

He moved around his lab, collecting the DNA and genome

charts for Troy Lee and Sylvester. The protein markers were so specific that both men's exact genealogical makeup and weaknesses in their DNA were displayed, as if pinpointed on a map.

Dexter knew Admiral Zoll now considered him a security risk. His bouts with insomnia and depression were getting worse. Twice in the last year he had attempted suicide. He had also flown into unexplained and uncontrollable rages, breaking up his own lab. Military guards, clean-cut men in pressed uniforms with ordinary backgrounds and intelligence, were posted to watch him constantly. Once he was finished with the human testing, he suspected, Admiral Zoll's plans for him would not include popping champagne corks. Dexter was running out of rope.

It was time to check the mosquito larvae boxes, so he moved out of the main lab down a corridor to the adjoining room where the mosquitoes were bred. He paused to put on the heavy canvas jumpsuit, gloves, and HEPA filter mask before opening the door stenciled with big red letters:

DANGER

BIO-CONTAINMENT AREA

LEVEL 3

Once he was suited up, he entered the smaller lab. He moved across the room and looked into the two glass boxes that were positioned on the center island. From a distance they almost looked as if they contained swirling smoke, but once you got closer it became apparent that the boxes really contained hundreds of newly bred, swarming mosquitoes. Some were still on the floor of the boxes, sitting on a tray of blood jelly, feasting on his newly designed Pale Horse Prion, PHpr: the deadly rogue protein that he had injected into the blood gel.

He looked in at the young, freshly hatched females still poised on long spindly legs over the gel, sucking up the Prion with their needle-nosed tubular labrums.

There were only a few of them left on the bottom of the glass box. Most were now blooded with his gruesome cocktail, flying around, desperately looking for a warm body to attack. He picked up the phone in the windowless bio-containment room and dialed the number for the gas chamber. Dr. Charles Lack answered the phone. Before he spoke, Dexter DeMille took a deep breath.

"I guess I'm ready," he said.

Troy Lee was screaming obscenities as they dragged him up to the old gas chamber, located in the tower of Center Block.

The door to the chamber was opened and Troy Lee's T-shirt was ripped off, then he was thrown into the small enclosure. He hit the far wall hard and slid to the floor. "Whatta you doing? Okay, please . . ." he was pleading now. "I'm sorry . . . okay? I'm sorry."

Two M.P.s in white helmets, armbands, and jumpboots grabbed Sylvester, removed his shirt, and walked him into the chamber. Then the door was closed and bolted.

The air lock hissed.

Troy Lee was screaming again, but nobody in the tower area outside the chamber could hear him, because the gas chamber was constructed out of two heavy glass boxes, one air-locked inside the other.

Then Dexter DeMille stepped forward. Dr. Charles Lack was adjusting two tripods with cameras that were placed where they could videotape the procedure. Lack was a young, new addition to the staff at Fort Detrick, recently recruited from MIT. He and Dexter DeMille had been clashing over several important aspects of the Pale Horse Program. One area of intense disagreement was whether to use mosquitoes as the vector agent. Dr. Lack preferred the more primitive methods of ingesting the cocktail, by corrupting water supplies or foodstuffs. DeMille couldn't convince the cocky younger doctor that mosquitoes offered a much better delivery system. If the enemy found out the Pale Horse Prion had been placed in water or food, they could just stop consumption. In order to avoid mosquitoes they would need to put every soldier in Level Three bio-gear, almost impossible under attack time frames. Also, mosquitoes were territorial and didn't migrate to new areas. Most important, they had short life spans and died in about three days, clearing the area of dangerous infestation. Despite the logic of this, Dr. Lack continued to object, saying mosquitoes were cumbersome and hard to deliver, and could be swept to new areas by strong winds.

Dr. Lack finished his adjustments to the video equipment, then two M.P.s moved up and stood behind each camera. Dr. DeMille picked up the "Governor's phone" nearby.

"Can you see that okay, Admiral?" he said.

"Yes. Go ahead." Admiral James G. Zoll's rough voice came through the line from the communications room at Company A, First SATCOM Battalion Headquarters at Fort Detrick.

Now Troy Lee was on his feet, screaming silently at them through the soundproof glass. His too-white skin was turning red with the effort.

Dexter DeMille walked over to the two boxes affixed to brackets on the side of the gas chamber. He removed the canvas covers, revealing the newly hatched, swarming female mosquitoes.

Then he pulled up the air lock on each of the boxes, allowing the x-ray-sterilized and Prion-primed female mosquitoes to fly through a small one-way filter valve into the gas chamber. First one, then three, then fifty entered the enclosure. In a few moments, most of the deadly insects were in the gas chamber.

Quickly both Sylvester and Troy Lee had dozens of mosquitoes on them. They danced around in the gas chamber, trying to get them off, slapping at them with their hands, rubbing against the sides of the glass chamber, smearing specks of blood on the chamber walls.

Dexter waited until he was sure both Sylvester and Troy Lee

had been thoroughly bitten, then he released an insect spray into the chamber. It flowed from newly installed valves in the ceiling, and quickly a fine toxic mist settled over Troy Lee and Sylvester, turning their shoulders wet and shiny.

One by one, the mosquitoes in the gas chamber died, falling off the two prisoners and off the walls where they clung. Hundreds landed dead in black clusters on the floor. Then one of the white-helmeted M.P.s turned on an overhead shower nozzle that drenched the chamber with water. The dead mosquitoes were washed from Troy Lee and Sylvester, rinsed off the glass walls and floor. Finally, they all disappeared down a drain, into a bio-container that was affixed under the scaffolding.

Dr. DeMille picked up the second intercom phone and dialed three digits. "Okay," he said softly.

The door opened downstairs and four M.P.s in full HEPA gear climbed the metal steps. The soldiers left their cameras, and everybody exited the tower for their own protection. The M.P.s in HEPA gear moved to the gas chamber door. They looked like visitors from the space program in their canvas suits and oxygen helmets.

They opened the air-locked door and dragged the confused prisoners out of the gas chamber.

Dexter DeMille went back to his quarters to begin what he assumed would be a three- to four-hour wait.

It began at 1:56 A.M.

Suddenly, without warning, Troy Lee Williams got up off his bunk on the fifth tier and hurled himself at a passing guard, crashing headfirst against the steel bars of his prison cell, splitting his forehead open. The M.P. had passed too close to the cell, and Troy Lee managed to grab his hand, jerking it through the bars. In a homicidal rage, he clamped his mouth over the guard's hand, biting hard, snarling and tearing the soldier's flesh.

"Get the fuck off me!" the soldier screamed, as he snatched

out his side arm and fired into the cell, hitting Troy Lee in the leg, throwing him back. Then the startled M.P. pulled his bleeding hand back through the bars and looked at the wound in horror. Troy Lee, with his own blood from the bullet flowing down his leg and the guard's blood running from his chin, stood in the center of the cell, screaming and drooling like a rabid animal.

Dr. DeMille ran up the stairs and onto the death row tier. Video cameras had also been set up in the cellblock, to record both Sylvester and Troy Lee. Dexter had been watching a monitor in his room and had seen the attack. Sylvester Swift was standing at his cell door, unchanged, but looking worried.

"Troy Lee, can you hear me?" Dexter asked the wild-looking murderer, who was in the center of his cell, blood and spit foaming at his mouth, his breath coming in gasps. "Tell me, tell me what you're feeling. What's it feel like? The rage you feel—is it uncontrollable?" He had a tape recorder out and pushed toward the bars.

Troy Lee's mind was somewhere else; he was homicidally insane. He charged Dexter DeMille and smashed against the metal bars, grabbing for Dexter's hand holding the tape recorder. Blood from the deep cuts on his forehead splattered out into the corridor. The microbiologist had been ready, and jumped back, avoiding the lunge.

"Get this soldier to sick bay," Dexter ordered.

They took the M.P. with the bleeding hand away. For almost twenty minutes more, Troy Lee raged in his cell.

It was worse than anything Dexter had ever seen among the Foré Aboriginal tribe in New Guinea in '73. They also had rages in the early stages of the disintegrating brain disease they called "Kuru," but it was nothing like this. He and Carleton Gajdusek had tried to save them, but one by one, the Aborigines first went mad, then died. It took the microbiologist a year of doing autopsies in grass huts to isolate and identify the likely cause as a rogue protein that was eating away the mood control center in their midbrains.

After he returned from New Guinea, Dexter had not been able to find funding to continue his Prion research. While he was teaching microbiology at Sam Houston University he was approached one evening by the head of the department and offered a research sabbatical at Fort Detrick, Maryland. It was there that he met the frightening Admiral Zoll, who surprised him with a thorough knowledge of his work in New Guinea. He was introduced to Zoll's bioweapons program at the Devil's Workshop. There he began experimenting with mixing Kuru and mad cow disease, a similar protein-based illness that had recently surfaced in English cattle, making them crazy by also attacking the mood center in their brains.

The initial problem with his concoctions was that the total destruction of the midbrain took over two years—way too long for a bio-weapon. To accelerate the devastation, DeMille had finally mixed in a strain of human Epstein-Barr virus. E.B. virus proved a perfect accelerant. He continued to tinker and adjust, finding other ways to speed the result. His tests on primates were extensive, and finally he had a strain of Prion that ran its course in hours. He named his discovery the "Pale Horse Prion," PHpr, and it now had several unique characteristics that made it an excellent choice as a bio-weapon. One was stealth . . . the Prion appeared to be just another "normal" protein. It was undetectable by ordinary lab tests, and it was impervious to sterilization. PHpr was a "Dr. Jekyll" protein that transformed into a vicious "Mr. Hyde" Prion when activated.

He watched now in fascination as Troy Lee's hands clawed insanely at his own throat. His eyes were red-rimmed and resembled no eyes Dexter DeMille had ever seen.

Then, as with Kuru and mad cow, the rages started to subside and Troy Lee began to lose his balance, each time falling on his right side. During the next hour came the onset of tremors and dementia.

"The patient has gone into the severe ataxic stage," Dr. DeMille said into his tape recorder.

Twenty minutes later, Troy Lee was on his back, gurgling fluids out of his mouth as occasional grand-mal seizures ravaged his trembling body.

"It is four thirty-five," Dexter said softly into his tape recorder. "The subject now has badly impaired swallowing and has gone into status epilepticus."

At five-fifteen, Troy Lee Williams was pronounced dead. He was put into a bio-containment bag and removed to the hospital for autopsy.

The entire course of the disease, from infection to death, was less than six hours.

Despite over twenty mosquito bites, Sylvester Swift was unchanged. His good health proved that Dexter DeMille had done something that had never been achieved before . . . he had successfully targeted a bio-weapon to a specific genetic group by hitting Troy Lee and not affecting Sylvester at all.

Admiral Zoll called Dexter DeMille and congratulated him. "I'm very pleased," the sandpaper voice said. They both knew the weapon would devastate the enemy, first with the terrifying homicidal rages, then with the horrible death cycle.

"Thank you," Dexter replied.

Then the Admiral asked to speak to Dr. Lack. Dexter handed the phone reluctantly to his assistant, who asked softly, "What do we do with Sylvester Swift?"

"He has to be collateralized," Zoll replied.

Five minutes later a gunshot sounded in the empty corridor of the fifth tier of center block.

Dexter DeMille didn't hear it. He had already returned to his quarters.

He poured a strong drink of Scotch and sat on the edge of his bed. His hands shook, while his mind wandered. He had started studying Prions in New Guinea, trying to save lives, but after that there was almost no practical application. Nobody seemed to care about his discovery, except for Admiral Zoll. Somehow his once humanistic science had led him to Fort Detrick, and then to this gruesome new discovery.

"Dear God, what am I doing?" he finally whispered to himself. Then he got off his bunk, walked into his bathroom, and threw up.

Chapter 7

HOBOS

Hollywood Mike glowered. "My old man. What a prick! Know what the worst day of that asshole's life was?"

"Whaaa?" Lucky slurred.

"The day Heidi Fleiss got busted."

Lucky took another pull on the half-empty bottle of Gallo Red Label.

It was seven A.M. Sunday morning. They were both drunk, sprawled against the wooden slats of an empty boxcar coupled in the middle of a manifest freight—a train with many different types of cars—that was making a slow climb up the face of the Black Hills of East Texas. The train creaked and groaned as the scenery drifted lazily past the open door, strobing fingers of pale sunlight into the boxcar and across both of them.

Somebody had recently done a job on Lucky. One of his front teeth had been knocked out; his lip was split and maybe needed stitches. He also had some open sun sores on his lips, caused by passing out in the park on a ninety-degree day. Most of the discoloration and swelling from the beating was hidden under his tangled blond beard. He was thirty-seven, but seemed ageless. Greasy, shoulder-length hair hung limp; his blue eyes were rimmed in red and remained unfocused as he rocked with the motion of the car.

Lucky didn't know who had beaten him up, because he'd been passed out in a hobo encampment, known as a jungle, when it happened. He woke up just in time to be knocked unconscious again. He'd lost five dollars that he'd earned in Waco, Texas, chopping wood, but more important, he'd lost his torn Nikes to the vicious unseen jungle buzzard who'd attacked him. Now his feet were wrapped and tied in black plastic garbage bags that he'd stolen from containers behind the Salvation Army mission, known as a "sally." The mission director had thrown both him and Hollywood Mike out after a two-day visit, two days being the limit you could stay in one of those preachy "ear-bangs."

They had gone to the switching yard in Waco and had "caught out" on this manifest train.

Hollywood Mike, at twenty-two, was fifteen years younger than Lucky, and he still had his shoes, but aside from these two advantages, there was little difference between them. He was just as scruffy, and almost as drunk. His curly hair was plastered on his head with just as much road muck. His one wardrobe statement, which was responsible for his nickname, he wore under torn coveralls. It was a movie premiere T-shirt that read:

ARNOLD SCHWARZENEGGER

IS

HOMEWRECKER

HOLLYWOOD PREMIERE

JULY 3, 1999

"Heidi Fleiss, man, Heidi fuckin' Fleiss," Lucky said, in mindless reflection. Then he straightened up and took another hit from the bottle, being careful to pour the wine down the right side of his throat to avoid the open cut and festering sun blisters.

"Gimme a hit off that," Mike demanded.

Lucky leaned to pass the bottle and the two of them, drunk as they were, almost fumbled the prize. Both lunged to catch it. Finally Mike wiped the neck with his dirty palm, a concession to proper oral hygiene, then took a deep swallow. "Yeah, everything in that prick's fucked-up life is only about him. I might as wella been dead."

"Selfish motherfucker," Lucky commiserated dully.

"I only stayed with the prick one summer, but that was enough. Know what his drug bill is in one day? Just one lousy day?"

"One fuckin' day?" Lucky repeated, his dull eyes locked on the bottle of Red Label.

"Thirty-two thousand dollars."

"Thirty-two . . ." Lucky stopped and looked up at his friend. "Huh?"

"I'm not sayin' like every day he spent that." Mike took another hit from the bottle. "I'm sayin' I found this one bill like in the pool house, or some fuckin' place. I can't remember now where it was. Bill from a Malibu pharmacy, March tenth, thirty-two large. This shallow cocksucker is stickin' it up his nose, or in his arm, and then he has the balls to piss on me about one little misdemeanor pot bust. Fuck him." Mike took another swallow.

"Fuck him!" Lucky repeated. "Gimme it back."

Mike reluctantly handed the almost empty bottle to Lucky, who was now so gone he was lolling against the side of the empty boxcar, swaying with the rhythm of the rails, his lidded eyes half open.

"Fuckin' guy has, whatta they call it . . . ? Acute mania," Mike went on. "No shit. From all the drugs. Acute fuckin' mania. He takes Thorazine every four hours, and Valium and Vicodin and lithium and fuckin' Xanax and Desyrel and fuckin' who knows what else? He's on more shit than the Russian weight-lifting team . . . and this doofus gets all bogged down over my one crummy pot bust. Dear ol' Dad. Man, if I never see that shallow fuck again, it'll be two months too soon.''

The train was slowing for the summit now, and out the door they could hear footsteps running up the gravel embankment beside the track. Then four heads appeared alongside the train, running for all they were worth.

"Giddyap, motherfuckers!" Lucky yelled drunkenly.

One of them dove into the boxcar, followed by two more. They then turned and grabbed the last guy, who was hanging by the door handle, skipping along just above the gravel. They finally got him in. The new arrivals were just as scruffy as Lucky and Hollywood Mike, but they weren't anywhere near as drunk.

"Look't what's in here," one of them said, surveying the current occupants of the car. "Got us a coupla track tunas." He was fat and greasy, with long gray hair knotted in a ponytail. His accent was West Texan.

"It's Miller time," a second hobo said, looking at the bottle of Red Label. He was short and muscular, and also had a Texas twang.

Next to him was a thirty-something black man. The one who they'd just pulled in was a skinhead covered with homemade prison tattoos.

"Gimme the bottle, asshole," the skinhead said.

"You got it . . ." Lucky grinned, dully. He quickly drained the bottle and threw it out the door of the slow-moving car. "All gone," he slurred through his already busted lips.

"Fuckin' Yankee," the black hobo growled when he heard Lucky's accent.

"You're in my place," the short, muscular one said, moving toward Lucky.

Lucky tried to get up, but before he could rise, the hobo kicked his legs out from under him and he landed back on his ass.

''Where'd you get them great patent-leather shoes?'' he said, leering at Lucky's garbage-bagged feet.

Lucky and Mike were in deep shit and they knew it. One way or the other, they were about to get the crap kicked out of them for no reason at all. That was the way it went on the rails sometimes. It was an unforgiving life.

The boxcar they were on was known as a ''sleeper'' car, and was favored by train-riders because it was a vacant car in the center of a loaded train that had been left on when the train had been assembled. It was sometimes easier for the switch crew to leave it engaged than to move lines of cars all over the yard in an attempt to drop it. Every train had one or two sleepers, and they were prized spots for hobos. This one, however, was about to change ownership.

''Why don' we all jus' take it easy?'' Lucky slurred, trying to get his senses to function correctly.

''Fuckin' Yankees is just like hemorrhoids,'' the gray-haired hobo droned. ''It's okay if they come down an' go right back up. But when they come down an' stay down they irritate the hell outta ya.''

'' 'At's good,'' Lucky said, trying to grin, but feeling the scabs cracking around his mouth.

''You two track tunas is 'bout ta be flyin' fish,'' the skinhead said, and without warning, the four Texans rushed the two Yankees.

It wasn't much of a fight because Lucky and Mike were so out of it. After head-butting the short one, Lucky was grabbed by two others and thrown out of the moving train. His backpack followed. Lucky summoned what sobriety he could as he sailed high over the graded shoulder. The train was going only about fifteen miles an hour. At the last moment, Lucky ducked his head, rolled awkwardly down a slight grade, and finally came to a painful, bone-jarring halt. Moments later, he could see Mike also being hurled through the air with his back to the ground, struggling to get his body turned. He landed badly, with a loud thump and grunt, and no bone-saving roll. He didn't move once he hit.

"Shit," Lucky mumbled. "That ain't how you do it, Mike."

The train roared on. They could hear a diminishing rebel yell from the faraway sleeper car and soon they were left in still mountain silence.

Lucky stumbled to his feet and checked his scrapes and bruises. Then he moved drunkenly to Hollywood Mike, who was still on his back, unconscious. Lucky went hunting for his pack, then brought it back. He opened it and pulled out an old refilled Evian water bottle and a torn T-shirt. He poured some water onto the shirt, then put the compress on Mike's forehead. Mike groaned and his eyes finally opened. He looked up at Lucky. "Whaa happened?"

"Bubbas threw us off the motherfuckin' train," Lucky slurred, and looked around. Off to the north he could see a deep meadow and lush green bushes. "Looks like water over there."

Hollywood Mike tried to sit up. "Think some ribs are broken," he groaned.

"Bubbas threw us off the motherfuckin' train," Lucky said again, trying to clear his vision.

He helped Hollywood Mike to his feet. The twenty-two-year-old groaned and let out a sharp cry of pain.

"Schwarzenegger is de 'Homewrecker,' " Lucky mused, looking at Mike's T-shirt, "but you an' me is de homeless wrecks."

The greenery was located at the edge of a large lake. The water was cold and clear. Lucky stripped off his shirt and pants, unwrapped the garbage bags from his feet, and waded in. He scrubbed the grime out of his hair with his fingers and sluiced the grit off his body with his hands. He was careful not to open the sores on his mouth. The cold water and the half-mile walk had sobered him up some. "This life is sure gettin' old," he said, as he came out of the water and sat on a large rock in his underwear. "Maybe I should stop ridin' high iron an' go pick fruit in California, or maybe yer old man will give me a job, make me a movie star?"

"You don't wanna work for him, he's an asshole," Hollywood Mike said softly through gritted teeth, still holding his ribs. "But sometimes I miss him. . . . I don't know why. . . . I guess because . . ."

" 'Cause he's your only relative," Lucky finished. Mike had made this zigzag several times before . . . pure anger and hatred, followed by loneliness and longing. Mike desperately needed a father, a service the older 'bo was not prepared to perform. Lucky was mostly on a search for his next bottle. Surfing a cresting wave on a slippery board, he was always just a few hours in front of the D.T.s, those scary hallucinations caused by alcohol withdrawal and the destructive imaginings of his own brain. He had fallen into that snake pit twice before, once screaming so desperately that four hobos had hand-delivered him to the hospital ER in Wilmington, Delaware, while he slapped at hallucinatory snakes and bugs that crawled all over him, feasting mostly on his eyes.

Lucky was now out of money and booze. He needed to start working on finding that next bottle before the dangerous curl on this alcohol-induced wave collapsed again, driving him under.

Lucky looked out across the lake. A half-mile away there appeared to be a fishing village. Then he swung his gaze back in the other direction, where there was a mammoth stone prison.

"The fuck is that over there?" Lucky said, pointing at the huge building. He could also see a small plume of dust from a fast-moving vehicle on a dirt road a mile or so away.

"Looks like a prison," Mike said.

They watched in growing panic as the vehicle now headed right at them. As it got closer they recognized it as a jeep painted military green. Lucky and Hollywood Mike quickly gathered up their things and started to retreat from the shore as it came nearer. They scrambled up into the tree line and crouched down in the ground cover of heavy, tangled forest growth. The jeep pulled up to where they had been standing. Two soldiers were in the back of the jeep and another one was driving. All were heavily armed.

"They got rifles," Mike whispered.

"Those're German MP5s," Lucky said. "Submachine guns."

Then the soldier closest to them pulled up a bullhorn and pointed it in their general direction. "We aren't gonna chase you in there and flush you guys out, but this here is all military property. We saw you through field glasses. Here's the deal. . . . Get off this land. It's posted. Get back past the highway or over to Vanishing Lake Village. We see you in here again, you're both goin' in mummy sacks."

The man with the bullhorn then nodded to the other man in the back of the jeep, who fired his machine gun into the high branches over their heads. The gun chattered nine-millimeter death. Bullet-riddled tree limbs rained down where Lucky and Hollywood Mike were hiding. Then the jeep pulled away, heading back the way it came.

"How come if we're in Texas, the side of that jeep said 'Fort Detrick, Maryland'?" Lucky asked.

"Who cares. Let's just get outta here."

They picked up their tattered gear and, with Hollywood Mike still holding his ribs, they moved off toward the fishing village, about a mile away.

The town of Vanishing Lake was very small and very quiet. Crude log-cabin A-frames were the main architectural flavor. A hardware store, market, and gas station were lined up on both sides of the main street. There was a wharf, with rental boats, and next to it was a small bait shop and restaurant with a sign out front that read:

BUCKET A' BAIT
COFFEE SHOP

As Lucky and Hollywood Mike moved slowly down the center of town, several people came out of the hardware store to look at the two unwelcome apparitions. Lucky's feet were back in the plastic bags; Mike was doubled over, holding his ribs.

"Let's try over there," Lucky said, pointing to the coffee shop. "Lemme do the hee-haw. We need ta get money fer a bottle."

They went around to the back, where they could smell breakfast being cooked in the kitchen.

"Hey . . . hello in there," Lucky said, and banged his hand on the screen. In a minute, a very pretty blond woman came to the door. She was wearing an off-the-shoulder blouse and jeans. An order book was shoved in her waistband, a stubby pencil behind her ear.

"Yes," she said.

"Uh. Mama . . . good morning," Lucky smiled, beginning his panhandler shuffle. "Me and Mike are real hungry. Bein' it's Sunday mornin', and bein' as Sunday is a Christian time a' charity an' giving, we were wonderin' if we could work for some food? Or, better still, a little money for necessities? Shampoo, a razor, and the like. Anything ya could spare would be appreciated, ma'am." He smiled wider, showing the broken tooth and split lip.

"I'll ask Barry—he runs the place. The raccoons got into the trash, so maybe you could clean that up. Wait a minute, I'll go ask," she said, disappearing. She reappeared a few seconds later with four large sugar doughnuts. She handed them to Lucky and Mike. "Wait over there," she said, pointing to a bench under a pine tree.

"Thanks. I'm Lucky, he's Mike."

"I'm Stacy," the pretty woman said.

Chapter 8

HOBO PRIEST

Eve was seduced by the serpent and bore by him a son. So that first seed revealed in Genesis was the seed of the devil,'' Reverend Kincaid shouted to the congregation. ''That son was Cain, who eventually slew his own brother, Abel.''

It was ten o'clock on Sunday morning, and Reverend Fannon Kincaid stood before a makeshift altar in a lean-to chapel constructed from materials scrounged or stolen from houses all up and down the Southern Pacific Railroad track. A huge green nylon tarp was stretched overhead to create a ceiling for the chapel, which was located in the hills above Vanishing Lake not two miles from the prison. The morning sun shone through the nylon and cast an eerie green hue on the worshipers. They sat on logs and boxes or on the hard ground. They looked up at Fannon Kincaid in wonder. Even in these meager surroundings, he seemed larger than life. He towered above his flock.

''So what does this tell us about the second creation?'' Fannon thundered, pausing as if to wait for the answer, but, of course, no one dared interrupt. ''Tells us Cain was not the son of Adam; Cain was the seed of the devil. Adam was the first and only true white man created by the Lord God. Later Adam gave the second seed to Eve, and they begot Seth, and with him came the glorious beginning of the white godly civilization.''

His voice thundered off the back wall of the chapel, which was a piece of plywood leaning up against some grocery store siding.

There were forty worshipers in the congregation: scruffy, unwashed men, and a few tired females with snarled hair. All of them looked homeless. All of them were bending forward slightly to catch every bit of Fannon's holy wisdom; all except for Dexter DeMille, who sat between his two uniformed M.P. guards, wearing pressed Dockers slacks and a pink Ralph Lauren shirt.

"Now, there are those who will say this is heresy. These heathens ask, 'Where in the scriptures does it tell of a second creation?' ''

Fannon Kincaid looked out at his flock. His silver-white hair seemed to shimmer in the backlight that came through window holes cut in the makeshift chapel. "For that, we have to turn to the forty-eighth and forty-ninth chapters of Genesis, the prophecies of Jacob for his twelve sons, and look at how the Tribes of Israel were founded and came down to eventually rule the nations of Europe."

The two M.P.s who had brought Dexter DeMille to this Sunday service were Bobby Faragut and Lewis Potter. They were both from the rural South and had been assigned to Vanishing Lake Prison. Dexter thought they were dumb white trash in uniform. Bobby and Lewis had discovered this church while wandering in the hills doing some hunting. Dexter overheard them at the prison one afternoon, talking about the strange hobo priest who lived up here with a band of misfits. After talking to Bobby and Lewis, Dexter thought that Fannon Kincaid might be just what he was looking for. He had petitioned Fort Detrick for the right to attend church services. He had been told okay, but that he had to go under guard. Dexter accepted this condition and had left that Sunday to attend the hobo church with the very M.P.s who had originally told him about it.

"Okay," Fannon thundered. "Let's go to the begats." He glanced down at his Bible for a moment, then looked up, reciting, more or less, from memory. " 'And Israel said thy issue begettest and shall be thine and shall be called after the name of their brethren and I shall bless them. And when Joseph saw that his father had laid his right hand upon the head of Ephar-im, it displeased him and Joseph raised up his father's right hand and tried to put it on Manas-seh's head. This is my first born, Joseph said. Put thy hand on his head first. I know it, my son, Israel replied, but truly his younger brother shall be greater. His seed shall become a multitude of nations! And Israel set Ephar-im before Manas-seh.' " Fannon paused to look at his congregation. "Y'all listening to that? Lemme say it again, 'cause it's real damn important. *Israel set Ephar-im before Manas-seh.* Joseph's father, Israel, chose one race to be supreme over the other. And that was the White Christian race." The congregation nodded and murmured at this holy wisdom.

What a crock of shit, Dexter thought. He turned his gaze to the congregation of misfits and lost souls. They wore ragtag clothing and weathered complexions. Most had tattoos on their biceps that read "F.T.R.A." One thing about the congregation was horribly out of place: They were all armed to the teeth. The men were carrying every imaginable kind of firearm. The hardware dangled from their belts as they worshiped. Live ammunition hung across their chests in army surplus webbed bandoliers.

"Our Father who art in heaven," they whispered, as Fannon led them, "hallowed be thy name . . ."

Dexter bowed his head, reciting with them. He didn't know how he would use this collection of throwaway people, but he knew they offered his best possibility of escape. Since the murder of Troy Lee Williams and Sylvester Swift, he'd suspected he was on a very short clock. Admiral Zoll was not above disposing of him once he was satisfied that Dexter had delivered an operational strain of Pale Horse Prion. What had happened to Max Richardson was a testament to Zoll's brutality. Reverend Kincaid could probably get him out of the Black Hills of Texas. Dexter assumed Kincaid had four-wheel-drive vehicles that could climb over the hills and avoid the roadblocks that would instantly be thrown up if he tried to escape.

After the service, they drank lemonade in a three-sided yellow tent with an open flap. Fannon Kincaid sat in an old discarded upholstered chair, his hands out on his knees like the last Pharaoh of Egypt. Dexter sat on a wooden crate, and his two M.P. guards squatted in the dirt near him.

"I never heard of the two-seed theory of creation," Dexter said. "I found that uplifting, very edifying."

"I'd figure a mo-lec-u-lar biologist like yerself would more likely hold with Darwin. Man like you can't possibly believe all that shit I was spoutin'."

Dexter smiled slightly; they were circling each other like wary combatants looking for handholds. Both wanted something from the other. Dexter could see that the old man was much more than he first appeared. A bright intensity shone from his blue eyes. "How do you mean that?" Dexter said. "There are lots of ways to view creation. Darwin doesn't have to dispute biblical creation."

"Y'mean, God creates life by bringing accidental single cell clusters of microbes together, and they become bacteria growing in the moisture on the leaves of prehistoric trees, then they fall to the ground and the bacteria mixes with the mud protein, which then evolves over billions of years into a more complex organism, capable of splitting in two and reproducing itself until there is a flood that turns it into a tadpole. Then this fish, or whatever, becomes an air-breathing lizard, starts walking around on his tail, and, after a zillion years, develops up into a biped or some shit like that." Fannon's blue eyes were twinkling as he spoke, amusement and intelligence burning there bright and shrewd, surprising Dr. DeMille with their piercing energy.

"That's pretty good, although you forgot a few important steps like the first sexual beginnings where chromosomes divided, called meiosis. But who's to say that Darwin's kind of evolutionary process isn't God's Creation? Creation can be molecular *and* divine, can't it? Do we need the biblical lumps of clay?"

"Don't know, maybe not," Fannon said. "Probably don't need all yer fossilized skeletons either."

"I'll tell you something that bothers me about Darwin," Dexter said, smiling. "I don't like missing links. We go from *Australopithecus* through *Homo erectus* to modern *Homo sapiens*, but lots of mysteries still remain. We've still got huge gaps in the evolutionary chain."

"You wouldn't be shitting me, would ya, Mr. DeMille?"

"Dr. DeMille," Dexter corrected.

"You got a doctorate. That only makes you a Ph.D. A real doctor cures sick people; a Ph.D. don't do nothin' but read books or write 'em. I ain't making you call me Colonel. And I'm sure God wore the Oak Leaf and kicked some dink ass for this beautiful God-blessed country. You ever in Vietnam, or did ya serve in Canada?"

"I was Four-F."

"I was for America," Fannon shot back, "all the good it did me." Then he smiled, and seemed to relax slightly. "You must be curious why I allowed you t'come up here and visit with us."

Now Dexter could see something else in Reverend Kincaid's eyes. . . . There was a gleam there, a shining connection to some hidden truth that nobody else could share. "I wasn't aware that these were closed services," Dexter finally said.

"Don't shit me, bub," the Great Man said from his old stuffed chair. "You know better'n that. I gave Bobby here permission ta invite you. See, I know what's happenin' in that prison. Bobby

and Lewis tell me what's going on. You guys are cookin' up a
heap of nasty shit over there.''

"Really?'' Dexter looked over at the two young hillbilly guards,
who suddenly seemed uneasy. "What else did they tell you?''

"They told me you're making chemical weapons. I'm real interested in strategic chemical weapons.''

"They're wrong. I'm not a chemist, I'm a molecular biologist,
as you said. I don't deal in chemicals. I'm a different kind of
scientist.''

Fannon looked at the two M.P. guards, and some voiceless command seemed to pass between them. Both men simultaneously rose
from their squatting positions beside Dexter and moved out of the
tent, stopping about fifty feet away and turning so that their backs
were to Fannon Kincaid. They looked out at the religious compound that sat on a rocky bluff.

"What'd you really think of the sermon?'' Kincaid asked, a
small smile playing on his rugged features.

"I thought it was unique. As I said, you hit on some things I'd
never thought of before.''

"I did, huh?'' Again, that small smile hovered. "I think,'' Fannon said very slowly, "that you and I are going to be friends.''

"It's my hope.''

"But friends, Mr. DeMille, tell each other the truth. Bobby and
Lewis told you about my little church, my settlement, 'cause I told
'em to, and they told me about yer situation over at the prison.
Not being able ta go places without bein' watched.''

"It's been a problem,'' Dexter concurred.

Fannon reached down and pulled up a long blade of grass, stuck
it in his mouth, and chewed it pensively. "You got any idea what
it is I'm doin' up here?''

"No, not really.''

"The church I run is called 'the Christian Choir and the Lord's
Desire.' ''

"I saw that on the banner in the chapel.''

"We're a chorus of angels and sub-angels, Mr. DeMille. In Revelation it foretells of the Choir of One Hundred and Forty-four Thousand."

"Really?" Dexter said. He was an agnostic and was not sure where this was headed.

" 'For the great day of his wrath is come,' " Fannon recited from Revelation. " 'And I saw four angels standing on the four corners of the earth. And there were sealed one hundred and forty-four thousand of all the tribes of the Children of Israel. And one of the elders said, What are these which are arrayed in white robes and whence do they come? And I said, These are they which came out of great tribulation, and have washed their robes, and made them white in the blood of the Lamb.' " He paused and looked hard at Dexter, who once again felt he needed to say something, to comment, but he was badly off rhythm and wasn't sure what his response should be.

"I see," he finally muttered.

"I am one of those four angels standing on the corner of this earth. From the iron rails of this great nation, I will lead my people to God's greatest victory. I will wreak havoc on a government of lost idolaters who have chosen to worship material values sold to them by Levites. Our government today is far more corrupt than the British Empire that our Continental Congress declared war on in 1776. Our leaders today choose to favor the Children of Satan handed down from the loins of Manas-seh over the godly descendants of Jacob and the twelve tribes of Israel. As prophesied, we will become a Choir of One Hundred and Forty-four Thousand and we will throw off the chains of this corrupt administration. What I'm doin' is I'm leading the Second American Revolutionary Army. Whatta ya think of that, bub?"

Dexter DeMille was forced to make another quick reevaluation. He finally knew that the intense gleam in Fannon Kincaid's eyes was more than shrewd intelligence. He now realized the silver-haired man sitting in the old chair leaking stuffing was insane.

Chapter 9

DISASTER AT VANISHING LAKE

'll have the deluxe cheeseburger, the small chili, and a Bud Light,'' Dr. Charles Lack said, looking at Stacy Richardson's trim figure as she leaned across the table to pour his water.

The Bucket a' Bait was filling up. It was Sunday lunch, and there were the usual after-church retirees, some anglers, and at the far end of the restaurant, a table full of soldiers from the prison, raising hell. She glanced over as they let out an ear-piercing whoop.

"I can talk to 'em if you want," Dr. Lack said.

"That's okay, they're just puppies tearin' up a shoe," Stacy said, using a pretty fair country accent she'd developed playing Ado Annie in her high school production of *Oklahoma*.

Charles Lack was trying to figure a way to shuck this beautiful new waitress out of her tight jeans and into the sack. He had never been very good with women. He had lost most of his hair before he got out of grad school, and at thirty-four had only been laid twice. He looked at the dumb blond waitress and decided to play his best card . . . the old black ace, his scientific mind.

"You wanna hear something we found out that's really incredible?" he asked.

"You bet yer shabooty," she grinned, tucking the pad into her waistband and her chewed pencil behind her ear. "I usually only hear complaints about Barney's food."

"You were telling me those hobos working out there in the yard were cleaning up after raccoons that got in the trash . . ." he said, trying for a smooth scientific segue.

"That's right," she said, looking out the window at Hollywood Mike and Lucky, who were just finishing up raking trash from around the Dumpster.

"Well, I did some 'index case' research on raccoons a few months ago."

So did I, Stacy thought, remembering the paper that had earned her five hundred dollars from *Animal Science Magazine* and Augie, the ceramic raccoon from Max.

"My study," Dr. Lack continued, "showed the relationship in raccoon HIV-1 variants that infect brain-derived positive cells in humans."

She knew the study. It had been done by three Japanese microbiologists. Nowhere had she ever read that a Dr. Charles Lack was involved. "You and Dr. DeMille must be awful busy over at the prison," she said, refocusing the conversation.

"You know Dex DeMille?" Charles asked.

"Not to talk to. I seen him in town at the grocery store once or twice. He always has guards protectin' him, like he was a national treasure or some damn thing."

"Well, not exactly." Dr. Lack was choosing his words carefully now, working up to a hatchet job on his rival. "Dr. DeMille is a troubled, highly dissociative personality, who needs to be watched constantly. I don't like to use terms like 'suicidal,' so let's just say that they're watching him for his own good."

"Son of a gun, an' I thought it was 'cause he was so important," she said, shaking her head in wonder. "Well, lemme get this order in 'fore y'all faint from hunger." She moved away, and as she passed the table full of soldiers, they whistled at her, pawing out as she swept past.

"Need another round of beer, Stace," one of them shouted.

"It's comin', sugar," she chirped, and darted past them. "And hold it down. This ain't the rodeo." She gathered some dirty plates off a sideboard and backed through the swinging doors into an over-hot kitchen where Barney, the harassed owner-chef, was flipping burgers, stirring chili, and falling behind on the orders. He patted his damp forehead with the towel he always had around his neck.

"One Bud Light and another round of long-necks for the table from hell," she said to Barney. "Dr. Lack wants a CB, full-house, and a side bowl of red. And the two 'bos are almost through with the raccoon cleanup, so you better decide what ya want to pay 'em and throw their steak an' eggs on."

"I'm goin' inta the trees here, Stace," Barney said. "I'll get to the hobos when I can."

He put the beers on her tray with an opener, then shoved two fruit salads through the pass-through. "Here's yer two number fours with yogurt sides for table nine."

"Right," she said, scooping them both up, balancing them on one hand. Then she picked up the tray of beers and backed through the swinging doors, into the restaurant. She set the salads on a side bar and took the long-necks over to the rowdies.

"Here's the rescue lady," one of the soldiers yelled as she snapped the tops off with a church key and passed the beer around. The one closest to her tried to slip a hand around her waist as she leaned in to distribute the last beer to the soldier by the window.

"Easy there, babe," Stacy said, playfully slapping his hand away. "Don't be messin' with the wagonmaster."

The others hooted their appreciation.

After her parents died, she had waitressed all during her teens to save up enough to put herself through college. The first thing she had learned was how to serve a meal without getting tackled.

She finished distributing the beer and scooped the salads up off the back console and moved with them to a nearby table occupied by a mid-sixties couple named Sid and Mary Saunders.

Sid was a retired dentist, with a full supply of old jokes. Mary was gray-haired and always pleasant. They told her they had just had their silver wedding anniversary and had moved to Vanishing Lake to live out their golden years. Mary was glaring at the table full of rowdy soldiers.

"How do you ever put up with it?" she asked angrily.

"Sorry, Mrs. Saunders. I just got through asking them to hold it down. Here's yer two low-cal pineapple boat salads, each with a side a' peach yogurt," she said, sliding the plates in front of them. "I'll get yer two iced teas."

Mary went on, "When it was a prison we were so worried somebody would escape and kill us in our beds. We thought it would be so much better when the University took it over, but now we have all these soldiers."

"Oh, why don't you quit yer damn complaining," Sid growled uncharacteristically, startling both Mary and Stacy.

"All morning you've been sullen and mean," Mary said. "What on earth is the matter with you, Sid?"

"I'll be right back," Stacy said, wanting to avoid this strange domestic quarrel. As she turned away to get their iced tea, she heard Mary say, "Don't glare at me like that!" Then Stacy heard a commotion behind her at the Saunders table. She turned and saw Sid scramble unexpectedly to his feet. He was glaring angrily at his wife.

"What is it?" Mary demanded.

"God damn you!" he shouted.

"I beg your pardon?" Mary Saunders said.

Now everybody in the restaurant fell quiet and looked at the round-faced dentist, who was cursing at his wife in public for no apparent reason. His face was suddenly contorted, his complexion pumped with blood.

"You hush up, Sidney," Mary hissed. "Sit back down and behave. What's gotten into you?"

"Fuck you!" he screamed in rage. Then he reached down and picked up a serrated steak knife from a basket on the console. Without saying another word, he lunged at his wife and plunged the knife deep into her chest. Mary Saunders let out a gasp as the knife was slammed into her up to the handle. Blood, thick as motor oil, oozed down her white silk blouse and pooled in her lap. Then she began to scream as her husband turned and bolted from the coffee shop amid the startled shouts of the other patrons.

Stacy had momentarily frozen, but now reached out for the old woman, who was still seated upright in the booth, looking down at the knife in her chest in horror and disbelief. Then Mary went into her first death spasm. Her whole body jerked uncontrollably, her right hand banged hard against the table. The blade had pierced her heart, and Stacy knew that the convulsions signaled oxygen starvation in the cerebral cortex. The old woman spasmed several more times as Stacy held her, trying to give her comfort. Then Mary Saunders let out a long sigh and fell sideways onto the upholstered couch.

Stacy reached out and felt for a heartbeat, but Mrs. Saunders was dead.

Sid was standing in the middle of the street between the restaurant and the dock. His teeth were bared. He was still yelling obscenities. Two soldiers had chased him out of the restaurant. They stood on the porch of the Bucket a' Bait, looking with alarm at the growling, snarling dentist in the center of the street.

"Let's go. Let's take him. He's just an old guy," the tall Army Corporal said. "You go right, I'll go left."

They separated and moved off the porch, toward Dr. Saunders. It was then that the old man charged. He attacked with such fury that both twenty-year-olds could not restrain him. He clawed at them. His teeth snapped savagely as they tried to tackle him.

Two other soldiers from their table could see through the window what was happening outside. They got up and followed their buddies onto the porch. They watched in disbelief as the old dentist seemed to actually be overpowering two men one-third his age. The rage and adrenaline that drove him were, in that moment, too much for them. The two remaining soldiers bolted into the street. It took all four of them to finally subdue Sid Saunders.

They tied his hands behind his back, using their belts. Then they dragged him, screaming and cursing, into the restaurant. Barney suggested they put him in the empty food locker out back. It was a sturdy, windowless room with a padlock. They shut the door and snapped the latch. They could still hear him shouting incoherently after the door was closed.

"What the fuck was that all about?" Barney said, his voice a whisper of shock and dismay.

Nobody answered.

Stacy Richardson had a theory. Only Charles Lack knew exactly what had just happened.

"We got an event over here," Dr. Lack said to Dexter DeMille over the telephone from inside the restaurant. "I think . . . I think . . ."

"You think what?" Dr. DeMille snapped impatiently. He was in his lab in Building Six at Vanishing Lake Prison.

"We've got a problem. A guy at the restaurant just went nuts and killed his wife." Dr. Lack lowered his voice. "He behaved exactly like the test case yesterday."

"That's impossible," Dexter DeMille shouted. "How could that be?"

"Obviously, some of your damn mosquitoes got loose," Dr.

Lack hissed. "I told you that it was a mistake. We should never have used an aerobiological vector."

"Let's not go into that now," Dexter said. "Stay there, I'm on my way," and he hung up.

The bio-hazard team from the prison roared into town fifteen minutes later. Dr. DeMille was the first one out of the windowless van. He moved into the restaurant with his medical bag, followed by three M.P.s. Barney unlocked and cautiously opened the door to the food locker. Stacy Richardson moved to where she could see into the room over their shoulders.

Dr. Sidney Saunders was now kneeling on the floor leaning against the sidewall. His hands were still tied behind him. The rage was no longer in his eyes. Instead, there was a look of desperate confusion. He tried to stand as they entered, but staggered, and like Troy Lee, fell over, going down on his right side. He had lost his equilibrium; drool was streaming down his chin.

"Look for a labrum injection mark," Dr. DeMille said to Dr. Lack, referring to a mosquito bite, knowing the scientific language would elude the civilian restaurant patrons. "See if you can isolate it. We can do a tracking scan later," DeMille finished.

They were working feverishly, pulling Sid Saunders's shirt off, checking around his hairline.

"Here," Dr. Lack said, and pointed to a mosquito bite on the back of the dying man's neck.

"Get him in the van," DeMille said. "Forget bio-containment. We've gotta move fast."

"What's going on here?" Barney said again. "Does this have something to do with yer experiments over at the prison?" But Drs. Lack and DeMille were already following the uniformed M.P.s, who had picked up the dying sixty-year-old dentist and were carrying him out of the restaurant. They put him in the back of the truck. The M.P.s pushed Barney away from the van and slammed the back door before scrambling in and roaring away.

Mary Saunders still lay dead in the booth at table two. Only after the van left did Barney make calls to the County Coroner and Sheriff, which were fifty miles away in Bracketville, a town with only a two-man substation. The Sheriff said they would get up there as soon as possible, and suggested that Barney take Mary over to the big walk-in fish cooler on the dock and put her there until the County people showed up.

Stacy Richardson slipped out of the restaurant in the confusion and moved up the hill to a little two-room wood cottage in the back that Barney sometimes rented to employees. She noticed absent-mindedly that the two hobos had finished their cleanup, but had left without waiting to get paid or fed. She assumed that, like homeless people everywhere, they were sensitive to their vulnerability and had fled during all the frenzied activity.

Stacy took out a key, opened the door, and moved into her cluttered cottage. She went directly to her small desk and pulled a binder down off the shelf, which read:

PRIONS

She opened it to a section she had labeled:

SYMPTOMS AND DISEASE

Then she turned the binder to a fresh page and wrote:

"Dr. Sidney Saunders, DDS."

"Near death at 10:30—07/16/99. Condition appears to be neuro-related."

Below that she wrote: "The death resembles no condition before observed. Probable iatrogenic infection, homicidal rage, followed by status epilepticus. Mosquito vector." Then she wrote a detailed medical account of Sid Saunders's bizarre homicidal pre-death behavior.

Also pasted in the binder were several long-lens photos of

Charles Lack and Dexter DeMille, along with both men's scientific histories. Under Dr. DeMille's bio, Stacy wrote the new information Dr. Lack had provided: "DeMille is unstable, dissociative, and suicidal." Yet it was stable, fun-loving, nonsuicidal Max who had supposedly stuck a twelve-gauge shotgun in his mouth and pulled the trigger.

Chapter 10

DAMAGE CONTROL

They were seated in the old parole board hearing room in the big, rectangular pale brick administration building. Out the windows across the yard they could see the high tower that contained the gas chamber in center block.

Admiral James G. Zoll was seated with his back to the windows that streamed sunlight past him and lit the unhappy faces of Dexter DeMille, Charles Lack, and Colonel Laurence Chittick. Seated at the end of the room, with his back to a large map of Vanishing Lake, was Captain Nicholas Zingo. He and his "Torn Victor" Delta Force Rangers were assigned to Admiral Zoll for program security and had arrived with the Admiral and Colonel Chittick half an hour ago from Fort Detrick, in three unmarked Blackhawk helicopters.

Captain Zingo was a muscular thirty-year-old, who Dexter DeMille feared would be ordered one day to kill him. Torn Victor was a unit combat designation and included ten event-trained Delta Force Rangers, who immediately upon arriving had commandeered the available jeeps and two half-tracks at the prison, then quickly deployed them around Vanishing Lake. Captain Zingo had an earpiece attached to a belt radio and was monitoring his deploying Rangers through his headset, while at the same time listening to what was going on in the briefing room.

"I assume it's your cocktail that caused this?" Admiral Zoll asked Dr. DeMille, his sandpapery voice filling the room and raising the hair on the back of Dexter's neck.

"Before we know that for sure," Dexter said, "we'll need to do a brain slice and examine the tissue under an electron microscope at forty-seven thousand power to see if unusual amounts of amyloid plaque are present in the cells and if—"

"Cut the shit, Doctor," Admiral Zoll interrupted. "I don't need a buncha nano-chat. Is it our stuff that caused this or not?"

Dexter couldn't bring himself to answer. He looked around the room and his eyes accidentally caught Dr. Lack's.

"It's us, Admiral," Charles Lack said, as if invited in by Dexter's helpless look.

Admiral Zoll got to his feet and walked around the table slowly. He moved over to the map. "How did the goddamn mosquitoes get out?" he asked, and when Dexter hesitated again, Charles Lack answered.

"We did a colored smoke test an hour ago. There's a leak in one of the vents. It appears that there were bad exhaust seals in the old gas vents that were never properly addressed."

"Why didn't we do a smoke test *before* we put those two grunts in there?" Admiral Zoll asked softly.

"Good question, sir," Charles Lack said. Then he looked to Dexter as if he should suddenly have the answer.

Dexter had no answer. It was a mistake, and the Crazy Ace was not a man you confided your mistakes to.

Dexter was beginning to slide into one of his deep depressions. The room seemed to be getting smaller. It was almost as if the

walls were closing in. Even his breath was coming faster; his heart
was slamming so uncontrollably in his chest that he was alarmed
he might actually have a coronary.

"Okay, forget it," Zoll snapped. "We got the problem now, either way. What I need is a varsity play from the deck," he said, using an old aircraft carrier expression. "I want full containment on
that little town over there. Nobody leaves. How many people live
there?"

"A few hundred or so," Dr. Lack said.

"I also want the phone system shut down. We need to impose
a total information blackout. If any word of this slips out, this
whole program goes back to the taxpayers and all of us are gonna
be up on the Hill trying to find a way to explain it." They were
all quiet, but everyone knew if this got out, they wouldn't be going
to Capitol Hill, they would be going to Leavenworth. "First priority is containment, then we need to make sure we kill all of the
escaped mosquitoes," Zoll continued.

Captain Zingo got out of his chair and moved over to the map.
"We have ultra-sensitive directional microphones set to the exact
high frequency female mosquitoes make when they fly. They've
been tested on mosquito vectors before, so they're accurate, and
efficient. My men are checking the marshy areas around the lake
to see if we can determine where they're breeding."

"What makes you say they're breeding?" Dexter asked.
"They're sterilized females. They can't breed."

Dr. Lack got to his feet. "Not to disagree, Dex, but apparently
they weren't sterilized properly."

"The hell they weren't," Dexter snapped. "I did it myself."

"After this happened, I took some unhatched larvae out of your
lab and hatched them. You have unsterilized females, and, I regret
to say, I also found quite a few functioning males."

"That's impossible!" Dexter exclaimed. But he was now beginning to suspect that Dr. Lack had been sabotaging the mosquito

experiment. "Those insects and the larvae were hit with huge x-ray exposures. There's no way they could reproduce."

"Well, one way or another, that's what they did," Charles Lack said, his face grim. He had chosen this moment, with Admiral Zoll present, to destroy Dexter DeMille.

"If they're breeding," Captain Zingo said, "we've got an even bigger problem. We need to find the places where they're nesting on the lake, and get in there immediately with either insecticides or defoliants. I think we should set fire to the marsh areas and burn them. That way we'll get the unhatched larvae."

There was a cold, angry silence in the room. Finally, Captain Zingo spoke again. "I have half my team working the high-frequency mikes, looking for breeding areas. The other half are doing phone and field containment."

"Mosquitoes swarm at sunset," Dr. Lack said. "I think we need to hit them before that."

"Okay," Captain Zingo said, looking at his watch, "that gives us two hours." Then he turned back to the map. "As far as civilian containment, we deployed our people here and here," he said, pointing to the two roads that surrounded the lake. "I've got the Angel Track parked across the main road leading up here," he said, referring to a half-track ambulance that could travel off-road on treads. "We're going about two miles down the highway and cutting some lumber so the trees will fall across the road. We'll put a two-man team there and turn all traffic around, but this probably buys us less than a day. Then the county cops are gonna chopper in here."

"What about phones?" Admiral Zoll asked.

"We're working on that." Captain Zingo had a shoulder mike, which he now clicked on and spoke into: "This is Zippo-1 to Zulu Field Command. Gimme a communications update." He listened for a minute through his earpiece, then triggered the mike again. "Okay, roger that. Stand by." He looked at Admiral Zoll. "We've just shut down the main cellphone pod on this hill, here"—he pointed to a low hill on the west side of Vanishing Lake—"and we've located the main telephone junction box. It's off Highway 16. They're in the process of disabling it."

"Anything else?"

"One of our scout teams said they just learned there's some kind of hobo camp up by the rail line, to the east. Soon as they can, they'll go up there and secure those people."

Dexter DeMille straightened up abruptly when he heard that. Fannon Kincaid was a delusional, heavily armed fanatic. He doubted that two men in a jeep would have much luck securing one of God's four revolutionary angels.

Stacy and most of the other residents of Vanishing Lake Village had heard the three Blackhawks coming up the canyon, heard the heavy whomp-whomp-whomp of the rotors as they reverberated against the hills and mesas. Ten or twelve townspeople came out, stood on the wharf, and watched through binoculars as the combat helicopters landed a mile away on the baseball diamond, which the soldiers had cleared on the far side of the prison.

"What the hell are those people up to?" Barney said, a nervous sense of impending doom gripping him.

They were all trying to comprehend the bizarre events of that afternoon. Stacy stood on the edge of the dock, looking across the lake at the unmarked choppers through her camera's telephoto long lens. She snapped a few shots as they landed and tried to decide what she should do next. She had little doubt that they were in the middle of some kind of aerobiologic outbreak that was mosquito-borne. She wondered if all of the people in Vanishing Lake would end up dying, following the same horrible homicidal paths set by poor Sid and Mary Saunders. She suspected that the strange neural encephalitis that had claimed Sid was a Prion very much like the

rare New Guinea disease Kuru, discovered in the early seventies
by Carleton Gajdusek and Dexter DeMille. Max had told her that
Kuru was caused by a rogue protein that, when ingested or injected, wasn't broken down by the body's enzymes, as all other
such proteins were. The Prion eventually went to the brain, where
it attacked the mood center, eating holes, turning the midbrain to
jelly, causing a condition called spongiform encephalitis. If Dr.
DeMille had developed some juiced-up strain of Kuru, it could
constitute the worst strategic weapon ever conceived. She also
knew if mosquitoes were the vector, and if they were breeding, it
might be only a matter of hours before more people went berserk.

One other thing that Max had included in his e-mail had been
rattling around in her head. He had said that what made a protein
bio-weapon so dangerous was that it adapted to the target victim's
own body chemistry. It didn't cause an infection or swelling, like
a virus, so it often went undiagnosed. It became, in effect, a stealth
weapon that silently and efficiently attacked your brain. Your immune system would not even be aware that it had infiltrated your
body. It could therefore spread quickly, with the body producing
no anti-toxins to fight it.

Twenty minutes later the first jeep full of bio-garmented soldiers
appeared in the sleepy fishing village. The troops drove slowly
down the street. One of the soldiers in the back of the jeep was
holding a very scientific-looking long-nosed directional mike.

"What happened to Sid? Is he dead?" Barney asked the driver
of the jeep when it slowed at the town's only intersection.

"Go inside, sir. We'll take care of it," the soldier said.

Stacy was standing nearby, and she saw a cold menacing look
in the three soldiers' eyes. It was a look of complete disregard for
all of them. Stacy knew as the jeep pulled away that this was going
to escalate. She knew that if she was going to remain viable, she
had to get out of Vanishing Lake Village immediately.

She went back to her cottage and tried to dial Wendell at the

University of Southern California. Her phone wouldn't work—she couldn't even get a dial tone. She tried her cellphone, snapping in a fresh battery. Again . . . nothing.

"Shit," she said softly, realizing that they had already cut off communications. She figured she wouldn't be able to drive out either. The one road out would be blocked. She grabbed her back- pack and her science notebook and began throwing everything she thought she would need on her bed. She found a few Power Bars she had kept in the room for snacks. She fished an empty Evian bottle out of her wastebasket, rinsed it, filled it, and screwed the plastic cap back on. She grabbed her nylon windbreaker and last, but not least, her long-lens camera and all of her unshot film. She put everything in the backpack and then stripped the blanket off her bed, rolled it as tight as she could, and lashed it to the backpack with her extra leather belt.

"Max, what did you get us into?" she said softly. Then she checked the room one last time for anything that might be useful. She could see nothing else to take, so she slipped out of the cot- tage.

She took the wooded path that led up to the trash area, behind the restaurant. Once there, she set off across the hillside, staying in the trees, making her own trail. She went around the lake, mov- ing toward the old prison. She didn't know whether she would die from deadly mosquito bites or at the hands of the cold-eyed sol- diers. All she knew was that these were the same pricks who had killed Max, and they were about to kill more innocent people.

Stacy Richardson intended to make a photographic record of their crimes.

Chapter 11

APOCALYPSE

Asshole!'' Dale Cole screamed. He was pointing his side-by-
side twelve-gauge at the overweight, sweating Douglas Ballard. They were in front of the Vanishing Lake Hardware
Store. Douglas turned and made a desperate, lumbering run up the
steps toward the door. Dale fired one barrel, blowing away part of
Doug's right arm and shoulder before he got to the threshold.
Douglas slumped against the doorjamb, groaning in pain. Then
Dale stalked his old fishing buddy like a predatory animal, moving
slowly and deliberately up the steps, screaming at him. He aimed
the weapon and fired again, turning Doug Ballard's head into a
blood mist, then Dale started digging in his pocket for a reload.

Barney saw it from the front window of the Bucket a' Bait.
''I've had enough of this,'' he said, and grabbed a meat tenderizer
off the counter. He grabbed Stu Marshall, one of his customers,
''Come on, let's stop this,'' he said. Barney and Stu ran out of the
restaurant and tackled Dale Cole just as he was snapping the re-
loaded barrels shut. They drove him back against the wall of the
wooden front porch.

Like Sid Saunders, he fought them insanely, his eyes rimmed with red, shining with madness. While Stu tried to hold Dale, Barney hit him with the meat tenderizer, knocking him down. They both finally subdued him, tying him with their belts, as they had seen the soldiers do earlier. Barney and Stu then stood over Dale Cole. Both were shaking.

"What's going on? Why is this happening?" Barney asked, bewildered.

Stu couldn't speak, unable to grasp it.

"I'm gettin' outta here. Gonna go get us some help," Barney said. He moved off toward his car and, without even a look back, he jumped behind the wheel of his pickup and drove out of Vanishing Lake.

He was doing over seventy when he came around a bend and saw three fallen trees across the highway. He slammed on the brakes, going sideways in a free-wheel skid, stopping just a few feet from the massive trunks. Then two uniformed soldiers in biocontainment gear moved up to him, appearing almost from out of nowhere. They looked to Barney like a NASA flight crew, with their canvas suits and oxygen-fed helmets.

"You've got to go back," one of them said, his voice tinny through his filtered HEPA mask.

"What the fuck are you doing at that prison? What got loose up here? People I've known all my life are shooting each other in the streets!" he shouted. "People are going crazy!" The adrenaline was coursing through him, making him rage with anger.

The two soldiers took several steps back and pulled their side arms from web-gear holsters strapped over their bio-suits. "Go back," they said to him.

Barney didn't see how he could get around the armed soldiers and the fallen trees. After a minute of frustrated deliberation, he returned to his vehicle. "You people are gonna burn in hell for this!" he shouted. Then he got back into his idling truck, slammed it into reverse, and backed up fast. He spun the pickup around, burning rubber as he headed back to town.

"Two more cases," Nick Zingo reported. "One in town, one out on Lake Road. A few civilians are trying to run."

Admiral Zoll was seated in the parole boardroom, listening. It was dusk and he was looking out the window, trying to organize a new containment plan.

"These civilians are going to start hiking out. We're gonna need a strong N.P.D.," Nick Zingo said, referring to a night perimeter defense.

Admiral Zoll stood up. Out the window, in the fading orange sunset, he could dimly see the prison tower and shimmering lake beyond. He couldn't believe this was happening. He had been nurturing this program for twenty-seven years. He had fought to save it when Nixon had ordered it shut down in 1972. Zoll was just a Naval Commander then. He was recently back from Vietnam, had been the liaison to Fort Detrick, and was stationed at the Pentagon. He had quickly become a total believer in the work being done at the Devil's Workshop.

A strategic weapon was defined as anything capable of killing large numbers of people with a single strike. Zoll realized that in this category, bio-weapons far outperformed nuclear weapons. First, they were much cheaper. The huge sums of money that were spent on nuclear armaments could be redirected to more practical conventional military operations. Second, bio-weapons didn't destroy the enemy's infrastructure. They didn't turn captured cities into smoking piles of radioactive rubble. Twenty-four hours after a toxic event, occupation forces could secure an area, and the telephones still worked. Third, devastating as they were, they attacked only people, not the environment.

He convinced several members of the Joint Chiefs and had quietly pursued a covert bio-weapons program at Fort Detrick, under the guise of running a defense against chemical and biological terrorist attacks. He had carefully masked it from Congress, setting up Pentagon funding through colleges and universities, disguising it all as research grants. He had brought troubled scientific geniuses, like Dexter DeMille, into the program at Fort Detrick to do the R&D. When the CIA had sniffed his program out, he had been forced to include Agency spooks, and had skillfully steered the program through the dangerous white-water rapids of multiple Congressional hearings caused by unauthorized CIA cowboy tactics. They'd brought heat on the program with their mosquito tests at Carver Village, the asinine San Francisco and Minnesota open-air experiments, and the incredibly foolish subway debacle in New York, when CIA agents had attempted to determine if germs placed in one subway tunnel could be spread by the trains' backdraft, eventually leaking out of air vents all through the city.

He had been dragged to Washington, but had managed to convince a wary Congress that despite a few lapses, the work being done at Fort Detrick fell inside the Presidential Order, allowing for the development of anti-terrorist science.

Now, all these years later, on the eve of their greatest bio-weapon triumph, because of a few escaped mosquitoes, the entire program might come crashing down. Worse still, despite his patriotic motives, he knew he would be vilified. He would be categorized with monsters like Adolf Hitler, or Saddam Hussein, who practiced wholesale genocide. The politicians and the American public would not accept the truth in his arguments. They would insanely prefer nuclear armaments, with their world-ending potential, to the far more practical bio-weapons.

Admiral Zoll knew this situation at Vanishing Lake was probably not going to be fully contained. Someone would slip out and tell the story. He needed a scapegoat to pin it on. Dexter DeMille was the obvious choice. He was the scientist who had designed the killer Prion in the first place.

DeMille was a temperamental, suicidal genius who often broke up his own lab in fits of uncontrollable rage and had been under constant suicide watch. It wasn't too big a stretch to believe that he had developed this bio-weapon without Admiral Zoll's approval, and that when his unsolicited research had been turned down and condemned, he had cracked and set his killer insects loose, and then, in a final self-destructive act, killed himself.

"I want you to get Dr. DeMille and put him in one of the jail cells over in C-Block," Zoll finally said to Captain Zingo, who touched his shoulder mike and gave the order. "It's sunset. How're we doing locating the mosquitoes?" the Admiral asked, turning his thoughts back to tactics.

"We have two sites so far," Zingo said, pointing to marshy areas on the map.

"Okay, let's get started. We can't wait. Put two of the Blackhawks up there and burn 'em out."

"Yes sir," Captain Zingo said, and moved out of the parole boardroom, leaving the Admiral in the dusky space alone.

The last rays of sun were now barely lighting the edges of the tables and chairs. Zoll stood for several moments, lost in thought. After a while, he heard the "helos" winding up and taking off. Then he saw them fly across the prison yard and over the lake. He watched them until they became small specks in the diminishing light.

"Dash Two, this is Dash One. Our time over target is just ten minutes," Zingo said, going air-to-air on the rocking-horse band. He was talking to the Blackhawk flying just off his starboard side.

"Dash Two, roger," he heard Captain Don Abrams respond woodenly from the second helicopter. Nick Zingo was in the passenger seat of the lead bird. They were flying low over the lake. Silver-blue water tinged with late-afternoon sun was flashing by under them. He had decided to limit their T.O.T. to avoid problems with civilians. The mission plan was to fly just two passes over the coastal marsh, dumping the JP-5 jet fuel into the water and along the shore on the first pass. Then both zippo gunners, who were strapped in the waist door amidships of each Blackhawk, would lean out at the end of their tethers, holding machine guns that shot explosive white phosphorus-tipped bullets, called "Willy Petes." Once they were over the target area, they would fire them into the fuel-soaked grass as they flew the second sweep. The phosphorus-tipped bullets would ignite the gas-soaked marsh, flaring white-hot, even underwater. Their total Time Over Target was supposed to be less than ten minutes.

Nick had done this once before on an illegal CIA ground op in Panama. He knew that they had to be ready to grab altitude quickly, because the jet fuel would go up fast, causing an updraft, which could scorch or even break the bird. He glanced at the second Blackhawk, forty feet to starboard, and grabbed the mike.

"Okay, Dash Two, let's cover the tires and light the fires," he said, as they approached the marsh. The second Blackhawk peeled off and headed right. For some strange reason, Don Abrams didn't roger the transmission.

Zingo's bird made its first slow pass over the marshy area, while the tail gunner opened the pump valve and dropped thousands of gallons of JP-5 into the water and onto the reed marsh. They all felt the helo lift slightly as they lightened their load. Then they made a turn and started the torch run. The waist gunner, holding his weapon loaded with Willy Petes, leaned out the door on his tether as they flashed back over the Drop Zone. He triggered the W.P.s. Phosphorus-tipped bullets shot toward the marshy ground and exploded on impact. The fuel ignited with a terrible *whomp*. A huge ball of orange fire rolled up, singeing the underbelly of the Blackhawk as it climbed fast and to the right, then flew back along the quickly spreading fire line at the perimeter of the lake.

.   .   .

In the cockpit of the second Blackhawk, Captain Don Abrams was performing the same operation a half mile to the north. Captain Abrams was a solid combat pilot. He had flown countless ground-pounding missions during the Gulf War. He had an easygoing disposition, which kept his crew calm even on low nut-pucker sorties, but he had been feeling very strange all afternoon. Occasional waves of intense anger had swept over him for things that he would usually laugh off. He had had two or three dizzy spells, which had come and gone quickly. He found himself questioning this mission, something he had never done before. He was a strict chain-of-command officer, but all afternoon he had been wondering angrily, *What the hell am I doing up here?*

He looked over at Zingo's Blackhawk less than a thousand yards away. It was flying low, and he could see the vapor trail of the Willy Pete, streaming out of the waist door, followed by huge "ca-whumps" that, seconds later, would send concussive shock waves across the water that bounced against the side of his own chopper, rattling his plastic radome pod, which covered his sensitive radar equipment. The turbulence from the concussions shot unreasoning venomous anger through him.

"Okay, we're ready for the fire pass," his zippo gunner said over the crackling ear mike.

"I'm in fucking charge here, Deek," Captain Abrams snapped, uncharacteristically. "I'll fly the mission plan on my timetable, not yours."

"We gotta light the fires, Sonar," his waist gunner said, using the nickname his crew had hung on him because of his huge ears.

"Shut the fuck up, and let's use rank designation, Corporal," Don Abrams shot back, feeling a flash of anger so intense his hands shook. It was followed by a frightening momentary loss of equilibrium. For a second he could barely control the Blackhawk.

"Have it your way, *Captain*," his waist gunner snapped.

Don Abrams was feeling increasingly strange. He felt "out of it," almost as if he were somewhere else. Why was he so angry?

What was this dizziness? Then he heard Nick Zingo's voice on the rocking-horse band: "Let's go, Sonar. Your T.O.T. is half gone. Get it shakin'."

Suddenly, Don Abrams snapped. He pushed the collective forward and peeled unexpectedly left, heading directly at the other Blackhawk. Somewhere in his mind he wondered why he was doing this, but that one sane thought was immediately lost in a rage that swamped all reason.

"What the hell is Abrams doing?" Zingo said, as he saw the Blackhawk swerve and head at them, flying at attack angle.

Then before Zingo could get on the radio, they saw the nose cannons on the approaching Blackhawk winking fifty-caliber death.

"He's got his fangs out!" Zingo's pilot shouted. A second later they heard the rounds tearing into the side of their helicopter.

"The motherfucker has us padlocked!" Zingo screamed, as more rounds slammed into the Blackhawk, rocking it badly.

His pilot abruptly spun left, pointing his nose into Don Abrams's charging Blackhawk to present a smaller target, then he began a zigzag evasive action as the attacking helicopter flew directly at them, all of its nose cannons firing.

"Splash the motherfucker!" Zingo yelled at his pilot, as Captain Abrams flashed directly over them. What happened next was hard to understand.

Suddenly, Don Abrams aborted his attack on Zingo's helicopter and turned toward Vanishing Lake Village. He flew low, at full throttle. Moments later he flashed across the treetops at the lake's edge and turned toward the center of town. He hit his stick "hot button" and his nose cannons started tearing up chunks of asphalt and blowing cars over, killing the drivers with explosive beehive rounds. Then, without hesitation, the fourteen-ton Blackhawk flew directly at the Bucket a' Bait restaurant and, diving low, crashed through the front window. The entire building exploded, going up in a huge ball of white fire. The concussion from the explosion rocked the town and shattered glass windows two blocks away.

Drums of outboard fuel started exploding on the dock from the white-hot heat.

"This is Dash One to Firebase," Nick Zingo said into his mike. "Dash Two just crashed. Sonar went nuts—he attacked us, strafed the town, and then boltered into the restaurant. We've got a major situation over here."

"Roger, Dash One. Stand by," the firebase R.T.O. said quickly.

Zingo's Blackhawk hovered over the town, and they watched in amazement. Building after building caught fire from the intense heat. Men and women ran into the street, their clothes and bodies burning.

"Mother-grabber," the pilot said in dismay.

Admiral Zoll had heard the explosion and had climbed up into the gas chamber tower in Center Block. He looked out of the window, and with binoculars he could see the huge fire burning across the lake. Occasionally something over there would explode. He listened to Zingo describe the devastation on the radio. He knew he had no choice.

Admiral Zoll had wiped out entire Cong villages from behind the joystick of his Intruder. He hadn't liked it, but back then, he came to accept the fact that some missions were ethically more difficult than others. He triggered his handset and came on the radio; his voice was surprisingly calm. "Dash One, this is Firebase. The situation has progressed beyond contain," he said, slowly. "Collateralize the area, begin Charlie Fox-trot."

.   .   .

Nick Zingo had never turned down an order, but now he hesitated. There was a moment of static on the radio, followed by a squelch. Then he heard Zoll's sandpapery voice. "I know," the Admiral said sadly, responding to Zingo's silence, "but do it anyway, goddammit!"

Chapter 12

RUNNING

They had left Vanishing Lake quickly when the soldiers poured in. They found a footpath in the hills, and climbed up into a wooded valley a few miles beyond. It had taken several hours. It was just after dusk, and for the last ten minutes, they had heard the sound of the two Blackhawks miles away. The engines alternately roared and whined, while the distant rotor blades changed pitch as the helicopters turned.

The two hobos were sitting on their bedrolls, resting, to catch their breath before moving on. Lucky still hadn't been able to get a bottle since he'd been thrown off the train, and he was beginning to feel the onset of delirium tremens. Colors seemed too bright, his skin felt crawly. He could always feel things walking on his skin before he saw the bugs and spiders with their probing antennae and spindly legs making the hair on his body stand on end. While his flesh crawled, he sat very still, awash in a wave of self-pity. "Shit," Lucky said. "We need some money for wine."

"We ain't gonna get any money up here, man."

"Then we gotta steal us somethin', car radio, or something we can sell," Lucky mumbled.

Then they heard the first concussive "ca-whump," coming from far away down the valley.

"What the fuck was that?" Mike blurted, jumping to his feet.

"Beats me." Lucky was still sitting on his bedroll, with his back against a tree. He knew from experience that if he didn't get a drink, he would soon plunge into a terrible delusional nightmare.

Then they heard two more loud "ca-whumps," and Lucky looked off toward the sound. "You know what that sounds like?" he finally said.

"Uh-uh," Mike answered.

"It's like when you turn on the gas and it won't light, and you leave it on, and 'whomp,' it finally catches."

"Fuckin' A," Mike said, nodding. "That's exactly what it sounds like."

Then they heard distant machine-gun fire, followed a few moments later by a loud crash and a huge explosion. The sound rolled like thunder up the valley. Lucky jumped to his feet as well. "That sounded like a chopper crash," he said, his mind momentarily distracted from the oncoming D.T.s.

Then they heard several smaller explosions, almost like distant fireworks.

Mike was scratching some mosquito bites on his arm, and they began bleeding. He wiped his arm against his pants and looked over at Lucky, who was now moving farther up the hill.

"Where you going?"

"Up there, to that bluff. I wanna see what's going on."

They both climbed farther up the mountain until they got to a mesa. Lucky moved across to the eastern edge, and from there he could see down to the town, almost three miles away. What he saw shook him badly. The whole shoreline was an inferno. One Blackhawk helicopter was still buzzing around down there like an angry dragonfly, moving out of the dark into the flickering firelight, then disappearing again into blackness. The distant whine and roar of the engine seemed far away on the night air.

"Son-of-a-bitch," Lucky whispered. "They blew up the fuckin' town."

While they were watching, the hardware store's roof crashed in. It took almost five seconds for the sound of the falling beams to reach them. Then in the distance they heard the sound of chattering gunfire.

"Must be bullets exploding in the hardware store," Mike said.

"Uh-uh," Lucky said, remembering his Marine training. "That's fifty-caliber. Like they got in the nose guns on that Black-hawk." He couldn't understand why that would be happening unless it was some kind of new alcoholic figment. "You see all this too, right?" he suddenly asked Mike.

"Of course," Mike said, startled at the question.

Suddenly, the gas station at the end of town went up in a ball of flame as the underground tanks blew. The explosion rattled their eardrums.

"You know what I think?" Lucky said slowly.

"What?"

"I think it's time for us to catch out."

"I can make it," Mike said, feeling his sore ribs.

Lucky and Mike climbed back down the hill and picked up their bedrolls.

"Shouldn't we do something?" Mike whispered in the darkness.

"Whatta you wanna do, throw rocks?" They started climbing across the moonlit slope toward the Southern Pacific railhead, which was two miles away.

"We're better off just gettin' outta here. We should take the SP up to Waco," Lucky said. "I need ta get my hands on a bottle. . . . I'm gettin' one a' my whaddayacallits."

Mike nodded his head. He'd been through one set of the D.T.s with Lucky, and it had scared the piss out of him.

"Or maybe we catch out on the UP to California," Lucky said.

He was talking again, trying to keep his mind off the imaginary spiders, as well as the horror of the fishing village on fire. *Why was the chopper strafing the town?* he wondered.

One thing Lucky knew was that he was through being a hero. Then they heard more machine-gun fire directly up ahead.

"What the hell is that?" Mike asked.

"Shhhhh. Stay here," Lucky commanded, some remembered piece of his old life taking over. Lucky dropped his pack and moved toward the sound. It took him almost two minutes, forging through the thick forest, trying not to rustle leaves or branches or give away his position. Then he came to the edge of a tree line. In a meadow, about a hundred yards below him, he could see thirty armed men. They were shabbily dressed and looked to him, from a distance, like hobos. The headlights of an Army jeep, which looked like it had just had its tires shot out, lighted all the men. Two uniformed soldiers were lying facedown on the ground, while several of the hobos held guns on them. While Lucky watched, a tall, silver-haired man moved up to one of the facedown soldiers. He appeared to be talking to the man for a minute, and then, without warning, he pointed his pistol down and shot the soldier in the back of the head. The second soldier tried to rise, but the tall, silver-haired man put his foot on the back of that soldier's neck, pushing his face into the dirt. Then they appeared to have a lengthy conversation, all of it too far away for Lucky to understand. The prone soldier seemed to be talking fast, telling the silver-haired man something important. Then the man took his foot off the soldier's neck, stepped back, and shot him.

Lucky was frozen by the two cold-blooded murders. He could still hear the remaining chopper wheeling, turning, and strafing the burning village. He wondered again if the whole thing was some sort of never-before-experienced hallucination, some alcohol-induced mind trick that was turning his world into an apocalyptic nightmare. Then, as he watched, the silver-haired man stood over the two dead soldiers and lifted his hands to the sky. It looked to

Lucky as if he was praying over the bodies of the men he had just executed. It was crazy. He scrambled back to where Hollywood Mike was waiting.

"What was it?"

"Tell ya later," Lucky said grimly, as he grabbed up his back-pack and bedroll. "C'mon, I wanna get outta here before the space-ship lands."

The towering flames had spread all along the east side of the lake, and Stacy had to move fast to stay ahead of the inferno. In the darkness, she heard the rustle of animals fleeing from the fire. She was afraid she would run into the soldiers in the hills. She had caught occasional glimpses of the patrols before sunset. The dust plumed up from their speeding jeeps, marking their positions in the distance.

Her camera was banging against her chest, her heavy backpack cutting into her shoulders as she grabbed onto rocks and pulled herself up a mountainous slope, to a spot where she could get a better look at the prison.

She finally found a protected area, and was shocked when she looked back at the blaze. It now consumed hundreds of acres, burning out of control all over the mountains around the lake. Flames and glowing embers lit the night sky. She could feel the strange fire-induced winds swirling. In her nose was the heavy, sooty smell of burning trees.

From where she was, she could look down into the prison. She put her Nikon up to her eye and, through the five-hundred-millimeter lens, she could see men moving around down there in the darkness. Two soldiers had huge canisters strapped to their backs. Others were moving in and out of the temporary low build-ing in the center yard, carrying boxes out and putting them into trucks.

She watched them for almost forty minutes. It was obvious to her that they were emptying the labs of any evidence. Stacy knew that this was going to be a huge national news story. There was no way they could cover it up—a whole town burned, a Blackhawk and its crew crashed, thirty or forty civilians killed, a raging forest fire out of control in East Texas. She wondered how Admiral Zoll and his team would attempt to spin it.

She took a roll of long-lens shots of the men as they loaded the boxes of files and research onto the trucks. She hoped if she "pushed" the film in the lab, she would be able to get exposures in the low light. After the trucks were loaded, the men with the canisters on their backs moved up. Suddenly, streams of liquid flame shot out of the nozzles in their hands and into the buildings. The men deliberately moved around the structures, setting fire to all of them. She used another roll as the buildings burned.

Then Stacy moved off the rocks and started to pick her way down, getting closer. She wanted faces. She wanted to get pictures that would allow the authorities to identify these people.

Twenty minutes later, she was close enough to the prison to feel the increased heat from the fires burning in the yard. She could see the flames through a double razor-wired chain-link fence. She kneeled down in the dark, hoping she was out of sight of the soldiers. They had driven the trucks out of the yard and were now packing the crates that they removed from the center buildings into the remaining two Blackhawks, which were still parked on the makeshift baseball diamond.

It was then that she saw Dexter DeMille. Admiral Zoll was leading him out of the prison's front gate. Dr. DeMille was walking on stiff knees, holding his left hand painfully. She thought he looked like a man being led to his own execution.

They had come to his room at six o'clock in the evening. Without speaking to him, the two soldiers had put him in handcuffs, then moved him out of his living quarters across the yard to the huge tower in C-Block. Dexter had been forced to climb the metal stairs to the fifth tier, where Sylvester Swift and Troy Lee Williams had been held two days before.

"Why are you doing this?" he had asked the stone-faced Rangers several times, but they refused to speak. He felt their strong hands on his arms, propelling him along the metal walkway and into one of the cells. The door was slammed and the lock buzzed shut.

He sat there on the cold steel bunk with no mattress, and waited in fear. He had heard a huge explosion around eight o'clock and then the distant clatter of machine guns. He knew the whole thing was coming apart, and that he would probably die before the night was over. He sat there in the dark and cursed himself for the waste he had made of his once-promising life. Depression circled him like a cold, gray mist.

At ten-thirty he looked up and saw Admiral Zoll standing in the corridor. It surprised him that he had not heard the huge man approach. The Admiral was in a tan uniform and a Navy flight jacket. His gold Navy wings glistened in the naked overhead light.

"Dexter, I need your signature on something," Admiral Zoll said.

Dr. DeMille looked up, fear gripping him. Admiral Zoll handed a single sheet of paper through the bars. Dexter took it, and held it up to the light to read:

I, Dr. Dexter DeMille, take full responsibility for my actions. I cannot live with the consequences my research has brought. I know now my illegal work with Prions is ungodly and that I should never have pursued it. The accident here at Vanishing Lake was entirely my fault. Mosquitoes carrying PHpr got loose from my lab. Nobody at Fort Detrick knew of my work, and I take full responsibility. May God, and my country, one day see fit to forgive me.

Dexter looked up at Admiral Zoll. "I don't think so," he said, handing the letter back.

"Dr. DeMille, you are going to die tonight. The only question is whether you die easily or in great pain. Your time here is over. This paper will have no effect on you once you're gone, but I promise you, sooner or later you will end up signing it. . . . Sooner would be easier."

Dexter got up from the bed and backed up until he was standing against the far wall of the cell. "I won't sign it," he stammered. "It's a lie. This whole program is your doing."

The Admiral nodded to Captain Zingo, who stepped forward and opened the door of Dexter's cell. He grabbed the frail scientist by his left hand and, finding a pressure point on the nerve between his thumb and index finger, pressed down hard and shot a bolt of agonizing pain up Dexter's arm to his shoulder.

Dexter screamed.

"Captain Zingo knows every nerve point in the body." Then Zoll nodded, and Zingo repeated the pressure.

This time Dexter's knees collapsed; the agony it caused was so excruciating he could barely stay conscious. He withstood the torture for only three minutes before he begged them to stop.

He was sobbing as he signed his name to the document.

Admiral Zoll, Nick Zingo, and the two Delta Rangers led Dexter DeMille out the front gate of the prison. He walked on rubbery legs. Over his shoulder, he could see his labs on fire in the main yard. Then Admiral Zoll got into one of the loaded helicopters, and without saying another word to Dexter, closed the hatch. The Blackhawk started. The blades began stirring the air around them. As the rotors spun faster, several of the soldiers covered their eyes from the flying dust and small rocks. The huge helo lifted off. Once airborne, it dropped its nose and whisked Admiral Zoll away into the firelit night.

.   .   .

Stacy was down to her last roll of film. Besides Dexter DeMille, there were only five men and one Blackhawk left on the baseball diamond. She moved along behind the brush line, crouching in the dark, shooting as many shots as she could through the tall grass.

Then she watched in horror as Nick Zingo pulled his nine-millimeter Beretta and pointed it at Dexter. She could hear Dr. DeMille pleading as he stood there helpless, his voice tinny and shrill as it came across the baseball diamond. Stacy froze, the camera forgotten for a moment in her hand. Suddenly gunfire erupted from the third-base side of the diamond. Captain Zingo's chest was instantly riddled with red blots.

Dexter spun around in confusion as gunfire erupted from behind home plate. One by one, the soldiers in the compound fell, clutching at their wounds, unable to even get their weapons free.

Stacy shrank back behind the foliage in horror. Only Dexter was left standing.

Then she saw a tall, silver-haired man step out of the darkness. With him were half a dozen more men. All of them wore grimy overalls; most were holding automatic weapons. She could see that each had the same tattoo in black letters across his right biceps: F.T.R.A. The silver-haired man walked to where Dexter was standing. They were only twenty feet from her.

"I told you we were gonna be friends," the silver-haired man said.

"He was going to kill me," Dexter stammered. "How did you know?"

"I know all about you, brother. Your coming is foretold in Revelation."

"What?" Dexter asked, confused.

" 'One of the four beasts gave unto the seven angels seven golden vials full of the wrath of God,' " Fannon quoted. " 'The first angel poured out his vial onto the earth, and there fell a noisome and grievous sore upon them which had the mark of the beast, and upon them which worshiped his image....' " Fannon smiled at Dexter. "You an' me, we're gonna pour some a' that wrath you been cookin' outta your vial onto the earth. We're gonna destroy the lower races. Niggers and Jews. Whatta you think a' that, bub?" Then Fannon took Dexter by the elbow, and along with his band of armed hobos, he led the bewildered microbiologist off the baseball diamond.

As they passed, Stacy Richardson used her last exposure on a firelit close-up of Fannon Kincaid.

Chapter 13

CATCHING OUT

He's dropping air," Lucky said, after the freight crested the pass. They could hear air brakes hissing, indicating the engineer was slowing for the long downhill grade ahead. The freight crested the pass and began rumbling down the northern range of the Black Hills. The diesel engine was a big black-and-orange SD 45-2 high-hood road locomotive. "These were used by the Denver Rio Grande Railroad for long hauls," Lucky said, realizing that probably meant it was a "mixed" train containing a variety of different kinds of cars. Lucky was "scoping the drag," looking for one that would be easy for Mike to board with his broken ribs. Thankfully, the onset of D.T.s had subsided for the moment, killed by the exertion of climbing the rugged terrain to the rail, or by the earlier jolt of adrenaline as he watched the two soldiers die. But Lucky's stomach was rolling. For the last hour he'd felt as if he was about to throw up.

They were in a perfect place to catch out. The train had slowed to five miles an hour at the mountain pass. Lucky and Mike were crouched low, out of sight, as the big yellow MoPac diesel rumbled by. Then came a long line of piggyback cars, known as "pigs." Lucky was looking for a sleeper, because often one was left between two long lines of the same kind of cars. Not this time. The fifteen pigs rumbled past immediately followed by twenty stack cars, not good for hoboing. The double-decker stacks were thickly loaded with huge metal containers, which often shifted and had crushed more than one sleeping 'bo. Then came a dozen closed grainers, followed by a line of gondolas.

"About to get boned here," Lucky murmured. "Shoulda caught one a' them pigs."

They were running out of train when he finally saw a few "ledged grainers" coming toward them. They were old cars, not very common anymore, characterized by a narrow ledge on each end just wide enough to sit on. It wasn't the best option, but at least it was an easy car to get on.

"Okay, let's take the green one, second old grainer after the row of reds," Lucky said. He held his hands out in front of him to check his nerves. His hands were shaking badly. "Shit, these fuckers are comin' back," he muttered.

Mike didn't answer. When Lucky looked over at him he saw a strange, troubled look in Hollywood Mike's eyes.

"Let's go!" Lucky said. They took off running up the tracks. Lucky sprinted along next to the car, trying to find his coordination, which was just about lost now. He was feeling awkward, as his neurons and muscles trembled inside his body, on the verge of turning on him, attacking his voluntary nervous system. Lucky grabbed the ladder handle with his left hand and swung himself up onto the small ledge at the back of the car. He moved over as Mike grabbed the handle, gritting his teeth in pain. Lucky grabbed Mike's shirt, and with great effort, finally hauled him aboard.

They were now sitting backward, looking at the front of the grain car behind them. The tracks were flashing past; under their feet the huge metal coupling was groaning and creaking with the changing stress of the car.

"How's the ribs?" Lucky asked, his own nerves rioting in his alcohol-ravaged system. Again, Mike didn't answer.

The train had crested the peak at the top of the grade and was now picking up speed, heading downhill.

The ledge they were on was only two feet wide. If they fell off, they would land in the space between the cars and be run over and maimed, if not killed, by the car behind.

Lucky sat with his feet dangling, looking at the back of Mike's head. "You okay?" he asked.

Mike spun his head around. "Stop askin'. You're not in charge a' me," he snapped.

Now Lucky could see a shiny menacing glare in Mike's eyes that he had never seen before. "Calm down," he said. "I was just—"

"Screw you," Mike said, and then without warning the train went into a tunnel, and they were both in diesel-choking, inky blackness.

"Been through this tunnel before," Lucky screamed over the echoed racket. "Only a mile long. Hold yer breath."

"Shut the fuck up," Mike screamed back.

Suddenly and strangely, Lucky could feel Mike's hands clawing at him in the dark.

"Whatta you doin'?" Lucky yelled, knocking Mike's hands away. "Don't screw around. Dangerous back here." There was no light at all, and worse still, the tunnel was becoming thick with throat-closing exhaust.

"Fuck you!" Mike screamed. Then Mike's hands were back up by Lucky's throat. Before Lucky could defend himself, Mike had him in a strangulation grip, and was squeezing hard, shutting off Lucky's air supply.

"The fuck you doin'?" Lucky croaked, letting go of valuable air. He could hear Mike's teeth snapping close by his ear. His friend was actually trying to bite him! "Leggo! Leggo me!" Lucky protested, inhaling heavy diesel smoke that was closing his constricted windpipe.

Lucky did not want to hit Mike, but he was beginning to feel his consciousness dimming. He couldn't see anything in the black tunnel. Finally, in desperation, he swung a short-chopping right hand in the general direction of where he thought Mike's busted ribs were. He landed the blow and heard Mike scream in pain. Mike's grip on his neck loosened slightly, and Lucky inhaled another quick breath of lung-choking smoke. They were struggling in the pitch black, fighting each other on the narrow ledge. Lucky was trying to save his own life without throwing Mike off the grainer and under the steel wheels.

He couldn't fathom why Mike was attacking him. The noise of the train was magnified in the tunnel, but over the racket Lucky could hear Mike screaming, "You're dead, fucker!"

Once Lucky had pried Mike's hands off his neck, he instinctively fell back on his old Marine Special Forces Recon training. Instead of pushing Mike away, he pulled him closer, encircling Mike's trunk with both arms. Fueled by adrenaline from the unexpected attack, Lucky began to squeeze Mike hard, using as much force as he could. Mike screamed as his broken ribs shot pain through his torso, then Lucky head-butted him.

They flashed back out of the tunnel into pale moonlight. Overhead lights attached to a parallel trestle strobed over them. Lucky now spun Mike away from him and quickly looped an arm around Mike's throat. As he struggled and fought, Lucky choked him out, compressing his carotid arteries until Mike was unconscious. Then Lucky held his slumped friend tight, so he wouldn't fall off the narrow platform.

"What the fuck?" he screamed at the twenty-two-year-old. "I'm your friend, dammit. Whatta you doing?"

Mike couldn't respond.

Exhausted, Lucky finally stood up with shaking legs on the rocking platform, then dragged his friend across the ledge and laid him down. Lucky took Mike's pulse. It was uneven. He sat back and tried to clear his lungs of diesel smoke. He prayed he hadn't crushed Hollywood Mike's larynx. Then he saw the first bug. It was crawling up his arm, under his shirt. "Get the hell off me!" Lucky wailed, beating at the hallucinatory insect. They were coming now. He could feel them crawling up his neck. They were in his scalp, going for his eyes.

Mike was regaining consciousness, but he seemed unable to talk and was having difficulty swallowing. He was lying flat on the ledge of the grain car, with spit drooling out of his mouth. Lucky was beginning to think he had done some life-threatening damage.

"What the fuck's wrong with you, man?" Lucky asked. He tried to tell himself the bugs were imaginary but was, nonetheless, raking stiff fingers through his hair, trying to clear his scalp of the crawling bastards.

Hollywood Mike still couldn't answer. Worse still, his gaze was unfocused, and when he looked at Lucky it was with vacant, glassy eyes.

The sun had not appeared above the horizon, but already it was lighting the eastern sky. Lucky could see the ribbon of cars stretching out before him as the train, still heading down the slope, made a long gradual turn. Off in the distance Lucky could see a ravine with a big metal trellis. The rumbling diesel engine was a quarter of a mile ahead, just crossing the ravine. Then Lucky sat down with his back to the car and began to whimper. He felt bugs crawling on his face. He saw them moving under his T-shirt. "Nooo . . ." he wailed. "Go away, I can't take this." He began slapping at himself, trying to get them off, while Mike lay close to death on the ledge beside him.

Unexpectedly, Mike went into a huge spastic convulsion. Lucky jumped back, startled, and watched in horror as his friend spasmed uncontrollably on the narrow ledge.

"Fuck, man!" Lucky screamed, "Fuck . . . oh fuck. We're getting off!" he yelled.

Lucky needed to slow the train in order to jump. To do this, he knew he had to cut the air on the car. Once the air line was cut, the brakes on the center section of the train would automatically come on, slowing the entire train.

Lucky pulled out an old pocketknife and crouched down with his feet on the uncoupling lever, one arm holding on to the coupler, as the track strobed by beneath him. With his life hanging suspended above the tracks and his heart beating wildly, the bugs disappeared. Lucky didn't know what part of his subconscious was driving him, but at least the D.T.s had been washed away by his pumping adrenaline. He quickly grabbed the rubber air line with his right hand and slashed it. It whipped all around the uncoupling lever where he was precariously perched, slapping his face like an unattended garden hose. As he crawled back onto the grainer's narrow ledge, he heard the brakes come on under the car. The train slowed slightly.

They were now crossing the trestle. He looked down at a thousand-foot drop below the tracks through the open metal rails. When Lucky pulled Mike up into a sitting position, more spit drooled out of his mouth and down his shirt. Mike coughed, but said nothing. His eyes seemed cloudy and distant now, almost as if he had already passed on.

The train was going only ten miles an hour as they came off the trestle. Lucky knew the engineer would stop somewhere down the line and check the cars for the broken air hose, but he needed to get Mike off now.

He stood Mike up and grabbed him in a fireman's carry. Then Lucky took a deep breath and two running steps, leaping off the grainer with Mike over his shoulder. He was trying to get as far out from the wheels as possible, sacrificing himself by landing on his feet instead of taking his patented bone-saving roll. He hopped once, feeling his knees jam. The pain shot up his thighs. He went down, still holding Mike over his shoulder, trying to keep Mike's head from banging into the hard ground. He rolled once and came to a stop.

Mike's eyes were open, but were now like no eyes Lucky had ever seen on a living person. He was conscious, but it was as if nobody was in there, as if Mike's soul had disappeared.

Lucky sat up and saw that he was in a small switching yard. The sun was peeking up over the horizon. Off to his right was a very small town, only a couple of buildings and a store. The town probably supplied the switching station.

Lucky hoped there was a doctor nearby, and a bottle. *Christ, I need a bottle,* he thought. He couldn't deal with the bugs, not now, not with Mike dying.

Chapter 14

ROSCOE MOSS, JR.

Roscoe Moss had crashed on an old sofa in the back of his brother's feed and grain store. He'd been up half the night helping deliver Shep Holworth's new Appaloosa foal. The animal had not been right; one eye on the colt was missing and his reflexes were shot. The poor animal couldn't stand, no matter how hard they tried to get him up. Then his lungs collapsed. Roscoe had done everything he could, but he had learned his rudimentary medical knowledge as a Marine Corps ambulance driver, and he didn't have the veterinary skill to save the animal. In the end, Shep had decided it was easier, and cheaper, to just put the foal down.

It had bummed Roscoe out, and he had come back to Moss Feed and Grain, pulled down the bottle of Scotch, and while watching the late late movie on the old black-and-white, gotten completely hammered. Sometime before sun-up he'd fallen asleep on the couch.

Roscoe's main job was to guard the switching station for the old Southern Pacific and Union Pacific Railroad. Often, long lines of loaded boxcars were parked on the Badwater siding for several days, waiting for one of the high-hood switchers to connect the line and pull it north to the switching yard in Pueblo, Colorado. Roscoe was the "yard bull." He had been deputized by the County Sheriff and could make arrests if thieves tried to steal radios out of the Japanese automobiles left on his siding waiting for the Pueblo hookup. Roscoe had made over twenty arrests, mostly Native Americans off the nearby Ute Reservation. Unless they were repeat offenders, he usually ended up just holding them in the Feed and Grain for a few hours before turning them loose. He was half black, half Ute himself and didn't have the heart to call the Sheriff on the poverty-stricken Indians.

It was six A.M. when he was brought out of a deep sleep by a racket at the store's back window. It was an incessant pounding, and he could hear someone shouting, "Hey you!" Roscoe sat up and rubbed his eyes, then he ran a hand through his tight black Afro hair. He looked out at the source of the noise and saw a very scruffy, long-haired blond man with wild eyes pounding on the windows with dirt-scarred knuckles. Roscoe's head was still thick with whiskey, as the bum continued pounding on the glass. Finally he stood. "He ain't open till nine!" Roscoe shouted at the man through the glass.

"I need a doctor. Where's the doctor?" the bum shouted.

"Ain't got a doctor here. There's six people live in this place. You want a doctor, gotta go t' Government Camp, 'bout sixty miles yonder, toward the mountains." Roscoe turned and moved back to the couch, but the man started hammering on the window again.

Roscoe spun around, and this time anger flared. "Hey, listen, you," he shouted. "There ain't no doctor. Stop yer bangin' or I'm gonna come out there an' fold ya over."

An ex-Marine and bull-riding champion, Roscoe Moss, Jr., was generally up to that task. He was forty-eight years old, but there was not an inch of fat on him. His brown skin was rippled with slabs of muscle.

"Open the fucking door. I need a phone," the bum yelled and continued his incessant, brain-jarring racket.

Roscoe moved angrily across the floor. He snapped the lock and, in one motion, pulled the door open, grabbed the scruffy man by the shirt, and yanked him forward.

Without exactly knowing how it happened, Roscoe Moss was suddenly spinning half off balance, half in the air. He pirouetted out of the door and, in a matter of seconds, was flat on his back in the dirt behind the Feed and Grain. The bum was somehow miraculously sitting on his chest, holding a cocked fist a few feet from his nose.

"I said I need a phone," he snarled.

Roscoe was not used to being tossed around like a rag doll, but he was still groggy and hungover, he reasoned. As he looked up at the threatening hobo astride him, he saw the rage in the man's blue eyes suddenly change to pleading desperation.

"You gotta help me. Please," the bum said. "I'm in trouble. My friend's dying! I got the shakes. . . . I need a drink."

"Just get the fuck off me," Roscoe demanded.

The bum got off and the embarrassed yard bull got up, brushed himself off, then looked around in the dirt for his dignity. "For a guy with the shakes, you move pretty good."

"My friend's dying," Lucky repeated.

Roscoe looked closely at the bum. The man had moved so quickly he had been just a blur in that moment before Roscoe felt himself flying through the door, landing helplessly on his back. The 'bo was a mess, his feet wrapped in garbage bags.

"Need a doctor," Lucky said.

"Gonna take 'em more'n half an hour to get here from Government Camp."

"We can't wait that long. He's choking to death!"

"I'm kinda a veterinarian. I'll get my doctoring bag. Maybe I can help."

"Come on then," the bum said, and moved away from him at

a run. He turned to look back at Roscoe, who still hadn't moved. "Come *on!*" the bum shouted.

When they got back to the tracks, the train Lucky and Mike had been riding on had stopped and there were two brakemen looking down at Mike. One of them was kneeling, taking the gold ring off Mike's finger.

"Hey, whatta you doing?" Lucky said. "Leave that alone! His dad gave him that." He snatched the ring away.

"He ain't gonna need it. This piece a' shit already caught the westbound," the kneeling brakeman said.

Lucky pushed him away in frustration, got down on his knees, and put his head over his friend's heart. "Can't hear anything," he said fearfully.

Roscoe pulled the stethoscope he had used on Shep's Appaloosa out of his bag, opened Mike's shirt, and placed it on the young hobo's chest. He also could hear no heartbeat. He checked from several places, then put his hand on the young man's forehead. The body already seemed cold.

"I'm sorry," he said softly.

"You two're the ones that cut the brake hose, aren't ya?" said the brakeman who had been trying to steal Mike's ring.

Lucky was still looking down helplessly at his friend.

Suddenly, the other brakeman standing behind Lucky moved up and hit him as hard as he could in the back of the head with a long metal spanner. Lucky's knees buckled and he collapsed right on top of Mike. The blow opened a nasty cut in the back of Lucky's head, and blood immediately ran down onto his T-shirt collar.

"What'd ya do that for?" Roscoe screamed at the brakeman.

"These motherfuckers cut our air just so they could jump off the train. Fuckin' hobos. They do it all the time. We're gonna be stuck here for half a day. Gonna get reamed. The Trainmaster'll be up here from Sierra Blanca fuckin' us over, screamin' about his shitty timetables. I'm callin' the Sheriff; at least this bum's gonna do his thirty days.''

"Ain't no need ta call 'em," Roscoe said. "I'm the yard bull here. I'll call the Government Camp substation." Roscoe dug around in his pocket for his deputy's star to show them, but it wasn't in his pocket. Maybe he'd left it back in his motor home, which was parked behind his brother's house. Or maybe it was still in the glove compartment of his pickup. He wasn't sure.

When Lucky regained consciousness the bugs were all over him. They were crawling in his eye sockets, eating his eyelids. He sat straight up, screaming, trying to get them off his face, but for some reason he couldn't move his hands.

"Fuck, fuck . . . fuck!" he screamed.

"Shut up!" Roscoe commanded, his own headache from the whiskey nearly unbearable

"On me. They're on me. . . . Oh no, oh no, get 'em off!" Lucky was in the back office of the Feed and Grain, handcuffed to the heavy wooden bench there.

"Ain't nothing on you. What the hell you talking about?" Roscoe Moss, Jr., said, stepping back, startled.

Lucky was completely lost in the D.T.s and was no longer able to separate the dementia from reality. He felt the bugs nibbling on his face, and what made it worse, he couldn't move his hands to knock them off.

"Shheeeiiiittt!" he screeched. "They're eating my eyes, they're eating my fucking eyes! Help me, fer Chrissake!" He was thrashing on the bench, desperately yanking against the handcuffs. When he opened his eyes he saw Roscoe's shocked face, but he also saw a giant tarantula on his left wrist. It moved slowly up his arm, until it wiggled under his T-shirt, crawling in through the armhole. He could see it writhing under the cotton, and was helpless to fight it. His mind started to spin out of control, his vision blurred.

"They're all over me! Get 'em off, please!" he wailed.

Roscoe was knocked back by the ferocity of the hobo's scream and the violence of his actions. Lucky was yanking his handcuffed wrists so hard that blood was squirting from cuts where the metal shackles dug into him.

"Shit!" Roscoe said. "Stop it!"

Roscoe was panicked; he didn't know what to do. He grabbed a phone off the counter and dialed. "Gimme Doc Fletcher," he said to the nurse. "'Mergency!" After a minute the doctor came on the line.

"What can I do for you, Roscoe?"

Roscoe explained the problem, and when he was finished, Lucky was pulling his handcuffs so violently he was deeply scarring the wooden arm of the bench.

"OHHHHHH, GOD . . . PLEEEASE," he wailed.

"Go to the liquor cabinet, get some liquor, and pour it in him till it stops. That's all I can tell ya t'do for now," the doctor said. "Other than leave him be till he comes out of it."

Roscoe hung up and ran and got his bottle of Scotch off the store shelf. He opened it and poured four shots into Lucky, who swallowed them like a man parched on the desert. The effect was like cold water going into an overheated engine. Lucky started to calm down as the whiskey hit his bloodstream and sedated his rioting nervous system.

"Shit," Roscoe said. "You got a problem, Mister. You better go get yerself straightened out." Lucky slowly leaned back on the bench. His wrists were soaked with blood, but he was grinning, showing Roscoe the gap in his smile as the warm circle of Scotch expanded in his stomach, taking away the pain and delusion as it spread. "Man, that feels better," he finally said, then blissfully closed his eyes. He was so tired he could barely sit up.

An hour later when Lucky woke up, he was still handcuffed to the bench inside the Feed and Grain. The heavily muscled ex-Marine was sitting on a wood-backed chair nearby, looking at him studiously. "How'd you learn t'throw a man 'round like that?" Roscoe finally asked.

"Marines," said Lucky.

"Me too, I was a jarhead. In for four years."

"My head's killing me," Lucky groaned.

"That fella opened it up fer ya pretty good. Hit ya with a foundation brake spanner. I cleaned the wound off, taped it up, but you oughta get stitches."

Lucky was trying to sit up, but he felt dizzy, so he slumped back again.

"Tell me what happened to yer friend. How'd a kid like him die like that?"

Lucky wasn't about to share the details of what happened, no matter how bad he felt about it. If he told the yard bull about Mike's attack and the fight on the back ledge of the grainer, they would probably arrest him for murder. So he gave an abridged, reconstructed version of the story: "We jumped on the freight up by Vanishing Lake. I think he banged his throat real bad getting on. I got worried, so I cut the air and we jumped off the freight down here."

"Vanishing Lake," Roscoe said, alarmed. "They say some kinda killer bug is loose up there, people goin' nuts, attackin' each other. Somebody started a big ol' forest fire. It was on the radio."

Lucky was still trying to get a grip on his wavering consciousness. He sat up straighter. "Whatta you mean?" he said. "What killer bug?"

"Don't ask me. They got the whole place quarantined. Maybe your friend got the bug!" Roscoe said, alarmed.

"Don't think so. Like I said, I think he crushed his larynx when we were getting aboard. The door handle whacked him in the throat,'' Lucky lied.

His mind was spinning with what the yard bull had just said. He started to replay the strange events he had witnessed at Vanishing Lake, ending with Mike, for no reason, clawing at his throat in the darkness of the tunnel, screaming obscenities while they fought desperately on the narrow ledge of the grainer.

Lucky looked down at the handcuffs holding his wrists to the wood arm of the sofa.

"Yer under arrest,'' Roscoe explained. "I'm holdin' ya here for the Sheriff. He ain't gonna make it for a bit, on accounta the substation at Government Camp is workin' with the military right now, lookin' for some scientist that started the fire. They got roadblocks up for two hundred miles."

"Where'd you put Mike's body?"

"Got him in the other room. My brother's gonna shit."

"Whatta you gonna do with him?"

"I ain't gonna do shit with him. I just watch parked freight cars for the SP,'' Roscoe said. "I ain't got nothin' t'do with this. Once the Sheriff gits here, he'll figger somethin', probably pack him off to the Medical Examiner in Government Camp, then they'll probably do him like all the other 'no names' we find dead 'round here . . . just drop him in a potter's grave with a sack a' lye."

"You don't wanna do that."

"Yeah? Why's that?"

"You just don't wanna,'' Lucky repeated.

"Yeah? Well, it ain't gonna be none a' my doin'."

Lucky didn't want to wait around for the Sheriff. He knew he couldn't dry out cold in some cell, covered with bugs. He cleared his throat and leaned forward.

"He hoboed under the name 'Hollywood Mike,' but his real name was Michael Brazil."

"Yeah?'' Roscoe said, not really caring.

"His father's a big-time movie producer."

Roscoe Moss now started to smile and shake his head in be-wildered amusement. "Sure," he said. "Sure."

"Go look in his mouth."

"What's that gonna tell me?" Roscoe smiled. "He got his daddy's name engraved there?"

"Just go look in his mouth, you'll see." Lucky could still feel the Scotch, warm inside him. It had settled him, given him new courage. "Go on, take a look," he prodded.

After a long moment Roscoe got up and moved out of the back room of the store, muttering to himself. He had laid Hollywood Mike on the floor behind the counter, out of sight. He peeled back the tarp he had covered the body with, then took a pair of pliers and a screwdriver off the shelf and carefully pried Mike's mouth open. It was harder than he expected. The joints were already be-ginning to lock from rigor mortis, a condition that Roscoe knew from his ambulance-driving days would have the body board-stiff in an hour. After he got Mike's mouth open, he looked in. He couldn't see much in the dim light behind the counter, so he got a flashlight down off the shelf and shined it into Mike's mouth. "What'm I supposed t'be lookin' for?" he called to Lucky.

"His bridgework," Lucky called back.

Sure enough, Roscoe could now see a complicated dental repair job, complete with gold fillings. "That sure musta cost a few bucks," he shouted. Then he snapped off the light and moved back into the room where Lucky was seated. "So?"

"He told me he was in a car accident up on Mulholland Drive last summer. He trashed his dad's Porsche and broke out a buncha teeth. How many twenty-two-year-old hobos you know got ten grand in dental reconstruction?" Then Lucky stretched open his own mouth, showing his own broken tooth for emphasis. "You don't wanna be the guy who dumped Buddy Brazil's kid in a hole with a bag a' lye."

"Whatta you think I should do?"

"Take a Polaroid of him and send the picture to his father in

Hollywood. He's gotta be at one of the movie studios.'' Lucky paused. "Who knows...maybe he gives you some kinda reward.''

Roscoe Moss finally nodded. "And what's in all this fer you?''

"He was my friend. I want him to get a proper funeral.'' Lucky hesitated, then added, "I can't go to jail, man. I can't go through that. I helped you, you gotta help me, one Marine to another. Semper Fi, brother.''

Roscoe looked troubled. He moved over and sat down next to Lucky. "I let you go, there's gonna be hell t'pay. Not that I wanna give you no grief, but that Trainmaster is gonna drive up here from Sierra Blanca. I know him. He's a tough old buzzard, an' them two brakemen gonna be yellin' 'bout how you 'bos're all the time cuttin' the air t'slow trains. He'll go on 'bout how them products on that train is worth money—'The interest on that trainload a' stuff would pay my salary fer ten years!' I'm gonna have t'listen t'that shit fer hours.''

The two of them held each other's gaze.

"So, y'learned that trick a' yers fightin' in the Marines?''

Lucky decided to humor him, and smiled warmly. "It's called ground fighting. The idea is that all fights end up on the ground anyway, so you take it there first. Use the other guy's force against him. There's half a dozen choke points. You should be able to kill an opponent silently in seconds.''

"You was a Ranger?''

Lucky nodded. Roscoe looked at him hard and said, "See, thing is I don't really like bustin' people. It sorta ain't in me.''

Finally, Roscoe Moss, Jr., got up and left the room.

Lucky looked down in wonder at his bloody wrists cuffed around the arm of the sofa. Then he looked out the back window of the Feed and Grain. The dusty Texas-Oklahoma landscape was barren and bleak, like the last four years of his life. He wondered what had happened to Hollywood Mike. He remembered the horrible way Mike had choked on his own spit. His friend's eyes had

burned with insanity, then had been empty and expressionless, devoid of soul. Suddenly Lucky wanted to run, wanted to get the
hell out of there. He had never felt such a compelling desire to be
someplace else. He wanted a new life . . . a life without alcohol,
without dementia tremens, and the poverty of hopelessness and
homelessness.

For three and a half years he had been riding the high iron,
living in main stems or hobo jungles. He would catch out on the
SP rails and head west to the Burlington tracks, then north to
Oregon. Once there, he would have no reason to be there, no reason to stay, and would catch out again on the UP, heading east
until he got to New York. Then it was the main central line to Fort
Kent and back west again on the CN, fueled by restlessness and
cheap wine. Around and around he went, human lint on a big
useless spin cycle, sleeping under cardboard with the Sunday paper
for a mattress. Then up again, with no reason or direction, wandering aimlessly to nowhere important, from nowhere special.

Suddenly, he wanted to sleep someplace warm, where he
wouldn't wake up being hammered into oblivion for his shoes.

Then all at once, with Mike's death weighing on his mind,
Lucky knew the journey was over. He was through with the liquor,
through being a drunk. He would go home. He would talk to his
old friend Clancy Black . . . Clancy would help him find a way to
beat it.

Ten minutes later, Roscoe returned. He unlocked Lucky's handcuffs and opened the back door.

"Git on outta here. I'll figure somethin' t'tell the Trainmaster
when he gets here."

Lucky moved to the door, past the half-empty bottle of Scotch.

"What's yer name?" Roscoe asked.

"Lucky," he replied.

Roscoe thought the greasy hobo was about as lucky as road kill.
"Where you gonna go?" the yard bull asked.

"Pasadena, California."

"Why there?"

"It's home."

"Good luck, Marine," Roscoe said. They shook hands, and then Roscoe turned and went to the front of the store. As Lucky walked out the back door, he slipped the half-empty bottle of whiskey under his coat. He was through drinking, he told himself. That was settled. That was a done deal.

He had stolen the bottle just in case.

Chapter 15

ZOPHAR

The Aryans conquered the Indus Valley fifteen hundred years before Christ,'' Fannon Kincaid lectured. "India was a strange exotic place that didn't have enough white women. Eventually primal lust drove the Aryan conquerors to the beds of dark-skinned Indian women.''

They were riding on a unit train, heading east. The big, slat-sided boxcars were all filled with cattle. The smell drifted back to the sleeper car they were riding in. A fetid stink of cattle and manure mixed with diesel fumes clogged Dexter's nose; the sermon clogged his ears.

"In time, the pure white Aryans made an ungodly mistake and married the dark-skinned Indian people from Bangalore and, inevitably, their pure white blood mixed with the blood of that lesser race.'' As he looked at Dexter, his intense gaze burned with this special truth.

The train was moving slowly down the east face of the Black Hills, on a stretch of Northeastern Texas Track that would eventually take them into Louisiana. Dexter was amazed how easily the forty members of the "Christian Choir and the Lord's Desire" had escaped the military roadblocks that had attempted to seal off Vanishing Lake. The rails went completely unguarded, and the forty heavily armed men and women had boarded the eastbound cattle train without trouble. They were gathered in two separate sleeper cars. Fannon and half the men were with Dexter in this boxcar, twenty more armed Crusaders of the Choir were huddled in an open-top gondola a few cars back.

One of the men in Dexter's boxcar was a tall, hardened man named Randall Rader. He was Fannon's second-in-command, and Dexter had been told he was a sub-angel. Randall never took his cruel gaze off of Dexter.

Randall, like many of the others, had the big F.T.R.A. tattooed in block letters on his right biceps. Fannon had explained that it stood for Freight Train Riders of America. F.T.R.A.s, he told the frightened scientist, were a group of outlaw train riders who had originally formed after Vietnam. Eight disillusioned, disenfranchised vets had met in a bar in Dallas after the war and decided to escape a society that had branded them baby killers by riding the rails. Fannon had been one of the founding fathers. They became a rail-riding cult of murdering thieves, and in twenty-five years, their number had swelled to over a thousand. No longer just a collection of disenfranchised vets, they were now train-riding outlaws of all ages. They had no code and no initiation. To be a member you only had to say you were. But any self-proclaimed member of the F.T.R.A. had to be ready to prove his or her tyranny. They usually banded in groups of five or ten. They would derail trains and steal from the wreckage. Sometimes they killed hobos for no apparent reason. They totally escaped prosecution for their crimes, because they lived in the netherworld of the railroad system that was not adequately policed by state, county, or federal law. They all took assumed names and carried no identification, traveling undetected from city to city. Fannon boasted that there were more than thirty of these killers in his Choir.

Scratched on Randall's arm was also the number 88. Dexter had been told that H was the eighth letter in the alphabet, and that 88 stood for "Heil Hitler." The other strange tattoo on Randall's scarred body was an Indian caste mark that he wore between his slanted eyebrows. Now Dexter was enduring that explanation as well.

"So as the White and Indian races mixed," Fannon continued, "it was hard for the true Aryan to tell which blond-haired women or men were his genetic equals. The Aryan gene being as strong as it is, it often did not produce dusky-skinned children when crossbreeding with Indian women occurred. It became necessary for the governing Aryans to devise a way to determine which of the righteous were true and pure-blooded and which had tainted their bloodline by fornicating with the mud races. They devised a system of marking pure children at birth with a caste mark. This custom has been carried down. Today, the Indian caste mark is only a sign of class superiority, but in old times, it depicted racial purity as well."

Dexter nodded his head. He knew this was pure nonsense, but he didn't want to engage Fannon, who, he had witnessed, was capable of killing in an instant without remorse. Dexter shifted his gaze off Randall Rader and his tattoos symbolizing racial hatred and Aryan purity.

"Many in our company have been able to establish their racial integrity, and once I have approved their genealogy, I designate the correct caste mark of purity."

"I see," Dexter said, the chill of this insanity enveloping him. They rode in merciful silence for several minutes.

"I'm sure you wonder why I went to the trouble of saving you from the godless purveyors of your government's criminal military conspiracy."

"You want me to share my research with you," Dexter said bluntly.

"It's not what I want, friend, it's what *God* wants. You have been delivered into my hands by the Lord God. You are to be His Sword of Vengeance. We have been holding up banks to get money to buy arms, shoulder-mounted Stingers, or perhaps one day a Russian suitcase nuke. But it will be a long, dangerous proposition, and I have been praying to the Savior for a better way. You and your genocidal weapon are God's answer to my prayers.''

''The ingredients to produce the Pale Horse Prion are very hard to acquire, and harder still to construct. They require extreme purification and strict bio-containment.''

''Nonsense,'' Fannon said softly, his voice barely audible over the rattling cars and the lowing cattle.

''You can say nonsense, but that doesn't change it. You're not a biologist—you have no idea how sensitive this material is.''

Then Fannon took out an automatic that was tucked beneath his shirt. He slowly chambered it.

Dexter's eyes shone with fear. ''What're you doing?''

''If you ain't gonna be part of this victory, then you gotta go stand with the heathens, and be part of the defeat. The Lord has christened my journey. The holy water of retribution has been sprinkled on His cause. There is no time to waste on nonbelievers.'' He aimed the pistol at Dexter DeMille.

''I am not afraid of death,'' Dexter bluffed, his heart beating wildly in his chest. He could feel his arteries pulsing. ''I'm suicidal. Three times this year I've tried to kill *myself*. You can't scare me with death. I've been courting it.''

''Suicide is an acute but temporary form of self-pity,'' Fannon drawled. ''To have meaning, *you* have to pick the time, place, and method. To have meaning, it has to be *your* ritual, not mine.''

He swung the barrel of the nine-millimeter automatic directly at Dexter.

''Wanna see?'' Without warning, he fired two rounds. One blew a chunk of wood out of the slat at the right side of Dexter's face; the other disintegrated the board on his left.

Dexter screamed in terror as splinters of wood flew into his eyes and bloodied his cheeks.

Then Fannon pulled back the hammer and aimed it directly at the bridge of Dexter's nose. "I'm doing the Lord's work here, bub, so don't fuck with me."

"Please . . . please, don't shoot. Please. I can do it for you. I can make your weapon," Dexter pleaded.

"How?"

"We need to go back to Vanishing Lake," he murmured.

Fannon turned back to Randall Rader. "Go back to the others, tell them we're getting off this train."

Randall Rader climbed the ladder at the back of the car. They could hear his footsteps overhead as he surfed the cars to the open grainer that contained the others. Fannon turned back to Dexter.

"Welcome, brother, you are now an Acolyte of the Choir. As an Acolyte, you can have a biblical designation. I name you Zophar," Fannon smiled. "Do you know about Zophar?"

Dexter was still shaking. He had lost control of his bowels and was now sitting in runny shit that filled his underwear and was pushing up against his balls. "No," he finally murmured. "Who's Zophar?"

"Zophar was one of Job's friends. In the Book of Job, he learns a great lesson. God allowed Satan to inflict evil onto Zophar, and he lost everything. The Lord questioned Zophar on this loss of position and wealth, and Zophar finally admitted the limits of human wisdom and bowed before the will of God. This is what you are doing right now. With this new humility, Zophar eventually finds everlasting peace, and so, my friend, shall you."

Chapter 16

SPIN DOCTOR

I can't say exactly how the fire got started," Admiral Zoll said, his rough-hewn voice spilling out over a sea of reporters gathered in his press briefing room at Fort Detrick. "I've explained to you that Dr. DeMille was unstable and that, despite his brilliant work in counter-terrorist biology, he had several bouts with suicide and deep depression. It's hard to understand the choices this kind of psychosis leads to. But let's suppose Dr. DeMille chose to try and destroy a line of research that he had been working on illegally. In so doing, some strain of his experimental virology might have gotten loose. Under this scenario, he could have set the fire to try and contain it. That fire itself became a terrible tragedy causing many deaths, both to people in the town and to many brave soldiers stationed at our research facility there. You all have copies of the suicide note we found in his quarters. Beyond that, I can't comment until more facts are uncovered."

"How much longer will the area be quarantined?" a reporter from AP asked.

"Until it's safe."

"Where is Dr. DeMille now?" CNN asked.

"We are assuming that he perished in the fire. However, until we can completely sort out the military Medical Examiner's reports and do all the dental identification, that is simply conjecture. I know you people thrive on conjecture, so please quote me accurately. This is just an assumption."

"The reports of some sort of strange microbe getting loose persist," NBC said.

"Yes, I know. And right now we can't confirm or deny that. If a product of DeMille's illegal research got loose, then perhaps some biological illness could have escaped. Right now we just don't know. We'll have to monitor the area carefully. Twenty-four hours should give us the answer."

"If DeMille's research was illegal, what exactly was the nature of the *legal* research being done at Vanishing Lake Prison?" a woman from Reuters asked.

"Classified," Admiral Zoll said.

There was an angry murmur from the reporters, so he quickly added, " 'Classified' is not a pseudonym for 'illegal.' There was no underground science taking place at that test site. Most antiterrorist research loses its effectiveness when declassified. For example, as soon as we develop an anti-toxin in a natural environment for a bio-weapon, and the enemy finds out, they simply alter their bio-weapon to defeat the anti-toxin. Much of what we were doing at Vanishing Lake was experimental defense work aimed at protecting the population from waterborne bio-weapons. That lake behaves very much like a water reservoir, which would be a natural target for waterborne toxins. Vanishing Lake is a crater, making it useful for all kinds of deep-water research. It enabled us to test anti-toxins under extreme cold and high pressure. Beyond that, I don't want to comment."

"Was there an ongoing danger to the people living up there?" another reporter shouted.

"Absolutely none. All of the strains we were working with were dormant, as required by government health standards. We were simply tracking dormant toxins to see how viruses will react in large, open bodies of water.''

"Who is investigating the disaster?''

"We are. The area conceivably contains an outbreak of a non-sanctioned bio-organism designed illegally by Dr. DeMille. For health and public safety reasons, the C.D.C. in Atlanta and the bio-weapons experts here at Fort Detrick will be in charge of the investigation. That's all I can say at this time. Further briefings will be scheduled by the Provost Marshal's Office.'' He turned and walked off the stage, leaving the reporters with hundreds of unanswered questions.

Admiral Zoll knew that the only way to spin the disaster was to do it in waves: First give them provable facts to appear to be open and honest; later, bore them to death with complicated microbiology.

He moved to his makeup room, where Colonel Chittick and Dr. Lack were waiting. "Fucking vultures,'' Admiral Zoll said, as he started taking off the thin layer of powder, which he detested, but had come to realize was an absolute necessity in this TV media age. Nothing looked worse during a military Code Blue than a startled Pentagon official with sweat on his upper lip.

"Sir, we have got to open Vanishing Lake to the media,'' Colonel Chittick said. "We've had a medical quarantine on the area since this morning, but we've found no more infected mosquitoes in the insect traps. It looks as if the fire did its job. The media pressure is building. Lieutenant Nino DeSilva is up there with the remaining Torn Victor commandos we deployed from here this morning. He says that the area seems clear. The longer we hold the press out, the worse it looks.''

"Okay, let 'em in. But I want our people with them. I don't want a buncha fucking newsies poking around, diggin' up stuff we can't explain.''

"I can restrict their movement with medical quarantine guidelines. They're all spooked by the bio-weapons angle. They don't want to go in there and come out with Black Death.''

"We've got to play that one just right," Admiral Zoll warned. "We have to scare 'em enough to slow 'em down, but not so much they sense a huge story and start risking their lives to get it."

Then Captain Wilcox came in and handed Admiral Zoll a fax of a newspaper article.

"What's this?" he snapped.

"Nino DeSilva just sent it to us. It's from a local paper up there . . . the *Clark County Crier*. Clark County is about a hundred miles from Vanishing Lake, almost in the Oklahoma panhandle."

The headline read:

HOBO FOUND DEAD

Under that was a brief description of Hollywood Mike's death. Admiral Zoll scanned the article, then read part of it aloud:

" '. . . Twenty-two-year-old Michael Brazil, known among hobos as 'Hollywood Mike,' jumped aboard the Southern Pacific westbound freight to avoid the huge forest fire that was consuming Vanishing Lake. Yesterday, he and his companion were aboard the freight for the short distance to Badwater, Texas. Sometime after that ride, Hollywood Mike began having trouble swallowing, the Southern Pacific spokesman said. According to his hobo friend, he could have crushed his larynx getting on the train. They jumped off at the Badwater switching station to seek medical attention. Before they could get a doctor, Michael Brazil died.' "

Admiral Zoll looked up at the men standing in the makeup room. "Trouble swallowing . . . son-of-a-bitch! The bug is out of the containment area."

"Sir," Dr. Charles Lack said, "we need that body. If that dead hobo had the Pale Horse Prion, it's still inside him. It's a protein. It doesn't break down. It's like DNA—it'll still be there ten years from now. All our research, all the years of study, could be in jeopardy if somebody draws half a cc of blood or cerebrospinal fluid. If they know what to look for and get their hands on that body, we could lose control of this strategic weapon."

"Tell Lieutenant DeSilva to take his four men and get over to . . . where the hell is it?"

"Badwater, Texas," Captain Wilcox said.

"Badwater, Texas?" Admiral Zoll repeated softly. "Not a good omen."

"Are you Roscoe Moss?" Stacy Richardson asked when he opened the door of his motor home.

"Yes ma'am," he answered.

"I was wondering if I could talk to you for a minute about this article that was in the newspaper." She showed him a copy of yesterday's *Crier*, which had the account of Michael Brazil's death.

He glanced at it. "Ain't much t'tell," Roscoe said. "Mostly it's all in there. He was supposed to be a big movie producer's son. I sent the body down to Government Camp and I heard they put it on a plane, sent it to the coroner in Santa Monica, California, this afternoon."

"Oh," she said, and seemed disappointed.

"I do something wrong?" he asked, momentarily stunned by her beauty.

"I was hoping it would still be up here, that's all."

"Well, it ain't." He smiled at her. "I got some coffee in the pot. It's just recooked grounds, but if you want some . . . it's hot."

"Thanks," she said.

He led her into the motor home, which was littered with souvenirs. He had dragged the old GMC bus all over West Texas during his three years on the rodeo circuit, right after he got out of the Marines. He had a few pictures on the walls, shots of him riding Brahma bulls. Bull-riding had been his best event until a two-ton monster named Evil Thunder had gored him, taking half of Roscoe's stomach and his short rodeo career in one gruesome moment.

"The article said that the train rider was having trouble swallowing," Stacy said. "I was wondering, if you saw that, could you describe it to me?"

"He was dead by the time I got there," Roscoe said. "That's what the other guy said."

"The other guy?"

"The other hobo."

"Oh yeah, right. He's mentioned in here. Did he tell you anything else?" Stacy asked.

"He told me that the kid banged his throat getting on the train, but he was lying. Doc Fletcher down in Government Camp checked the larynx and he said nothing was broken."

"Why do you think he lied?"

"Don't know why. He was a scruffy-looking bird. Both a' them looked and smelled like hell. Just a minute, I'll show you. I think I got a picture a' the kid. . . ." He moved to a table and poked around in some papers. "I hadda send a picture by fax to his father's office at Paramount Pictures Corporation. Can you believe that? A movie producer's son livin' a hobo's life. Don't add up."

He turned away from the stack of papers he'd been looking through and went into the back of the motor home to continue his search.

Stacy had gone without sleep for almost twenty-four hours. After the hobo with the silver hair had killed the soldier on the baseball diamond, she had hidden in the hills around Vanishing Lake until morning. Then when the County Sheriff's helicopter came in with the news trucks, she had used the confusion to trek over the hills to Highway 16 and hike out. Stacy had been in Bracketville, drinking coffee at a diner, trying to figure out her next move, when she saw the article in the *Crier*. She rented a car and drove straight to Badwater. Now, as she waited for Roscoe to get Michael Brazil's picture, a wave of fatigue hit her. She shook it off, determined to go on.

Stacy was worried about a lot of things. She was sure Pale Horse Prion had escaped at Vanishing Lake, but she didn't know what the incubation period was. There was no way to tell when a mosquito vector had bitten an afflicted victim like Sid Saunders, so there was no way to set the clock. She also knew that if the Prion was in the blood there was the possibility of secondary infection. If, for instance, a noninfected mosquito bit an infected victim, by sucking up the blood and then injecting it into another healthy person, the Prion might be passed. During a medical procedure it could also be passed. For this reason, she wanted to warn any doctor attempting an autopsy, as well as warn the other hobo.

She could hear a drawer opening and closing in the bedroom of the motor home. While she waited, she wandered around and looked at the rodeo pictures that were up on the walls. Shots of a younger Roscoe Moss, one hand high over his head, the other holding the bull knot. They were impressive photographs. She turned as he reentered and handed her a Polaroid headshot of Michael Brazil. The hobo's eyes were open, but he was dead.

"There it is," he said.

She looked at the picture and immediately recognized him as one of the hobos who had cleaned up the raccoon mess at the Bucket a' Bait. "I'll be damned," she said.

"You know him?" Roscoe asked.

"Not really," she replied. "The other one was named Lucky?"

"Yes ma'am. Had the D.T.s right in my office. Not much left there, I'm afraid. Long hair, busted-out tooth. Wouldn't tell me his last name, just wanted to get the hell out of here 'fore the cops showed up."

She tapped the Polaroid against her thumb. "You mind if I keep this?"

"Sure, help yourself. I was just gonna throw it out. Don't even know why I brought it home with me—just had it in my pocket."

"Lucky didn't happen to say where he was going . . . ?"

"Home to Pasadena, California. That's all."

"Where's the closest airport?"

"Sierra Blanca, 'bout fifteen miles down the road. But they don't have no commercial flights outta there. T'get a commercial, you gotta go to Waco."

"Thanks," she said, and hurried out of the trailer. First she had to call Wendell at USC and get him to warn the coroner in Santa Monica that Mike Brazil's body was "hot." Any accidental blood or fluid transfer during the autopsy procedure could pass the deadly Prion to the Medical Examiner. Then she had to find Lucky. Despite his D.T.-ravaged condition, she had to find out if he, too, was infected. She got into her rented car and pulled away from Roscoe's motor home, sending a dusty plume up against the cold blue Texas sky.

That night, Roscoe changed into his crisply ironed blue-and-red saddleback cowboy shirt with the arrow pockets. He put on his new Tony Lama boots with the fancy leather inset on the toe. Then he got into his pickup and headed toward town. He decided to eat at the Sierra Blanca Bar and Grill, maybe play some pool with the farmers who always spent their Friday nights there. He was going almost seventy, so he was surprised to see a car speeding up behind him, closing so fast it was almost as if he were standing still. He pulled the truck to the side to let the speeding car pass. Suddenly, it swerved to the left, pulled alongside of him, then started to run him off the road.

"The fuck you doin'?" Roscoe yelled at the gray sedan with the tinted windows. Then, without warning, it smashed his left fender, and the truck was off on the shoulder, skidding badly. He hit the brakes and fought to stay in control. Before he even came to a stop his driver's-side door was yanked open and three men in ski masks dragged him out of the truck into a choking cloud of billowing dust. They were all armed. One of them stuck a gun into Roscoe's face and thumbed back the hammer.

"What's the problem?" Roscoe stammered. "Whatta you want?"

"Get him up there," one of the men said, pointing to some brush away from the road.

They yanked Roscoe up the hillside and into the dense foliage.

"What's going on? I ain't got much money, just a few bucks. It's yers."

Once they were a few hundred yards off the road, they spun him around and pushed him down into the dirt. Again, the gun was in his face, pressed against his forehead by Lieutenant Nino DeSilva, who was wearing a ski mask.

"Where's the body? The hobo's body?" DeSilva demanded.

"Gone . . . to Santa Monica, California. I drove it down to Government Camp this afternoon. They took it to the airport."

"Shit," DeSilva said, spitting the word out with venom. "When? What time this afternoon?"

"It left the airport 'bout four. Why is everybody so interested in that dead bum?" Roscoe asked.

"Somebody else was askin' about him?" another commando in a ski mask said.

"Yeah."

"Who?"

"I didn't get her name. She said she knew him from before. That's all."

"And you told her where the body went?" Lieutenant DeSilva asked through the ski mask.

"Why not? She wanted to know. What's this all about?"

"Luke, get on the phone," DeSilva said to one of the masked

commandos. "Tell Colonel Chittick where we're going." Then he shifted the nine-millimeter directly between Roscoe Moss's eyes.

It happened so fast Roscoe never heard the gunfire or felt the bullet that exploded his head. One moment Roscoe Moss, Jr., was there, the next he was gone.

Part Three

Part Three

Chapter 17

THE PRODUCER

Buddy Brazil shot his Porsche Spyder out the front gate at Paramount Studios and hung a wide right, barely missing a westbound bus on Melrose Avenue. He was on his cellphone screaming at his assistant, Alicia Profit, because he had no idea where the Santa Monica morgue was.

"It's in fucking Santa Monica is all I know!" he yelled impatiently. "That's all the guy said, 'the Santa Monica morgue.' Do I have to do everything? Call 'em, get me an address, and get back to me. . . . Shit!" he said, as he accidentally ran a red light at La Brea.

Buddy Brazil was loaded. He had done two lines in his bathroom at the studio before he got the call telling him that his only son, whom he barely knew, was dead. It would be another twenty minutes before he got level. Driving when he was wired had already cost him his black Testarossa and his license. He had flipped the Italian sports car on Angeles Crest Highway, then had bricked the substance abuse test. As a result, he was driving without the permission of the State of California.

He decided to go down Fairfax and get on the Santa Monica Freeway, south of Olympic.

He wasn't sure how he felt about Mike's death; lately all his introspections were puzzles. His personal feelings had become more hidden from him than his asshole. Of course, he reasoned, he'd just done two lines of primo rocket fuel, blocking some neurons, along with his faltering internal voice.

He got to Fairfax and turned left. The guy at the morgue had mentioned that the family physician would be permitted to witness the autopsy, so Buddy snatched up his cellphone and called his pool house out at Malibu. The phone was answered on the twentieth ring. Dr. Gary Iverson's voice sounded like he'd just been dragged up from drug hell.

"Fuck," Gary croaked, as he answered the phone, then dropped it and got it back again. "What is it? Who is it?"

"Jesus, Gary, it's three-thirty in the afternoon. What'd you take last night?" Buddy yelled over the rushing California air that was slipstreaming over the windshield into the sports car.

"Buddy . . . geeze, just a minute. I'm putting the phone down. I'll be right back."

"No! Don't put the fuckin' phone down, Gary. I need help now! Sit up and put your feet on the floor. Don't zone out on me, man."

There was a long pause, and then he heard Gary Iverson's voice again. "Jesus, my head is buzzing. What a cocktail . . ."

"What'd you and Ginger take? You gotta get straight. I need you. I need a *doctor*."

Dr. Gary Iverson had been prescribing most of Buddy's drugs since Buddy'd flipped the Testarossa. Buddy had pulled every favor he had in city government to keep the D.A. from filing DUI charges against him. As a result, he had given up street dealers and cultivated Dr. Iverson's friendship.

They had met at a party at Charlie Sheen's, where Gary was set up in the bar, prescribing the alphabet, everything from Atarax to

Xanax. It was too good for Buddy to believe. Later that night, Buddy had driven a wasted Dr. Iverson home. When he found out that Gary had lost his residence to his ex-wife, he moved the doctor into his pool house, where Iverson took root like a mushroom fungus, writing prescriptions faster than freeway graffiti. In return, Buddy got the geeky doctor laid with A-line hookers from Heidi's old stable. He told Gary they were actresses. When Dr. Iverson had become so unreliable that he had lost most of his practice and was in danger of losing his medical license, Buddy paid for him to take the cure at Windsong Ranch in Montana. Buddy had detoxed there three times himself.

The doctor had returned from drug camp twenty-eight days later, freshly pressed and ready to go, and they had taken up where they'd left off. It was an ideal solution for Buddy, who could now get his prescription of morphine or Seconal or gamma-hydroxyl barbiturates by simply walking down the garden path. Buddy had neatly switched from street drugs, with their potential for serious medical and legal risk, to Dr. Iverson's squeaky-clean drugstore prescriptions.

The problems came from a totally unexpected place. Buddy had agreed to fund a hair transplant for the balding doctor. After Windsong, Dr. Iverson had cut back to a baby habit, taking only sporadic hits off of someone's ganja stick, or doing an occasional half-line of white ghost. But the pain from the transplant had quickly driven him to self-prescribe some heady painkillers. He started shooting Toradol, which caused him depression, so he began taking Prozac for mood swings, but that caused anxiety, so he shot a few loads of Vistaril, and so on. Now Gary Iverson could barely haul his drugged ass and new plugs of bushy gray hair out of bed to piss. Worse still, Buddy was having trouble getting the doctor's eyes to focus long enough to write his own prescriptions. He began to fondly remember the good old days when he could just meet his dealer and get hooked up in some gas station bathroom.

"Mike's dead," Buddy said to Gary, going for shock value and getting nothing.

"Who the hell is Mike?"

"You're sleeping in his bedroom, asshole. Michael my son . . . he's dead! They sent his body to the morgue in Santa Monica. I'm on my way there now."

"Oh," Gary said, and from his tone, Buddy knew that was going to be the whole reaction.

"You've got to meet me there on the double. Get out of bed and get truckin'. If you're too zooted, have Consuelo drive you."

"What's the hurry?"

"He's in the Santa Monica morgue. We gotta go! I don't know where it is yet, so get the address out of the phone book!"

"Is he deceased or have they got some new back-from-the-dead Code Blue unit that's gonna revive him?"

Shit, he's right, Buddy thought, and backed his foot off the gas. "Look, Gary, I wanna know *why* my son is dead, and I don't want those county clucks sawing him up. I want him . . . y'know, in one piece for the funeral. . . . I'm thinking like, doing the whole deal. A temple funeral, sit Shiva at the beach house, invite everybody. You gotta meet me at the morgue, kill this idea they got of doing an autopsy. It's against my religion to desecrate the body," Buddy said, forgetting to mention he hadn't been to temple in ten years, not counting Bar Mitzvahs. "You gotta do this. You know how to talk to doctors."

"My scalp is on fire," Gary whined.

"Don't go back to sleep, Gary. You go back to sleep, I'm gonna evict you. You'll be writing prescriptions under a fucking bridge someplace." He hung up.

Before he got to Olympic, Alicia Profit called back and gave him the address of the morgue. "They said you can't get in there. It's not open to the public."

"I ain't the public!" he snapped maniacally, and hung up.

. . .

The morgue was on Lincoln Boulevard, halfway between Wilshire and Olympic. He parked in an emergency lot in a space marked "Doctors Only" and walked toward the hulking five-story concrete structure that looked like it had been designed by the same people who made Lego.

He had still not focused on the loss of his only son. He was sort of hoping he'd get some kind of emotional reaction, maybe even cry, so his faltering opinion of himself wouldn't take another direct hit. So far, he felt nothing. Of course, he told himself, he barely knew his son. Mike had been a love child with a beautiful but vapid model named Tova Conte. She didn't want the baby because it's hard to screw Italian royalty with a kid sucking on the other tit. For almost six years, Buddy had legally avoided being Mike's father. Then Tova hired Gloria Allred. That evil cunt had chased him with papers until they made him give blood. His DNA had sealed his parental obligation. Mike had become his legally designated offspring, which meant Buddy now had to pay for boarding school and summer camp, while Tova traveled through Europe bone-dancing with her fop princes. His ex had eventually died in a speedboat accident off the coast of Cannes. It didn't even make *USA Today.*

After Mike had spent two abysmal years at Pepperdine, Buddy finally agreed to let him move into the pool house. It lasted for six months. They barely saw each other, because Buddy had been in production on *Silver and Lead,* which was ten million over budget after only three weeks of shooting. He was practically sleeping on the set. During that summer, Mike had crashed the Porsche on Mulholland, trashed all his front teeth in the accident, and been busted three times for possession. Soon there was a small tent city of vice cops with long lenses living in the hills behind the Malibu house because of Mike's drug parties. That surveillance had inevitably overlapped to Buddy, who was now also under police observation. Buddy explained to his son that he had to be more discreet, but Mike just told him to eat shit, a flavor Buddy had never acquired a taste for despite twenty years in Hollywood.

Buddy entered the county building and found the morgue on the third floor. He'd approved half a dozen morgue sets in his thirty or so movies. He always thought morgues should be low-lit dungeons with no sunlight. The theatrically dead needed low lighting and dank windowless privacy. This morgue was sunny and bright.

He stopped a woman doctor and told her he wanted to talk to somebody about a deceased: Michael Brazil.

"Are you here to view his body and make an identification?" she asked.

"Yeah, yeah, that's what I'm doing. An identification." He was now well off the cocaine train and seesawing into a miserable paranoid snap. His mood swings were getting bigger and wider; he knew he had to head for another detox before he began hitting psychological curbs instead of concrete ones.

Buddy waited in the brightly lit human chop shop while the woman went to summon the right person to help him. After a minute, a fifty-year-old heavy-set man came out of a door at the end of the hall. "I'm Dr. Rackovitch," the white-coated, gray-haired man said.

"I'd like to make an identification," Buddy said. "Michael Juan Brazil." He'd always hated the "Juan," sitting like an uneducated brazero in the middle of an otherwise acceptable name. Tova had put it there to honor her liberal leanings and Hispanic mother.

"I'm afraid that's not going to be possible," the doctor said. "We've been contacted by a doctor of biology at USC and warned of extenuating circumstances. The County Medical Examiner is coming over this evening to personally conduct the autopsy. The body is in bio-containment."

"What're you talking about, asswipe? What extenuating circumstances?" Buddy snapped.

"You won't get anywhere talking to me like that."

"You know who I am?" Buddy said, glowering at this bone-cutter, who was obviously such a schmendrick they'd only let him practice on dead people.

"I'm afraid who you are really isn't the point."

"I'm Buddy Brazil," he said, spitting it out. "Buddy Brazil? *Movies?* I wanna see my son's body. This *is* going to happen, so let's not shed blood over it." Buddy didn't really want to see Mike's body, but he hated anybody telling him he couldn't.

"It's not going to happen, Mr. Brazil. Leave, and in a day or so, we'll release the body to the next of kin. If that's you, fine."

Buddy moved to the payphone in the lobby, which was only a few feet behind him. "Okay, who gets me past you? Huh? Who's your scout leader?"

"Nobody gets you past me," Dr. Rackovitch said.

"That's not the way the world works, buster. Could the Governor of the State of California press your grapes?"

"We have reason to believe your son may have died of a highly contagious unknown fatal disease. You can call the Governor, the U.S. President, or the Crown Prince of Liechtenstein, but that body stays in quarantine until we find out what killed him."

"Is that supposed to be a joke? The fucking Crown Prince of Liechtenstein?" Buddy shrieked, thinking he remembered reading that Tova had actually gone out with the asshole. Why had this doctor mentioned that? Was it some kinda plot? Was this some crazy plan aimed at driving him nuts? Could the world be that small? Or was he just paranoid from all the drugs?

Chapter 18

CONNECT

They were on the 110 Freeway heading toward Pasadena. Wendell Kinney had been quiet ever since they transitioned off I-5. Stacy worried he was driving his green station wagon too fast. He was deep in thought, but his rumpled hair and personality still gave off their characteristic warmth. Finally, he pointed to a green off-ramp sign.

"There it is," he said, flipping on his blinker and pulling into the right lane. He shot up the off-ramp and came to a full stop before turning right onto Orange Grove Avenue, which she knew was the same manicured street that was seen by millions every New Year's Day as floats from the Rose Parade made their turns in front of banks of cameras at that exact corner.

"I've been running it over in my mind," Wendell finally said. "Everything you say, all the symptoms you witnessed, are almost exactly like Kuru, except magnified."

He was going slowly now, heading past cross streets looking for La Loma Road. Stacy had the *Thomas Street Guide* open on her lap as Wendell continued, "If Dexter DeMille was designing a Prion bio-weapon, he would have needed to shorten the incubation period to make it effective. We need to get a blood sample—more than one if we can—so we can isolate the components. We should get one from you too. You were at Vanishing Lake, so you were exposed.''

She nodded. ''If this bio-weapon is attacking proteins with DNA markers, that could explain why some people are getting it and others aren't. According to Max's e-mail, two prisoners were transferred to Vanishing Lake just before the fire. They perished in the blaze and nobody knows or will admit knowing why they were sent there. I've been checking into their backgrounds. One of the soldiers was named Troy Lee Williams. I did an Internet news article search when I got home last night and found some four-year-old stories about his trial. He raped and murdered a girl in Rosemont, California. I'm trying to get in touch with his family to investigate his genetic background. The other soldier was an African-American. There's got to be some reason Dr. DeMille chose them, if he did. . . . Max's e-mail to me said they were about to do human testing.''

Wendell furrowed his brow, but said nothing as he continued for several more blocks. ''La Loma,'' he finally said, pointing at a street sign and turning right.

They headed down a steep hill. The houses were beautiful and getting larger and more imposing with every quarter mile they traveled. When they got to the bottom of the hill they saw the arroyo which carried water down from the Angeles Crest Mountains. They turned left, then right, and passed over an old concrete bridge that spanned the aqueduct. Once on the other side, they found themselves driving past beautiful old Pasadena mansions with imposing brick or concrete driveways and acres of rolling lawns, guarded by ornate wrought-iron fencing complete with gatehouses. They pulled up in front of the address that Stacy had in her hand and looked at a huge Spanish-style house sitting behind an eight-foot spiked iron fence.

"There it is," he said. "Be it ever so humble."

"This can't be right," Stacy said, staring at the slip of paper in her hand.

They got out, moved to the walk-in gate, and rang a buzzer. After a moment, a man's voice came through the speaker, squawking angrily, "Who is it?"

"We're here to see Cris Cunningham," Stacy said.

There was a long silence, and then without further comment, the electric lock buzzed. They pushed open the walk-in gate and moved onto the three-acre estate. They walked up a brick path toward the imposing house. A hundred yards to the right, an Olympic-size pool glistened in the afternoon sunlight. Dragonflies hovered. On their left, an empty tennis court shimmered with late-afternoon heat. Dusty brown birds did showy aerobatics over the huge lawn before climbing abruptly, then landing in the leafy elm trees.

The front door opened, and a tall, thin, gray-haired man moved out of the house. He stood defiantly on the front porch. His unfriendly glower was muted by his slightly comic wardrobe: a lime-green shirt over dark green golf slacks. As Stacy neared him, she thought his body posture sent a mixed message. Like a defeated general, he seemed both overbearing and apologetic.

"Yes, what is it?" he said warily as they approached.

"Is this Cris Cunningham's house?" she asked.

"And you are . . . ?" He let the question hang in the unfriendly space between them.

"I'm Stacy Richardson, and this is Dr. Wendell Kinney, from USC. We wanted to talk to a man named Cris Cunningham. We understood this is his address."

"He isn't here right now," the gray-haired man said.

"I see. When do you expect him?"

"I'm Richard Cunningham, his father. What's this regarding?"

"It's about . . ." She looked over at Wendell. "If he's the one we're looking for, I really think we should speak directly with him. Although it's also possible we have the wrong person.''

"How so?"

"The man we're looking for doesn't really seem like he belongs in this neighborhood. He's sort of . . ."

"Rundown?" Richard said sadly, then nodded and relaxed his posture slightly. "Why don't you come wait inside?"

He led them into a large entry hall with polished hardwood floors and a curving staircase. A huge chandelier hung above the foyer dangling expensive crystal. He led them into a den. The room was furnished in the warm colors and textures of an old tavern. Prints of horses hung above red leather couches and antique wooden tables. Outside, intense afternoon sun filtered through dense oak trees and fell without heat in dappled patterns on the emerald-green carpet.

"Would you like something to drink?" Richard asked.

"Ice water, if you have it," she replied, and Wendell nodded.

"The maids take Sunday off. I'll be right back."

Richard Cunningham turned and moved out of the den, leaving them standing alone, looking at the masculine decor. Behind the bar was a large framed color photograph that was almost four feet by three, mounted under glass. It froze a moment and a memory. In the photo, a lithe quarterback in the powder-blue-and-gold uniform of the UCLA Bruins was crossing the goal line. The number 9 on his jersey was full to camera. His gold helmet glinting in the Coliseum sunlight was turned away, looking toward the coffin corner of the end zone just inside the marker. In the picture, the quarterback held the ball tightly in both hands, slightly in front of him, while stepping through the outstretched arms of a USC Trojan tackler. The Coliseum scoreboard was out of focus but readable in the background: USC 9, UCLA 7. There were fifty-three seconds left in the fourth quarter. It was a picture of the moment before victory.

"That was Cris," Richard Cunningham said, strangely using the past tense.

They turned and looked at him as he handed them cold glasses of water. "He won the game." There was a soft, wistful quality to the way he said it, as if the memory was too fragile to address forcefully, hanging only by a very slender thread in his mind.

Also on the back wall behind the bar were a Silver Star and a combat ribbon from the Gulf War, in a frame with a picture of a young, extremely handsome blond man with Marine-short hair.

Stacy recognized the decorations from her years as an Army brat. She looked hard at the Marine, but didn't recognize him at all.

"This is Cris?" she asked.

"That was taken the day he graduated from Special Forces Recon training," his father said. Again his voice contained the wistful echo of faded memories.

"I got this address from the police," Stacy said. "They have an alias database on people with police records. The man I'm looking for was using the name 'Lucky.' The Pasadena police had a Lucky in their files. He'd been arrested for vagrancy and plain drunk in Old Town, up by Colorado Boulevard, four years ago. They said his real name was Cris Cunningham and gave me this address, but I don't think this is the same man."

Richard Cunningham shifted his weight slightly. "After Kennidi died, he was drunk all the time. He left home and was sleeping in doorways. I'd go find him, but he wouldn't even look at me. His wife, Laura, divorced him. Then he left town on the rails." Richard looked suddenly very fragile. "Cris doesn't look like that picture anymore," he said.

"Who was Kennidi?" Stacy asked.

"His four-year-old daughter. When she died, it changed him." Richard paused, then corrected himself: "It destroyed him."

"I'm sorry," Stacy said softly.

"Why do you want to see my son?"

"He was at a place called Vanishing Lake, in Texas. The man he was traveling with died of a new, fatal disease. It could be contagious. We don't know yet what the incubation period is, but he needs to be checked immediately, and we need to take a sample of his blood."

Richard stood, silently dealing with this information. Then he nodded, as if it was just another chapter in his family's horrible medical odyssey.

"He left early this afternoon. His mother took him to the doctor and the dentist. They should have been home hours ago, but I think I know where they went. . . ." Then he added, "I've been kind of worried, so if you want, we can go check. I'll lead you there."

The clothes from his past life were too big, and draped him like oversized memories. He had been standing beside the grave for an hour. His mother had finally gone back to the air-conditioned visitors' center to wait. He was looking down at the small brass plaque that silently screamed his daughter's name in uniformly correct ten-inch-high letters:

KENNIDI BISHOP CUNNINGHAM
BRAVE BEYOND HER YEARS
1991–1995

He seemed rooted there, looking for something meaningful, but he could find no elevating factors. The remembered taste of the "heart starters" he had snuck from his father's bar that morning consumed his thoughts, intensifying his need for a booster. As he stood looking down at the grave, he no longer wanted to blame himself for his daughter's sickness, but self-loathing hovered on the shifting winds of grief and loss. Then his thoughts jumped. Perhaps when he'd started drinking, he'd really only been looking for a way to escape his golden life. Had it been intentionally self-destroyed? Had he been afraid to raise the bar one notch higher, as he had time after time since elementary school, until even heroics in the Gulf War weren't enough to validate him? Had Kennidi's torment been his escape? Had he ducked out on his life using her death as his exit card? Was it possible that he was that hollow, or that selfish? Why, he wondered, did he have such an emptiness? Why was it that nothing he did fulfilled him?

He had begun to suspect that he had lived his life in pursuit of the wrong things, but how could he find the strength to redirect himself or even know what to aim at? His life before Kennidi died had been about trophies and medals; now it was about self-pity and despair. He had jumped out of his comfortable life almost in desperation, but the chute hadn't opened. Instead, he had experienced four years of free fall with his silk canopy streaming uselessly above him, flapping and tugging at his shoulders like ghostly memories. There was almost no time left; the ground was coming at him fast. The impact would be sudden and devastating. He had no solution.

The sun was finally setting, and the approaching night cooled his freshly shaved head. He wondered what he should do. He didn't want to sleep in doorways or under railroad bridges anymore, but he couldn't stand his old bedroom. No place seemed like home. He desperately needed a drink.

"I still owe you a meal," a voice said, pulling him out of these thoughts.

Cris turned and looked at a pretty blond woman standing just behind him. He could see his father down the hill, waiting by the car. He couldn't place her for a minute, but she looked familiar.

"Stacy," she said, reading the confusion in his eyes. "You cleaned up after my raccoons."

Then he nodded and smiled weakly, exposing the temporary tooth put in that afternoon.

Stacy almost couldn't recognize him. The long, greasy blond hair had been completely shaved off. He stood before her, bald-headed and sallow-cheeked; the skin around his eyes was mottled and unhealthy-looking. His shoulders were hunched, but at least the garbage bags had been replaced by expensive brown loafers.

"That's not much of a haircut," she said, smiling at him.

Absent-mindedly he rubbed his hand over his shaved head. "It's not a haircut, it's a medical procedure. Guy hit me with a wrench. Took fifteen stitches." He turned and exposed a nasty cut on the back of his head.

"Ouch," she said, then after a moment, "Listen, Mr. Cunningham . . . Cris . . . I need to talk to you."

"About what?"

"It's about Mike Brazil and Sidney Saunders, and that whole horrible disaster up at Vanishing Lake."

"Oh," he said, and then they both fell silent as a gust of wind blew dry leaves across the raised metal names of the dead.

Chapter 19

THE FAME IN DEAD MEN'S DREAMS

They had switched trains at Amarillo, and were now on the old, lyrically named Atchison, Topeka and the Santa Fe, heading back toward Vanishing Lake. Now that Dexter was an Acolyte of the Choir, he had been assigned his very own sub-angel to guide him to the path of godly reckoning. Dexter's sub-angel was the cruel, war-hardened Randall Rader. When Dexter wasn't listening to Fannon Kincaid's long, dissociative lectures, he was forced to sit with Randall and read scripture from the "Available Light Bible," which was just a long rolled-up filmstrip and a plastic viewer that they held up to the sunlight. The filmstrip only contained the Old Testament and the last chapter of the Bible, Revelation. No mention was made of the fact that all the other chapters of the New Testament, Matthew through Jude, were missing. Randall started Dexter's Bible study by concentrating mostly on Deuteronomy, which, he explained, was the Fifth Book of Moses and necessary for a new member of the Choir to fully understand. Fannon was a latter-day Moses, Randall told him. He was fighting for the Lord while attempting to lead his flock out of metaphoric Egypt, which in today's world was not a corrupt state, but a corrupt state of mind. Although hardened by war and life on the rails, Randall still cried as he read Deuteronomy: " 'Surely there shall not one of these men of this evil generation see that good land, which I swear to give unto your fathers.' " He whispered reverently as he read Chapter Two, Verse One: " 'Then we turned and took our journey into the wilderness by way of the Red Sea.' " Dexter learned the new metaphor for the parting of the Red Sea. Randall explained that the rail system from which Fannon led his flock parted a sea of corruption and misplaced moral values in America. As they read through the Available Light Bible, looking for appropriate passages, Randall explained that his biblical name was "The Angel in the Church of Per-ga-mos," a long, exalted title. Randall was, after all, a sub-angel.

As they scrolled Deuteronomy, they skipped right over a few important Commandments that caught Dexter's eye, like Chapter Five, Verse Seventeen, "Thou shalt not kill," or Verse Nineteen, "Thou shalt not steal."

When Dexter asked Randall Rader about these two cornerstones of religion, Randall simply explained, "How can one steal something that was itself stolen?" And regarding killings, Randall recalled a quotation from Luke 22:36: "He that hath no sword, let him sell his garment and buy one."

Dexter had given up, and was now just going along with everything. He had been captured by maniacs.

In the evenings they sat in a circle in the moving freight car, warming their hands over "canned heat," which was tins of Sterno. Fannon would give political, social, and religious lectures as the train rumbled back up the east face of the Black Hills.

"Prison is a kiss on the lips of defeat," Fannon said softly one evening, as they discussed their inevitable incarceration, *if* they allowed themselves to be caught alive. Moon shadows moved slowly across the floor of the moving car. The members of the Choir all looked at Fannon as if he had just uttered something so profound that a pause was needed to completely digest it.

"The field of Armageddon will be either in Kansas, or Nebraska, or Maryland," he said, for the umpteenth time. They all sat in silence and contemplated the great wisdom. For this reason the Choir rarely, if ever, ventured into those states.

"The filthy Levites control the banking system," Fannon continued. "This was predicted in Revelation with Apostle John's nightmarish vision, where he foretold that nobody could get a job or even buy in a store. The capability already exists for us to live in a cashless society." He rambled on, "Computer technology has accomplished this feat for the Jew. Already the banking system is increasingly multinational, and Levites are now managing the world's wealth. Their private banks issue computer credit, which is a debt against the currency of nations, instead of how it always was before, where nations issued currency backed by their own people's productivity. This change has delivered the financial powers into the hands of the International Jew Bankers, who now control the ability to throw us into financial dungeons."

His lectures were even more emotional when he turned to the mud races. He ranted endlessly on mixed marriages and the blurring of bloodlines. "The White men in America are 'sheeple,' " he announced. "Our White brothers are blind to what's happening in the Jew-nited States of America."

Dexter listened and nodded. He was trapped. He had made a horrible mistake when he told Fannon about his deadly secret, hidden in sealed containers in the freezing water at the bottom of Vanishing Lake. He had intended to escape from the Devil's Workshop and then retrieve the containers to continue the next phase of his research alone. He had only told Fannon in a moment of white fear, when he thought he was just seconds from death. It had been his only bargaining chip. Now he knew that if the deadly bio-weapon fell into the hands of this maniac, he might indiscriminately wipe out huge sections of the population. Still, he couldn't figure out a way to undo what he had done.

Dexter's attention drifted back to Fannon, who was now talking about death. It was clear from what he was saying that he didn't expect to survive his war with the U.S. Government. He was telling them that he would only strike the first blow before perishing. Others would have to pick up his lance and march to victory.

"Bob Matthews said it before he died," Fannon lectured. These last few days, Dexter had been hearing a lot about Bob Matthews, the martyred White separatist who went down in a hail of government gunfire. "Matthews said it, and remember his words," Fannon ordered. " 'The only thing I know of that does not die is the fame in dead men's dreams.' " All of them sat quietly in the rumbling freight and thought about their own death and fame as martyrs to the Cause. All, that is, except Dexter, who was only thinking about escape. But with Randall Rader never more than a few feet away, it seemed increasingly impossible.

Chapter 20

AUTOPSY

I t was already dark, and Buddy was still waiting for Gary Iverson in the overlit waiting room of the morgue. In the twilight afterglow, out the third-floor windows, he could just barely see the surf hitting the moonlit ribbon of beach south of the Santa Monica Pier. Paranoid thoughts still followed him, like refugees trailing a defeated army. He was fighting the urge to scoot down and retrieve his stash from the Porsche spare tire, which had a hole cut in the underside for easy access. He knew that would be a mistake. When he was snapping paranoid, cocaine put him in a despair so deep he would sometimes be blighted for days.

He began to think more seriously about rehab.

Only occasionally did his mind drift to his dead son lying in frosty silence somewhere in the overlit morgue.

The elevator doors opened, and Gary Iverson stepped off, his bloodshot eyes blinking rapidly in hollow sockets. He had a two-day stubble, and was wearing his Malibu chic grunge attire. He moved to Buddy, dragging visibly.

"You don't look like a doctor, you look like fucking afterbirth," Buddy complained.

"It's the nineties, man," Gary sighed. "I'm not okay, you're not okay, but that's okay. What's going on?"

"These guys are talking about doing an autopsy with some County Medical guy, some dipshit supervisor. They got Mike's body in bio-containment, whatever the fuck that is. Why would they do that?" Gary shrugged. "I want Mike's body released to Mount Sinai *now!*"

"God, why's my head killing me," Gary said, rubbing his eyes.

"Your head's killing you 'cause that whore Ginger hooked you to a G.H.B. ride. I told you not to shoot that stuff. Heidi promised me Ginger was off it." When Gary didn't answer, Buddy went on, "That shit's lethal. That's what gonked River Phoenix."

"Ginger's a whore?" Gary asked, dumbfounded. "She's one of Heidi's girls? You told me she was an actress."

"Whores *are* actresses," Buddy backtracked. "Listen, Gary, you gotta get down there and stop that autopsy. Somethin' ain't right," he said, paranoia driving suspicion.

"Ginger's a fucking whore?" Gary repeated. "All that time I thought she was enjoying it and getting off."

"Who gives a shit?" Buddy riled. "You don't pay whores to come, you pay them to leave. Now will ya please go find out why they got Mike in bio-containment. They won't let anybody but doctors in there."

In the second-floor autopsy section of the morgue, a heated argument was taking place between two M.E.s and Colonel Laurence Chittick, who had just flown in from Fort Detrick. All of them were in a sterile hallway that fronted four autopsy rooms.

"Excuse me," Iverson said softly as he approached, "I'm here to make arrangements to transport the body of Michael Brazil to the mortuary at Mount Sinai."

Nobody paid any attention to him, or maybe they hadn't heard him, because his voice was a low drugged whisper. Colonel Chittick was arguing loudly with Dr. Ernest Welsh, the Santa Monica Coroner, who was tall, with a hairline shaped like a laurel wreath.

"You don't seem to understand. I don't care who at Fort Detrick authorized it," Dr. Welsh said. "My chain of command is municipal. This body isn't leaving here without the correct authorization, period."

"I'm Dr. Iverson, the Brazil family physician," Gary stated more forcefully. They both turned.

His ripped-at-the-knee jeans, flip-flops, and fatigued appearance argued with this statement. "Sorry, I've been up forty-eight hours," he alibied, reading their disbelief. "Camping trip. Got here as soon as I could. I'd like to make arrangements to have Mike's body delivered to Mount Sinai—"

"He's not going to Mount Sinai. He's going air-express to the bio-containment facility at Fort Detrick," the Colonel said.

"Who are you?" Gary Iverson demanded.

"I'm Colonel Chittick, with the E.I.S. at the Centers for Disease Control."

"E.I.S.?" Gary asked.

"Epidemic Intelligence Service," Chittick said.

The Santa Monica M.E. turned back to Colonel Chittick.

"The only way to accomplish what you want is to supply me with the proper paperwork," he said. "I need a written request that states E.I.S.'s reasons why this body should be transported to Fort Detrick. Without that I can't let it go. My ass will get sued by his family." He turned to Iverson. "Right, Doctor?"

"Count on it," Gary said, with over-the-top conviction.

"Where will the body be kept?" Chittick asked.

"We'll keep it right here. The autopsy is scheduled for nine this evening. You should be able to get the correct paperwork to me by then. Have the EPS duty officer frame the request, then submit it with the C.D.C.'s recommendation and copy it to the State

Health Department in Berkeley. Fax it to me and the body will be turned over to you. Otherwise we're going to do this procedure as scheduled.''

Colonel Chittick nodded and moved out of the morgue, using the side elevator. He went down to a rented windowless van parked around the corner from the County Medical Building. Once inside, he turned to face Lieutenant Nino DeSilva. The Lieutenant was only twenty-two, but his dark Latino looks burned with a fierce intensity that made him seem older.

"They want a paper from E.I.S. or they won't turn the body loose.''

"Then let's get the paper,'' DeSilva said.

"We go through channels on this and C.D.C. *will* demand delivery on the body,'' Chittick explained. "They're gonna find the brain disintegration and see the spongiform encephalitis. Once that happens, they're gonna run more tests, take some C.S.F., and eventually discover the Pale Horse Prion. They'll turn it over to the FBI, who will notify Congress, and we're fucked.'' He paused and rubbed his forehead. "We have to contain this ourselves. They are doing the autopsy at nine. We've got to stop it,'' Colonel Chittick said darkly.

"This was the original Bob's Big Boy,'' Wendell told Stacy and Cris as they pulled up in front. "I haven't been here in ages.''

It was a large, old-fashioned fifties-style restaurant. The huge plate-glass windows looked out on Colorado Boulevard in Pasadena. Mr. and Mrs. Cunningham had gone directly home from Forest Lawn. Cris and Stacy got out of Wendell's station wagon. She leaned back in the passenger window and winked at the ever rumpled doctor, who was still seated behind the wheel.

"You sure this is okay? I could stick around,'' he said.

"It's better if you go over and witness the autopsy in Santa Monica. They did us a big favor by moving it up, and doing it on

Sunday night.'' She looked at her wristwatch; it was eight-fifteen. "You'll just about make it. I'll catch a cab, drop Cris, and meet you at my place around eleven.''

He hesitated, so she gave him a subtle head movement that said, "Get outta here.'' She wanted to talk to Cris Cunningham, and she thought she would get more out of him alone.

Wendell blew her a kiss and pulled the station wagon away from the curb, leaving them standing in front of the restaurant. They moved inside and were greeted by the chill of too-cold air-conditioning, and a hostess who led them to a table by a window overlooking the parking lot.

"Jesus, it's a fucking malt shop,'' Cris said. "Let's go someplace that at least has a bar.''

"Order anything you want,'' Stacy said, ignoring that, as a waitress handed them menus and moved off. "You and Mike did a good job around that Dumpster,'' she smiled. "This is on me.''

He took the menu and held it without opening it. "Why did you go to all the trouble of finding me?'' His suspicious, feral eyes studied her, eyes that had lost their trust in humanity. "You wanna tell me what's really going on here?''

"You're right, I came a long way looking for you,'' she admitted, then dug into her purse and pulled out the rolls of developed pictures she had taken at Vanishing Lake. She slid them across the table toward him. "Do you recognize him?'' she said, pointing to a shot of Fannon Kincaid taken moments after he had murdered the troops on the baseball diamond. "Most of the men with him had 'F.T.R.A.' tattooed on their arm.''

Cris looked at the picture for a long time, weighing his jeopardy before answering. It was the same man he'd seen shoot the two soldiers. When she mentioned the tattoos, he suddenly knew who he was. He'd heard stories whispered over jungle campfires.

"F.T.R.A. stands for 'Freight Train Riders of America,' '' Cris said. "I think his name is Fannon Kincaid. He runs some White supremacist church. Rides the rails to stay underground. He's killed hobos for just being on the same train. Legend says, if you see a crazy silver-haired fanatic that looks like the abolitionist John Brown, run like hell.''

''Great,'' she said. ''He's got Dexter DeMille. God only knows what that means.''

''Who's Dexter DeMille?''

''He's the other reason I came looking for you. You need to go to the hospital,'' she said. ''I'll set it up, but you need to get checked over immediately.''

''Why?''

''Hollywood Mike didn't die from a crushed larynx.'' She watched as his eyes shifted slightly, then came back and found hers.

''Who said he had a crushed larynx?''

''You did. You told Roscoe Moss in Badwater.''

''Christ, lady, you've been covering a lot of ground.''

''Roscoe Moss sent the body to someplace called Government Camp, and they looked it over. The doc there said there was nothing wrong with Mike's throat. That's not what killed him.''

Cris hesitated, then let out a long, slow breath. ''I thought I'd killed him,'' he finally admitted.

''You didn't. Something else did.''

When the waitress reappeared they both ordered full house Big Boy burgers and vanilla shakes. When she left, Cris looked back at Stacy.

''That still doesn't explain why you want *me* to go to a hospital.''

Stacy looked across the table at Cris and decided that the best way to get him to cooperate was to level with him. Despite his scrawny, alcohol-ravaged state, he was still a college graduate and a Silver Star winner. She hoped the truth would motivate him.

''I think Mike died because of exposure to a new kind of bio-weapon designed by Dexter DeMille,'' she finally said. Then she filled him in on the bio-weapons program headquartered at Fort

Detrick, Maryland, including Admiral Zoll and Dexter DeMille's work at Vanishing Lake Prison, and lastly describing the Prion illness. "He's designing killer proteins that attack the mood center, causing rage, then they destroy the midbrain, which controls swallowing and the other reflex actions. In the final stage there are violent seizures."

"That's what happened to Mike," Cris said softly.

"Mosquitoes were the delivery agents up there," she said. "I think Mike was bitten by escaped mosquitoes that got away from them at Vanishing Lake. It's possible you were bitten too."

"Wouldn't I have it by now? He's been dead two days."

"You may have antibodies in your system that are able to slow it down. You might be somehow immune, or you could become a carrier without exhibiting any of the symptoms yourself. If that's the case, your blood could be invaluable in helping us develop an antibody."

The hamburgers and shakes were delivered, and the waitress left. In the few seconds it took for this to happen, Cris seemed to change slightly. His posture straightened; his chin came up; anger now burned in his blue eyes. "My daughter, Kennidi, died from something I picked up in the Gulf, some chemical mix," he said. "I was a carrier. It didn't affect me at all, but Kennidi was born with her body full of . . ." He stopped, took a deep breath. "Tumors. She had hundreds of tumors. They grew everywhere inside her, until finally they killed her."

"I'm sorry," Stacy said gently. He nodded, and seemed momentarily overcome by the memory.

As Stacy waited for him to regain his composure, she suddenly remembered something Max had once told her about a strange incidence of Gulf War Syndrome. It defied all current explanation. "In Huntsville, Texas," she began slowly, "there was an outbreak of what looked like Gulf War Syndrome. Over twenty people were infected. There was a prison there, just like at Vanishing Lake, and there was also a science pod that was funded by Sam Houston

University, just like at Vanishing Lake. According to the news articles that I read, the prison medical personnel were suddenly moved out, and doctors from Sam Houston University restaffed the prison overnight. These new doctors were all former military personnel. Apparently, some top-secret scientific tests were performed on the prisoners. All of this would have gone unreported except quite a few of the civilian workers at the prison started coming down with the same symptoms as the prisoners and had to be rushed to local hospitals. Several civilians died. The disease they all had tracked exactly like Gulf War Syndrome: muscle aches, vomiting, malaise, and fatigue. Some had horrible rashes and body sores. What makes this so strange is it happened in 1985, a full six years before the Gulf War.''

"How could that be?" he asked.

"In 1985, Saddam Hussein was our ally. Iraq was at war with Iran, and Iran was holding our hostages. We know there were ex-military types in Iraq serving as 'advisors.' Maybe we also shipped chemical weapons to Saddam, for use against the Iranians. Six years later, he could've turned around and used them on us. At the very least, we know Pentagon higher-ups had our troops blowing up Iraqi bio-weapons depots at the end of the Gulf War, then claimed ignorance when they came home with Gulf War Syndrome.''

He seemed to consider that for a moment. He had only eaten one bite of his hamburger, and now he put it down and pushed the plate away. "Let's get this food wrapped to go. I'm not really hungry,'' he said, wishing he could get a drink to calm his nerves.

She waved a waitress over, and the burgers were whisked off the table and back to the kitchen for packaging.

"So, who are you? You're obviously not just some little country girl flipping burgers in a mountain restaurant. You a government spy or something?''

"No,'' she smiled. "I was almost a doctor of microbiology.'' She held up her thumb and index finger. "I came that close.''

"And didn't finish?'' he said.

"Long story," she said curtly.

He didn't speak or pursue it. Instead, he sat in absolute still-ness, a thousand-yard stare in his eyes. He was very far away. Suddenly, Stacy remembered Dr. Martin Duc at Fort Detrick and the autopsy he was performing on the baby female chimp with the clusters of hemangiomic tumors. *"We're testing pyridostigmine bromide with some of the Gulf War insect repellent we used. I think, by mistake, there was a bad chemical cocktail over there. . . . It resembles a condition we're studying in children of Gulf War vets,"* he had told her.

The waitress returned with the wrapped hamburgers and put them down in front of them. Stacy paid the bill, and they stood.

"Let's go," she said. "We've got a lot to do."

Wendell arrived at the Santa Monica morgue at a little past nine.

He hurried to the elevator and took it to the third floor, exiting into a bland waiting room with picture windows overlooking the ocean. He had never been in this facility before, and he looked around for someone to tell him where he could get scrubbed. Be-cause he had sounded the first alarm, he had been cleared by Dr. Welsh to observe the autopsy. He saw a tanned dark-haired man dressed in an Armani suit and T-shirt looking out the window at the ocean. The man didn't turn when he moved past.

It took Wendell Kinney ten minutes to get scrubbed, gowned, and gloved. A female lab assistant then led him down one flight of stairs to Autopsy Room C. He quickly entered and found the autopsy already in progress. The Y-cut had been made. Dr. Welsh was acting as the prosector, or lead physician. He was looking down and sawing the breastbones with a Stryker vacuum saw.

The vacuum saw was the right tool, Wendell thought as he ap-proached. It sucked up the bone particles and tissue before they could accidentally fly around, possibly into the eyes of the assisting autopsy doctor, known as the diener. There was one other man in the room; he had new, angry-looking hair plugs, and his disposable smock was belted over torn blue jeans. They were all wearing plastic goggles and plain plastic nose masks instead of the correct full-face, filtered HEPA masks that Wendell had suggested.

"We should have maximum containment," Wendell said.

"How ya doing, Dr. Kinney," Welsh said. "We don't have a Level Three facility here. Grab a spot at the table. Don't worry, we're going slow and being very careful."

Dr. Welsh now started to remove the heart. They all watched as he put his rubber-gloved, scalpeled right hand into the open chest. Holding the heart with his chain-mail glove, which protected his left hand from an accidental knife cut, he began the procedure, severing the left subclavian artery at the aortic arch.

Wendell Kinney watched as Dr. Welsh carefully and methodically separated Michael Brazil's heart from the remaining ten coronary veins and arteries.

Nino DeSilva was already on the third floor when the autopsy began. It was Sunday night, which was not normally a working night at the morgue. Only emergency autopsies took place on weekends. This bio-hazard constituted such an emergency, but there were very few people on duty. DeSilva had divided his four-man squad: He kept Luke Peterson with him; Calvin Watts was already outside the autopsy room with Tommy Sparks. The hall was empty, so DeSilva quickly moved out of the stairwell and subdued the one nurse on duty in the nurses' room. Silently, he choked her out. Once she was unconscious, he gagged and tied her, using plastic riot cuffs, then DeSilva and Peterson moved down to the second floor.

Sergeant Watts had found a medical gurney, and they parked it outside the door of Autopsy Room C. All of the Torn Victor commandos were wearing HEPA masks, and now removed MP5 submachine pistols from their backpacks.

Nino DeSilva kicked the door open and moved into the autopsy room. The four men inside turned as one at the intrusion.

"What the hell . . ." Dr. Welsh sputtered through his surgical mask.

"Everything goes back in the body bag. Everything!" Nino demanded.

Dr. Welsh stood dumbfounded along with the others. "We're performing an autopsy here. What do you think you're after? This man is dead."

Wendell Kinney knew exactly what they were after.

Nino DeSilva walked toward Dr. Welsh and slammed the butt of his MP5 into Welsh's mouth. The doctor went down like cut lumber. Blood started to seep out from under his plastic nose mask.

For some reason that Gary Iverson would never understand, he was considering trying to grab the gun out of the hand of the man nearest him. Gary had never been in a fight in his life. He was the last one to try to be a hero, but the armed man standing directly in front of him was paying no attention. Gary saw the gun dangling from his right hand. It looked tantalizingly easy.

Without knowing why, or even debating the odds, he made a grab for the weapon. The commando sensed the motion behind him, and with lightning reflexes, he spun, grabbed Gary Iverson's arm, and hurled him across the room toward the autopsy table and the cut-open body of Michael Brazil. Gary threw his hands out in front of him to block his crash, but one of Michael's freshly sawn ribs went through the rubber glove on his right hand, puncturing him. He screamed in pain and scrambled away from the table. Four machine pistols were now trained on him. He was seconds from death. "I'm sorry, I'm sorry. . . . Please," he whimpered. "I'm sorry, don't shoot me."

"Bag this body!" Nino yelled at the Torn Victor commandos.

They took Michael's heart, which was already safely inside a plastic container, and set it in the body bag. Then two of them put on heavy rubber gloves and slid Hollywood Mike into a double-zip bio-containment bag they had with them. They closed it up, carried him out of Autopsy Room C, and flopped the bag down on the rolling gurney.

Nino DeSilva pulled the phone out of the wall and turned to face them. "One of us is going to hold a position outside this door for five minutes. Anybody sticks his head out before then is gonna eat it." Then he backed out of the room and was gone.

Gary stood there, blood dripping from the puncture wound in his hand. Dr. Welsh was conscious, but still bleeding beneath his mask. They watched the clock on the wall, like obedient school-children waiting for recess. Nobody said anything.

When three slow minutes had passed, Dr. Welsh grew impatient. He got off the autopsy room floor and exited the room. One by one, they all followed. Wendell Kinney was the last to leave the room. He looked around and saw Dr. Welsh's autopsy scalpel still lying on the table. Wendell reached over and got an organ bag, then carefully retrieved the bloodied instrument, dropped it in the bag, and sealed it. Then he slipped the bag into his pocket, and he too exited the room.

The hall outside was empty except for a lab assistant tied up behind the counter. Dr. Welsh cut the plastic cuffs and released her, then dialed the police.

Gary Iverson made his way up one level to where Buddy was waiting.

"Is it over?" Buddy asked. "Does he still look okay? 'Cause I wanna do this right. The rabbi says the body has to be buried within twenty-four hours."

"Let's get the fuck outta here," Gary hissed, entering the elevator.

"Did they find out what killed him? Do they know yet why he died?"

"Let's go," Gary said, and pulled Buddy into the elevator, stabbing at the button for the ground level.

As they rode down, Buddy saw the blood seeping from Gary's palm and dripping off the end of his fingers. "What the hell happened to your hand?" he asked.

Chapter 21

DON'T GIVE UP ON THE MASKED RODENT

Augie, the ceramic raccoon, lay on the floor in at least fifty pieces. Stacy kneeled and started to gather him up. "Shit," she said. "How did this happen?"

Cris Cunningham was standing behind her. "Maybe the earthquake," he volunteered. "We had a four point one, day before yesterday."

She hadn't even heard about an earthquake. She had been in Badwater and missed it. She suddenly felt tears coming to her eyes as she looked at poor broken Augie. Carefully, she started putting the pieces of him on the table in the dining room.

Cris looked at the shattered ceramic raccoon, and at the silent tears coming down Stacy's cheeks. "Get all the little ones," he said. "I can fix him if you've got glue."

She looked up. "That's okay," she answered, and then unexpectedly changed her mind. "I've got nail glue."

"Get it. I did all of the dish and vase repairs at my house, growing up. I have a knack for this."

She left to go into the bathroom to look for the nail glue, and as Cris picked up the remaining pieces, he took a look around the living room. There was evidence of a man's presence in the apartment: a football leaning against the TV; a rowing machine in the corner with a Stanford boxing sweatshirt draped over the seat; a punching bag visible through the bedroom door. He looked at the bookshelf. Several of the books were by Dr. Maximilian Richardson. Cris wondered if that was her father, or brother, or if Stacy was married. He saw a bar set up in the living room and moved over to look, studying the bottles: Kahlúa, Drambuie, Grand Marnier . . . all liqueurs. It was a damn candy counter. Then he saw a bottle of sherry, and poured himself a glass.

At the emergency room at Huntington Hospital in Pasadena, both he and Stacy had given blood and skin scrapings. Stacy said that Dr. Kinney would collect samples from the hospital tomorrow for study at the USC lab. Cris realized when they weighed him that he had lost fifteen pounds.

He had decided to get his father's car and drive her back to her apartment. He wanted to talk to Wendell and find out what had really happened to Hollywood Mike. They had cabbed to his father's house; Cris had gone inside for a coat while Stacy waited in the car. On the way out, he stopped at his father's bar and took a hit of vodka straight from the bottle. That had been an hour ago. Now he knocked back the shot of sherry, feeling its warmth. He quickly poured another and took it back to the project on the dining-room table. Like most alcoholics, he was an expert at ''riding the buzz.'' He could drink just enough to stay loose, but not so much he became a fall-down. Mornings brought hangovers, but he would quickly flush them away with a shooter.

Stacy returned from the bathroom with the glue and sat down across from him. Cris started to separate the slivers and chips by color. ''The trick is to start with the small ones. The big pieces are easy.''

She watched him sort. "I wonder where Wendell is," she said, looking at her watch. "It's eleven-thirty. The autopsy should be over. He should be here by now."

"It probably took longer than you thought."

She nodded, and started to help him sort. Her eye fell on the glass of sherry at his elbow. She decided not to comment. "I saw the picture in your father's den. . . ."

He didn't answer, just kept looking down at the broken pieces of Augie.

"You were the UCLA quarterback?"

"And you were almost a doctor of microbiology," he answered.

"Don't want to talk about the good ol' days?"

"Same as you," he said, taking another slug of sherry. "Gimme the glue."

She handed him the nail glue, and he uncapped it, put a few dabs on a white sliver, then stuck the sliver on the edge of what would soon be Augie's reconstructed left ear. "This is gonna take me a while."

"Don't give up on the masked rodent," she said, and her voice caught as she said it. He heard her sob once, and looked up.

"Who's Maximilian?" he asked bluntly.

"He was my perfect fit," she said after a few seconds. "He made me complete. Before Max, I was doing everything for the wrong reason. Max showed me what I could be. He wanted things just for me. I'd never had that before."

"Where is he now?" he asked.

She bit her lip and pushed some brown chips over at him. "Work on finding a home for these."

"Stacy," he said slowly, "back at the restaurant, you said something about Gulf War Syndrome showing up in the eighties. I'd like to read those articles about Huntsville, Texas, if you have them around."

His long fingers were turning a broken piece of Augie's hindquarters. He put it aside and picked up another piece, turning it, looking for a match in the pile of chips. "Do you still have the articles? Could you loan them to me?"

"Yeah, somewhere in my files in there." She stood and moved into her pantry office and started to rummage around in drawers. "Nobody will ever be able to prove Gulf War Syndrome was our concoction, first designed and tested in Huntsville, Texas," she said. "It's just a theory supported by some very strange occurrences."

"That's okay," he said, knocking back the rest of his sherry. "I want to read it anyway."

"The only reason I mentioned Huntsville was because it so closely resembles Vanishing Lake." She returned, carrying a folder, and dropped it beside him on the table. "Here."

He was holding a piece of Augie's broken nose in place, while the glue dried.

"There was something called 'TRIES' at Huntsville," she continued. "It stands for the Texas Regional Institute for Environmental Studies, and I found out that same outfit was funding the bio-research at Vanishing Lake. The Huntsville operation got its money through Sam Houston University. When you trace the cash back, it comes from a Washington think tank that's funded by the Pentagon Special Projects Division, which at the time was run by Admiral Zoll." She watched as he found another piece and glued it on, but his face had suddenly hardened.

"One of the people who got the disease in '85 was a woman named Julie Medely," she continued. "There's an article in there about it. Her husband, Clayton, was a food worker at the prison in Huntsville, and they think he passed it to her. The left side of her body started wasting away like polio. The story of the strange illness started getting into the press: 'Mystery Disease,' stuff like that. Some TV station in West Texas picked it up. Several other civilians with ties to the prison came down with the same symptoms. The doctors at Huntsville took blood samples and claimed to have isolated a strange unknown microorganism, which was sent to Walter Reed Hospital to be studied. Somebody there leaked the result.''

"Which was . . . ?"

"The microplasma found in Julie's blood had a very unusual DNA sequence, indicating that the microorganism was probably genetically engineered. Seven years later that identical DNA sequence turned up in the blood of veterans suffering from Gulf War Syndrome."

Cris looked up at her, his eyes intense now, anger glinting, as he held two pieces of Augie's hindquarters in his hands while the glue set.

"So Gulf War Syndrome might never have come back in our troops if we hadn't shipped it to Iraq first, back in the eighties," he said.

She nodded, and there was a knock at the door. When Stacy opened it, Wendell was standing in the corridor, looking tired and even more rumpled than usual.

"What happened?" Stacy asked. "You're two hours late."

"I've been at the Santa Monica Police Department," he growled as he entered the apartment and flopped into Max's old club chair. "Four guys with HEPA masks and guns broke into the autopsy room and stole the body."

"You're kidding!" Stacy said.

"Whoever they were, they know Mike died of Prion disease. They stole the body to keep that fact from getting out."

Stacy's mind was racing. "Maybe they were from the Devil's Workshop . . . ?" she said.

"God help us," Wendell Kinney sighed. He leaned his head back and closed his eyes, never mentioning Dr. Welsh's autopsy knife that he had stolen.

Chapter 22

THE BLACK ATTACK

I t was almost one A.M., Monday morning.

Cris drove his father's new Lincoln Continental slowly. He made deliberate stops at all intersections. He made sure he used his blinker. He knew that he had enough unprocessed alcohol in his blood to "pin the needle," and he didn't want to get busted for DUI.

He was back on the Nickel (Fifth Street), driving past remembered alleys. The old thirties buildings of downtown L.A. loomed incongruously, leaning against the new glass skyline like shabby relatives at a posh wedding. Old crates and boxes were pushed up against chipped brick; annex dwellings of the homeless. Deep in narrow alleyways trash-can fires burned like hunger.

The Midnight Mission was on Fifth, a block south of Wilshire. Cris found a parking space across the street from the Salvation Army church. He fiddled with the Lincoln's expensive alarm until it chirped at him, then moved across the street and disappeared inside the "sally," where two years before he had spent many nights on a hard cot, curled around a hangover or a bad dream.

"Clancy around?" he asked an old man, who looked up from a broom. They had never seen each other before, but traded the instant recognition of men who had once found the bottom and been content to rest there.

"Upstairs in the cafeteria," he said, and as Cris headed off, added, "Hey, we're full up, and we got a sign-up sheet now."

Cris didn't answer as he climbed the wood stairs of the Spanish-style building to the second floor. All of the non-load-bearing walls on the second floor had been removed, to make room for a dining hall that was filled with wooden tables and metal chairs. Cris's polished loafers clacked against the tile floor. As he moved into the room, he heard Clancy in the back arguing about something. Cris headed in that direction, pushing through freshly painted double doors.

Clancy had his back to Cris. He was sixty, but still had the quick movements of a "promising boy."

Clancy Black was a legend on skid row. As a young man, they called him "the Black Attack," a middleweight who tended to cut too easily. He'd been matched badly by unscrupulous promoters, who used him like disposable goods. Still, he had the heart of a lion, and finally fought Art Aragon for the middleweight title in the sixties, but Clancy was a bleeder and got decisioned. When his career was over, he had nothing left but memories and a bottle. He became a "client" of the mission, puking up blood from esophageal hemorrhages with the rest of the heavy drinkers out in the alley behind the sally. It was back then that Clancy Black got his miracle. In a drunken stupor, he had a vision: "It was the Lord Jesus come to me at my lowest, fillin' me with his glory," Clancy had proclaimed in a reverent whisper. From that moment on, he had dedicated himself to a higher calling, a higher power. It stopped him from drinking, filled him with the Holy Ghost, saved his life, and gave him a future. God now walked inside Clancy, as surely as the demons who trailed behind the rest of the Fifth Street alcoholics. As Clancy put it, he had gone from a "helpless client" to "God's compliant," from "what's-it-to-ya" to "hallelujah." He found Jesus in the nick of time, just before he puked his life out with his last bottle of 49.

Now Clancy ran the Midnight Mission. He was the only one that had ever been able to get Cris to stop drinking. Clancy got him on the wagon for thirty days before he lost it, three years ago, and took off in shame to ride the rails.

"We can still use them fuckers," Clancy said to a cook, both of them looking at the date on a can of corned beef. "I think you're wrong, Danny, it don't say December, least it don't now." Clancy rubbed the date off with his thumb, and handed the can back. "Git alla them from this batch outta storage, and put 'em in with to-morra's stew. Sure beats eating outta Dumpsters, where rats been pissing." His bald black head was shining in the heat and stark neon light of the kitchen. Now he turned and looked directly at Cris, and his punched-out, slightly lopsided face broke into a smile. "And speaking a' rats," he said, "you musta rolled a banker to get them loafers."

Clancy didn't miss much.

"How ya doin', Clance?" Cris said, feeling slightly awkward, as well as light-headed and ashamed. It always started that way with Clancy. You wanted so bad to please him, to be straight for him. Lucky knew what he looked like, knew that Clancy could see the invisible residue of his addiction leaking out of his sweat glands, turning his skin to a boozer's blush.

"Reckless Reggie and Alabama Jack told me you was off seeing the great USA from under a boxcar."

"I need to talk to you, Clance," Cris said, suddenly wringing his hands uncontrollably in front of him.

"Let's get some joe; this ear-bang still has the best fucking coffee on the Nickel."

They poured two cups and moved into the empty dining hall. It was now after two, and the mission was strangely quiet. Lights out, Cris remembered, started at ten. Clancy sat across from Cris, and waited. Clancy was good at letting you get at it your own way.

"I gotta get straight," Cris finally said.

"Yep, no doubt about that," he answered.

"How?" Cris sort of croaked it out. "I keep telling myself I'm through, but I keep cheating."

"Like I told ya before, you gotta get yourself a higher power, you gotta find your miracle."

"Since Kennidi died, I can't go to God. I used to, but now . . . I just . . ." He stopped and lowered his head. "I know it works for you, Clancy. Me, I got doubts, y'know. I got things I can't reconcile."

"You thinkin' what kinda asshole God would take my little girl, torture her like that?" he said.

Cris didn't move or say anything, but Clancy read the agreement in his eyes.

"Yep. Well, sometimes it's like that. Hallelujah won't always do ya," Clancy grinned.

Cris couldn't help himself, he smiled back. "I think the people who gave me and Kennidi this problem are in Fort Detrick, Maryland, at a secret facility called the Devil's Workshop. They're also at a CIA-influenced company called Merck Laboratories. Maybe *we* shipped bio-weapons to Iraq. Maybe *we* made Gulf War Syndrome. It was tested here first in the 1980s."

Clancy looked at him, and finally nodded. "So?"

"I want to stop them, Clancy. I want to get them for Kennidi and for Laura and for me. It's the first thing in my stupid life I think I really care about. The first thing I give a shit about."

"Then do it."

"I can't. I can't make myself stop drinking. I try, and then I get the shakes and feel the D.T.s comin', and I just break all the promises."

"I seen guys in here every day for five years, trying to find the answer. They listen to the ear-bangs, look for Jesus to be their higher power, but they can't do it, and ya know why? 'Cause they're compulsive. Mosta my clients could use up a lifetime supply a' anything in three days. For you and them, there's no such thing as moderation." Cris nodded, and Clancy continued, "So, when a man can't find his higher power, he just keeps plowin' a furrow out there on the Nickel. One day somebody else comes in here wearing his shoes, and they tell me my guy's gone 'n' died in his cardboard box, with nobody to say his prayers to, and I be here knowin' it's 'cause he never found his miracle. Ya gotta have a higher power, Lucky. People like us, obsessive compulsives, we can't do it ourselves."

"Why?" Cris said. "Why can't I do it myself?"

"Anybody can stop for a while. Shit, I seen guys quit for a week, so their wives will stop yellin' at 'em, but that ain't no permanent thing. What you got, Cris, is a cravin', and a cravin' is a physical allergy, coupled with a mental obsession. That's a tough combination, so ya gotta have a higher power, something above ya to hang on to, to pull ya through when your resolve crumbles."

"But not God. I'd feel like a hypocrite praying. I've got to find my way back to Him when I'm ready. When I'm not . . ."

"So pissed off," Clancy finished.

Cris didn't answer.

"If ya can't fall on yer knees to God, then get down on yer knees to vengeance. You want these guys who made the chemicals? Then go get 'em. Make vengeance your higher power. Shit, man, anything works if it means enough to ya. Money, hatred, love, even pussy." He grinned at Cris. "Ya just gotta want it bad, you gotta serve somethin' bigger than yourself."

Cris looked at him for a long moment, then nodded slowly.

"I've known guys, took 'em five years of praying, to get thirty days of sobriety." He reached out and put a hand on Cris's arm,

"You gotta take this second-to-second. You're walkin' on a floor that may not hold ya, and each day of sobriety is just a day, and nothin' more."

"How do I beat the D.T.s?" Cris asked. "I can't get past them."

"You gotta go through 'em, son. You gotta buckle yerself in and just do it. There ain't no drugs for that. You got your body all fucked up. Comin' off just ain't no fun. Then you stay clean by seeking vengeance for your daughter's death. That's your higher power."

"Will you sit with me?" Cris asked. "Keep me from falling?"

"It's why I come to work, man. It's how I serve my higher power."

So Lucky went upstairs, got in Clancy's unmade bed, and wondered how long it would take the bugs to find his eyes.

Chapter 23

THE HIGHER POWER

The bugs came the next morning while he was eating breakfast. It was ten o'clock, and he was poking at some eggs, looking at the dining room full of listless and tattered men. Their faces were the faded plastic masks of empty souls. A few that he had shared bottles with in years past nodded at him and then moved on, not happy to see him, not sad he had returned. They shuffled past to find good spots out on the sidewalk, where they would warm their thin blood in the sun, like desert reptiles.

When he saw the first big hairy bug, it materialized like a movie special effect right on his hand. He dropped the fork he was stirring his runny eggs with and shook his hand hard. But the huge, furry spider clung to him, drawing blood. He watched the blood ooze as he screamed in terror.

Two men from the kitchen held him down while others ran to get Clancy. They took him to the D.T. ward, which was just a concrete-block room in the basement of the mission. More than one howling drunk had fought his demons in that cold, tight enclosure.

Cris writhed and jerked with insane madness as the beasts crawled on him. They went straight for his eyes. Others clung to the slick painted walls; they hung upside down on the ceiling over his head and waited for their turn. He screamed until he was hoarse.

It was afternoon before he began to find a few stretches of sanity. Clancy sat with him, leaving only to piss. He held his hand, whispering encouragement. He held the metal bucket while Cris vomited, until all he could heave up was long, drooling lines of transparent yellow bile.

Cris finally went to sleep at two A.M., and woke up a few hours later. He opened his eyes and lay still, sure he was still being invaded by insects and spiders. His skin was crawling, but he saw none of the furry eight-legged demons. He tried to stand; he was extremely weak. He desperately needed a drink. He needed to get in the Lincoln and go home to Pasadena. He couldn't stop thinking about the bar in his father's house, the rows of bottles with their colorful labels: vodka, Scotch, bourbon, rum. The memory of that parade of spirits made his dry mouth water. He licked his lips, and tried to open the door of the D.T. room. It was locked. In a second, he heard a key in the lock and the door swung wide. An old sandy-haired man with a concave chest was standing there.

"How y'doin', brother?"

"Gotta go," Cris said, trying to push past him.

"Clancy wants t'talk to ya."

"Gotta go," Cris said, and moved around him.

The man hurried off, up the hallway.

Cris climbed the stairs and found the front door of the mission, more or less by instinct. He started down the steps, moving slowly, holding the metal banister for support. He could see the Lincoln across the street, and set his sights on getting there.

"Lucky!"

Cris turned and saw Clancy standing on the steps above him

in the door of the mission. He had obviously just gotten out of bed, and wore only a pair of shorts with no shirt, shoes, or socks.

"Where you going?"

"Gotta go," Cris said.

"You're through the D.T.s, boy. You're out. Now you wanna go get a drink. That's what they all do. Don't be like them. Clean up. Look up! Grab fer yer higher power. You can do it!"

Cris was so weak his legs were shaking. He had to hold the metal railing to stand. "Gotta go, Clancy," he said softly. "Gotta go home."

"You ain't goin' nowhere," he said, " 'less you go through me."

The Black Attack was sixty and weighed only 135, but he still had the heavy shoulders and trim waist of a fighter. He now moved quickly on bare feet, down to face Cris.

"Don't make me wreck ya, Lucky. Don't make me do it. Come on back inside."

Cris licked his lips.

"The men who made that Gulf War shit are laughing at you, Cris. They're in their big houses, laughing. 'We got ol' Lucky Cunningham 'cause he can't serve his power. We gonna piss on him, an' we gonna go piss on his dead baby.' "

Cris looked at Clancy with pleading eyes, then he started across the street, toward the car. Clancy moved with the lightning speed he'd used in the ring, got around in front of Cris, and stopped him, pushing him hard in the chest, back toward the mission. The two of them faced each other in the middle of the empty mist-wet street.

"I can't do it, Clancy. I can't."

"They sayin' Cris Cunningham don't got it. They sayin' we can all go piss on that little girl's grave."

Now Cris swung at Clancy, who ducked easily under the blow and then popped Cris once on the breastbone with a short, chopping left hand. Cris bent over and started wheezing. Clancy grabbed him by the shirt and straightened him up.

"Yep. Cris Cunningham, he never gave a shit about nothin' but hisself. Everything is always about Cris, poor Cris. Cris gonna go feel sorry fer hisself, drown hisself in a buncha booze. His little baby girl? He don't give a shit about her. We can jus' give her the sickness, fill her up with tumors an' the like . . . any damn thing we want. Don't mean shit, 'cause Cris Cunningham only worries about hisself. He ain't gonna serve nothin'. He ain't got no higher power."

Now Cris was sobbing. He was crying in the street, and as Clancy put an arm around him, Clancy's own heart was breaking. "I can't, I can't," Cris wailed.

"Wanna bet?" Clancy said, and he led his friend back inside the mission.

Twelve hours later, at six o'clock that night, Cris was showered and dressed. His face was shaved, and his clothes had been washed and ironed. Clancy took him across to the Lincoln and stood with him in the gathering darkness. Cris had been at the mission less than twenty-four hours. He was shaky, but sober.

"I want you to tell me who the man is who killed your little girl," Clancy said.

"There's a guy named Admiral Zoll. I read some articles. He runs the program at Fort Detrick. Headed the Pentagon Special Project that did the tests in Huntsville Prison back in the eighties."

"What's he look like?"

"I don't know. I've never seen him."

"Tell me anyway. Look inside and make up a picture."

"He's . . . he's big."

"Big guy. Yep, he'd have t'be," Clancy nodded. "What else?"

"He's got black hair and real black, mean eyes."

"Yeah, that's the one. That's the guy. Black eyes, mean eyes, like the devil's. Yeah, you got him now."

"And . . . he doesn't give a shit about anything, about people."

"Fuckin' guy never did, Cris. Never gave one hoot in hell."

"And he, and . . ." Cris stopped and looked down. "Everybody in the Gulf said I was a hero. Shit, Clance, I was just trying to stay alive. I woulda run from that Republican Guard unit, but I didn't know where the fuck I was, which way to go."

"We don't give a shit about you, Cris. Not anymore. We're here servin' vengeance. Admiral Zoll . . . tell me more."

"He doesn't care that his bio-weapon killed my little girl, that he ruined my life."

"Fuck you. I don't care about you. This ain't about you. Get that through yer head. I don't wanna hear about how you got fucked. Stop cryin' about poor Cris Cunningham. Vengeance's gotta be aimed, son, gotta be pointed *out,* not in. It's a *higher* power. You gotta serve *it,* it can't serve you."

"He . . . killed her, and he doesn't care. He doesn't, because all he cares about is money and power."

"And who's gonna get this rotten son-of-a-bitch?"

"I am," Cris said softly, but it lacked conviction.

"Go serve yer vengeance, Cris. Hold it out in fronta you. But the first time you take a sip outta that bottle, this guy is gonna know. First time you take a sip, this motherfucker's won. Vengeance is your power, but this motherfucker's got rearview mirrors. He can see ya back here. He's gonna know if you fuck up, so you ain't gonna drink. You're gonna go get this godless prick."

Cris nodded. Then Clancy slipped forty bucks in his hand. "There's some money and my phone number. Don't go home, son. Don't go to yer Daddy's house. I don't know why, but a lotta your bad feelin's is there. When you're there, you look inside, you start feelin' sorry for yerself. You drink. You gotta look to your higher power, nothin' else."

"Thanks, Clancy."

Clancy nodded and watched while Cris opened the door of the Lincoln, started the engine, and drove off.

Cris didn't know where to go. He didn't have anybody he trusted. He drove around aimlessly for hours. He craved a drink, but instead made his mind blank and thought about Kennidi. Poor helpless Kennidi. He wouldn't let himself think about his hurt, his pain; he focused only on hers. He would seek vengeance for her. Several times he slowed as he saw bars. One had a neon sign, which pictured a glass that filled with neon liquor. He must have watched that glass fill twenty times. He almost went in, but forced his thoughts back to Kennidi. *"Daddy, hold me. Daddy, it hurts so much."* Cris slammed down on the accelerator and the Lincoln roared away, up the street.

At midnight, he found himself back at Stacy's apartment. He knocked, and after a long time, the light came on. The door opened and she was standing there in her bathrobe.

"Where have you been?" she said. "I called your house . . ."

"I . . . I had to go see a friend."

They stood looking at one another. She thought he looked different, weaker, even more unhealthy and fragile.

"I know we don't know each other very well," he said softly, "but I can't go home. It's a long story, but I need a place to flop. Could I use your couch?"

She stood there in the doorway for a long moment, hesitant.

"I've decided I want to help you get Admiral Zoll," he said. "I want to get him for what he did to Kennidi."

After a moment of appraisal she unlatched the door and let him in.

Chapter 24

GUNFIGHT AT THE I'M OK, YOU'RE OK CORRAL

He was carrying three loaves of baked bread; one was whole wheat, one was a rich brown multi-grain, and one was some sort of black bread the color of a Hershey's chocolate bar. Of course, he was on a no-carb diet and was strictly prohibited from eating bread.

His son, Mike, was walking beside him. They were going to look at a new house, and a Realtor magically appeared, opened the door, then disappeared. They walked into the place alone. The house had no yard; in fact, there was no property at all. It was artfully suspended between two high stone canyons. The living-room floor was a metal grate, perched thousands of feet above a valley. Somehow Buddy and Michael could walk on the grate without falling through, but the effect was unsettling. Below them stretched a horizon as far as the eye could see. There was also a pool that hung suspended, but it was empty, formed out of the same metal grates.

"Don't worry, Dad, it's a fixer-upper, but we can do it. Once we get furniture and some flooring, it's gonna be great."

His son was now standing next to him. Close to him. Buddy craved closeness. He craved unconditional love. Nobody ever loved Buddy. They tolerated him, or partnered with him, and sometimes slept with him, but love was never the reason. Money was the glue. Then unexpectedly, Michael put an arm around Buddy's shoulder and squeezed him lovingly, easing Buddy's longing, taking away the ache.

"A project for both of us. Aren't you gonna eat your bread, Dad?"

"My nutritionist says I'm not supposed to eat carbs," Buddy said. "Strictly off my diet."

They walked up to the "picture window," which had no glass, and stood on the heart-stopping grates, somehow not falling out of the house through the floor. They marveled at the spectacular view, but when Buddy looked down, his stomach lurched. Thousands of feet below, the green valley beckoned. It was fertile land, ripe with promise.

"Y'know, Dad, I bet if we worked on the house together, we'd learn to love each other. . . . Aren't you gonna eat any bread?"

"All my life I've been on some diet," he told his son. "All my life, I've been hungry, trying to be what I'm not. Maybe that's why you and I could never find each other. I was always pretending to be an outlaw, a rebel. It's what I thought everybody wanted from me, but I was just acting." And then the difficult admission: "Underneath, I'm always scared, Michael."

"Call me Juan, Dad. I go by Juan now."

Buddy nodded. He was starving; he wondered what the rich black loaf would taste like. When Michael looked away, he snuck a bite of the bread It was surprisingly good, and tasted just as he'd hoped . . . a sweet, rich chocolate flavor. As he chewed, he knew he had been wrong. He never should have rejected his son. If he had loved Michael unconditionally, then Michael would be the one who'd naturally love him back. How could he have been blind to that before? After all, Michael was his son, his flesh and blood.

As he realized this, he felt tears of gratitude. Then he heard scream- ing, looked up, and saw that Mike was way too far out on the edge of the suspended pool. His arms were pinwheeling. He was falling forward, off balance. His screams got louder, more hyster- ical.

"Mike, what're you doing?" Buddy yelled, tears still welling in his eyes. He tried to run toward his only son, juggling the loaves of bread. He thought he could pull him back by grabbing his shirt using his one free hand, but he could not run on the tricky grates. Although before he had walked easily across them, now his feet fell clumsily between. He went down, almost plummeting through himself. His son was falling . . . falling out of the house, right through the grates in the bottom of the pool, getting smaller. Buddy couldn't move, but he could see Mike's diminishing form. The son he had never cared about but now longed for was screaming in terror, and for some unknown reason, he was screaming in Spanish. *"Dios mío! Dios mío!"* Mike wailed.

"I'm sorry," Buddy yelled to his disappearing son. "I'm sorry I couldn't get there. We could have fixed the house. We could have loved each other." His screams mixed with Mike's.

Buddy sat bolt upright. "I'm sorry . . . !"

He was on his bed in Malibu, screaming at the top of his lungs, tears wet on his face. For a minute he didn't know where he was. His arms were across his chest, still clutching his invisible loaves of bread. His heart was beating fast. Suddenly, he stopped screaming and was quiet, but he could still hear Mike crying out in Spanish. He was far away. Buddy's head snapped around toward the bedroom balcony windows. He was disoriented. His conscious mind was fighting to take control, as the distant screams continued.

"Mike?" he said softly.

Then he realized he'd been in an extremely vivid dream. The suspended house, the three loaves of bread, and his dead son were all gone. Only the distant screams remained. *"Dios mío,"* a woman's voice pleaded. He realized it was his Mexican maid, Consuelo. She was outside somewhere, out by the pool, screaming for somebody not to shoot. *"No me dispare, por favor!"* she pleaded.

He got out of bed and moved uncertainly to the window. He could see Gary Iverson down by the pool. For some crazy reason, Gary had a gun in his right hand and was waving it at Consuelo, who was on her knees, begging him not to kill her. Gary pointed the gun at her head as Buddy snatched open the balcony door.

"The fuck you doing, Iverson?" he yelled.

Without hesitation, Gary spun and fired the pistol at him. The pane right next to Buddy's head shattered. Glass shards rained against his bare shoulders.

"Fuck!" Buddy yelled as he ducked for cover inside the house. Then he heard Gary screaming, and Consuelo pleading. "What the fuck?" Buddy whispered, his half-asleep mind racing to catch up with a shitload of adrenaline that had just hit his heart like a shot of ice water.

Buddy had one of the most extensive gun collections in Hollywood. He loved guns. He even had a gun dealer's license, which he got when he was in pre-production on *Grunt,* a Vietnam War epic he'd made at Columbia. He'd cherry-picked the prop department for the best ordnance. He had a U.S. M203, which was a single-shot pump grenade launcher, and five hot pineapples to go with it. He had an M60 machine gun called a "pig," and a selection of mini-lights, including the MP5, and the LMG version of the AUG machine gun. He also had a selection of Russian ordnance: the PKM-7 machine gun and the MG3. He had another whole case full of handguns: Glocks and Kochs, Brownings and Berettas. Although his war collection was mostly late-seventies stuff, he had sophisticated laser sights on a lot of them, and always kept his guns loaded.

Buddy would tell guests at his Hollywood parties that he just prayed some wired-up, celebrity-stalking fanatic would try for him, sounding like a ballsy hero from one of his action pictures. He would often field-strip a weapon in front of his coked-out guests, talking trash, while he tore the piece down. "I'll kill the mother-fucker if I'm ever transgressed," he'd promised, his eyes shining with a deadly mixture of cocaine and testosterone.

Now, with Consuelo screaming in the yard and glass splinters from Gary's quickly aimed shot still pricking his shoulders, his ballsy resolve evaporated. His hands were shaking. His dick crawled up inside him and his asshole slammed shut.

He was at his gun cabinet, clawing for his new short-barrel Colt Commander with the state-of-the-art Sentry Laser-Lite sight and the filed-down two-ounce trigger pull. He tromboned the weapon, inadvertently ejecting the live round that had al-ready been chambered onto the carpet at his feet. He snapped off the safety and clicked on the laser sight. A red pinpoint of light appeared on the carpet near his bare feet. He heard an-other gunshot, then Consuelo screamed in agony. As Buddy moved away from the cabinet, he saw that his Charter Arms Mark II target pistol was missing. Buddy was now cowering under a window, afraid to risk his life by exposing his head to look down again at the pool. Consuelo was still crying and pleading in Spanish.

He scrambled to his feet and ran downstairs. He was in one of his silk thong briefs, which Heidi Fleiss had given him last Christ-mas before her trial. When he had tried it on for her, she had told him the pouched thong made him look "killer." He always wore one to bed. Now it made him feel stupid and unprotected. He was in the living room, wondering if he should just run to the garage, take the Porsche, and split. *Fuck Consuelo,* he thought, *I'm at risk here! She doesn't even have papers. It's every man for himself.* Then he saw movement out the plate-glass window. Gary was standing on the pool deck, his back to Buddy, screaming insanities at Consuelo, who Buddy could now see had indeed been hit in the arm, near the shoulder. She was seated on the pool deck beyond, crying, begging for her life. The dim pool lights gave eerie cinema verité ambience to the area.

Then Iverson aimed again at Consuelo. Before the crazed doctor could pull the trigger, Buddy cringed and flinched. Because of the Colt's hair trigger, he inadvertently squeezed off a round. The shot shattered the living-room window near where Gary was standing. The slug bounced off the pavement and whined away into the Malibu night, splashing harmlessly in the ocean a hundred yards beyond the surf line.

"Fuck! Oh fuck, oh fuck!" Buddy screamed, as Gary turned and faced him through the now glassless opening. Buddy had never seen such confusion, terror, or craziness in another man's eyes. It was even worse than when Jack Nicholson, zooted on uppers, had taken a fire ax to Buddy's desk at Warners after he'd seen the re-cut on *Dead Before Dawn*.

Gary's eyes were terrifying.

"Oh fuck, oh fuck, oh fuck," Buddy kept saying, the laser sight on the forgotten Colt Commander burning a red dot in the carpet.

Gary Iverson aimed the Charter Arms Mark II at Buddy. He was yelling something. Buddy strained to make out the words, but couldn't.

Then Buddy was moving, screaming in terror as he went, with no idea where he was going. Gary had him in his sights; he would never escape.

Gary fired just as Buddy tripped over the marble coffee table. The bullet whined past his right ear, missing him.

"Fuck, fuck, fuck!" Buddy screamed at nobody. Then he got up and ran into the kitchen. "Help! Help me! Please!" The Colt Commander was still at his side, as he was fumbling for the phone to dial 911. Then his heart froze. Gary was clawing at the back door. Buddy turned and screamed at the door, "Leave me alone! Leave me alone! Why are you doing this?"

A shot shattered the lock, and then Gary kicked the door open.

Buddy had both hands out in front of him to ward off the certain killshot. He knew he was scant seconds from death.

"Don't shoot! Please, Gary . . . please! I'm your friend, man! I love you!" Then he saw a strange red dot between and slightly above Gary Iverson's eyes. It was sitting there like the ruby on Cleopatra's forehead. Buddy wasn't sure what it was.

Then Gary cocked his pistol.

Buddy spasmed in fear. The Colt Commander kicked unexpectedly in his hands and Iverson flew backward, out the kitchen door, landing on his back on the pavement. The new transplant plugs that Buddy had paid for, and half of Gary's forehead, were now missing.

"Fuck, oh fuck, oh fuck," Buddy mantraed, still in the kitchen, not sure exactly what had happened. Then he saw the gun in his outstretched hand, and realized that he had again pulled the hair trigger. He moved on weak, unsteady legs out the back door, where Gary now lay dead. He looked down at the doctor, who had written the prescriptions that had kept them both in a drugstore daze for the last two years.

Buddy's teeth were chattering; his bare ass felt cold from a panic sweat that was drying on his cheeks in the chilly air. A clammy sweet-sour aftertaste lingered in his mouth like the memory of rotten chocolate bread.

"*Muchas gracias, señor,*" Consuelo was blubbering from ten yards away. She was still on the pool deck, holding her bleeding arm.

Buddy's knees wouldn't stop shaking. He didn't think he would be able to keep standing, so he walked over and sat on a nearby pool chair, never taking his eyes off Gary Iverson's body. He tried to steady himself. He was trembling uncontrollably, but euphoric to be alive. He took several deep breaths to calm down. For a long time, he just looked down at the lifeless doctor.

"Transgress me, you motherfucker," he finally growled at the dead body.

Chapter 25

J E W

How and why this shooting took place are still pretty much
a mystery, Steve,'' field reporter Shannon Morrison said.
She was standing in front of the gate of Buddy Brazil's
multimillion-dollar Malibu Colony home. "The body was wheeled
out at about six A.M., and the police left a few minutes ago. The
way the bizarre story pieces together: Dr. Gary Iverson, a Long
Beach pediatrician, who had been living in famous 'bad boy' producer Buddy Brazil's pool house, apparently went crazy around
midnight last night and tried to kill Mr. Brazil's maid"—she
glanced at her notes—"Consuelo Gutierrez. The Oscar-winning
producer heard gunshots and Miss Gutierrez's screams, then got a
pistol from his gun cabinet and apparently saved Miss Gutierrez's
life, shooting the doctor out by his pool. This strange incident
occurred just hours after Buddy Brazil's son's body was inexpli-
cably stolen from the Santa Monica morgue."

The TV shot switched to Steve Edwards, seated at his in-studio
desk at KTTV in Los Angeles. Steve shook his head in dismay.

"Any idea if those two events are connected, Shannon? It would seem they must be."

"Again, Steve, it's all very tentative right now, so we'll have to wait until the police issue their statement. Possibly, one connection, according to neighbors, was that Dr. Iverson had been heavily involved in drugs, and had recently been to Windsong Ranch in Montana to take the cure. Michael Brazil also had a history of drug arrests when he lived here with his father two summers ago. But for right now, people out here in this secluded Malibu beach community are calling Buddy Brazil a hero for saving Consuelo Gutierrez's life, and it would certainly seem that's exactly what he is."

Similar reports were on every local channel and all the network news shows. There were "file" shots of Buddy with famous actresses smiling at premiers, waving at the press, showing his tanned, surgically enhanced face and white-capped teeth. They spewed out lists of his hit movies, along with opening weekend grosses. He was called a hero, a handsome hero, the bad-boy producer with the golden touch, a romantic outlaw. And on and on it went. . . .

Upstairs in his bedroom, Buddy was watching it all from his bed, with the covers pulled up around his chin. He had been forced to endure the police for almost three hours. *Thank God,* he thought, *that dumb bitch, Consuelo, got it right, or I would probably have been arrested for killing Iverson in cold blood.*

The body had been taken out two hours ago, and after the cops left, Buddy locked the front door, wearily climbed up to his bedroom, then stripped and flopped. He turned on the TV and watched, deadpan, as his legend grew right before his eyes. He was on every channel. This sort of heroic notoriety was something he had struggled to achieve for twenty years. It was suddenly happening on a level far beyond his wildest dreams, but he felt corrupted by it. He could still feel the fear. . . . He knew now that beyond any doubt,

he was a coward. He had always styled himself as a bad-boy outlaw who played by his own rules, kicked ass, and was afraid of
nothing. Ironically, now that the world was finally embracing that
image, he wanted to run from the lie.

He stared at the TV in dead-eyed stupor, feeling nothing but a
low-level dread about his future.

Consuelo knocked on the bedroom door. "Señor Brazil . . . ?"

"Yes, what is it?" he snapped, and struggled to see over his
barrel chest to the bedroom door. She was standing there, her fresh
paramedic bandage covering her right arm, which was in a sling.

"Señor, dere ees mans downstair . . ." she said in her broken
English.

"I don't wanna see anybody."

"Dey heff dis por jew."

"That's *you*, Consuelo, not Jew. Jews are agents, Sephardic ten-
percent assholes."

"No. *Por favor,* dey *give* dis por jew." She was holding out
something in her hand.

He sat up in bed, exposing his furry chest, and nodded. She
came to him on tiptoes and handed him a gold ring.

Buddy had never had a particularly good personal relationship
with Consuelo. He used to shout at her and tell her she was an
idiot. Consuelo had told her sister in Cuernavaca that he was a
pendejo, a *gringo malo,* who used bad drugs and took advantage
of women and had kinky sex with prostitutes. She had called him
el diablo pequeño, the little devil.

Now that he had saved her from the mad doctor, she didn't know
how to treat him or what to think.

"Thank you! Leave me alone," he snapped coldly, and she
quickly left, quietly closing the door behind her.

The ring in his hand looked familiar. He had seen it before . . .
a gold band with two snakes entwined. Then he remembered. It
had been a gift to him from the head of the studio, when *Snake*

Dancer went over one hundred million in domestic grosses. That was back in the seventies. Now when that happened, they gave you a fucking Mercedes. He hadn't liked the ring. He preferred bigger jewelry with diamond settings, but what the fuck had he done with it? Who could have taken it? Why wasn't it somewhere in the back of his jewelry box?

Then it hit him. He had given the ring to Michael when his son moved into the pool house after being thrown out of Pepperdine. A sort of "welcome home/bury the hatchet" present. He had lied and told Michael he'd had it designed especially for him.

Now, as he sat holding his dead son's ring, the taste of sour chocolate unexpectedly filled his mouth, startling him. He rolled over and hit the intercom.

"Jes?" Consuelo's voice came over the speaker into his bedroom.

"Tell them to wait out by the pool house. No . . . no, hold it, fuck the pool house, I'm never going in there again. Tell them to wait in the den."

And then Buddy Brazil got out of bed and put on a pair of new black jeans and a black silk shirt, his patented "Outlaw Buddy" attire. He slipped into a pair of custom-made black rhino cowboy boots that gave him an extra three inches in the heel. After inspecting his bloated face in the bathroom mirror, he gargled some Listerine and went downstairs.

There were three of them waiting, not in the den as he'd instructed, but in the living room, which was a mess, filled with shattered glass, empty Coke cans, and police cigarette butts. There was a slender, underweight man with a shaved head, and a rumpled, gray-haired porpoise with a bow tie. Last, but hardly least, a drop-dead gorgeous blonde of exquisite proportions, with aqua-blue eyes and a world-class bumper kit. Buddy focused on her, ignoring the two men. He slipped easily back into his old outlaw persona.

"How may I help you?" he said, trying to sound tired, but heroically resolute, like Alan Ladd after the big gunfight in *Shane*, his favorite movie, growing up.

"I'm Stacy Richardson. This is Dr. Wendell Kinney and Cris Cunningham," she said.

He looked over at the skinny, bald-headed man. "Cris Cunningham? There used to be a guy with that name who played quarterback for UCLA. They called him Lucky Cunningham 'cause he'd always complete some bullshit Hail Mary pass with seconds left on the clock. A real gamer. Not a bad player for a Bruin. Livin' in L.A., I bet you hear about him a lot," Buddy said, never for a minute suspecting that this underweight, bald, unhealthy-looking character in front of him was, in fact, that same man.

"Yeah," Cris said, "now and again." And that was all he said, so Stacy let it go.

"Sir, we've come to ask you a few questions about your son."

Again, it was the beautiful blonde doing the talking. Buddy would have truly liked to fuck her, but he hadn't had sex with a non-pro in almost five years. Now that Heidi Fleiss was out of the business and standing trial again, he was just using the few remnants from her old stable, who were still flat-backing around Hollywood. He preferred hookers. He had always been afraid of rejection. Prostitutes never rejected you. If you pre-ejaculated, or couldn't sustain an erection because of drugs, or whatever, they never said anything. Hookers always made you feel like your tool was a diamond cutter and you were the blue-vein prince of the city. He looked at this girl and desired her, but knew he would posture and strut, then probably never get up the nerve to take a cut at her.

"First, maybe you should tell me where you got this ring," Buddy said, holding it up between his thumb and forefinger.

"I got it off Mike when he died," the underweight young man said.

Buddy moved farther into the room, coming closer. He could see now that Cris Cunningham was surprisingly tall, at least six-three. Even in his custom boots, Buddy was a few inches shorter. "Why don't we go in here," he said, leading them into the den, which contained all of his showbiz trophies and pictures of him with celebrities, including shots with three different U.S. Presidents. "I'm sort of played out, so if we can make it fast," he said, going for a heroic pose by the bar, making it sound like his fabulous gunfight was nothing to really talk about, but maybe had tired him slightly.

"Sir," the beautiful blonde said.

"Buddy," he corrected her.

She rewarded him with a smile and went on, "Mr. Cunningham was with your son for several weeks just before he died . . ."

"And where was that? I heard he was hoboing up in Texas, for God's sake. Why Mike would be riding the rails, hanging with a buncha bums, sure beats the shit outta me."

"He was searching for himself," the tall, head-shaved man said. Buddy showed him to a seat on the sofa, while taking a high stool by the bar for himself. Buddy never let his head be lower than another alpha male's if they were both in the vicinity of prime pussy. From this angle, Buddy could now see a stitched wound in the back of the man's head.

"He was riding trains," Buddy said. "How do you look for yourself doing that?"

"I hoboed with him. We rode the SP line all across Texas. We had long talks about what he wanted. To tell you the truth, Mr. Brazil, he was lonely and confused, and didn't think anybody loved him. He was looking for a father, and I told him he should give you another chance. I took his ring after he died."

"You mean you *stole* his ring," Buddy snapped, angry that this stranger had asserted himself into his nonexistent relationship with Mike.

"No sir," Cris said. "I just gave it back a minute ago, but if I hadn't saved it for you, some railroad brakeman would have it now.''

Mike was lonely, he didn't think anybody loved him. . . . Like father, like son. "You said you wanted to ask some questions. What do you need to know?'' Buddy asked the blond woman.

"Was your son Jewish?''

Buddy first looked annoyed, then amused. Then he had no expression at all, as he leaned his elbows on the bar, and went for some Jack Nicholson cool. "How the hell is that any of your business, lady?'' he said slowly, immediately regretting the remark because it made him sound like he was hiding something. He seemed to be having trouble staying in character. The Buddy Brazil outlaw thing he'd perfected over the years was suddenly wavering badly.

"I assume the doctors at the morgue explained the unusual conditions surrounding your son's death,'' Wendell said. "I'm sure they explained their suspicions about the reason somebody stole Mike's body.''

Buddy nodded. Dr. Welsh had said to him that they feared his son had been infected by some rare bio-weapon that had gotten loose, and that somebody, maybe even a foreign government, had stolen Mike's body to get a sample of it. He'd been sworn to secrecy. They didn't want that on the news.

"I think that the weapon he was exposed to might have been designed to only attack people of Jewish origin,'' Stacy said. "So far, in almost every case we have confirmed, the victim was Jewish. Troy Lee Williams, who died from an illegal test of the weapon, was adopted. His natural parents were Jewish. Dr. Saunders, the retired dentist; your friend Dr. Iverson; the man who crashed his helicopter at Vanishing Lake, Captain Abrams—all Jewish. Only Sylvester Swift, an African-American who was transferred up there, wasn't Jewish. That still puzzles me. I've been giving a lot of thought to the fact that this is a protein bio-weapon. I've been reading up on it, and Wendell and I think it may be possible for a protein to genetically target an ethnic-specific section of a genome.''

"Do what?'' Buddy asked.

"If Dr. DeMille had attempted to use the protein markers that are in all human blood, I think it's very possible to target specific genetic groups. Blacks, for instance, are the only group to get sickle-cell anemia. Only Ashkenazi Jews get Tay-Sachs disease. This is because each genetic group has its own unique DNA, with its own specific protein markers. Prions could be engineered to attack only one set of genetic DNA markers. When you think about it, it makes both scientific and tactical military sense. . . . If we were at war with the Arabs, or the Chinese, it would be devastatingly efficient to infect only that genetic enemy.''

Buddy was starting to panic. "Is this shit contagious?'' he shrieked, losing his Nicholson drawl.

"It can be passed, but it needs to be transmitted by ingestion, direct blood transfer, or mosquito bites. It's not a virus, so it's not very contagious. I wouldn't be too concerned,'' she said.

Now Buddy was wondering if he'd touched Iverson after he'd blown half his head off. Shit! Had he stood in the blood with bare feet? He barely remembered any of it. He'd been in emotional shock for an hour after the shooting.

"Was Mike Jewish?'' Stacy asked again.

"Yes,'' Buddy stammered. "My name is . . . it used to be Peter Olenchuck.''

"Polish?'' she asked.

Buddy winced. "Yeah, it's fucking Polish. What about it?'' he snapped, and again immediately regretted it, because she looked startled and hurt.

"Look, Miss . . . what was it . . . ?''

"Richardson. And it's Mrs.,'' she said.

Now Buddy winced inwardly. She was married.

It was news to Cris as well.

"Mrs. Richardson,'' Buddy continued, "I'm very sorry. It's

been a while since I killed anyone. I guess I'm a little outta practice." At last, a good delivery. He had put just the right amount of tired distress into the reading.

"I understand," she said. "And Michael's mother, was she Jewish?"

"With a name like Tova?" Buddy smiled ruefully. "Tova was one of the great Eastern European Jewish Princesses. She was Tova Rosen, and before you think we're all running around Hollywood changing our names to deny our heritage, this is a billboard society we're in out here. Olenchuck. I didn't want to go around town dragging that Polish piano behind me."

"It's okay," she said softly.

Again he felt stupid. He'd overreacted. He was all over the road.

"Mr. Brazil, I think you should get your blood checked immediately. It's just a precaution, to be on the safe side. Not that I think you have anything to worry about."

Then the chocolate bread thing was back in his mouth, tinny and gross. He wanted to turn and spit into his bar sink, but he restrained himself.

"And just what are you people going to do?" he asked.

"We've decided to go back to Vanishing Lake," Cris Cunningham said. "We want to find out what really happened up there. Stacy thinks we should look at the prison. See if we can find anything they missed when they pulled out. Wendell is going to stay here and work on the science in case we turn up something."

"Vanishing Lake? Where the big fire was?" he said, remembering it from the news.

"It's where your son was infected," Stacy said.

"Isn't that dangerous, going up there?" Buddy asked. "If there's been a bio-weapon outbreak?"

"The government says that all infestation has been contained. They've even reopened the highways," Stacy said.

"I hope they're right," Buddy said. Then, apropos of nothing, he added, "Will your husband be going?" Buddy smiled, trying for some of the old Brazil bullshit, but missing by a mile. Without even looking in the bar mirror, he knew that his smile was lecherous. He had never felt more awkward.

"My husband is dead," she finally said softly. "He was murdered by the people at Fort Detrick, Maryland. They said he committed suicide, but they murdered him because he found out what they were doing."

So Maximilian Richardson was her husband, Cris thought, *and he was murdered because he stumbled onto this.*

"They killed Mr. Cunningham's four-year-old daughter, with U.S. Government–manufactured pyridostigmine, part of a chemical weapons cocktail used by Iraq in the Gulf War, and brought home inside some of our soldiers," Stacy went on. "And now they've killed your only son. We're not going to quit till we prove they were all murdered."

Buddy Brazil suddenly felt a range of new, different emotions sweeping over him. In his car on the way to the morgue he had wanted to cry, or have some reaction to Mike's passing, but he couldn't. Then in his dream, when Mike was falling, he knew he had lost something very important, and had cried in his sleep, although that had just been a slice of his subconscious. Now he felt guilt, overwhelming Jewish guilt, and burning, unreasoning anger.

He also knew he couldn't live with himself as a coward. He would rather die than carry that around with him. His self-loathing was swamped by his cowardice. He had denied Michael at birth, and accepted him only at DNA gunpoint. Now he felt crushed by Mike's loss.

"There's a hospital a mile from here. Let's go get my blood checked," he said softly. "And then if you want, I'll go with you. We can use my private jet."

It was the first sentence he had uttered since they arrived that felt right. The taste of stale bread was no longer in his mouth.

Chapter 26

RETURN TO VANISHING LAKE

t's a good thing I've got bank credit," Buddy Brazil muttered to himself, as he threw the Writers Guild credit arbitration finding aside. "If I had to depend on screen credit, I'd go broke." He'd put in for "written by" after doing a pencil revision on the last draft of a western he was producing called *Trail of Tears,* but the Arbitration Committee at the Writers Guild had denied it. He flipped the rest of the mail he'd brought with him onto the tray table and looked out the window of his Gulfstream III.

They were still climbing, just leaving the flight pattern at Van Nuys Airport, and he could see the San Gabriel Mountains falling away under the left wing. It was a typical smoggy L.A. day, and everything looked tiny and brown down there; a miniature town through a number six light filter. He turned away from the window. The tall man with the stitched-up head and the quarterback's name was sitting on the plush sofa. He was looking at the expensive seat controls in the Gulfstream, like an indigent trying to pick the right dinner fork at a five-star restaurant. Buddy loved the magnificent jet. The burlwood was varnished and glistening; there were three video screens, a full bar and galley, and a gorgeous uniformed stewardess named Carmen DeLuca, who was one of Heidi's ex-hookers. Carmen had hit the lockup for her third prostitution bust last May and had decided to retire from high-roller sport fucking. He'd given her a job on his new G-III, which he had just painted black, with the word "Outlaw" scripted on the tail.

Buddy got up and moved forward as Stacy Richardson came out of the forward bathroom and joined Cris Cunningham on the sofa. Even in his cowboy boots, Buddy could stand up in the plane without ducking his head. The Gulfstream had a six-foot-high cabin, so Cris Cunningham was too tall to accomplish that feat. It pissed Buddy off.

"Let me show you something," Buddy said. He took a gold key from his pocket and unlocked a cabinet forward of the galley, pulling out a Colt Python with a Tasco dot scope affixed to its three-inch barrel. He flipped the sight on and spun the pistol like a gunfighter in a bad western.

"Jesus, take it easy," Cris said. "Is it loaded?"

"Fucking A," Buddy said, still waving the gun around, sighting the dot on several things in the cabin. "This is an O.E.G. That stands for—"

"Occluded Eye Gunsight," Cris said. "Kick the thing open and drop the loads out, will you?" He was looking at the gun like a man who had been on the serious end of more than one firearm.

"Don't be alarmed, Cris. I know what I'm doing." Buddy was on familiar ground. He would often wave loaded guns around to scare the shit out of someone and establish his alpha-male superiority.

"If you knew what you were doing, Buddy, you wouldn't be handling a loaded gun like that," Cris said, feeling a familiar knot in his stomach.

"I can understand why you're a little nervous," Buddy said,

holding the gun carelessly pointed at Cris, "but I'm a certified sharpshooter . . . an expert. You're in no immediate danger," and he pulled the hammer back.

Cris moved as fast as he could. He came up off the sofa, grabbed Buddy's wrist, and twisted it to the left, immediately pulling his finger off the trigger. Cris simultaneously pivoted in the jet's cabin, turning inside of Buddy's outstretched right arm, yanking it upward, and miraculously coming away with Buddy's Colt Python. It was a move he'd learned in Special Forces Recon. He used to be able to do it so fast you almost couldn't see it. Now, with his reflexes shot, the move felt clumsy and dangerous. If Buddy had been for real, or had known what he was doing, Cris would have been dead. He snapped the sight off, then kicked the round wheel open, dumping all six magnum loads in his hand.

"Full Metal Jackets," Cris said softly. "What're you hunting with these, rhinos?" He dropped the six FMJs into his pocket, then handed the empty revolver back to Buddy. Cris's legs were shaking. He was amazed that a combat move he'd once been so good at he could now only perform at half speed. *What am I doing?* he thought. *I don't belong here. I'm going to get us all killed.*

"Jesus Christ, how'd you do that? One second I had the fucking gun, next you did." Buddy was impressed by any macho feat that he couldn't duplicate. So, while Cris was cursing his sad performance, Buddy was putting him a few notches higher on the alpha-male testosterone chart.

"Cris was a Delta Ranger. He won the Silver Star," Stacy said.

Buddy looked over at her. "That's not hard to believe. I never saw anything on two feet move so fast," Buddy gushed, notching Cris up even higher. "Let me show you something else." Buddy returned to the unlocked cabinet and pulled out another loaded pistol. It was a customized Beretta. He handled this one more carefully as he showed it to Cris.

Stacy thought they looked like little boys comparing toys.

"Know what this is?" Buddy asked.

"A nine-by-nineteen NATO Beretta selective-fire 93R," Cris said. "You got the stock?"

"Sure do." Buddy grinned. "You really know your guns." He reached in and pulled out a hand-carved wood stock that could be attached to the piece, turning it into a nine-millimeter carbine.

Cris's stomach was turning sour. He desperately wanted a drink. *Higher power*, he thought. *Serve vengeance. Get justice for what they did to Kennidi.*

Buddy reached in the cabinet and pulled out a Heckler & Koch 5.56mm G3SG sniping rifle, with a Zeiss 1.5×6 telescopic sight and a twenty-round clip. He handed it over to Cris, who removed the clip and dechambered a round. "Didn't anybody ever tell you not to keep a stored weapon chambered, Mr. Brazil?"

"I like to be ready," Buddy said.

"This plane could hit a wind shear and one of these things could discharge. Put 'em back empty," he said, his hands visibly shaking again, wishing he hadn't decided to come.

Buddy did as he was told, and put the unloaded weapons back in the locked cabinet. In that instant, Cris had somehow placed himself in charge.

The plane headed southeast, across Arizona and New Mexico, then down to Texas. On the way, Stacy filled Buddy and Cris in on everything they didn't know about what had happened at Vanishing Lake and Fort Detrick, ending with Admiral Zoll's weird behavior at Company A, First SATCOM Battalion Headquarters. Then she showed Buddy the picture of the silver-haired man who had ambushed the soldiers on the baseball diamond and who Cris had seen murder two soldiers in cold blood on the high plain above the lake.

"Who do you think he is?" Buddy asked. Cris sat up straighter and explained about the legendary hobo priest and his army of F.T.R.A. murderers and religious fanatics, who had captured Dexter DeMille.

After two hours, they began their descent. Cris Cunningham had fallen asleep on the couch. Stacy and Buddy had played two competitive rubbers of gin rummy, at the end almost breaking even on points.

When they heard the wheels come down, they woke Cris, then landed in Texas, at the Waco Regional Airfield.

Buddy had already asked the pilots to call ahead for a four-wheel-drive vehichle, and a big Chevy Blazer was waiting for them at the Executive Jet Terminal.

"You wanna take the guns?" he asked.

Cris nodded without speaking. He seemed strangely troubled, and that upset Buddy. If a Silver Star winner was worried, it must be much worse up there than they had confided.

They loaded the weapons and extra ammo into the back of the Blazer. Cris felt dull and listless as he helped transfer the guns. He hadn't eaten in hours. He was weak and ravaged by years of alcohol. He prayed he wouldn't be called on to react. He wasn't up to it.

Once the jeep was loaded, Buddy told the pilots to stay on the beeper; he'd notify them when they'd be returning.

"Do you think this is really dangerous?" Buddy finally asked, as he pulled the Blazer off the field and took the highway west, toward the Black Hills. He sure didn't want to meet the commandos who had stolen his son's body, and he certainly didn't want to come face to face with a silver-haired murderer and his band of freight-train-riding fanatics.

"I don't think it's dangerous, not anymore," Stacy said. "The whole place caught fire. I think the people from the Devil's Workshop are gone."

Buddy nodded, and the freeze in his stomach thawed. Maybe he could regain his self-respect without getting himself killed. After all, he *was* stepping up. He *was* driving into a threatening situation, risking his life. If nobody was up there, that wasn't his fault. He hadn't chickened out. He'd put himself in harm's way. Would that allow him to reclaim his outlaw persona? he wondered. Thank God Cris Cunningham knew what the hell he was doing.

A hundred miles to the east, Fannon Kincaid, Dexter DeMille, and forty heavily armed members of the Christian Choir and the Lord's Desire jumped off the slow-moving freight where the tracks passed a mile from Vanishing Lake. They walked down a wooded incline toward the burned-out village at the far end of the lake.

"We'll need to get a boat," Fannon said. "There's probably some still down by the dock." His white hair was billowing wildly in the breeze, making him look more and more crazy, Dexter thought.

They marched him resolutely toward the burned-out fishing village, near where the Pale Horse Prion was waiting in the deep.

Chapter 27

SNAKE EATER

In Special Forces Recon, they always said Cris Cunningham was best after dark. They said he came alive at twilight, like a coyote. He could find an enemy as if by magic. It was uncanny. He would be on reconnaissance patrol when suddenly he would just point right and there would be a bunch of unfriendlies dug in some hole, ass down in the mud and completely out of sight. On more than one A.A.R. (After Action Report), under Initial Enemy Engagement it stated, "Captain Cunningham smelled them."

As they approached the town of Vanishing Lake, Cris felt the same uneasy prickle on his neck. He felt his body tense in the eerie blackness. "Turn off your headlights and pull over," he instructed Buddy.

"We're not there yet."

Cris leaned over and pushed in the headlight button. "Get on the shoulder over there!" he commanded.

Buddy reluctantly pulled over and parked.

"What is it?" Buddy asked.

"I don't know," Cris said, his senses tingling.

There was a tense silence in the car as Stacy and Buddy waited for him to tell them what he was doing. Cris sat with his nerves jumping, feeling stupid. Then, to cover his embarrassment, he opened the door and got out.

"What the hell is it?" Buddy whispered impatiently.

"I don't know. Sometimes I get hunches," Cris said, feeling lame and unsure, but Buddy easily accepted it as wisdom. It was like John Wayne in *The Green Berets* knowing Charley was hiding up in the hills without ever seeing them.

"I'm gonna go take a look," Cris whispered, and moved away from the car. He was now almost sure that what had caused the "combat sensation" was his alcohol-shot nervous system. He wandered a short distance away from the car and unzipped his pants to take a leak. He froze again. This time the sensation was more pronounced. His instincts were screaming at him. He stood absolutely still and listened. He strained to filter the multiple sounds of night: Wind? Bugs? Nightbirds? Mansounds? What was it that had alerted him? He didn't know. Then he emptied his bladder. In "Snake Eater" school, when they were in survival training, he had been taught that sounds carry a long distance over water. So he quietly zipped his fly and moved cautiously down toward the lake. . . .

He could feel the old Recon training kick in as he descended, but it was like looking at something through a gauze curtain. His senses were muted and sluggish. It had been eight years since he had called in an air strike on his own position. He had been on Recon with Sergeant Tom Kilbride, with orders not to engage. They were hopelessly lost when they stumbled into a Republican Guard unit, bivouacked on the desert. Cris ignored his orders and wormed up close, dropping a homing package, then backing out and calling for an Alert-5, Fly-by-Wire air strike with a ten-minute E.T.A. A scant two minutes after their request, six F-16s were catshot off the deck of the *Constitution*. Cris and Tom had still been trying to retreat out of the fire zone when the F-16 ground pounders came in low, three minutes ahead of schedule. The Falcon pilots zeroed out their position and fired before Cris and Tom could get away, so they found a hole in the sand and dug in. The Republican Guard unit panicked, running in all directions. Cris and Tom opened up on the confused troops as the F-16 missiles targeted on the ground package. Tom Kilbride had been blown away when one of the Iraqi soldiers machine-gunned him from ten feet away, before Cris was able to shoot. The way Cris saw it, all he had done was get Tom Kilbride killed. He had put that damning self-evaluation in his A.A.R.

That night he got roaring drunk. He had a bad case of survivor's guilt over Kilbride's death, but the war needed heroes, especially ground troops. He got the Silver Star for gallantry under fire and Kilbride got a battlefield grave.

He hated the medal. He refused to wear it, and had thrown it in the trash. His father wrote the Marines, got it replaced, and hung it in his bar, right next to the picture of Cris scoring the damn touchdown. These had been Richard Cunningham's victories. They defined him, but left Cris empty and confused.

As Cris moved out of the trees, the lake came into view. His hands and senses were tingling as he crouched down at the water's edge and looked out. He slowly swept his gaze 180 degrees, looking for anything that seemed out of place: a glint of reflected moonlight off distant metal; a sound; a smell. Anything that might point to an enemy position. As he sat there, he again distrusted his alert system. He felt foolish squatting in soft sand wearing dress loafers, trying to convince himself that despite three years of drunken malnutrition, he still had combat sharpness. Then, almost without thought, he was moving slowly along the perimeter of the lake. He moved in total silence, stepping light. Then again, without knowing why, he suddenly froze. Something was wrong. He remained still, his head pivoting, both ears straining. He could smell the minty-green scent of pine needles. This patch of ground had escaped the devastating fire. He could smell the deep, fragrant richness of moist earth. He could hear the slight, rippling sound of water lapping against the shore. He remained very still for almost a minute, identifying nothing out of place, wondering what the hell it was that had alerted him. Then, after a moment, he sorted it out. It wasn't something that he *had* heard; it was something he *hadn't*. A distant chorus of night insects had suddenly stopped keening, causing a slight change in the background sounds he had subconsciously set his ear to monitor. Something, some foreign sound, had frightened them. It was only when they started up again that he realized it.

He moved slowly, one foot carefully placed in front of the other, choosing safety over speed. After he had traveled almost four hundred silent yards in the sand by the edge of the lake, he heard a distant soft tapping sound, metal on metal. This was not a sound made by wind against a loose door. This was a man-made sound, a controlled tapping with a rhythm. Again, he moved forward, then went to his stomach, snaking along the ground. In the pale moonlight, he could see the burned-out dock that had once fronted the Bucket a' Bait restaurant. He could see the burned-out husk of the coffee shop, with its few remaining cedar posts poking up at the sky, charred reminders of that night of insanity. He inched toward the shoreline and slipped silently into the lake.

The cold chill of the mountain water soaked through his clothing, freezing his skin like the promise of death. He reached down and scooped handfuls of dark mud off the bottom and quietly rubbed it all over his shaved white head. He rubbed it on his cheeks and chin, then submerged silently to his shoulders. He grabbed handfuls of moss in the shallow water and pulled himself quietly along, with only his mud-caked head above water, being careful not to send out a wake of moonlit ripples. He was still desperately trying to regain that sharp combat edge from years ago. That feeling that he was no longer a visitor in the environment, but part of it. Instead, he felt like a clumsy intruder, slow, loud, and easy to spot. He sank down to his ears, giving up his ability to hear in favor of better water camouflage. Now only his nose, eyes, and mud-caked head were above the water, moving toward the burned rubble that had once been the restaurant pier.

As he got closer, he saw that the metal pounding sound was coming from a man standing in a small boat tied to a piece of dock on the far side of a low piling. The man appeared to be tapping a small hammer on an outboard engine. He had the engine cowling off and seemed to be trying to dislodge something that had damaged the engine, perhaps a piece of flying debris from one of the dock explosions. Cris stopped moving and slowly brought his head up to clear the water from his ears. Suddenly, he could hear several men whispering in the dark behind him. *Shit!* he thought. *I completely missed them.* He had gone right past their position, overshooting them in the dark. A blunder he would never have made during his Ranger days.

"Okay, I think I got it," the man with the hammer whispered.

"Good," a man on the shore replied. "We're coming out." Cris was trapped between them.

Without warning, four men crashed into the water directly at him, not ten feet from where he was. Quickly, he submerged, cursing himself.

As one of the men moved to the boat he kicked Cris in the side. Cris heard the man call out, "Whaaa? Fuck!"

Cris reached up, grabbed the man's belt, and yanked him under. He had been trained in U.D.T. (Underwater Demolition Teams) and water combat. At one time he had had excellent underwater combat survival skills. He pulled the man under and tried to roll on top of him, but the man got his feet down and, using the bottom, reared up, bringing Cris with him. As they broke the surface the man hit Cris full in the face with a pistol gripped in his right hand. Cris momentarily blacked out, but the impact of the blow somehow knocked the gun from the man's hand. Cris hung on to him to keep from falling down, and the gun got pinned between them.

They struggled in four feet of water, thrashing awkwardly, as several other F.T.R.A.s ran to help their comrade.

The gun was slipping down between their bodies. Cris put his hand down and miraculously caught it, coming away with the stubby automatic. He turned and fired two shots at the charging men, then quickly hit the man in the face with his own gun. Cris grabbed the stunned man and yanked him under again. He could hear his victim choking through the water. Over his head, Cris heard voices screaming, but he could not make out any of it. He concentrated on taking his captive farther and deeper into the lake. Cris was now operating completely on instinct. The man was gaining consciousness, and began to struggle fiercely. Cris momentarily lost control, and the man shot up to get air. As he broke surface, he choked out, "Help me! Help me!"

Cris reached up and pulled him down again. In U.D.T., he had once stayed submerged for three and a half minutes. Back then he was in terrific shape; now he was a physical wreck. He wasn't sure how long he could stay under. Then, thankfully, he felt the thrashing of his victim turn to spasms, but his own lungs were exploding. Finally, Cris came up, rolling his mouth across the surface as he'd been taught in U.D.T., taking in a breath without completely breaking out of the water. He could hear chaos in the boat near him.

"He's got Cleve!" somebody yelled.

Then Cris dove again, keeping Cleve pinned under him, pushing him down lower and lower.

Cleve was not moving now, buoyant, unconscious below Cris. Cris wanted him alive, but was afraid if he surfaced, he would be target practice for the men in the boat. Then he heard the outboard starting. Cris was five feet under. The engine was a muffled whine, the prop stirring water and moonlight in a bubbling silver froth, as the boat slashed across the lake above him. Then the whine of the engine faded. After the boat left, Cris dragged Cleve to the surface, pulling the unconscious man toward shore.

He was exhausted as he pulled Cleve up on the sand. He tried to sling his captive over his shoulder, but didn't have the strength, so he just flopped him onto his back.

First Cris cleared the man's tongue, then he rolled him onto his stomach and tried to pump water out of him. Nothing. Cris rolled him onto his back again and began mouth-to-mouth. He blew air into Cleve's lungs. He felt the man's heart sputter and stop. Cris banged his fist on Cleve's breastbone, trying to shock the man's heart into starting.

"Shit," he whispered between breaths.

The CPR went on for almost five minutes. It seemed futile, but Cris continued. Then, unexpectedly, the man groaned. Encouraged, Cris kept going, blowing more breath into Cleve's lungs. It took Cris almost ten more minutes before he heard Cleve exhale, but the man still hadn't opened his eyes.

"Don't go brain-dead on me, asshole," Cris whispered. "I need you alive."

Cleve didn't open his eyes. He didn't twitch or move. It was then that Cris suspected that the groan, and later the exhale, was just his own breath coming back out. The man was dead. Cris lay back against a tree, exhausted. He tried to catch his breath. He knew he was incredibly lucky to be alive.

Chapter 28

MUD DEMON

Fannon Kincaid heard Cleve Robertson scream and saw him thrashing in four feet of water. Then, almost like a creature rising from the slimy lake floor, something reared itself out of the water, caked in black mud. The apparition attacked the Reverend's Acolyte like a monster from the deep.

Fannon pulled his nine-millimeter and aimed it at the roiling bodies, but couldn't make out who was who. So he held his fire, looking for a clean shot.

"Something's got Cleve," someone behind him shouted.

Then he saw the bald mud man clearly. His mouth was open in a silent scream, and he looked like a vision from hell. Blood was streaming down his face onto his shirt; an anguished look was on his face. Fannon finally had a clean shot. He squeezed off a round, but the gun didn't fire because the chamber was soaked with lake water. Then the bald man fired two shots in their direction, and Fannon panicked, afraid Dr. DeMille would be hit. "Get him in the boat!" the Reverend screamed at his men.

Dexter DeMille was wallowing along clumsily in shallow water, making no headway. He screamed when the gun was fired. One of the Choir grabbed the skinny scientist by the arm and dragged him. They clambered up onto the one small piece of dock that remained from the inferno. The section was held in place by a concrete piling that had protected the wooden float from the blast. An eighteen-foot metal boat was tied there. Fannon pushed Dexter into the craft, then jumped in along with the three surviving Choir members he had brought with him on the mission. "Let's go," Fannon shouted, deciding in that instant to leave Cleve to the mud demon that had risen from the watery depths and grabbed him.

"We can't leave him!" Randall Rader shouted, looking off at the area where the fight had taken place. Now there was no sign of the combatants. They had disappeared under the water's surface.

"He's in the hands of God. Move out, R.V.!" Fannon screamed at Robert Vail in the stern.

R.V. was the man who had been tapping on the engine. Despite his ropy build and long, stringy hair, his most distinguishing features were his two facial tattoos: "Fuck You" on the right side of his forehead and "Eat Shit" on the left. R.V. pulled the starter cord and the engine caught on the first try. Holding the handle of the seven-and-a-half-horse Evinrude engine, R.V. steered the boat right over the place where Cleve and the bleeding bald apparition had been struggling.

"Race and Faith!" Fannon shouted at the bubbles in the water as they sped away.

They were soon out in the middle of the lake. Fannon wondered who, or what, had risen from the water's depths to capture Cleve. The bald man had not resurfaced. Fannon had pulled the nine-millimeter, firing a shot directly at the mud-demon from the lake. But the gun had refused to discharge. Was it a sign? Was this the devil of the mud races rising from a crater lake that stretched deep down to the gates of hell? Fannon believed that signs were messages from God. The taking of Cleve was a message. The mud man in the lake was proof that God's enemies from the mud races were trying to destroy Fannon's mission. He was being told by God to hurry. He now pushed these thoughts aside and turned his attention to the shivering scientist huddled on the middle seat of the boat.

"Where is the position?" he demanded of Dexter, who jerked his head up like a frightened child and engaged the fiery gaze of Fannon Kincaid. Intense mania shone from Fannon's eyes, revealing the madness inside his head.

"It's halfway out," Dexter said softly. "Position the boat directly off the flagpole on the prison tower, then line it up on the other side with that large silver pine over there." He pointed off to a huge tree that stood down by the water's edge on the east shore.

Fannon nodded to R.V., who slowed the boat and moved it into line with the prison tower. From across the water they could see that most of the wooden prison buildings had suffered extensive damage in the fire.

"Right about here," Dexter said dully. "There's an underwater buoy anchored to the bottom. It has a pull cord attached through rings. Find the buoy and then pull up the cord," he said. "The bio-weapon is in two orange watertight pressure containers attached to the cord."

Fannon nodded at two members of the Choir, and they stripped off their shirts and pants. Clad only in ratty underwear, they dove into the cold waters of the lake, splashing moonlight around the perimeter of the boat before kicking hard and disappearing under the surface.

"God is a refuge and a fortress," Fannon said softly.

"Bless Jesus," R.V. muttered from behind Dexter, who jerked his head around and saw that the man with "Fuck You" and "Eat Shit" tattooed on his forehead had bowed his head and was praying reverently.

God in heaven save me, Dexter thought, issuing his own desperate plea to the Almighty.

Then, as if by magic, one of the divers poked his head above the surface. "We found it!" he yelled.

"Praise Jesus," R.V. and Fannon said in unison.

Fannon looked at the old Timex watch with the broken band that he carried in his overalls pocket. It was almost eleven-fifteen. He knew that even though the Sons of Manas-seh had sent the mud apparition in the lake, God had managed to use the demon to warn Fannon of the need to hurry. Once Dexter had told him of the secret plague, he had looked up the verses in Revelation that foretold of this event and found some striking details: "The fearful and unbelieving, and the abominable, and murderers, and whoremongers, and sorcerers, shall have their part in the lake which burneth with fire and brimstone." *This lake had burned with fire and brimstone,* Fannon thought. The verses continued: "This will be the second death. . . . And there came unto me one of the seven angels which had the seven vials full of the seven last plagues, and he carried me away in the spirit to a high mountain, and showed me that great city, the Holy Jerusalem, descending out of heaven from God." This had all been written in the words of the Prophets two hundred years after Christ, but surely it was no coincidence that these events so perfectly described in Revelation were coming true here in Texas, as prophesied.

Suddenly his divers came to the surface, carrying two large orange canisters. The men pulled themselves into the boat. Fannon looked at the wet canisters in wonder. "God has arranged our timetable," he said. "We have been given a sign from heaven to leave this place immediately. The Southern Pacific unit train will pass through the Black Hills in twenty minutes. If we hurry, we can make it."

Then R.V. started the boat, and they headed toward the eastern shore of Vanishing Lake.

·   ·   ·

After Cleve died, Cris had washed the mud off in the lake, then went back to the Blazer. He got the sniper's rifle with the long sight out of the back.

"What is it? What happened? Why are you wet?" Buddy pestered, and Stacy waited for Cris to explain.

"Follow me," Cris said, and carrying the gun, he moved off in front of them, heading back down to the lake.

When they got there it was quiet. Then suddenly, from across the water a mile away, they could hear the outboard engine start. Cris found an old tree and slammed the heavy sniper rifle into the crook of a limb and sighted through the scope. He adjusted the focus, and could now see the boat starting to move, its wake a moonlit tail of silver, heading away from them toward the other side.

"Are you gonna shoot 'em?" Buddy asked, surprised.

"No, I'm just tryin' to see. Here, take a look, Stacy." He pulled his eye away, allowing her to take his place at the scope. She could just make out the five men in the boat. One of them definitely looked like the silver-haired Fannon Kincaid. Huddled low, in the middle, she thought she recognized Dexter DeMille.

"It's them," she said, pulling away from the scope, so Buddy could see. Her heart was pounding. "What're they doing back here?"

"Maybe Dexter's doing the same thing we are—looking for evidence to use against Zoll," Cris said.

"No," she said. "No, it wouldn't be that." Then she fell silent.

"What are you thinking?" Buddy asked.

"I can think of only one reason why Dexter DeMille, who's wanted by every law enforcement agency in the country, would ever come back to Vanishing Lake." They waited for her to finish. "He's hidden some of his Pale Horse Prion here," she said.

Chapter 29

LAST TRAIN OUT

They had turned off the highway and were moving too fast along a rutted dirt road that Stacy remembered would cut several miles off the distance around the lake.

"Are you seriously trying to catch them?" Buddy yelled.

"They have to be heading for the rails." She looked over at Cris, but he said nothing.

"Let's slow down and think this out," Buddy yelled from the back seat. "We screw this up, we'll never get the toothpaste back in the tube."

Neither Cris nor Stacy answered him.

"We're just three people. They're armed lunatics. This is nuts." Buddy was more or less shrieking now. "Isn't that right, Cris?"

Again, Cris didn't say anything. He just sat in the passenger seat of the Blazer with his eyes on the road and a grim look on his face.

The headlights swept the darkened road ahead of them each time they rounded the frequent and sharp switchback curves. Several times, Stacy had to reach down and shift into four-wheel drive as they climbed steep or sandy sections of the firebreak. Then she would shift out of four-wheel and rocket dangerously along on the narrow rain-rutted path.

Suddenly, they heard the low, mournful whistle on the eleven-fifteen unit train.

"Shit," Stacy said. "There's a train coming. We'll never get there in time."

"Turn right up ahead and shoot across the meadow," Cris said. "It's a shorter way to get to the tracks." It was the first thing he'd said since they got in the car.

"Can we fuckin' please slow down and discuss this a minute?"

Nobody answered Buddy. Cris could feel a heavy fatigue settling over him, like a fatal shroud.

"We need to have a plan!" Buddy yelled. "Fer Chrissake, you're just gonna drive up and fuckin' yell at 'em? We're gonna all get killed!"

"Do you wanna get out?" Stacy yelled back, as she geared down and stopped the Blazer. "You can walk back." She glared at the movie producer with fire in her eyes.

He had never seen a woman look so dangerous. "All I said was, I wanta know how we're gonna do this."

"We'll think of something. My husband died trying to stop these killers. If DeMille has this Prion and I can get my hands on it, I can prove what went on here. Without it, I can't prove shit. I'm going to get the bastards who killed Max, so either stay in the car and shut up, or get out and walk. But make up your mind, and stop whining!"

In the back seat, Buddy was jerking slightly, little conflicting reflex movements, as if one second he was starting to get out, the next instant some invisible cord was holding him there. Then the low moan of the train whistle drifted across the night.

"Shit," she said, still looking at Buddy, who nodded his head weakly.

She put the Blazer in gear and gunned it, throwing stones and gravel as she shot up the next hill, then cut right off the dirt fire-break they were on and headed across the two-mile-wide meadow as Cris had suggested.

The car was first bogging, then accelerating as it hit mud and then hardpack. Occasionally a wheel would go into a hole, so she would hit four-wheel drive and blast out. The progress was slow, but a mile up ahead and to the left, she could see the train head-lights wigwagging on the engine's nose, cutting figure eights over the steel rails in front of it. "Cris," she said, and he looked over at her. "Are you okay with this?"

He said nothing.

"The train's coming. You need to tell us what to do," she said. "They're going to get away." He just sat there with his shoulders slumped, looking out the windshield as the Blazer bounced along. "What the fuck is wrong with you?" she yelled.

"I don't know what to do," he said.

Cris had told Stacy about the man he had killed at the lake; after that, Stacy thought, he had stopped functioning. She put the Blazer in low and started powering up the hill, trying to head off the train. As they got to the rise, in the moonlight they could see forty men and women crouching down in a ravine about four hundred yards away, waiting for the train to pass. One of the men saw the Blazer and pointed at them.

"Turn off the lights," Cris said softly.

"Huh?"

"Turn off the headlights and move the car. You're about to take fire."

Then the Blazer rocked, and they heard the shrill whine of ric-ocheting metal. A second later they heard the report of the gun.

"We're taking rounds," Cris blurted. She finally flipped off the headlights and turned left, exposing Cris as she started to drive along the top of the hill.

Several more shots rang out. Then the right front tire blew and they were riding on the rim, swerving badly until they plowed to a jarring stop.

"Out of the car," Cris ordered.

He and Stacy scrambled out. Buddy decided to stay huddled down on the back floor. Cris came back and snatched open the door. "Get the fuck outta there," he yelled.

"Safer in here."

"This thing is gonna draw fire parked up here. Those are armor-piercing slugs! Get out." Then he grabbed Buddy and dragged him. They ran along the hill, although visible in the moonlight, so Cris found cover behind some rocks and pulled them out of danger.

The Southern Pacific locomotive flashed past the place where the Christian Choir lay in the low ditch, trying to stay out of view of the engineer.

"They're getting away," Stacy said, as she stuck her head up and watched.

Cris was sitting with his back against the rock; his hands were shaking, his muscles twitching. He was done and he knew it. Then he rolled over and vomited bile onto the ground.

"What're you doing?" Buddy asked, appalled. "This sucks! You're puking 'cause you're scared?"

" 'Cause I'm sick," Cris said softly. "I'm an alcoholic. My body is fucked up. Nothing's working right."

"Great," Buddy whined. "Just great."

Stacy was looking at the F.T.R.A.s, who were beginning to make their parallel run up the embankment toward the slow-moving train. In twos and threes, they boarded the cars. "Dammit! We've gotta do something."

"Whatta you wanna do?" Buddy snarled. "We can't make it over there in time."

Off across the meadow one of Fannon's men was facing her, his hand out in front of him.

"Why's he pointing at us?" she said, as a bullet hit the rocks by her head and zinged off into the night.

Cris reached up, grabbed her, and pulled her down hard. "He's not pointing at you, he's *shooting* at you."

She sat beside him, her back against the boulder, until the train was gone. Then she stood and looked at the spot four hundred yards away where the hobos had been. "Where're they going?" she asked.

"Waco," he answered. "There's a big switching yard there. It's a hub. From there they could catch out to anywhere."

"What're we gonna do?" she said, her voice frail with distress.

He sat there in silence, so Buddy threw in his opinion. "I think we need to go to the authorities," he said. "Let them handle this."

"And what if the authorities are in on it?" Stacy shot back. "The Pentagon, the CIA, a lotta people had to be fronting this, and they'll want to see it covered up. We can't prove anything. We need evidence." Then she looked at Cris. "What do you think?"

"I need a drink, that's what I think." After a long moment, he stood. "Why don't we put on a new tire, go down to the lake, and see if we can find their boat. Maybe they left something behind."

Chapter 30

THE OLDEST CLICHÉ IN MOVIES

uddy didn't want to go to the lake, he wanted to go home. He had been shot at twice now in two days, and quite frankly, it was nothing like the paintball tournaments he'd had in the hills above Malibu, where, dressed in brand-new cammies, face guard, and shooting gloves, he had crawled around giggling, armed with his top-of-the-line CO_2-operated paintball "Devastator" rifle. He had done mortal combat with a hand-picked gang of stone-eyed killers from the William Morris Talent Agency. During those tournaments, Buddy had been dismayed to learn that he was surprisingly easy to hit. He was usually the first to get knocked out of the game. Geeks from the studio mailroom outlived him. Even so, he always enjoyed the contests. This was much different. The sound of bullets impacting deep into the side of the Blazer, or pinging off the rocks where he was cowering, was like nothing he'd ever before experienced. He visualized a bullet heading right at his surgically enhanced profile.

He'd spent hundreds of thousands of dollars on plastic surgery. He'd added surgical implants to his cheek and chin bones. He'd liposuctioned the fat from under his chin and stitched his forehead up under his scalp to eliminate the onset of forehead wrinkles. Buddy and Dr. Eugene Haliburton had spent at least ten fascinating hours adjusting his look on the virtual reality computer in the doctor's office, turning the image of the new square-jawed Buddy from full face to profile to three-quarters. They added a little mass here, nipped some there. He watched the screen in awe as the little stylus erased wrinkles and added a chin dimple. All of this facial artwork took place before Buddy nervously submitted to surgery. The idea that his expensive cosmetic redo would end up being splattered all over the Texas landscape by a whining piece of lead fired by some religious zealot with a fourth-grade education appalled him.

After Buddy and Cris changed the bullet-punctured tire, they drove along the east shore of the lake looking for the discarded metal boat. Buddy wished he had the inner strength to persevere, but the fact was, he desperately wanted to split. He played out a few excuses, looking for a usable exit line. "*Shit,*" he might say, "*I forgot I have a damn music and effects run at the studio on Friday for 'Starfighters.' It's a fucking command performance. I'd do anything to not have to go, but . . .*" Or perhaps, "*I gotta loop Barbra Streisand on Friday. Babs goes tits up if I don't stand there and feed her every single line. If it wasn't for that, you know I'd . . .*" Or some fucking thing, anything that would get him out of here with his outlaw rep intact. But every time he was on the verge of reciting one of these excuses, he would get the mild taste of chocolate in his mouth . . . which he had now come to dread, because it was immediately followed by such loneliness and self-disgust that he knew he had no choice but to stay.

His mind would then shift gears. They had killed his son. He had never been there for Mike. Never even tried to find out who Mike was. With his son's death, he could make up for it all by trying to catch the bastards who killed him. The problem was that Buddy couldn't escape the fact that he was so scared he could barely function. He wished he had some inner strength to fall back on. There was nothing for him in the arcane tradition of the Jewish faith. Buddy needed a hipper religious gig.

He had tried Scientology; Tom Cruise and John Travolta had gotten him enrolled. Scientology had been a fun excursion for a while. He loved their snappy military-style uniforms with the cool ornamental braid. He wore the uniform of an Operating Thetan. He had his tailored at the studio wardrobe department, so it fit him perfectly, no sags or wrinkles. He looked like Richard Gere in *An Officer and a Gentleman*. He also read the basic dictionary of Dianetics and Scientology from cover to cover. He had Scientology E-meter tracks made, which drew mental pictures of his state of being, graphing such notable psychic landscapes as his interior pain or perceived threat to his survival. He had tried, for almost six months, to obtain the level of Operating Thetan Three (OT-3), which was the State of Beingness, and would give him full control over Matter, Energy, Space, Time, and Form of Life. He had sat with his counselor and told her that he felt he was on the verge of going "clear," which in Scientology indicated a pure spirit. He had smiled blissfully and bragged about his spiritual purification to the actors at the celebrity center, but in reality, he attained none of the inner peace that he sensed the others derived from the religion. Worse still, he was paying through the nose for the experience.

After another three months of bluffing, he dropped out. The night that he quit, Heidi told him that life wasn't about control over energy or time or the form of life. It was just about getting laid, so she sent Michelle Fortner over to prove her point. Michelle gave him an incredible weekend of tube cleaning, but spiritually, Buddy was still bankrupt. Now he felt so alone and confused that he was on the verge of jumping out of the Blazer and running. But some invisible force wouldn't let him.

"Pull up," Cris said suddenly.

Stacy stopped and they all got out. Buddy followed Cris down to the water, where the aluminum boat Kincaid had been in was floating near the shore. Inside the boat, on the floorboards, were two orange canisters. While Cris and Buddy pulled the boat up onto the beach, Stacy took some latex gloves out of her purse and pulled them on as she walked to the water's edge.

"What is it?" Buddy said, his eyes on the orange painted canisters.

"They're waterproof bio-units. Good to three hundred feet," she said. "They're used for marine research." With gloved hands, she picked them up. Inside the canisters the black Styrofoam packing was still in place; the indentations where several vials had been pressed were still visible.

Then she carried one of the canisters back to the Blazer and examined it in the headlights.

"What do you think?" Buddy asked. He had trailed her there, hating this discovery; afraid it might lead to something and afraid it might not.

"I was just wondering if we should send this to Wendell. Maybe there were ink markings labeling the vials. We could get an ink transfer off these with chemicals."

"What for? We know what was in there."

"We think we know," she said. "But we can't be sure." She closed up the container and moved back to the boat to retrieve the second canister. When she got there, she saw that Cris was inside the boat, sitting on the center seat, studying a wet slip of paper in his hand.

"What's that?" she asked.

He handed the slip to her. On it she read:

FT W/DGNO, GV KCS, MERIDIAN NS ROANOKE

"Some kind of code?"

"It's a track warrant. It marks a train route. It means Fort Worth on the Dallas, Garland and Northeastern line, transfer in Grandview to KCS, which is the Kansas City Southern Line. It heads up into central Kansas. Then change in Meridian to Norfolk Southern, then to Roanoke, Virginia."

"It's a road map," she said, smiling. "Where'd you find it?"

"In the bottom of the boat, floating in an inch of water."

Buddy looked at the paper. "You know what the oldest cliché in movies is?" he said. "It's the fucking matchbook cover left at the scene of the crime. This is bullshit."

Cris considered this. Maybe Buddy was right. He was also hungry, exhausted, and longing for a drink. So he thought of Kennidi, for strength and resolve; he remembered the horrible headaches, caused by the clusters of tumors that grew in her sinuses and bulged her skull.

"We've got one thing going for us," Cris finally said. "These guys aren't exactly invisible. Forty guys with tattoos, guns, and Bibles are gonna be hard to miss. We could ask around in the jungles."

"Jungles?" Buddy looked puzzled.

"Hobo encampments. Hobos live in a narrow world. It covers the entire United States, but it's only as wide as the tracks. People congregate and talk. I think we should drive to Fort Worth, try and get there ahead of this train."

"Then what?" Buddy said.

"Then, if we don't see them, we pick up the trail and go on the rails after them. We ask around, try and run them down."

"Riding a freight," Buddy said, chagrined. "You can't be serious?"

"We won't find them any other way," Cris said.

"And we don't have time to talk each other out of it. I'm game if you guys are," Stacy said, and hurried back to the car.

"When we get to Fort Worth, I'll send these bio-containers to Wendell."

Buddy got in the passenger seat and Cris climbed into the back as Stacy got behind the wheel. She took off fast, heading back to the main highway, trying to catch up to Fannon Kincaid and his band of murderous train riders.

Chapter 31

BUCK

It was 8:45 A.M. and the Pentagon staff car was heading down Embassy Row in Washington, past the European embassies with their stone pillars and uniformed guards, past the ornate flagged buildings at the end of the street belonging to Mexico and Argentina. Then the car swung left and headed into the large, column-flanked driveway of the Naval Observatory, which contained the official residence of the Vice President of the United States.

Admiral Zoll was seated next to four-star Army General and Chairman of the Joint Chiefs Colin Stallings. Both men had been quiet on the long drive from the Pentagon, lost in their own speculations about what was going to take place.

It was promising to be a typically muggy Washington June day. The leaves hung like limp decorations from the heavy oak trees that surrounded the magnificent property. The Naval guards at the drive-in gate saluted the two staff officers in the back seat of the Pentagon car, then let the vehicle pass onto the ten-acre estate. It headed up the sweeping drive toward Admiralty House, where the Vice President lived.

Admiral Zoll often thought that Admiralty House, with its white turn-of-the-century splendor and acres of beautiful gardens, far outshone the White House, which seemed to him like little more than an antiques museum, full of boxy rooms, square architecture, and sweating tourists.

"This guy can sound like a hick, but he does his research and he knows how the fruit gets canned, so don't volunteer anything," General Stallings said in his Texas drawl.

"I know all about Buck Burger," Admiral Zoll said. "I did this whole dance in the late eighties to get funding, and again last year, when the Agency spooks fucked up. Buck sees the big picture. This will go down fine."

Nonetheless, Zoll was dreading the meeting.

The summons by Vice President Burger had followed a flurry of phone calls from O.T.S.G. (Office of the Surgeon General) and M.R.D.C. (Medical Research and Development Committee). The frantic calls started coming about an hour after the in-depth front-page Vanishing Lake story in *The New York Times* hit the Congressional doorsteps early that morning. Zoll got a wake-up call from the office of the Vice President requesting this nine-A.M. meeting. He and General Stallings had gathered their wits, compared notes, and rehearsed their defense over the phone. Now, without benefit of morning coffee, both were headed to a meeting that could easily spell disaster.

They were led into the Observatory Wing, where the V.P.'s residential suite was located, and shown into his massive office, which was empty when they arrived. Plate-glass windows looked out over rolling lawns and fountains. The room had blue velvet drapes, Early American furniture, and hardwood floors. The flag of the Office of the Vice President stood next to the American flag on gilded eagle-head poles. An old polished brass telescope, dredged up from the quarterdeck of John Paul Jones's ill-fated ship, the

Bonhomme Richard, sat in the window, pointing out at the gardens. Like both Admiral Zoll and General Stallings, it had seen its share of incoming cannon fire.

After a moment, the double doors at the end of the room opened, and Vice President Brian Burger briskly entered the room like a Lexus salesman smiling his greeting. He had been the senior Senator from Arizona and had once chaired the powerful Ways and Means Committee. Admiral Zoll had appeared before him for initial funding on his anti-terrorist bio-research program at Fort Detrick. Back then, the Senator had been known as "Buck" Burger, a folksy nickname he still favored.

"Colie, James, thanks for coming over on such short notice," he said, booming the greeting as he moved behind his desk.

"Mr. Vice President," they chorused, and both shook his hand.

His smile widened, giving them the whole campaign package. White teeth glistened like Ajaxed porcelain; thick, dark-brown, blow-dried hair helmeted a face highlighted by sky-blue eyes that projected warmth and intelligence. Barring a disaster, such as being exposed as the one who had approved funding for an illegal, covert bio-weapons program, he would one day make it to the Oval Office. He was carrying a heavy folder, and now sat behind the working desk near the observatory window, motioning them to the two chairs opposite him.

"Admiral, since Fort Detrick is your command, let's start with you. What the fuck is going on?" Buck Burger began.

"What exactly do you want to know, sir?"

"The President is concerned that we are engaging in illegal bio-research. He wants to know 'yes' or 'no.' "

"Absolutely not, sir."

"Glad to hear it. Very reassuring, but I need more. Your word won't be enough this time, Admiral."

"How about General Stallings's word? As head of the Joint Chiefs, the General would never let our program engage in a criminal endeavor," Zoll said. "Offensive bio-research has been illegal since Nixon signed the Geneva Protocol on Nonproliferation in '72. We are certainly not going to disobey a Presidential mandate, right, Colin?''

Colin Stallings nodded his big gray head. He was a remarkably fit sixty-eight-year-old who had had a brilliant career and was set to retire in six months.

"Here's the problem, James," Burger continued. "This is already a media fire dance. So far, on the negative side, we have Dr. Dexter DeMille, who was assigned to USAMRIID under your command, and who, you yesterday told the media, may have been suicidal and was probably nuts. Yet he was still, somehow, able to use your facility to work on illegal bio-weapons without your knowledge or permission. Second, he has mysteriously disappeared. Maybe he's dead, maybe not. Nobody knows. Next, we've got this town in Texas where lots of innocent citizens got horribly incinerated. We also just told the press some unknown sickness may be loose up there. No real reason given, except DeMille went berserk, set the bug loose, then burned the place. We have fifteen dead military troops, also under your command, stationed at Vanishing Lake, Texas—a facility, I might add, that isn't even listed on the government books. The prison, it now appears, was rented to the Science Department at Sam Houston University, but was being used by USAMRIID for defense bio-research. Making matters worse, some of these dead soldiers have been burned beyond recognition. Their remains are so charred there is almost nothing left to ship home. On the positive side, we have your assurance that nothing is out of order. I think you'll agree this scale is horribly out of balance. The President is getting swamped with calls from families of dead soldiers and civilians, and from some front-bench players in government, including Congress. The press is sharking every detail, and the President has very little to tell them except 'Don't worry,' 'Trust me,' and 'I'm looking into it.' This is not a good situation for the Commander in Chief of the Free World.''

Zoll replied with practiced sincerity, "I wish I could change it, but unfortunately it is what it is."

"Not the answer I'm looking for, Admiral." The meeting, and the vibes in the room, had become ice cold.

"I wish I had Dr. DeMille on hand, so we could debrief him and find out exactly what really happened up there. But until we locate either him or his remains, I don't know what else I—"

"This sounds like you guys have been freelancing again," Vice President Burger interrupted. "What is it, two, three times you've violated that treaty since '72? Not counting the times you didn't get caught."

"Buck, you know that I was as shocked by those transgressions as you or anybody else on the Hill. The fact is that the CIA was running a parallel program at the Fort. Congress accepted that explanation, and several Agency S.A.C.s lost their jobs and pensions over it."

"I'm not going to rerun that disaster, okay? The fact remains that it *did* happen, and that causes our Defense Oversight people to be goddamn suspicious of this thing that's goin' on now."

"Of course, Congress needs to be vigilant, but—"

"Come on, your history here is piss-poor! Y'get caught running a bunch of illegal aerobiological tests over San Francisco and Minneapolis, let shit loose in the subways of New York, kill people with yellow fever in the Florida panhandle testing mosquitoes," Burger lectured, rerunning the disasters from the mid-eighties, after promising not to. "The Congress and the press aren't gonna accept some promise of innocence, or your lame excuses." Buck Burger was getting worked up; his genial blue eyes had turned glacial.

"General Stallings and I are giving you our assurance that everything is as it should be."

"Fuck assurance, I want *evidence*. We had assurances last time. This is now a big media deal. *60 Minutes* has their nose up the crack of your ass, Admiral, and you two are standing on the end of the plank. Only way you get back in the boat is to come completely clean. If I have to push you two jugheads overboard, then that's what's gonna happen. The President is not going to be embarrassed *again*. You fuck up here, and you both are going to experience firsthand the meaning of the words 'political sacrifice.' "

"Mr. Vice President, you tell us what you want, and that's what we'll do."

"The President has instructed me to initiate an independent investigation. The Subcommittee on Bio-Defense is gonna conduct it. That's Senator Osheroff and Senator Metzger. They're gonna want full access to the facility at Fort Detrick, and to the records of the U.S. Army Medical Research Institute of Infectious Diseases."

"When?" Admiral Zoll asked. Ugly silence polluted the room, their collective thoughts dark and ominous as an oil spill. Zoll wondered if they had been called in here to be disciplined or to be warned.

"How long do you need," the Vice President finally said, "to get ready to receive the Committee Investigators?"

"Two days," Zoll answered.

"Okay, then I'll wait to call for the investigation until tomorrow. I'm sure everything will turn out to be fine, and they won't find anything, but we're gonna have to give this a complete once-over."

"Yes, sir," Admiral Zoll said. "I think it's always better to be vigilant and thorough."

"Best to Sally and Beth. Don't fuck this up, guys."

Without saying another word, the Vice President got up and left the office.

Admiral Zoll and General Stallings waited until he was gone, then moved out of the room. They said nothing until they were back in the staff car, heading off the property.

"I assume you'll need the White Train," General Stallings said.

"Yes, sir, but there's a lotta bio-active shit to get rid of. Some of it is toxic and unstable. You gotta find a place we can put it."

"I'll get the Train down to you tomorrow. Sweep the area carefully," the General ordered. "I'll find a secure dump site where we can lose everything without paperwork."

"Hell of a way to start the week," Zoll muttered.

Chapter 32

STEAM TRAIN JACK

They were forced to stay on Highway 16 out of the Black Hills. The two-lane road wound back and forth, meandering like a coiling rope down the fire-ravaged slope, heading west toward Howlings Junction. The denuded landscape and blackened tree trunks were monuments to a night of insanity. They had to double back to catch the four-lane highway toward Fort Worth. The Southern Pacific tracks that they suspected Fannon Kincaid was still traveling on followed a much more direct route. Those tracks were on the east side of the mountains, following a gradual slope that allowed the freight to attain speeds of over fifty miles an hour all the way to Fort Worth.

They arrived at the main SP switching yard just after nine in the morning. Stacy parked next to a split-rail fence and turned off the engine. They looked out the front window at acres of track and parked freight cars.

"What now?" she said.

"We gotta find what time that unit train got here, then find out what trains have left this yard since then, or the trains scheduled to leave later today. Then we need to check the Sugar Shack.''

"Sugar what?" Buddy asked. He had been sleeping in the front seat, and was trying to come awake. He felt sluggish and dull.

"It's a jungle, a hobo camp down by the river. I wanta see if I know anyone there, ask around about Kincaid. Somebody might have seen him.'' Cris pushed on the seat, forcing Buddy to get out, so he could exit the back of the Blazer. The Texas heat fell on their faces and shoulders like exhaust from a factory furnace. The relentless morning sun was softening the asphalt, and rippling their view of the distant shopping center. It was only shortly past nine, and already near a hundred degrees. Cris knew the temperature would soon soar to 115.

"So these train-yard jerkoffs who run the switching operation are just gonna tell you what's coming in and going out?'' Buddy said doubtfully.

"They won't tell me anything, so I won't bother asking.''

"If they won't talk, then you won't get dick.''

"This information is guarded, but not protected.''

"You sound just like a fucking agent,'' Buddy said, getting irate, rubbing his eyes and wishing he had slept better.

"Be right back,'' Cris said, and moved away, heading across the tracks, staying in between cars, moving toward the spot where he remembered the Southern Pacific Yardmaster's office was located. He'd only been in this place once before, and back then he'd been drunk and still suffering the aftereffects of the great tennis shoe robbery. Now, as he moved along, he could feel a terrible weakness in his legs, and it startled him. Then he realized that although he had stopped drinking, his appetite had not come back. He'd had no calories in almost twenty-four hours.

The Yardmaster's office was in a three-story tower at the east end of the switching yard. The observation windows overlooked the tracks and most of the railroad cars parked on the several acres of sidings. Cris skirted a line of parked grainers and then moved down between two rows of stack cars. Crouching on trembling thighs, he inched along, staying out of sight of the high, green-tinted windows until he got opposite the tower. He hoped that the three or four people in the office would be looking back the other way, at the incoming tracks. If the Trainmaster spotted him, he'd be arrested and questioned by the yard bulls.

Cris had been taught the art of carbon-sheet-spotting by an old-time hobo with the unlikely name of Begone John. *"These dufuses get their train line-ups and consist sheets delivered in sealed, locked pouches,"* John had once told him, grinning, his brown teeth and stringy pencil-neck belying a soul as crafty as an Arab merchant's. *"Everything has five copies, but with downsizing, a lot of these carbon copies are no longer necessary. The stupid pricks just throw the extra sheets in the trash. If ya know what trains are leaving and where the sleepers are, then ya don't have ta wait on the grade with forty other drunk assholes while the sun's fryin' yer brains. Ya just show up at the appointed hour and catch out on the exact right car."*

Cris snuck around to the windowless back of the Yardmaster's tower, where he found the trash cans. Three fifty-gallon oil drums were pushed up against the yellow-painted wood building. An aerial circus of black horseflies the size of gypsy moths, strafed the top of the oil drums, competing for airspace in the fetid containers.

Cris waved his hands over the can to flush away the angry flies, then began to gingerly pick through the refuse.

He quickly found one of yesterday's train line-up carbons on top. He began to gather up the three-page report, careful not to smudge the sheets as he folded them into an old newspaper he also found in the trash. After some more digging, farther down in the second drum he found the consist sheets. Cris included them in his newspaper package and made his way back to the Blazer, where Buddy and Stacy were waiting.

"Let's go over there," he said, pointing to a small park across the street. They walked to the nearest shaded picnic table, then Cris unfolded the newspaper and began to sort the track line-up carbons from the consist sheets.

"What the hell's all that?" Buddy asked, looking at the sheets.

"Each day, the Trainmaster gets a train line-up, which lists all the trains scheduled to come through the yard in that twenty-four-hour period. That's these sheets up here. He also gets 'consist' sheets, detailing what cars are on each train, and what cars need to be switched in his yard, or held for transfer to other trains. There are always five copies of everything: one for the Yardmaster, one for the Trainmaster, and one for the Engine Foreman; the extra copies are for us." He smiled, and finished spreading them out on the picnic table. First he studied the train line-up and thinned out the choices. He began by eliminating the "locals," trains that made multiple stops.

"A seasoned hobo will rarely ride a local," he explained. "All the stops increase his chances of getting busted by some nosy cinder bull. Plus, locals are slow, and often have to 'go in the hole' to let a 'priority train' pass. You can bet Kincaid and his band of thugs won't be on a local."

Finally, Cris ended up with three sheets: one for manifest trains, with many different types of cars and products, all headed to the same destination; one for unit trains carrying just one type of cargo; and one for passenger trains. He spread them out and started studying them.

"Okay, according to the slip we found in the bottom of the boat, the next place they said they would go is Grandview, on the Kansas City Southern Line. Grandview is up in Colorado, just across the Continental Divide. So if Buddy is right and this slip we found is bullshit, then we got three choices. Either they took this grain unit train to Sheriland, Louisiana, or they went south on this eight-o'clock manifest train to New Orleans. It left forty minutes after the train they arrived on hit the yard. They woulda just had time to catch it.... The third choice is this 'varnish' leaving for Portsmouth, at six P.M., in which case maybe they're still here.''

"This what?" Stacy asked.

"Varnish. It's an old-time rail term for a passenger train. But for Kincaid, riding varnish is both good and bad. It's good because it's fast and won't get sided, but it's hard to catch out on a passenger train. They don't pull many cars, so they don't slow much on a grade. They're also damned uncomfortable. You have to ride the 'blind'—that's a flexible piece of metal between the coaches, on either side of the coupling unit. Since there are almost forty men and women with Kincaid, I doubt they'll be 'blinding.' " He hesitated for a minute as a wave of nausea hit him, followed by such trembling weakness in his arms and legs that he had to sit down. "I need something to eat," he finally said. "I feel shitty."

"I saw a McDonald's on the way into town," Stacy said.

"Jesus, a McDonald's?" Buddy grumbled, "Let's just skip eating and go right to the Maalox."

"Gee, Buddy, I'm so sorry. Why don't ya gimme your cellphone and I'll make us reservations at Spago," Stacy cracked.

The air conditioner was broken, so they sat outside McDonald's on the deck under the colorful umbrellas. While sweat collected under their arms and ran in rivulets from their hairlines, they started breakfast.

Cris took two bites of his Chicken McNugget, excused himself, then went into the men's room and threw up. "Shit," he said to himself as he splashed water on his face and looked up at his scary reflection in the mirror. His eyes seemed to have receded deeper into his face. His cheekbones jutted. Then his stomach rolled, churned, and erupted. He spewed a mouthful of bile into the sink that was the color and consistency of 3-In-One Oil. "Fuck," he whispered softly. He gulped two handfuls of tap water, then returned to the table.

.   .   .

Sugar Shack Jungle was all the way down by the tributary that fed Eagle Lake on the northwest side of Fort Worth. The jungle was nestled into the elbow of the river and took up over three acres. It was out of sight of but near the SP track heading out of Fort Worth. Nearby was a two-mile stretch of track that had a two-percent grade and slowed most hundred-car freights to less than five miles an hour, making them easy to hop. Sugar Shack Jungle contained hundreds of hobos squatting in every imaginable kind of dwelling. It was the final parking place for half a dozen rusting cars that now served as upscale housing for the families that owned them. A graveyard of old tires and oil drums performed every imaginable task, from tire-swings for children to fire-pits and structural supports. The ''houses,'' like the residents who lived there, were the unwanted refuse of a steel-and-glass world that had no further use for them. Old wood cartons and scrounged or stolen lumber made up house sidings; corrugated tin created patches of shade; old, sagging chairs and three-legged tables leaned precariously on makeshift supports like wounded veterans. What really defined the place was the eyes of the people. As Cris led Stacy and Buddy into the camp, the eyes of the inhabitants tracked them like enemy radar . . . eyes vacant of emotion, like licked stones or holes bored in an empty box.

''I feel like the last piece of cake at a Weight Watchers party,'' Stacy said softly, as they stood on the edge of the camp and felt the silent, angry appraisals.

''Grab a seat over there,'' Cris said. ''Don't look at anyone directly, or lock eyes. Just watch the river.'' He left them and moved across the jungle, walking slowly, looking at the makeshift houses. He didn't belong here anymore, and the unfriendly stares were like silent curses, unmistakable in their hostility. Had Cris entered this camp a few weeks ago as Lucky, a long-haired, dirty man with garbage-bagged feet, he would not have merited a second glance. In his expensive loafers, new clothes, and recent dental work, he was now a class enemy, a representative of a world that first mandated their failure and then engineered their exile.

He had just about decided his quest was hopeless when he saw the old hobo poet Steam Train Jack. He was flat on his back near the river, looking like a pile of discarded clothes from the Goodwill. His snow-white beard and huge girth made him hard to mistake. He had an old, river-soaked neckerchief across his forehead cooling his eyes. Cris moved over and sat near him. He could tell the old man knew he was there, but Jack didn't move or take the kerchief off his face.

" 'I was walkin' down the street with my bundle on my back/When I saw a 'bo I used ta know/His name was Steam Train Jack,' " Cris recited. The poem had been written by the old man beside him.

Steam Train didn't move, didn't twitch. He just lay there. "Since I wrote that damn poem/I sure as hell should know him," Jack finally said. He took the damp cloth off his eyes and looked over at Cris. Then he propped up his enormous girth on one elbow and looked a second time.

Recollection dawned. "Lucky?" Steam Train asked, as he sat straight up, but in so doing, he gained only a couple more feet of altitude. Steam Train was oddly proportioned, with short legs and torso but unusually long arms. He had simian dimensions. "Lucky! Shit, that is you, ain't it? What happened, man? This can't be true/I can't believe it's really you/Yer lookin' thin as jungle pot stew," he rhymed.

"It's a long story," Lucky said.

Then Steam Train reached out and pounded Cris on the shoulder. "From the look of them tails/You ain't on the rails?"

"I'm retired from high-iron drifting. Stopped drinkin' too," he added, and watched Steam Train smile his approval.

Steam Train Jack was what they called a boxcar barnacle. He was a legend on the rails. He'd been riding boxcars since the early forties, and he almost never uttered a sentence that wasn't in rhyme.

Steam Train strained to pull his prodigious girth up to his feet. "Shit," he said, groaning. "Harder and harder ta git up an' go/ Got more pains than a stained-glass window." Standing, he was only slightly taller than sitting. He weighed over 250 pounds, and seemed a gravelly-voiced cross between Jabba the Hut and Santa Claus. He mopped his red face with the damp cloth. "So, if y'stopped ridin' trains and y'don't drink no more/What brings ya here ta my jungle door?"

"I'm looking for Fannon Kincaid. I was wondering if anybody's seen him and his F.T.R.A. bunch around. I know he was headed this way. I need to find out which train he caught out on."

Steam Train shook his head. "He's a Texas tomcat with an ass fulla buckshot. Kincaid's the devil, let him be, son/He'll kill in a heartbeat, without no reason."

"I don't care about his reason. 'Cause vengeance is my reason. It's my reason and my higher power," he said, more to himself than to the old man standing before him. Steam Train looked off toward the river where Buddy and Stacy were sitting, trying hard not to engage the cold-eyed stares around them.

"You wait over there, I'll go ask about/I heard he was around/ But he mighta catched out." Steam Train moved off, waddling on sore feet, then began to talk to people who were seated in leaning chairs in front of makeshift houses.

When Cris got over to Buddy, the producer was fidgeting. "Who the hell is that?" Buddy said. "Looks like a character from a Spielberg movie."

"It's a break he was here. If anybody in this jungle knows anything, Steam Train Jack will find out for us."

They sat by the river and watched undernourished children playing in the water.

Stacy looked at the camp in wonder. "This is amazing. I never knew something like this existed. It's like pictures I saw of Hoovervilles in the thirties. Why are they here?''

"These people are rejects.''

"You weren't a reject,'' she said, looking at him carefully.

"No,'' Cris said softly. "I was running from myself.''

After twenty minutes, Steam Train moved back to them. He must have returned to his shanty, because now he had a walking stick, a long piece of polished oak with a knotted handle. He hobbled down to the river and motioned to Cris, who left Stacy and Buddy and joined him.

"On the two-mile grade/Three hours ago/They left on the NETT/On a Burlington, MO.''

"The Northeastern Tennessee Track, Burlington MoPac Unit?'' Cris said. "That's New Orleans.''

Steam Train nodded. "Three 'bos I know were ridin' that hop/When they saw Kincaid/They decided to drop.'' He raised an eyebrow in concern, and it arched there like a huge furry caterpillar.

"Thanks, Steam Train,'' Cris said. "I'll be careful.''

The old man's face scrunched in thought for a moment, then he spun an old rhyme: "Mosta my pals caught the westbound freight, to the land beyond the sun/God had a time on His consist sheet for each and ever one/Heaven's great and fulla 'bos, for that ya can be sure/But it don't make sense ta push up front fer an' early departure.''

Steam Train hugged Cris, stepped back, turned, and poking the ground with his gnarled stick, limped slowly away.

Part Four

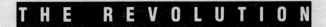

THE REVOLUTION

Chapter 33

ILL-GOTTEN GAINS AND THE TEXAS
MADMAN

They had been sided at Shreveport, Louisiana, to let a "hot-shot" intermodal train go by. The muggy air clung to them like foul cologne. Luther "Ill Gotten" Gains and the Texas Madman sat with Randall Rader and Dexter DeMille, watching Reverend Kincaid. The empty wood-slat boxcar was buried in the middle of the parked unit train, which contained a hundred grainers filled with Kansas wheat. They had been sided for almost an hour. "Milk is transported all across this nation on the rails," Fannon reasoned as he paced. "Moves in big refrigerated tankers ever day. So we're gonna send retribution to the Niggers and Jews in the milk they buy at the store."

"It's not gonna be that easy," Dexter answered, his voice strained and weak in the still air of the boxcar. "I'm trying to tell you that the Prion in this form is basically harmless—it hasn't been genetically tuned. This is simply a baseline protein. In order to turn what we have into a genetic binary weapon you'd need to change all the pH factors. The process is called acidosis. It's . . . it's very complicated and specific work."

Now Fannon kneeled beside Dexter and studied him like a crushed bug on the sidewalk. Dexter knew in that instant that he was nothing to Fannon Kincaid; that exactly like Admiral Zoll, Kincaid would kill him as soon as he got what he wanted. He needed to call on all of his survival instincts to buy time.

"Mr. DeMille, we are *going* to deliver this victory for Yahweh," Fannon said. "We are *going* to purge two cities of the counterfeit races. This will start the Revolution. People who know the truth, but have been afraid to act, will see this victory and take heart. Many will join the cause. You think this great victory can be delayed by some pissant piece of shit like you?" When Dexter didn't respond, Fannon screamed, "Answer me, you godless motherfucker!"

"No, sir. No . . ." Dexter flinched. He was now pressed hard against the side of the boxcar, straining to get away from Kincaid.

Luther Gains watched his discomfort with sadistic interest. Gains was rail-thin, snake-mean, and had a personality as twisted and coarse as hemp rope. After breaking out of a federal prison in Fayetteville, where he had been incarcerated for murder, Luther had started hiding out with the Choir.

The Texas Madman was an absolute contrast to Luther. Heavyset and soft, the Texas Madman spoke in a high-pitched whisper, never raising his voice above a breathy squeak. He was out of shape and overweight, a grotesque collection of bulges and curves. He had earned his moniker by brutally killing six sleeping hobos in one blood-soaked year, and he gloried in these fatal assaults. His eyes lost reason and focus as he hacked his victims to death with the short-handled ax he kept in his backpack. After "converting" to the Choir, he had become Fannon's chief executioner.

" 'Complicated and specific work.' You must really think I'm one gullible, outta-touch motherfucker," Fannon hissed, showing tobacco-stained teeth.

"It . . . I . . ." Then Dexter fell silent.

Fannon turned to the Texas Madman. "Kill this godless motherfucker.'' Then Fannon got up, went to the ladder, and started to climb to the roof, where he would ''car surf'' to the grainer behind and join the others.

The Texas Madman picked up his backpack and retrieved the ax, then he moved over to Dexter. Fannon opened the hatch and started to climb out to the top of the boxcar.

''No . . . no . . . please,'' Dexter said, looking into the soft face and soulless eyes of the Texas Madman.

''Talk t'me, brother,'' Fannon said from the top step of the ladder.

''I need a lab. I need pH meters, and the right acids and bases. I need pure blood samples from the target groups, African-Americans and Jews, so I can do the DNA stranding.''

''If I get what you need, how long will it take to make this shit right?''

''Coupla hours, maybe less.''

Fannon slid down the metal ladder, his combat boots hitting the wood floor, cracking the silence like a leather bullwhip. He moved back to Dexter and looked down at him. ''We can find a blood bank, steal whatever we need.''

''Blood banks don't keep those kinds of records. Government regulations prevent separating blood along ethnic or racial lines.''

''This fuckin' society. Whatta buncha bullshit. So, how do we do it?''

''There's only one lab that has everything I need, but it won't be easy.''

''It wasn't easy for Moses to get the stone tablets down from Mount Sinai, or to part the Red Sea. God's work ain't supposed t'be easy. God's will is dangerous to pursue. Where the hell's this lab?''

''At the Devil's Workshop in Fort Detrick, Maryland.''

Chapter 34

IMPORTANT TRAIN

We need a priority train," Cris said to Buddy. He was seated on the bed in the suite Buddy had rented at the Fort Worth Four Seasons Hotel, and was looking at the train line-up. The shower was on in the bathroom, and they could hear Stacy's splashing through the closed door.

"You got anything cooking with her?" Buddy asked unexpectedly.

"Give it a rest. Her husband just died."

"Sometimes you can catch a good bounce after a personal tragedy." Cris looked up at him in dismay, but the look seemed to please Buddy. The old outlaw was back, the "do anything/fuck everybody" Buddy.

"Leave her alone. She needs time."

Buddy started to answer, but the sound of the water cutting off stopped the conversation.

The bathroom door opened and Stacy walked into the suite. Her hair was wet, and she had on a big terry-cloth bathrobe belted at the waist, a hotel towel around her neck.

"God, that feels better," she said. "Who's next?"

There was a long silence, and then Buddy got up and headed into the bathroom. "Boy, it smells like girl in here, sweet and sexy," he grinned, then closed the door.

Stacy moved into the room and looked down on the bed at a map of Texas and Louisiana, and the carbons that Cris had fished out of the trash at the SP switching yard.

"You find what you were looking for?"

"Yeah, there's a unit train leaving at ten tonight. It's a priority train, full of expensive products, mostly Japanese cars. It should travel twice as fast as the grain train Kincaid's on."

"Why is that?"

"Important trains carry what they call 'Time Sensitive Freight.' All the cars on this train are worth millions. The interest on all that money means they have to get to market fast. That grain train Kincaid is on will have to 'go into the hole' to let a hotshot train like this pass. It'll slow him way down, and with some luck, we'll overtake him."

She sat down on the bed and started to dry her hair with the towel she had around her neck. "Why don't we just take the car?"

"Lotta reasons. First, we're not sure he's going all the way to New Orleans." He pointed to the map. "It's possible that Kincaid will switch trains in Dallas or Shreveport or Jackson. At any of those hubs he could change destinations—we'd be going to New Orleans, while he'd be heading off someplace else. I'm gonna have to get off and ask around at each of those hubs. Also, the rails are at least as fast, especially if we can catch this hot train at ten tonight."

She nodded, stood, and moved around the room, ending at the picture window. "It was nice of Buddy to get this room. It's beautiful." Cris nodded, but didn't say anything. He was starting to think that having Buddy along was a bad mistake.

The suite was a large corner room that overlooked a shopping center. The subtle colors and rich antiques were restful. The air-conditioning hissed perfect temperature.

She moved over and sat on the bed near Cris. "You don't look so good."

"Knock it off with the compliments—you're making me blush."

"You've lost even more weight since we met."

He dropped his head, and his eyes found the maps and carbon sheets on the bedspread.

"Cris, we need you. The three of us are in this alone, and the people at Fort Detrick have too much power. Plus, the Pentagon and God knows who else is involved. Conceivably, it could go all the way up to the President. They couldn't run a program this big without a lot of important people in the loop. We call the FBI, we could get locked up instead of listened to."

"I'm okay," he said. "I'll make it."

"You gotta eat. I'm ordering from room service. I'll get you some soup, maybe some oatmeal or yogurt."

"Okay," he smiled, "but I think I'll skip the yogurt."

"There's two showers in there. Go on, get washed up, and I'll get something up here for you."

He nodded, and got slowly off the bed. He had to admit he was getting weaker by the hour. He opened the bathroom door.

Buddy Brazil was naked and wrapped in a towel, standing by the sink with a rolled bill jammed up his nose. Two lines of chopped cocaine were tracked out on the tile counter. Buddy snapped his head up and grinned. "Oops," he said. "Kick that door closed, will ya? I've gotta Hoover up these two lines."

Anger flashed in Cris. He suddenly reached down and grabbed Buddy, spun him around, and threw him out of the bathroom into the suite. The towel fell off and he hit the floor naked, with the bill still up his nose. Buddy yanked the quilt off the bed and covered himself, then snatched the rolled-up bill out of his nose, as Stacy stood over him.

"This asshole was in there taking a sleigh ride," Cris said, adrenaline fueling his aching body.

"This is bullshit," Buddy shrieked, pulling the quilt all the way off the bed and wrapping it around him. The maps and carbon sheets fluttered to the floor.

"What other drugs have you got in there?" Cris demanded, as he moved into the bathroom and grabbed Buddy's shaving kit.

Buddy quickly moved after him, dragging the large quilt like a bridal train. Cris grabbed five or six prescription bottles out of his shaving kit and held them up to read the labels as Stacy joined Buddy at the door.

"It's for my asthma," Buddy chirped.

" 'Take one every four hours for depression,' " Cris said, reading the labels. "Morphine sulfate, Dexedrine, Clonidine. All of it prescribed by the poor asshole you shot in your backyard." He threw the bottles at Buddy. They hit him in the chest, then bounced on the floor.

"Look, I got medical problems."

"We all got problems. I'm vomiting up my breakfast 'cause my system's so shot I can't hold anything down. This is a joke. We're running a fucking clinic here. How're we ever gonna pull this off?"

"Please," Stacy said. "Please, let's stop shouting."

Cris moved out of the bathroom and sat on the edge of the bed, while Buddy slid into his pants and got down on the floor to gather up the vials of prescribed drugs.

"Flush them down the toilet," Stacy said.

"These are prescriptions," he whined. "I need these." Then, as he stood with the plastic bottles in his hand, he saw the disappointment in her eyes.

"I'm outta here. I'm goin' home." Buddy took the pills, threw them back into his shaving kit, and zipped it up. Then he packed up his stuff, dressed, and turned to leave.

"You can't leave. We need your help," Stacy pleaded. "They killed your son."

"I hardly knew him. The room's paid for until tomorrow." Then Buddy walked out, slammed the door, and left them standing there.

Chapter 35

POSSE

Buddy had left more out of embarrassment than anger. Now, as he sat in the Blazer under the porte-cochere of the Four Seasons with the engine idling, he was stuck for his next move. The sour-sweet taste was there again, filling the back of his mouth like sewer runoff; he was staggered by an unfathomable sense of loneliness so vast and full of self-hate that it pressed against him like a fateful warning.

His accumulated list of personal negatives was mind-boggling. He was a coward and a drug addict. He had no commitment to himself or to his craft. He had not one single relationship in his life that he valued or cared to maintain. All of his "intimate" associations were bought and paid for, professional friends who circled him like airliners stacked above a foggy field, waiting for his instructions, not one of them willing to give him a moment of unselfish concern. Buddy knew that it was his fault. He had constructed a world that was only about him. Buddy suspected that the hateful truth was that to gain respect, it was also necessary to give it. If he continued to focus everything inward, he would be nourished by nothing. Now, as the Blazer's engine idled, he had no place to go. He could not pick a new course of action. He only knew that he was through hiding; if he did not choose the right path, he would sacrifice what was left of himself.

He began grasping for solutions. Maybe he should call the Pelican, he thought.

Anthony Pelicano had been on his payroll on and off for almost fifteen years. The L.A. private eye had managed to get several actors and directors out of tight spots and drug busts while they were working on Buddy's pictures. Pelicano flushed more Hollywood toilets than the Polo Lounge bathroom attendant. Buddy had first employed the detective during his divorce. The Pelican had managed to turn up Tova's one lesbian affair, which Buddy hung over her like a sword of damnation during the property settlement negotiations. Pelicano would know what to do.

Buddy was startled by a tapping at his passenger window. He snapped his head around and saw a doorman in a high-collared braided coat, faintly reminiscent of his old Scientology uniform.

"Would you like me to park your car again for you, sir?" the attendant asked, smiling professionally.

Buddy shook his head and put the car in gear, pulling out from under the heavy stone awning into the shimmering Texas heat.

"I don't give a fuck what his office told you. Tell him it's critical I speak to him," Buddy screamed at Alicia Profit, who had just informed him, after ten minutes on hold, that the Pelican was in New Mexico getting one of Dick Zanuck's stars unhooked from a mescaline bust.

"They said he'll call you back," Alicia repeated, holding her ground like a Prussian general.

He could picture his beautiful assistant in his palatial Paramount office, standing behind his Ping-Pong-table-sized executive desk, flipping her black hair in stylish exasperation as he screamed at her over the speakerphone. He had spent more than one hapless night trying to talk her into the sack, but she had eluded him like an NFL running back, always leaving with both her honor and his grudging respect. Still, Buddy screamed at her endlessly.

"Is Rayce around?"

"Yes. He's in with Marty."

"Get him on the phone," Buddy snapped.

Then he was on hold again, listening to a recorded selection of his movie themes. After a moment he heard Rayce Walker; it was a comfortable, upholstered voice, soft and deep, like expensive furniture.

"How's it goin', pard?" the stuntman said in his Arizona–New Mexico drawl.

"Rayce, I need your help," Buddy answered. "I'm sending the G-III to get you. Get four or five guys who can handle themselves . . . like Billy Seal, and that crazy fucking Indian we used on *Sheriff of Apache Canyon,* Little Boy, whatever—the one who drove the burning pickup into the lake."

"John Little Bear," Rayce corrected.

"Right. And go to the Malibu house and collect up some firepower outta my gun case. I have the Dominator and the two pistols from the plane with me now. Get your ass to Fort Worth. I need you fast," he said.

"What's up, Mr. B.?"

"We gotta go kick some ass," Buddy said, trying to sound macho, but feeling weak and foolish. "Also tell Alicia I need her to come with you to handle details. Tell her to call Rob at the business manager's, and clear all my credit cards. Also tell her that I want her to line me up a motor home I can rent in Fort Worth—bill the studio location scouting account. Make it at least thirty-seven feet long, roomy, with a big engine. We're gonna be traveling. I'll need cellphones and booze. Bring some white lady and a bag or two of grass. I'm down to seeds and stems."

"Yes, sir," Rayce said. "What's going on?"

Buddy didn't answer, just hung up. He'd been driving aimlessly down a Fort Worth street with no destination. Now he pulled the Blazer over and parked it by the side of the road. His hands were shaking and he needed something. At first he thought it was a zoot of cocaine, a pick-me-up that would blur the edges and lift his spirits, but as he reached for the shaving kit, he stopped. He realized it wasn't dope he wanted. What was it? It wasn't something he *had;* it was something he was missing. A new craving much harder to recognize. His mind ran down a list of physical needs, but he could check none of the mental boxes. And then, like a TV uplink that finally locked on the right satellite, the picture became clear.

As Buddy Brazil sat in the heat of his rented Blazer on the side of a road in Fort Worth, he realized what he craved more than anything else was his own self-respect.

Chapter 36

HOT TRAIN

Max was a hero," Stacy said. "He went to Fort Detrick and found out about all this, and he tried to stop it. It's exactly the kind of thing he would do. He would risk everything, even his life, if he saw injustice or deceit. It's why they killed him." She whispered these words as if in church, kneeling in the gravel beside the SP tracks, bathed in moonlight.

They were a quarter mile east of Sugar Shack Jungle waiting for the ten-P.M. priority train carrying automobiles, which Cris had found on the Yardmaster's line-up sheet. The night was warm, and a few hundred yards up the grade they could see a cluster of hobos crouched below the tracks, also waiting to catch out, their voices rattling on the wind like water-churned rocks.

"Sometimes I think I'm going crazy, I miss him so much," she added.

Cris nodded his head. Her memories of Max brought back his own thoughts of Kennidi. He could feel his daughter's remembered warmth touching him, her child's breath on his cheek, her arm around his shoulder as she nuzzled up against him. The memory of her painful death couldn't destroy these tearful recollections.

"The thing about Max was he just seemed to understand. He could read your thoughts like a Gypsy. He would always know what frightened you, and then would find a way to help."

Cris looked over at her, struck by both her strength and beauty. The subtle moonlight lay in the shallows of her cheekbones, like pools of liquid silver, as she looked down the track for the freight.

After hearing Stacy describe her husband, Cris wondered why Max Richardson would work at Fort Detrick with such evil company. It didn't add up. "Why did Max go to study with Dexter DeMille?" he finally asked.

"Max had become extremely worried about Prions," she answered. "He told me that he felt they represented one of the most dangerous and potentially deadly situations in the global environment. He felt outbreaks like mad cow disease could be just the beginning. Mad cow was badly mishandled by the Brits in the early eighties. They didn't believe it would jump the species line, but it did, infecting sheep and cattle. The Brits have now identified over ten cases of human infestation, proving that Prions can also jump to *Homo sapiens*. These human cases of mad cow disease behave just like the Aboriginal Kuru that Dexter DeMille helped Carleton Gajdusek isolate in the seventies. Kuru was caused by a bizarre religious custom the Abos had of eating the brains of their dead relatives, so with both Kuru and mad cow, ingesting the rogue Prion is what passed it on. Max thought science was not equipped to deal with Prion sickness if it got out of control. Right now, in its pure state, it's slow-acting. We haven't seen too many human cases, but Max felt there could soon be a wave of human disease caused by infected beef. This was why Max wanted to work with Dr. DeMille—to find a cure and to understand how it spreads, and how long it incubates in humans before signs of the early stage of the disease show up, marked by mood swings and rages."

Cris was watching her closely, and she seemed to be kneeling at the altar of science.

"The problem in England was exacerbated because the government didn't fully subsidize the farms. If a farmer discovered a downer cow that he suspected had died of mad cow, the government only paid a tenth of the value of the carcass. Max said the result was that the farmer wouldn't report a diseased cow, but would sell the carcass to a feed company for full price without warning the chopping house of the cause of death. The feed company would grind it up and turn it into bonemeal and it would be used as food for other cattle. The Prions would survive in the bonemeal and would be passed to whole herds. Max was also studying the ease with which it jumped the species line. Wendell and Max ran a lab study last year and found that even vegetables fertilized with infected bonemeal carry the rogue Prion. Those vegetables could conceivably pass it to people if ingested. Not to be ultradramatic, but a case could be made that unchecked Prion disease could poison the whole earth, killing all mammalian species on the planet."

They were silent for a long moment.

"Max died trying to stop this," she went on. "We've got to get the Pale Horse Prion away from Kincaid before he further pollutes the bio-stream. The weapon that DeMille designed seems to run its course in hours, not years. That means DeMille and his team at the Devil's Workshop have juiced it up somehow. At Vanishing Lake it acted very quickly. A bio-weapon with a two-year lag time would be worthless. I know this sounds over-the-top, but if Kincaid tries to use these targeted Prions against large segments of society, he could perpetrate an event that would substantially alter the evolutionary process of mankind. If people with specific genes were eliminated, survivors who were not killed outright might share linked but weakened genes. In fifty years, who knows what downstream effect this could have on human development? We've got to prove that those bastards at the Devil's Workshop are actually developing this shit, and if we're going to get anybody's attention, we need a sample so we can choke Admiral Zoll on the evidence.''

When she finished, Cris was again swept by a sense of his own inadequacy. "Stacy, I'm not sure I have what it takes. I'm not a hundred percent. Things have changed for me. I'm not like I used to be. I'm just not sure I can do it.''

She looked at him, and wished Max were here. Max would take the challenge no matter the outcome. The ex-Marine kneeling beside her was no substitute for her dead husband, but with Buddy gone he was all she had. She couldn't let him quit. She finally reached out, took his hand, and squeezed it. "I know," she said softly. "I feel the same way, but we have to try. Too much is at stake.''

"I'm still shaky," he confided. "And I still crave alcohol. Sometimes it's all I can think about. I'm not sure I can even stay sober. Buddy took the guns, and we're outnumbered thirty or forty to one. We need a plan, and I haven't a clue. . . .''

When she looked over at him, for the first time she could see the Marine in the picture behind his father's bar. Cris's youthful intensity burned in blue eyes that reflected moonlight. Then, just as quickly as the vision materialized, it was gone.

Suddenly, a light appeared against a line of trees in the distance. Then the wide yellow-and-red nose of a five-thousand-horsepower MK5 engine came around the curve 150 yards away. The headlights now turned toward them and zigzagged figure eights across the rails as it rumbled slowly in their direction. The night birds and the distant hobos fell silent as the creaking, groaning monster moved up the tracks, straining to pull a hundred loaded stack cars up the 2.3 percent grade.

The engine moved past, followed by two B-unit power packs and a second MK5 hooked backward. As the four-piece multiple unit locomotive lumbered by, they felt the ground shaking. The hot wind from the blower duct that cooled the traction motor rippled their clothes like a desert wind. Then, for as far as they could see, there were car carriers. Three decks high, the multicolored Japanese, German, and American cars creaked and rocked on their chained-down axles. Shimmering acrylic rainbow colors glistened in the moonlight like endless iron necklaces.

"Now!" Cris shouted, as he grabbed Stacy's hand. They ran up alongside one of the car carriers. The train was moving only five miles an hour up the two-mile grade, and it was easy to get alongside the car Cris had chosen.

"Grab the front handle. Watch your feet!" Cris yelled, as he sprinted alongside the car. Then he jumped for the foot stirrup, caught hold of the side grab-iron on the car, and swung aboard. Once he cleared the space, she also lunged for the handle, catching it and jumping up onto the slow-moving foot stirrup.

The car they were on rumbled past a second group of hobos, who were now also running beside the train, trying to catch a ride a few cars back. The rattling, rocking freight now swayed energetically under their feet.

"Where do we sit?" she asked, her heart beating with exhilaration.

"Follow me," he said.

They began to climb a small red ladder, the metal wheels rumbling and growling on the steel rails below them.

"Be careful—don't slip. It's a Cuisinart under there," he warned.

They climbed up to the top of the train, where a line of new Mercedes were rocking on their axle chains. He edged along from car to car until he was at the front of the carrier. Then Cris took a pocketknife out of his pants, popped the chrome strip off the door of a white Mercedes sedan, reached through the crack, and released the lock. He opened the door and got in, sliding across the German leather to make room for Stacy behind the wheel. She joined him in the front seat and closed the door. He opened the ashtray and pulled out the keys.

"Let's get it going," he said, handing her the keys. She turned on the engine. He leaned over and checked the gas gauge. "Half a tank." He nodded in satisfaction, then turned on the climate control, setting it at seventy-two degrees. "Welcome to the hobo Dome Liner. What kinda music do you like?"

"Pop . . . or R and B," she smiled.

He found a station and set the volume low. Then he reclined the seat.

"And I thought this was gonna be a grim, dirty ride," she said.

"Every occupation has its points of craft, even hoboing, but there's also a practical side to this. We've got a three-mile tunnel up ahead, which would asphyxiate us if we were outside. In here we'll be fine."

They sat back and listened to the music, as the East Texas landscape floated past under a cloudless, moonlit sky. Half an hour later they flashed into the blackness of the long tunnel, and, as Cris had promised, they rode through the deadly diesel fumes breathing cool air-conditioning.

After they came out of the tunnel they rode in comfortable silence. Stacy glanced at Cris, who was pensively looking out the window at the passing scenery. "It must have been horrible losing your daughter like that," she suddenly said, reading his thoughts as accurately as Max used to read hers. "I can imagine how much you must miss her." She waited for his reply.

He bit his lip but didn't answer. Words couldn't possibly express Cris's true feelings.

Chapter 37

THE THRONE NEXT TO GOD

R obert Vail and the Texas Madman rarely spoke; they had
completely different agendas. R.V. saw Fannon Kincaid as
a savior, a godlike Messiah who had divine direction. The
Texas Madman saw Fannon Kincaid as a savior of a different sort.
Fannon provided the Texas Madman with permission to kill, his
acts of murderous "cleansing" easing the terrible ache inside him.

Now, R.V. and the Madman sat behind the Yardmaster's tower
in Shreveport, Louisiana, waiting for the Engine Foreman to deposit the unused carbon sheets in the trash. The yard was huge;
almost a thousand parked railcars cooked in the humid heat.
Shreveport had been a scrap metal center and had grown from that
into a "railhead," where train line-ups and track warrants for the
East Coast originated.

The two men didn't speak, nor did they look at one another, as
if even accidental eye contact would stir the contempt they naturally had for each other.

They had been sent ahead to get consist sheets on the milk trains
coming out of Harrisburg, Pennsylvania. Harrisburg was a dairy

center where the huge funnel-flow refrigerated tank cars were
loaded with milk for major cities in the eastern United States. Fannon had carefully chosen the two cities he intended to attack. Detroit, he proclaimed, was the capital city of the mud races. New
York, he declared, was the home of the Jew, an infested conclave
of Hasidic corruption. All Fannon needed now was the consist
sheets to tell him which milk tankers were going where. This was
the mission he had assigned to R.V. and the Texas Madman.

They hid in the shade behind the Yardmaster's office while flies
buzzed around their heads and landed in their hair.

At a little past ten in the morning the door opened and a skinny
man in jeans and a T-shirt carried a cardboard box down a wooden
flight of stairs and upended it into the trash. Then he turned and
moved slowly in the summer heat back up to the air-conditioned
coolness of the Yardmaster's office.

"Let's go," R.V. said, and the two of them moved out of a
magnolia tree's shade over to the trash can. They quickly retrieved
around twenty carbon sheets, then moved away from the tower.

"Hey!" a deep voice shouted.

"Huh?" R.V. answered as he turned, slack-jawed and indolent
in the oppressive heat.

A heavy-set yard bull in a Southern Pacific uniform was in a
doorway twenty yards away with a doughnut in his right hand.
"Whatta you two fuckheads think you're doin'?" the yard bull
growled, closing the door and moving toward them ominously, his
leather gun belt and Sam Browne harness creaking loudly as he
walked.

"Whatta we doin'?" R.V. repeated, glancing over at the Texas
Madman for help. The Madman was already beginning to smile in
murderous anticipation, slipping a hand inside his unbuttoned shirt.
His corpulent cheeks gathered in folds at the side of his fleshy
mouth as he spread a grin that showed teeth, but no humor.

"You heard me. Whatta you two dickbrains up to? You stealin'
carbon sheets?" the yard bull sneered.

And now, as the bull came closer, he put the doughnut in his mouth and held it there between his teeth to free his hand as he grabbed the carbon sheets out of R.V.'s grasp. "You fucks don't get to ride my trains, no sir, not today," he slurred around the doughnut, which was still in his teeth. "You two are headin' for the lockup."

As he reached behind his back to unhook a pair of handcuffs from his Sam Browne belt, the Texas Madman pulled a gun out of his waistband and shot him between the eyes. The nine-millimeter slug punched a hole in the center of the yard bull's forehead. The man's head snapped back from the impact, but defying all laws of physics, the doughnut miraculously stayed in his mouth. The Texas Madman was treated to the orgasmic thrill of watching the light go out of the yard bull's eyes. It faded slowly, like a rheostat dimming an incandescent bulb. The yard bull fell, first to his knees and then forward, banging his destroyed forehead and uneaten sugar doughnut into the dirt at the Madman's feet.

It was silent for a moment, and then R.V. heard something that sounded like high squeaks or fingernails being scratched on a blackboard. He looked over and saw that the Madman's huge girth was shaking. It was then that he realized that his murderous companion was giggling.

The Reverend Fannon Kincaid sat in the still heat of the sleeper boxcar on the sided grain train. They were parked waiting for a "hot train" behind them to pass and for the Texas Madman and R.V. to return. The unit train they were on had been forced "into the hole" and had been waiting for almost two hours.

Randall Rader was sitting at the far end of the car, his feet dangling over the graded shoulder of the tracks, reading the Available Light Bible in a low voice to Dexter DeMille. Fannon looked at their backs and listened to the resonant tone of Randall's gravel-strewn voice.

Fannon had started out years before as a patriotic Army Lieutenant from a Southern Baptist family who had idealistically gone
to Vietnam to serve his country. He had been told that he wasn't
fighting North Vietnamese, he was fighting Communists. He knew
that Communists were God's enemies, so he felt that his mission
there was just. However, what he saw and did in that godforsaken
place changed his perspective on mankind. He saw drug abuse and
chemical insanity's corruption and debauchery. Still he believed in
God and country, and through it all had distinguished himself under fire. He came home a combat-decorated Colonel. Once he got
stateside his world shifted.

He was called "Baby Killer" and spat on when he wore his
uniform, which proclaimed his victories against the godless Communists in neat rows of ribbons over his heart. There was no ad-
equate work. Affirmative Action took jobs from him and handed
them freely to protesters, Niggers, and Jews who had stayed home.
As he read passages in the Old Testament over and over he now
saw things he had never seen in the Good Book before. Things
that had had no meaning for him as a youth now screamed out at
him from the pages of Genesis and Revelation. It had all been
prophesied thousands of years ago. He read and interpreted and
understood how the devil had put the Levites and Mud Races on
earth to defy God's will. Over the next few years he drifted to the
side of the road, forgoing traditional political correctness in favor
of White separatist literature. He traveled to Hayden Lake, Idaho,
and to Richard Butler's Aryan Nations Church. It was there that
he had met and befriended Bob Matthews. He and Matthews took
a blood oath one night and swore to purge the Jewnited States of
corruption and evil. Fannon became a sort of Aryan Robin Hood,
holding up banks and markets and handing the money to men he
saw as defenders of the White Christian cause. He asked for nothing in return, save the purity of their uncompromised convictions.

Fannon's views on religion had changed from his long-ago
Southern Baptist upbringing. His new religious convictions were

like plaster poured on the imperfect imprint of humanity, hardening until they bore the veins and lines of what he saw as America's moral mistakes. Welfare programs and politically correct theories rutted the surface of his beloved nation like enemy trenches. More important, Fannon had gained a new sense of his own significance. Now he saw his calling as more profound, more exalted. He wasn't just a Robin Hood, he was now the new Messiah.

A whistle ripped through the silence, shattering these ruminations. The rail that the sided grain train was sitting on began to shake as the ground trembled. Then the priority train they had been waiting for roared past, trapping air between the cars, rocking the boxcar he was standing in.

Fannon snapped his gaze up at the thousands of shiny new automobiles as they flashed by three decks high, quivering on their axle chains. A godless tribute to man's endless need for material validation. The cars were speeding madly to market, where they would eventually fulfill their commercial expectations as gaudy containers for the inflated egos of heathens. Here he was, the new Messiah, God's avenging angel, waiting on a siding while they were rushed past. But Fannon knew that like Jesus and Moses before him, when he fell on the battlefield, he would be taken to heaven and asked to sit on the Throne next to God.

Chapter 38

SHREVEPORT, LA.

Cris and Stacy saw the SP unit train from the windows of the white Mercedes as the priority train they were on flashed past.

"There it is," Cris said, as he craned his neck to look back at the freight full of enclosed grainers.

"You think Kincaid is still on it?"

"That's gotta be the train he caught out on," Cris said, turning back to her. "At least according to Steam Train it is."

"What do we do?" she asked, as they rocketed past the parked line of grain cars, the trapped air between the trains shaking the Mercedes violently.

"We gotta get off. He could be changing trains here or he could be just waiting for us to pass. Either way, we have to check the switching yard and the local jungle. Shreveport's a hub—he could be heading anywhere from here."

"How do we get off?" she said, looking at Cris with her eyes wide now, because the train they were on was going over sixty.

"We'll slow for the yard in Shreveport, cut down to ten miles

or less. Come on!'' He reached over, turned off the engine of the
Mercedes, and opened the door. As they got out they could already
feel the train begin to slow.

They moved along, retracing their steps, finally getting to the
ladder. Cris climbed down and helped Stacy, until finally they
stood on the main floor of the car carrier, only four feet above the
tracks.

''Shit, you can't be serious,'' she said, as she looked down at
the rocky grade flashing by beneath them.

Cris climbed down the side ladder and was now only a couple
feet above the grade. Holding on to the grab-iron, he stepped down
to the stirrup at the bottom of the ladder, then slowly let his right
foot down, not quite touching the fast-moving gravel. Then he
dropped his foot a few inches lower until it touched the ground.
Almost immediately, it kicked back and behind him; his heel flew
up and hit him in the ass.

''Not yet,'' he grinned. ''Still goin' too fast.''

''What the hell are you doing?'' Stacy demanded.

''It's a way to find out whether the train's going slow enough,''
he explained. ''When you can put your foot down and it doesn't
fly all the way up and hit you in the ass, then it's safe to jump.
These are time-tested procedures.''

She wrinkled her nose in distrust as he smiled up at her. Again she
could glimpse the heroic man in the picture behind his father's bar.

The train was now near Shreveport, and wooden shacks marking
the edge of the town began to appear; their pebble-scared backs
turned toward the tracks like banished children. Cris pointed to
one of the old wood structures as it flashed by them. It had a
chevron painted on the side: ⑊

''See that?'' he said pointing to the drawing.

''Yeah,'' she said, whipping her head to watch the shack recede
behind them.

''A chevron on a wall outside of town means the cops in the
switching yard are assholes likely to beat the crap outta you before

making an arrest. It's a hobo warning . . . means we've gotta get off before we hit the yard.''

They could see that a couple of hobos had already jumped off the train and were rolling in the dirt as they shot past.

Cris put his foot down again, and this time it flew back, but didn't come all the way up and hit his butt.

"Okay, let's go." He gathered his strength and jumped, running a few awkward steps as he hit the ground, then went down, rolling onto his shoulder. Stacy climbed down after him, and without thinking, jumped. She hit and rolled like tumbleweed in the dust.

The train slowed further as it approached the yard. They could hear the brake valves hiss; tortured metal screamed as the brake shoes engaged.

Cris helped her up. "You just did your first train hop," he smiled as they brushed themselves off. "Welcome to the Knights of the Road. If I was still drinking we'd split a bottle over it. That was some dismount."

"Jesus, that's not as easy as it looks," she said, but she was smiling broadly, invigorated by the experience.

Now that the train was gone, keening insects took over, playing their field music. The other hobos had all magically disappeared like cockroaches under a baseboard. Stacy and Cris began walking along the track, toward the line of wood shacks. Cris pointed to some crude stick drawings on the side of one of the buildings. "See those?" he said.

She nodded.

"Over the years, hobos have put them there to tell other 'bos what's going on up ahead in the switching yard." He pointed to a triangle with two arms on either side: ⚡. "That means the cops in the switching yard carry guns." Then he pointed to another symbol: 🐈. "That means a kind lady lives here." Next to the cat were three triangles, each one larger than the last: ∆ ∆ ∆.

"What's that mean?" she asked.

"It means an exaggerated story will work with her. She's gullible. Come on."

They walked along the side of the shack with the cat and found the gate, pushed it open, then crossed a dirt yard strewn with rusting junk. Cris knocked on the back door of the weather-beaten house, which was badly in need of paint. After a minute the door opened, and an old woman with her hair tied in a bandanna appeared at the screen door.

"Well, lookie here," she said, smiling at Cris. Then she shifted her speculating gaze to Stacy. "Don't believe I've seen you two before."

"We just got off that train, and were wondering if you'd be kind enough to tell us more about the yard up ahead."

"Stay outta Shreveport. Them SP bulls is the worst." She smiled at Cris. "You got a name, son?"

"I'm Lucky, she's Stacy," Cris answered.

"Cinder-Ella," the old woman said proudly. "Cinder for the trains, Ella 'cause my given name is Eloise."

"Nice knowin' ya," he smiled, then added, "We need to know where the jungle is around here and what kinda place it is."

"That's Black Bed Jungle, but it ain't too healthy. It's east a' here, down by the river, but lotsa Low Enders hang there. Two old 'bos got murdered at Black Bed last year. The cops didn't do nothing, and the word spread. It's been fillin' up with F.T.R.A.s ever since. There's a new camp been forming 'bout two miles away, called Need More Jungle. It's safer." She smiled at Stacy, who smiled back. " 'Course things ain't like in the old days. Everybody's packin' guns. Some 'bos shot a cinder bull in the switching yard just this mornin'—plugged the bastard right outside the Yardmaster's office," Cinder-Ella said.

"No kidding," Cris said.

"Yep, been on the TV all day. News said the dead man was an SP yard bull, shot with a nine-millimeter."

Cris remembered it was a nine-millimeter that Fannon Kincaid had pointed at him when he'd been in the water at Vanishing Lake. "How far down the tracks is the switching yard?" he asked.

"Not far, 'bout half a mile. But them yard bulls is crazed right now. They'll be billy-jackin' anybody looks like a train rider."

"Would it be okay if my friend stayed here while I run a few errands?" he asked.

"Be fine with me," she smiled. "Can always use the company."

"I'll only be gone a little while," Cris said to Stacy.

Stacy followed him to the garden gate. "What're you gonna do?"

"If Kincaid's men shot that bull, I'll bet you anything they were carbon-sheet-spotting. I'm gonna go to Black Bed Jungle, see if they're still around. If I can find them, maybe I can figure out what train they're catching out on. I want you to stay here and listen for that grain train. It should be pulling through anytime. Move out to the side of the tracks and check out the cars as they pass. Look for a sleeper car, and look under all the cars at the suspension rods. Sometimes 'bos ride there, or up on the roof. There'll be around forty of them, probably riding in two or three cars. If they're still on that train, you should be able to spot them."

"If you think they're on that train, why don't we sneak back and check it?"

"I don't, 'cause they wouldn't have been at the Yardmaster's office and killed that cinder bull, but we gotta check in case I'm wrong. Besides, by the time we hike all the way back to that train, my guess is it'll already be moving. Just check it from here when it passes. Be back in a few hours." Then he smiled at her, and in a second he was out the gate. Stacy could hear his footsteps on the gravel as he moved along the side of the house and away.

She turned and faced the old woman, who was busy tucking loose strands of wispy gray hair into her scarf, making herself more presentable for the company. Stacy felt like Alice down the rabbit hole. She was in a whole new world where none of the rules of her old life applied. She could barely understand any of it.

Chapter 39

TEMPTATION

Cris stood in front of Cinder-Ella's house and tried to guess which way was east. He finally stopped a mail carrier and asked the way to the river.

In the fifties and sixties, Shreveport had been a big center for scrap metal, and as a result it had become a shipping hub in the south. Now, because of the extensive rail and shipping lanes, there were all kinds of local factories making everything from ball bearings to furniture. They were tucked in among lush trees heavy with Spanish moss.

The summer air was moist. Cris walked until his shirt was dripping. The majority of buildings he passed were fifties-style motel structures; an occasional antebellum house looked out from between its stucco neighbors like a beautiful mistake.

It took Cris almost an hour to find Black Bed Jungle. When he saw it through the trees, it lived up to the warning. There were almost no dogs or children, always a bad sign. Also, the dwellings were even more temporary and makeshift than usual. In other camps, hobos would often build a house of scrounged lumber and materials, then leave the dwelling behind for others to use. This jungle had no "permanent" structures; they were unfriendly hovels built by unfriendly men. As transients moved on, the hovels were immediately picked clean as vultures' prey.

Cris stripped off his inappropriate polo shirt, with the monogram horse and rider, and rolled it up out of sight, wrapping it around his waist. His once lean muscles had become thin and stringy. He still had the shape of a college athlete, but not the bulk. He reached down and grabbed some damp river mud, then rubbed it in his new head fuzz and on his face. It took a few minutes before it dried, then he shook his head and rubbed his face until he had knocked most of it off. It left him looking dusty and lost, as if he had not bathed in weeks. Then he removed his good Spanish leather loafers and hid them under the moss of a tree.

Barefoot and shirtless, "Lucky" Cunningham walked into Black Bed Jungle. No one bothered him; he had transformed himself into one of them. In his current state, he was of no benefit to anyone. After one glance, he was ignored.

He began to wander through the jungle, his gait uneven, as if dazed or drunk. He also had a growing desire to have a drink. . . . His mouth began to water and his stomach began to ache. He remembered reading once that if you were on a diet you should stay out of the kitchen, because once you entered a room where you were accustomed to snacking your hunger would overpower you. Cris had always been drunk in these jungles, and now an unreasoning thirst for a drink overtook him. He could feel his resolve crumbling, so he kept moving, remembering Kennidi and his promise of vengeance. But his hand was in his pocket on some money, certainly enough to buy a bottle from one of these 'bos. These conflicting thoughts were in his mind as his eyes scanned the transients in the jungle.

Then Cris spotted Ben Brook Bob and the Pullman Kid. They were down by the lake, away from the others. Cris remembered them from a few years back. Ben Brook Bob was a mean son-of-a-bitch, who was almost Cris's height and weighed at least 250 pounds. Worse still, he was half crazy. Cris recalled a time outside of Denver when he had seen Ben Brook Bob fly into a rage and attack a hobo with a hammer. He had almost pulverized the man before several 'bos had pulled him off. The Pullman Kid was a boyish-looking "bottom," Bob's personal property and homosexual lover. There were quite a few gay men on the rails, as the train-riding society had a scarcity of women.

Cris figured he could probably get good jungle scuttlebutt from the Pullman Kid if he could separate him from Ben Brook Bob, who would jealously protect his slender lover. Twenty minutes later the Pullman Kid moved off, leaving Bob by the river. Cris trailed him, staying out of sight by skirting the tree line at the edge of the jungle. He soon realized that the Kid was going into the woods to take a shit. The man-boy took a bottle out of his pocket and set it down on the ground. Then he undid his belt, dropped his pants down around his ankles, and squatted. Cris stood in the trees a short distance away, his attention split between the squatting Kid and the bottle of rye which was sitting tantalizingly before him. Then he must have rustled some leaves, because the Pullman Kid looked directly up at him. "Howdy," Cris grinned. "Been a long time, Kid. Go ahead and pinch that one off, then we'll talk." He moved out of hiding and picked up the bottle of rye. Just having his hands on the bottle made Cris's stomach rumble. He could already imagine the fiery warmth of the liquor going down his throat.

The Pullman Kid shot him a look of dismay and quickly stood, yanking his pants up and pulling his belt tight. "I don't know you," the Kid said, fear and excitement competing for control of his narrow face.

"We met a few years back at Gnaw Bone Jungle outside of Denver. You still swappin' spit with Ben Brook Bob?" Cris grinned lecherously, trying to keep the Kid off balance with attitude, holding his bottle in front of him.

"You better gimme that back and get the fuck away from here. If Bob sees you talkin' to me, he'll kill you."

"He won't know we're talkin' 'less you get dumb and tell him. All I need is some info. I heard Fannon Kincaid was here at this jungle. I wanna know where he went." And without even realizing it, Cris was unscrewing the cap on the bottle and raising it to his lips.

"Get the fuck away from me. You got any idea what will happen, Bob catches us together?" The Kid was panicking.

"Just answer me. You seen Kincaid around?" Cris took a mouthful of liquor and held it in the back of his throat. But something wouldn't let him swallow. He heard Clancy's voice somewhere in his subconscious: *"He's gonna know if you fuck up, so you ain't gonna drink. You're gonna go get this godless prick."* Cris stood there, unable to spit out the liquor, unable to swallow it. Then the decision was taken out of his hands.

"The fuck you doin' with my punk?" Ben Brook Bob's voice cut the momentary silence like a sickle slashing dry wheat.

Cris spun toward the voice, but he was too late. The huge hobo hit him in the face, and Cris went down hard, spewing rye whiskey. He rolled right, a split second before a knife thrown with deadly accuracy stuck in the ground and quivered in the exact spot he had just been. Cris came up to his feet in a fluid motion, just in time to take Ben Brook Bob's rhino charge. Bob buried a shoulder in Cris's stomach, screaming in rage as he hit Cris's thin wiry body, driving him back until they both fell painfully into a pile of rocks.

Ben Brook Bob was now snarling like a wild beast as he threw three quick punches at Cris, all of them hitting him on the side of his head, knocking stars into his eyes and blood into his mouth. The fight was already on the verge of being over; Cris was still conscious, but just barely. In a desperate combat-training reflex he pulled Ben Brook Bob in close, Ranger-style, taking away his chopping fists and pinning his arms to his sides. As Cris's head cleared slightly, he rolled once, scissor-kicking and pushing hard with his left leg, until he was on top of Bob. Then he shifted his grip for better traction around the big man's chest. Because Cris was weak, his hold slipped. Bob heaved backward and broke Cris's grasp, stumbling to his feet. Cris was dizzy and still on his knees. Ben Brook Bob turned and kicked Cris square in the face with his hard leather boot. Cris went over on his back. Bob rushed him, but as he charged, the ex-Ranger managed to kick his bare left foot up between Ben Brook's legs. The ball-shot doubled Bob over. While on his back, Cris reached up, grabbed Bob, and pulled him down. This time he shifted his grip quickly and got a choke hold on the muscled neck of the larger, groaning man, squeezing off the blood supply to Bob's brain. In a last desperate effort, Bob lunged up, and Cris heard something pop in Bob's neck. In seconds, Ben Brook Bob was facedown and out on the ground. Cris struggled up to his feet and faced the Pullman Kid.

"Don't hit me," the man-boy shrieked in terror.

"Talk to me, you piece of shit," Cris said, trying to scare the little pansy. He was completely spent by the two minutes of fighting, and he knew that if the Pullman Kid just turned and ran, Cris would never catch him. Fortunately, this tactic didn't occur to the skinny Kid.

"Leave me alone," he said, backing up a few steps.

"You tell me what I want to know or you're gonna get the same," Cris bluffed. His head felt light on his shoulders and his vision was blurred.

"I don't know shit about Kincaid or that fat killer he travels with. Me an' Bob, we only been here a couple hours."

"What fat killer? Who you talkin' about?" Cris took a threatening step forward, and the Pullman Kid looked to Ben Brook Bob for help, but the huge hobo was still facedown.

"The one they call the Texas Madman," the Kid blurted.

"Were they here in this jungle?"

"Two of them was over by that table. Down there by the trees, lookin' at some shit. That's all I know."

"Which two?"

"Just the Texas Madman an' some skinny mean fucker with tattoos all over his forehead . . . 'Eat Shit,' and 'Fuck you' over his eyebrows."

The Pullman Kid's lips quivered; he seemed to be only fifteen or sixteen, but Cris had been told once he was really twenty-five. "Bottoms" like the Kid were passed around among unparticular hobos, and Cris didn't know whether to feel sorry for him or just disgusted. "Why don't you go home? Get the fuck outta here," Cris finally said. "You don't need this guy up your ass. Get out before he wakes up."

"Maybe I will," the Pullman Kid said, but just stood there like a cornered animal.

Cris turned and moved out of the small clearing under the trees, leaving the emptied bottle of rye on the ground where it had fallen. He walked toward the table that the Pullman Kid had pointed out. In the dirt nearby he saw some sheets of paper. Other sheets were half submerged in the shallow water at the river's edge. A few carbons had been blown into the bushes. Cris gathered them up, then moved quickly out of the jungle.

He made his way back to the tree where he had hid his loafers. Then he began the long trek back to Cinder-Ella's house. Halfway there he found a garden hose coiled at the side of a building. He turned it on, then washed the dirt out of his hair and the blood off his face. Surprisingly, despite his fatigue and the aches from the fight, Cris felt a swagger coming into his step, like the last days before the Rose Bowl, when he was quivering with excitement and the thrill of competition. He had gotten what he had come for, but more important, he had withstood temptation. He didn't know if he would have swallowed the rye or not, but he had hesitated . . . he had gone to the edge, but had not crossed over. As he walked, there was a new lightness in his step and in his spirit.

Once he got back to Cinder-Ella's and was sitting under the shade of her gnarled magnolia tree, he spread the carbon papers in front of him. Stacy was looking at him strangely as he studied the sheets. Cris seemed to have been roughed up, yet was smiling. She could sense a change.

"Here," he said, pointing. "Somebody marked this one in pencil."

She read:

MAN-SH-PT-BR [KCS]

"It looks like a manifest train heading from Shreveport to Baton Rouge, on the Kansas City Southern track," he said. "Then they marked a transfer to this manifest train on the Norfolk Southern Line, which goes all the way up to Baltimore." He looked up at Stacy. "Why Baltimore, I wonder?"

They sat there for a long time, thinking.

"Baltimore is just about fifty miles from Fort Detrick," Stacy finally said.

Chapter 40

EMPEROR

When Caesar rode through the crowded streets of Rome, Buddy had heard, he'd always kept a slave standing next to him on the shaded litter. As the crowds cheered, the slave's job was to whisper into the Emperor's ear, "Caesar, thou art mortal."

Buddy had never had someone performing this mind-leveling function. Quite to the contrary, Buddy's slaves seemed to constantly bring out the worst in him. The more he paid them, the more obdurate and demanding he got.

Now he was sitting in the "command" chair, directly behind Billy Seal, who was driving the thirty-seven-foot motor home that Buddy's assistant, Alicia Profit, had rented. He was screaming at the black stunt driver, pointing frantically at a turnoff on the Interstate. "You fucking asshole, that's Interstate 20," he shouted, as they flashed past the connecting ramp, while Billy slowed looking for a place to turn around.

The motor home was full of "Brazil Nuts," his affectionate yet degrading term for his inner circle of employees.

Alicia Profit was on the cellphone, which was always attached to her head like a bracketed utility. She was rearranging the new dubbing schedule on *Deadwood County Countown*, a feather-covered gobbler that Buddy should never have shot. He was trying to rush it into the theaters so that it could perch on the screen during January, with all the rest of the major studio turkeys. January was the dumping ground for bad pictures in the film business.

Seated next to Alicia was Rayce Walker, dressed as always like a rodeo contestant in faded blue jeans, a silver conch belt, and dusty rough-out boots the color of sandpaper.

Then there was John Little Bear, who rarely spoke. His black eyes burned with intensity from a flat brown face that looked like it must have been hit at birth with the wide end of a shovel. John Little Bear had balls the size of cantaloupes. Buddy had seen him drive trucks off motel roofs, do high falls from twenty stories into air-bags, and set himself on fire. Crackling like a Christmas log, he would run out of an exploding building, the flames consuming him until the director yelled "Cut!" and the stunt safety team smothered him with blankets and doused him with fire extinguishers. With his hair and eyebrows already singed, Little Bear would shrug and repeat the life-threatening stunt if the director wanted a second take. All of this impressed Buddy, but he still failed to show John Little Bear any respect. Nobody told him when he was acting like an asshole, so Buddy abused them all like helpless orphans, his raging ego always out of control.

"This fucking guy has this Prion shit, and we're gonna find out where he's goin' and get our hands on it," Buddy blurted. He'd already said this three times before. "He can't be hard to trace. There are fifty people in his fucking congregation. He's a wild-eyed evangelist with silver hair. He'll leave a trail two miles wide. . . . Crank me up," he shouted at Alicia, who whispered something into the phone and hung up. She got her compact of cocaine out of her purse and expertly chopped two lines. While Buddy zooted the load, the Brazil Nuts tried not to notice, looking nervously out the window at the passing landscape.

He wiped the residue from his nose and glared down at a map, waiting for the rocket blast to hit. "Shreveport is just twenty-five miles up ahead. Rayce, when we get there, we go to the cops and show 'em your badge, see if they'll escort us to the jungle where these hobos all hang. Then we bust chops until somebody talks."

Rayce had a New Mexico Sheriff's badge, and it had been Buddy's "get out of jail" card more than once.

The Shreveport P.D. was in a brick building on Lee Street, in the old section of town. Heavy, gnarled oaks overhung the sidewalk and rested their twisted limbs on the low eaves of the police annex, leaning like tired soldiers after battle.

Buddy and Rayce were on the third floor of the building, in a cluttered two-man office with no window, talking to Detective Beau Jack "Bobo" Turan. He was a heavy-set cop who looked to Buddy like he would sweat in the middle of an Alaskan blizzard. Bobo was listening patiently as Buddy finished introducing himself, managing to get in three of his hundred-million-dollar-domestic-grossing pictures.

Rayce Williams's badge lay open in its leather case in front of them on Bobo's desk. "We just happen to be having a special on hobo assholes today," Bobo grinned. "First somebody killed that yard bull, then somebody else killed one of those jungle buzzards just four hours ago. I got a fuckin' roomful downstairs, all of 'em rummy-eyed dick-brains with memories like Nazi war criminals. I was just getting set to close the case, say my dead hobo killed my dead yard bull, call it a trick, and kick the whole sorry bunch loose."

"Killed a jungle 'bo?" Buddy asked.

"Yeah. The way I get it, the perp blew town already. Got in a fight in the jungle down by the river an' chilled the vic. Some fudge-packer named Ben Brook Bob, took him two hours t'die. Broke his windbox, Special Forces–style.''

Buddy looked at the Shreveport cop, but said nothing about Cris Cunningham. ''My son, Mike, was killed riding the rails,'' Buddy finally said, looking at the sweating cop. ''I'd like to talk to the men you have downstairs. I'm trying to find out who killed Mike. Maybe somebody down there . . .'' He let it drop in mid-sentence because Detective Bobo Turan started smiling. ''I said something funny?'' Buddy asked softly.

''This ain't a fuckin' movie, Mr. Brazil. These people, they don't stand around talkin' to guys in five-hundred-dollar shoes about who killed who. I got the dead asshole's butt-boy down there cryin' like an unwed mother, an' even so, the little faggot won't even give me the time of day.''

''You tried paying for the info?'' Buddy asked, letting a snide smile inadvertently fuck up a pretty good suggestion.

''Yeah, sure, that was gonna be my next move. The Shreveport P.D. gives me thousands in hustle money t'drop on these douche bags. I just ain't gotten around to it yet.'' Sarcasm was dripping like humidity on a flower shop window.

''My son died in the Oklahoma panhandle,'' Buddy persisted. ''That's way out of your jurisdiction, so it's nothing you have to worry about, but I need closure here.'' Buddy reached into his pocket, pulled out a sheaf of hundred-dollar bills, and started peeling them off. When he reached ten, he dropped them in a pile on the desk next to Rayce's badge.

''What's that for?'' Bobo Turan asked, cocking an eyebrow dangerously.

''That's for the widows and orphans of dead Shreveport police officers, or the Police Betterment Society, or it's for your new backyard patio barbecue. You choose. But me an' Rayce would very much like to spend a few minutes with the guys you have downstairs.''

Bobo looked at them and shook his head sadly. ''You Holly-

wood people think you own the whole fuckin' world, don't ya?''
When Buddy started to retrieve the money Bobo looked at him
sharply. "Leave it be. You got five minutes," he said, snapping
up the cash faster than a frog hitting a swamp fly.

Buddy thought the room full of hobos smelled worse than a sock
hamper. Rayce, who had actually spent five years as a cop in New
Mexico, isolated the group, quickly cutting it down to four people.
He saved the sniveling Pullman Kid for last.

When Buddy started passing out hundreds, they found out that
two members of Fannon Kincaid's Christian Choir had been at
Black Bed Jungle around ten that same morning. One of the hobos
in the room mentioned that a skinny tattooed man named Robert
Vail had said that the Choir was heading to Harrisburg.

"Why Harrisburg?" Rayce asked the hobo with tattered clothes,
brown teeth, and a slight stutter.

"Da-don't know, fu-fucker wouldn't say. Ju-just said,
'Harrisbu-burg.' ''

The Pullman Kid was useless. He sat in front of Rayce and
Buddy, sniveling. "I wanna go home," was all he said, over and
over, until Buddy wanted to hit him.

"Let's get outta here," he ordered Rayce, and they walked out
of the holding area. Bobo Turan was waiting in the lobby.

"You solve my 'who cares' murder?" the fat detective asked,
grinning.

"Nope," Buddy said.

"Them fuckers down there don't have much movin' around in
the way of brain matter."

"Sounds like the Writers Guild," Buddy sighed, then he and
Rayce moved past the detective, out of the police building, and
into the sunlight.

They crossed the sidewalk to the blue-and-white thirty-seven-
foot motor home. Billy Seal had kept the motor running and the
air-conditioning on. They entered the cold RV and Buddy slipped

into the command chair behind the driver's seat. "Harrisburg," he ordered.

The motor home moved away from the curb, went down the road, turned left, and took the state highway north. There was still no one standing behind Buddy whispering in his ear, reminding him he was mortal.

Chapter 41

WHITE TRAIN

It arrived at Fort Detrick at one A.M., taking a military rail that ran onto the base from the switching yard at Frederick, Maryland. The train had no markings, was painted pure white, and was only four cars long. The engine was a sleek EMD-F59PHI with slanted windows and a short hood. It had an isolated "Whisper" cab and a rooftop hump, which disguised an air scoop that routed the diesel fumes high up and over the trailing cars. The special cab was designed to have extra-wide visibility. Since the train was just four cars, the three-thousand-horsepower engine was fast, but light, rated and geared for 110 mph. The White Train also had an aggressive blended brake system with a high deceleration rate. Behind the engine was a pure white cylindrical, covered metal hopper car. It was specifically designed for toxic waste disposal, with both an inner and outer shell made of hard titanium and a special space-age superheated ceramic. It usually carried hazardous waste from either nuclear breeder reactors or military storage facilities disposing of inoperative warheads. The next car, also white, was a Pullman, with living compartments for ten Marines, who rode the roof of the cars in four-man shifts. They were armed with automatic rifles to protect the train from attack or theft because of the weapons-grade nuclear material that was often aboard. Behind the troop car was another white hopper car, identical to the first.

The White Train pulled to a stop on the isolated rail spur in a restricted area near Company A, First SATCOM Battalion Headquarters. The area was jeep-patrolled by units of the Torn Victor Special Forces group. As soon as the train stopped, two black Bell Jet Rangers with fifty-caliber nose cannons landed. One set down on a patch of ground in front of the engine, one behind the last car. The helicopter gunships were assigned to fly air cover over the train, wherever it went.

Colonel Chittick stood in the field and looked at the impressive arrival of the White Train. There was only one such unit operating in the United States. It was booked by appointment through the Pentagon; its missions included frequent runs carrying nuclear waste from Three Mile Island, through the Appalachian Mountain Pass, across the South to Texas, where its radioactive load was pumped from the covered caskets inside the hopper cars into a titanium pipe that went thousands of feet down into the hot inner crust of the earth. There it was swept away by the burning, molten inferno of inner-earth gases into the planet's core.

As the engine shut down, its diesel growled like an unfed beast. Colonel Chittick hoped that in a matter of hours, they would have all of the sarin and anthrax that had been developed and stored at Fort Detrick over the last twenty years pumped aboard the hopper cars and that the train would be safely out of there.

The troop car door suddenly opened, startling Colonel Chittick. Then a uniformed scientist from the C.D.C. branch at Walter Reed Hospital got off. He was in an Army Major's uniform, complete with medical insignias.

"Major Flynn?" Colonel Chittick asked, reaching out to shake his hand.

"Yes. Colonel Chittick?" the man replied. Flynn did not have a trace of military bearing; he was a narrow-shouldered, balding man with glasses. He wore no combat designations or ribbons. He looked to Colonel Chittick to be in his mid-fifties.

Chittick nodded as they shook hands. The two of them had spoken twice on the phone.

Now, several Marines got out of the troop car and looked around. They were all dressed in camouflage uniforms and high-laced combat boots with their pants bloused and tucked neatly inside; all were wearing white helmets with the HAZMAT seal on the back.

"Come on," Chittick said. "We can take my car to the containment area." As the two Bell Jet Rangers finished winding down, the whine from their engines was finally replaced by the sound of cold night wind blowing across open fields of tall grass. Chittick led the Major over to a sedan command car, parked on a concrete apron with its headlights on. They got into the car, Colonel Chittick behind the wheel. He had released his driver for security reasons. As he pulled off the apron onto the narrow lane, he looked back over his shoulder . . . The White Train was parked in the middle of the empty field lit by moonlight, looking like some ghostly apparition with the two black dragonfly helicopter gunships next to it.

"Pretty fucking impressive," Chittick said.

"We transport some very nasty stuff," Major Adrian Flynn said, in his quiet, unobtrusive, scientific voice.

The trip to the Underground Containment Room took about ten minutes, and finally Chittick pulled up to a chain-link fence where two uniformed M.P.s with fully automatic M-14s let him pass. They drove down a concrete ramp to a pair of heavy metal doors that were cut into the side of a hill, like a fifties-style bomb shelter. They got out, and Chittick motioned Major Flynn over to the back of the car, where he removed two HEPA masks and canvas bio-suits from the trunk, then handed one rig to the Major.

"What's this for? I thought the material was stable."

"Well, let's call it a precaution," Chittick said. "There's a changing room right inside the underground," he added.

They moved down to the metal doors cut into the concrete wall. Colonel Chittick punched in a code. The door lock clicked and he swung it wide, then both men stepped inside.

They were in a small ready room, lit by neon bulbs. It was spare, with only two benches. The ceiling, walls, and floor were all poured concrete. There was a lead-foil material on the floor that wrapped up around the baseboards.

"Are you getting leakage?" Major Flynn asked, looking with alarm at the metal sheeting on the floor.

"This stuff started getting stored here in the mid-seventies. Back then they were using steel drums. We didn't switch to bio-containment caskets until the mid-eighties." Chittick tried to make it sound matter-of-fact, but Major Flynn was now glaring at him.

"You gotta be kidding," he said. "And how much time do I have, again, to get all this out of here?"

"No time, Major. We could have Senate investigators down here in a matter of hours—days at the most. There's more than just a little shit in the wind on this deal right now."

"My invoice says I'm picking up hundreds of gallons of sarin, anthrax, and accelerated Prions. Now you're telling me some of this stuff's in old oil drums?"

"Major, let's spare each other the golly-gee-whiz bullshit. We all know it's never as neat and clean as everybody says it is. The world is full of careless assholes, and we have to be ready to defend ourselves."

Major Adrian Flynn didn't say what he was thinking, but in that moment, he definitely agreed that the world was full of careless assholes . . . and he was standing next to one of the biggest. After a moment of reflection, he finally started putting on the bio-containment gear.

Flynn and Colonel Chittick finished dressing, then moved to a security door, which was marked with stenciled red letters:

DANGER
BIO-CONTAINMENT AREA
LEVEL 3

Colonel Chittick had to place his palm on an electronic reader which identified his print before the lock clicked open. They moved into a huge underground storage warehouse, cold and windowless, lit with long banks of fluorescent tubes. Flynn estimated the room was almost an eighth of a square acre. Large metal drums sat on racks piled three tiers high. Each drum was marked with the type of biological or chemical weapon it contained, along with the date of manufacture and the date of storage. The classifications were stenciled on the front of each barrel in white letters.

There was another man standing in the room, also in full HEPA gear. Before they got to him, something caught Major Flynn's eye. He moved to inspect a row of metal drums.

"This shit is sweating," he said in alarm. "You've got rust here, and corrosion. How the fuck are we supposed to get this out without killing ourselves and half the camp?" He read the markings on the barrel. "This is pure sarin, for God's sake! From 1976!" Then he touched the barrel with a canvas-gloved hand, drawing his fingers across the sweating metal. "You people are outta your minds! This is about to start leaking. You've got enough stuff stored in this room to kill the entire population of the world twenty times over. Who's the idiot in charge here?"

"I am," a sandpapery voice came through the third man's HEPA mask.

"May I introduce Admiral James G. Zoll," Chittick said softly.

Zoll stepped forward and looked at the startled Major through the glass plate in his mask. The two men exchanged unfriendly looks.

"Here's the deal, Major," Admiral Zoll said. "You and your men get this stuff outta here and onto that train by tomorrow night, or the consequences will be staggering."

"That just may not be possible, Admiral. If one of these barrels breaks open, we'll have a bio-contamination disaster, which will take weeks to neutralize. I suggest you bulldoze the entrance and bury this room. Then pave the area over and pray you never get an earthquake."

"There are plans in the Pentagon that identify the location of every structure at Fort Detrick, including this underground facility. This bunker is clearly visible on the layout. Since I have a feeling the Senators are going to want to see it, one way or the other, you're gonna get it emptied out," the Crazy Ace growled.

"And if that's not possible?" Major Flynn said, his voice shaking with dread and anger.

"Everything is possible, Major. I just have to have the right man for the job and push him hard enough. You better be that man. What we have in this room is an international disaster waiting to happen. So let's not debate protocol, or operational difficulties, or your opinion on feasibilities. Let's just get this shit on its way."

Chapter 42

BLOOD IN THE FACE

Fannon said, "I've been studying the original Greek and Hebrew versions of the Bible, and I found out that 'Adam' actually is a word that when translated from its root means 'capable of showing blood in the face.' "

"Really?" Dexter tried to sound interested, while hiding his contempt. He had had almost all he could take of Fannon Kincaid and his endless, egotistic, self-centered sermons that dealt more and more with his own martyrdom. Fannon saw himself as a religious superstar, destined to be remembered in church hymns and on stained-glass windows.

They were in a gully south of Frederick, about half a mile from the train yard, waiting for the six-o'clock switcher that would pass by on the track above them with ten cars loaded with supplies for Fort Detrick. The switch engine was a "pusher," so Fannon had warned them to be careful boarding or the engineer would see them from the high-hood switcher's windows.

"This ability to show blood in the face is what defines a White

man. More proof that Adam was the father of the White race,"
Fannon said, after a long reflective pause.

"I see," Dexter said. "That makes very good sense." His mind
was wandering dangerously.

Once they got on the base at Fort Detrick, Dexter had to devise
a way to alert the Fort commandos. He was fairly sure that the
Torn Victor Delta Force Rangers would make short work of Fannon Kincaid and his Choir of fanatics.

It would take Dexter only a short amount of time to change the
pH factors on the Prions that were in the sturdy bio-containers,
which Fannon had given Randall Rader to protect. Dexter intended
to stall in the lab to buy time, and find a way to alert security. He
had decided to use the USAMRIID neurotransmitter lab in the
basement of Building 1666. He had chosen it for two reasons: It
was a well-stocked lab that he had worked in for two years, and
he knew where everything was; and, it was in an old building with
few exits. Once they were below ground, if Dexter could set off
one of the contamination alarms, they would be up to their asses
in commandos in seconds. Then all he had to do was find a way
to keep out of the line of fire until Fannon and his Choir were
mowed down with the armor-piercing Black Talons that he knew
the Fort commandos all used. Dexter had never been drawn to
violence, but he was hungry to see Fannon Kincaid and his "Blood
in the Face" Brotherhood riddled with bullets.

Then the high-hood switcher arrived right on time, pushing its
ten cars. Six or seven of Fannon's men charged up the bank, out
of hiding, and boarded the front cars as the train passed. Fannon's
war party was only ten strong, including Dexter. The Reverend
had elected to leave the majority behind, going for a small, less
visible strike force. Dexter and the rest of the heavily armed band
now raced up the bank of the gully. While a bend in the track
blocked the engineer's view, they jumped on the rods that were
under the cars. It was uncomfortable and dangerous, but Fannon

had already explained that they were only going to be on the train for five miles, until it arrived inside the Fort.

With Randall Rader lying under the railcar beside him, Dexter felt his heart beating with apprehension. He was only a few feet above the grinding metal wheels, resting on the narrow suspension rods, holding on for dear life.

In less than fifteen minutes, Dexter DeMille and all ten members of Fannon's assault team were inside the Fort. The train was only going twenty miles an hour, but the frightening sensation of speed caused by lying so close to the tracks was overpowering. Dexter locked his eyes on the scenery beyond and prayed he wouldn't lose his grip and fall. He had been hoping that they would be stopped and arrested at the perimeter of the Fort, but the rail system had proved to be a surprisingly good way of subverting all road-blocks and security measures.

Once inside Fort Detrick, the train slowed and headed across open fields toward the warehouse where the cars would be discon-nected, then left to be unloaded. As they neared the low black buildings, Fannon Kincaid was the first off the train, suddenly run-ning alongside the car that Dexter was on.

"Off now! Head for that gully!" Fannon screamed above the rumble of the metal wheels. Randall, who was riding the same suspension rod as Dexter, pushed him in the back, knocking him off his resting place and onto the gravel shoulder. Dexter rolled down a hill, with four other members of the Choir alongside him, until he hit with a thud at the bottom of the gully.

"Stay low," Fannon commanded, as the high-hood switcher rumbled past. The engineer appeared not to have seen them.

Suddenly, the air brakes on the huge train screamed; metal shrieked against metal, as the ten cars slowed dramatically. The engineer inched the cars closer, until they were alongside a con-crete loading dock.

Dexter was watching all of this from fifty yards away when suddenly Fannon Kincaid was at his shoulder.

"We're gonna hide in them woods, over there," the new Messiah said, pointing at a heavy stand of trees some distance off. "Everybody stay in this gully till we're outta sight a' them buildings," he ordered.

They moved in a group, crouching low, heading toward the wash near the tracks and finally up into the coolness of the wooded hillside.

"God's time is coming," Fannon said to them all, as they crouched in the leafy moon shadows created by the stand of trees.

"Faith and Race," the members of the assault team whispered in reply.

They had passed the first Fort Detrick security check with mind-baffling ease. At every turn, Fannon Kincaid had proved to be up to the task. Dexter DeMille wondered if he had made a huge mistake trying to trap him here.

Fannon led the way along a narrow path through the trees, moving single-file along the pine-needle-carpeted trail, heading back toward the main campus of the Fort. Finally, they crouched down and looked off across a meadow at a large windowless structure. Fannon put his field glasses up and surveyed the building.

"Company A, First SATCOM Battalion Headquarters," he announced, reading the flags flapping from poles in front of buildings bathed in the moonlight. Then he swung the glasses to the right. "What the fuck is that?" he asked, and then handed the glasses to Dexter. It took the scientist a minute to adjust the lenses. What came into focus surprised him. He had never seen it before, only heard about it . . . the ultramodern train that was painted pure white.

Chapter 43

ARMING THE PRIONS

s night fell they were crouched in the forest, east of the
medical campus. Dexter had drawn a map that showed where
Building 1666 was located. Fannon dispatched Randall
Rader and the Texas Madman to find the lab and scout the area.
Then he turned his gray eyes to look across the rich farmland at
the lights coming on in the buildings a mile from where they were
bivouacked in the stand of trees.

"Whatta ya think is going on over there at SATCOM HQ?"
Fannon finally said. "Looks like they're about ta move that
train."

Dexter looked over at the SATCOM Battalion HQ, which was
almost a mile to the east. The hill they were on sat just halfway
between the medical campus and the isolated SATCOM HQ,
where he could see the strange four-car White Train, lit by lights
from the building. Suddenly, they could hear the rumbling diesel
engine as the train started moving slowly toward the east end of
the Fort, where Dexter had heard the underground bio-weapons
storage facility was located.

"I don't know what's happening," Dexter said, although he had a pretty good idea, and it had huge ramifications.

Fannon smiled at him. "Look at me, Mr. DeMille," the Reverend said softly.

"I am looking at you."

"No, all the way, into my eyes."

As Dexter swung his head to look directly at Fannon, the Reverend swung a big fist. He had timed it so Dexter turned directly into the punch, and it knocked him flat; he was stunned and almost unconscious, and his displaced jaw shot such pain into his eyes it made them water. While he was still trying to get his mind to function, Fannon's face loomed over him like a pale rutted moon.

"You ain't quite being honest with me, bub. Only a profligate sinner would attempt ta lie ta one a' the Lord's angels."

Still out of it and half unconscious, Dexter felt himself being dragged into a sitting position by the front of his shirt. He became vaguely aware that Reverend Kincaid was astride him, pulling him up.

"Again, let us talk about what is happening over there."

Dexter could taste the coppery blood in his mouth; then he saw huge drops of it falling onto his pants from a badly split lower lip. His blood appeared black in the moonlight as it fell on his trousers in Rorschach-like splatters.

"Why did you hit me?" he whined.

"In the next life, God will punish all liars, Mr. DeMille, but I get ta kick the shit out of 'em in this one."

"I think it's the White Train," Dexter finally whispered, his tongue feeling the new, unfamiliar edge of a chipped tooth.

"Of course, I know it's a white train, you dip-shit. I got eyes. What I want to know is, what is it doing?"

"It's *called* the White Train," Dexter repeated. He was feeling a complete loss of energy now, a hopelessness verging on despair. The blow had more or less convinced him that no plan to trap this man would ever work. "I never saw it before, but I heard about it. The government uses it to transport toxic material."

"What's it doing here?"

"There's a lot of chemical toxins and bio-weapons on the base, hidden in underground storage. It's all illegal stuff we should never have manufactured. There's an underground warehouse out by the SATCOM HQ."

"You think they're putting toxic waste in that underground warehouse?"

"No," Dexter said, thinking what a dumb human being Kincaid really was. "They're taking it out."

"Why?"

"All I can do is guess, so don't hit me."

"Then do it! Guess!"

"After that mess at Vanishing Lake, the Senate Defense Oversight Committee must be getting worried that something isn't right here, so Admiral Zoll is moving his stash of illegal weapons before an investigation committee finds them."

Fannon Kincaid leaned back on his haunches, and in that moment looked like a painting of a great Apache warrior, looking off from his perch with weathered intensity. He studied the White Train through his binoculars as it came to a stop out in the middle of an empty field. It was a ghostly, moonlit apparition; its diesel was idling, the noise carrying across the windswept plain like the distant metallic purr of a mechanical beast.

"That's gonna work for us pretty good," Fannon finally said, still looking at it through the binoculars. He watched as long pumping tubes were attached to the top of the car behind the engine and hooked to a female shackle sticking up from a paved square on the ground. He could see men in full canvas suits, bathed in pale light, walking around like astronauts on the moon.

"How's it gonna help us?" Dexter finally got up the nerve to ask.

"Zoll's gonna have his hands full getting that shit outta here. Gonna make it easier for us to get into that lab, do what needs to be done, and get out."

He again settled back on his haunches, a modern renegade with his black metal Uzi full of hollow-points, slung on his back like a quiver of deadly arrows.

Dexter thought in that pose Fannon Kincaid looked as frightening and resolute as any man he had ever seen.

An hour later the Texas Madman and Randall Rader returned. They had found the building.

"We can get in through a side door. I dismantled the internal alarm system," Randall Rader said. "These fuckers have outside security boxes. The idiot who designed this system was asking to get his pocket picked. Ain't it just like the Army, 'Cost over function.' Cheap, but it don't work for shit."

Fannon pulled out a can of "black" and the members of the Choir, along with Dexter, rubbed it on their faces.

"Okay, let's get in and out fast," Fannon said, then turned to Dexter and looked at him strangely.

"Mr. DeMille, you are not important to me in any personal sense. Your value is in what needs to be done. You said you could arm this weapon, and you fucking well better do it. I suppose it might have occurred to you to try and arrange for us to be trapped inside that lab. You may have fantasized about setting off some hidden alarm, and finding a way to avoid getting hit in the ensuing battle. Let me encourage you not to try this foolish maneuver. We are not inexperienced. Every man here has seen action behind enemy lines. The Angel in the Church of Per-ga-mos is assigned to send you to your Maker at the first sign of trouble. A loaded gun will be at your head until we leave the lab. Are you straight with me so far, bub?"

Dexter looked at him, and what little was left of his willpower evaporated. He didn't answer, just nodded.

"Okay," Fannon said. "Let's move out."

They came out of the hills in three separate groups, moving quickly in the dark, hugging the shadows and gullies.

They made no noise and tripped no perimeter alarm as they skirted the edge of the hospital campus at Fort Detrick. They stayed off the walkways, using the landscaped common areas, always staying next to a building or clipped hedge. The members of the Christian Choir and the Lord's Desire headed stealthily toward Building 1666.

With Randall Rader and the Texas Madman in the lead, they were finally in front of the unlocked door that had been jimmied earlier. Fannon left four men outside to act as rear guard. They settled low in the bushes, positioned to set up a deadly crossfire that would cover the Choir's exit from the building.

Inside Building 1666, Fannon, Dexter, Randall, and three others moved down the stairs. It was ten P.M., but there seemed to be nobody around. Dexter wondered where the bio-containment people were. They were always stationed in this lab. It was a Level Three facility. As he asked himself this question, he instantly knew the answer. The crazy prophet had called it correctly. They were all with the White Train at the underground storage facility, or over at Company A, First SATCOM Battalion Headquarters.

Dexter opened the door to the basement lab, using his palm print, which miraculously had not yet been erased from the database. Then he entered the room along with Fannon and Randall. The last three Choir members took up positions in the hall outside. Dexter turned on the light, illuminating the tile countertops and animal cages; the stark fluorescent overheads threw a bright white light on everything. Dexter cast his eyes around at the familiar cabinets full of chemicals and beakers of acids. He had spent two years in this room working on the accelerant for PHpr. Everything he needed to change the pH factors and arm the Prions was here: the acids, the pH meters, the DNA blood strands for Jews and African-Americans. His hands were shaking, his head felt light.

"You got thirty minutes. Don't fuck it up, bub," Fannon Kincaid said softly.

Chapter 44

CLOSING IN

They were blinding on a passenger train, moving fast up the Eastern Seaboard sitting on the narrow ledge behind the baggage car. They had elected to ride outside rather than buy a ticket so they could dismount if they spotted the Choir hiding anywhere along the tracks. Cris read Stacy the hobo markings on the sides of the shacks outside each switching yard as they strobed past. Former train riders had also obligingly left "track options" scribbled there, telling what rail lines intersected in each town. Also inscribed on the weathered lumber were all sorts of useful symbols, like the ones he showed her in Shreveport. He explained them to her:

⬭ meant "No reason to stay here."

▣ "Beware, danger."

▣ "Bad water."
〰

✕ "Good jungle."

▦ "Bad jail."

They were a few miles out of Harpers Ferry, at the Maryland border, on the Norfolk Southern track, which would land them only ten miles from Fort Detrick.

"Sometimes, when it was late, we'd lie in bed and talk," Stacy said suddenly, picking up the strains of an earlier conversation about Max Richardson. "We'd discuss things I'd never really thought about. Sometimes Max could see around corners. He'd spot dangers or see problems where it seemed others in the scientific community never even bothered to look. He worried about the effect this science would have on evolution, and its environmental effect on human development. That's why he was so worried about what they were doing at Fort Detrick."

"He sounds pretty impressive," Cris said, looking at her as her eyes clouded with loss at the memory of her dead husband.

"Sometimes, in science, people get target fixation," she went on. "It's like you're so bent on succeeding and beating your competitors to the prize that you forget the collateral damage your discoveries might one day cause. Scientific history is full of these oversights, from thalidomide to the Manhattan Project to Dexter DeMille's work with Prions. His research started out as a life-saving cure for a horrible disease in New Guinea, but it ended up as a genetically targeted bio-weapon. I'm sure if you asked Dr. DeMille when it went from good science to bad, he wouldn't be able to pinpoint the moment. In his mind, it was undoubtedly all about a fantastic discovery and scientific acclaim. Max used to say that the Nobel Prize hangs in front of all of us, a big ugly carrot on a string, driving scientific ego without regard for mankind's capacity for moral mistakes. To get funding, you often make horrible compromises with the business community or the military—anything to fund the science, anything for academic glory. Some great scientific theories have turned into potential world-ending nightmares.''

"Like the whole Nuclear Age?" he asked.

"You got it. I'm sure Albert Einstein never imagined that his Theory of Relativity would turn into the basis for understanding the apogee of the neutron, which eventually produced nuclear weapons. Every time something good is discovered, there is also the potential for unforeseen and horrific applications. Max understood that. It's one of the things that made him so special.''

"Then why did he go study at Fort Detrick? From what Wendell Kinney said, everybody knew Dexter DeMille had started using Prion research for military reasons." Stacy didn't answer; she remained silent, so Cris went on, "Wendell said that the Pentagon funds lots of university programs, and that military research into Prions was aimed at creating antipersonnel weapons.''

"Max believed that he needed to find out what DeMille was doing," she finally said.

"So he was spying on Dr. DeMille?" Cris persisted.

"Look, it isn't as easy as all that. It's not black and white." She was getting angry now. "I mean, knowledge is precious, and sometimes you form strange alliances to mine certain truths that you'll ultimately be able to use for the betterment of mankind. Sometimes people like Dexter DeMille have to be temporarily part of that equation.''

"But if USC was getting military funding, along with all those other universities like Sam Houston and the University of Texas, then wouldn't Max be part of the decision-making process if he ran the Microbiology Department?''

"No!" she said. Now she was angry. "You just will never be able to understand how difficult it is to balance the need for funding against the moral equation. Max did that dance better than anybody!''

Cris realized that he had become annoyed at Stacy's worship of her dead husband. He wondered if he was subconsciously trying to tear down his memory because she was so obviously still in love with him. Cris was suddenly ashamed of himself. "You loved him," he said sympathetically.

"I adored him," she said, then fell silent as the train slowed for Harpers Ferry.

Cris knew that they would have to get off the passenger train in about ten minutes. Already the sleek ten-car varnish was slowing for the station. The ragtag buildings that seemed to announce every new town were now drifting past the car they were blinding on. On the outskirts of town were leaning, unpainted shacks with tar-paper roofs. Soon those structures were replaced by small boxy industrial brick buildings with low-slanted eaves, announcing that they were getting closer to the yard.

"We fought about just what you said the night before he left," Stacy continued softly. "I didn't want him to go. I was afraid of the research, where it was going. The last night he spent at home we argued about Dexter DeMille." She was speaking so quietly that he could barely hear her over the grinding metal brake shoes on the slowing train.

"We have to get off. You got everything?" Cris said, changing the subject.

She nodded and grabbed a small backpack she'd purchased in Shreveport. Then she shrugged her shoulders into the straps.

"Let's go," he said, as the train slowed to less than five miles an hour, and they easily dismounted the metal strip that was on the back of the baggage car.

Cris and Stacy moved away from the tracks and down into a gully. They crouched in the tall grass until the train was out of sight, moving very slowly into the yard.

"It's about a ten-mile walk into Frederick," Stacy said.

"How far is the Fort from there?" Cris asked.

"Not far. Just on the outskirts of town."

"If Fannon came here, he and DeMille must be collecting some-thing from the base," he reasoned. "A military installation that big should be fed by rail. We oughta be able to catch a supply train into the property."

They climbed down a long, sloping hillside to a spot where they could see the two-lane highway slanting across the valley.

"I think I can get us in through the front door of the Fort without sneaking in," she said. "I left Max's ashes there, in Colonel Chittick's office. He said he was going to ship them, but what if we just show up to collect them?"

"I don't like it," Cris said. "I think it's dangerous for them to know you're on the base. After what happened last time, somebody will call Admiral Zoll and you're gonna be sitting in some interrogation room trying to talk your way out again."

"So, what do we do?"

"Let's head over there and I'll check the rail line that feeds the Fort. Somebody along the track oughta know what time the rail deliveries are made. It's probably once or twice a day."

They moved down to the two-lane highway and walked along the shoulder, heading northwest. It was a perfect day, cool and crisp. A fall wind was beginning to gust leaves across the road; they danced and flipped along in their orange and gold colors like nimble circus acrobats.

Cris found the rail heading into Fort Detrick, more or less by instinct. Most experienced hobos could look at the general terrain of an area and discern where the track would be; railroad engineers would shun any grade that exceeded twenty degrees and didn't allow for a switchback. After looking at the shape of the valley, Cris thought the rail leading into the Fort would most likely lie on the eastern slope, so he and Stacy headed that way. Before noon they found the spur leading into Fort Detrick and began walking alongside the track.

Ever since Shreveport, Cris had been feeling his old energy coming back. He got the rhythm into his stride, swinging his arms and legs, moving briskly until he could hear Stacy huffing behind him.

His lean body glistened with sweat, and he glowed with newfound purpose.

Around eight-thirty A.M., they arrived at the perimeter fencing of the Fort, near where the trains entered. The terrain was wooded, and a few hundred yards past the fence his view was obstructed by a dense growth of trees.

"It's surprising nobody is guarding this entrance. At the front gate they have Marines with automatic weapons," she said.

"Rail tracks are the back door to the twentieth century," he said, somewhat poetically. "A freight train is a very efficient transportation system, but it doesn't fit in with the jet age. It's still used, but strangely forgotten."

They found an old hobo sitting under a nearby tree. He was eating a peach, the juice running into his white beard. His face and clothes were grimy. Cris moved over and squatted in front of him. "Howdy. I'm Lucky," he said.

"Don't have t'tell me that, not with a pair a' shoes like them you got on," the old 'bo said.

"What time's the feeder train come through?" Cris asked.

"Two of 'em. First one's already come through, goes by at nine ever' night. It was the military train, fulla shit from the Pentagon. Anytime from now on, ya got yer supply train, food, soft goods, stuff like that. They're both pushers. Hard t'get on, not that y'wanna. Line stops a few miles in. They got patrols all over . . . ridin' in jeeps. Ya can hear 'em runnin' around all the way out here."

"Those the only two? The nine-o'clock olive and the supply train?" Cris asked, looking at his watch.

" 'Cept fer yesterday night. Damnedest thing I ever saw came through here . . . Sum'bitch was evil-lookin', cold an' mean as a pale ghost." Then the old man gave Cris and Stacy a description of the White Train, with its two low-flying black helicopters.

"What's it for?" Cris asked.

"Beats the shit outta me, but it probably ain't here deliverin' cookies," the old 'bo said.

Chapter 45

PALE HORSE WITH NO RIDER

Dexter was scared shitless. He stood in the basement lab of the Devil's Workshop, in his white coat and gloves, looking into the deranged gray eyes of Fannon Kincaid.

"Okay, get goin'. Do yer magic," the crazed Messiah ordered.

Dexter had already taken the two metal vials of Pale Horse Prion they had retrieved from the bottom of Vanishing Lake over to the rack of acids and bases and set them down next to the pH meter that read the DNA markers. He had just finished setting up when suddenly Fannon moved over to him and stood very close. The voice in his ear was a hollow whisper, like a sour wind blowing into a dry well.

"Back in Vietnam, when we caught us a zip officer and we was debriefing him, we always had us a problem. . . . How d'ya know if the scummy dink bastard is lyin' or not? It was a big problem, 'cause I hadda send men into battle based on intelligence gleaned from them zipperheads. I developed my own pain interrogation technique that was more accurate than a fuckin' lie detector. Did you know, Mr. DeMille, that on a dolorimeter pain threshold scale of one to ten, a normal man can only stand a level eight for less than twenty seconds before passing out? Women can generally go for almost a minute. . . . Go figure that one.'' Fannon's tobacco breath was rancid and dank. ''When a man comes out of it, he's in a state of mild shock and psychosis, which is not unlike hypnosis. He's conscious, but it's kinda like a dream state. Only lasts about four minutes. Then the man wakes all the way up, and he's so fucked he'll start screamin' an pukin'. Strange thing I discovered was, in this state of agony and semi-consciousness, even the bravest men don't lie. And the few who try, I can look in their eyes and know when they're shittin' me. Are y'with me here, bub?''

''Please . . . please, I've done everything you want . . .''

''Yeah I know, but our problem is, I think you're still just a lyin' piece a'shit, and I don't trust you any more than I trusted them zips back in 'Nam. So, how do I know if you're givin' me honest-to-God, good-to-go shit here, or if you're just foolin' around mixin' up a batcha Kool-Aid?''

''I promise,'' Dexter said, his voice shaking with fear.

''Yeah, I know. I know you promise. Lotta dink motherfuckers gave me their word, and when I acted on it, I lost good, all-American White GIs because the fucks lied. Once I figured out that extreme, unendurable pain acts as a truth serum, I never lost a man on info I got from one a' them captured rice-burners.''

''Don't hurt me . . . please. I can't stand pain.''

''Okay, Dexter. Then make me a believer. Prove to me that what you're cookin' up here is more than just the measles. Otherwise, I'm gonna sit you in a chair and run my little 'truth machine' up your dick and start cookin' your prostate with wall current.''

From out of his pocket he pulled a small rheostat box with a cord and plug. At the other end of the electric cord was a long, slender needlelike object that looked like a metal catheter. Fannon held it up in front of the terrified scientist. ''There she is. Two dollars' worth of over-the-counter hardware that works better than a forty-thousand-dollar polygraph. I stick this puppy right down the hole in yer snake, then crank it to level eight and hold it there until either yer balls explode or ya start singin' 'The Star-Spangled Banner' through yer asshole.''

"I promise I won't lie to you, Reverend Kincaid. I thought I was Zophar. I thought I was a member of the Choir.''

"You ain't. We don't take heathen shitheads. But I'll tell you what . . . if you go fast here, and do this quickly, with no stalling and dallying, then I'll hold the Truth Applicator to a six when we debrief. I won't crank this baby up and we won't have t'smell yer pecker burning.''

"Oh, God . . . oh, God . . .''

"That's a good start. So, why don't y'get goin' and we'll see how I feel about the work when yer all finished.''

Dexter had originally planned to just fiddle for a while in the lab, then maybe pick the right moment to open a beaker of ammonium sulfur, which would set off the contamination alarm and bring in the Delta Force Rangers. But now, as he looked at the homemade electric rheostat and imagined the wire going up his penis to his prostate, he lost all resolve. If Fannon used that on him, he would scream the truth in seconds. He had no choice but to do as Fannon instructed. He no longer cared about the forty-five percent of the Detroit population that was African-American, and whom he was now targeting, along with New York's huge Jewish community. All he was worried about now was saving himself.

Dexter DeMille went to work arming the Pale Horse Prion. In the name of life-saving science he had once helped isolate this protein's ancestor in the mountains of New Guinea with Carleton Gajdusek. Now, like Adolf Hitler, he was about to use it to commit genocide. He couldn't fathom how he had traveled from one place to the other.

He pulled down the books on ethnic and racial DNA groupings and opened them to the appropriate acidosis graphs. He reached for the beakers that would alter the pH of the Prions. Then he went to work creating the second monstrous act of twentieth-century genocide.

Cris and Stacy waited for the supply train, and in the darkness, they easily boarded it. The car they rode on creaked and rumbled into the Fort. They dismounted only a hundred yards beyond the place where Fannon and his assault force had jumped off two hours earlier.

Now they stood in the gully and watched the train full of foodstuffs moving off, across the field. As they watched it go, it led their gaze to another, much more ominous train.

"There it is," Cris said, pointing at the White Train parked out in the field. "I heard about this in the Marines. Some guys knew a sergeant who worked the guard detail, and he said they would ride up on the roof with automatic weapons, but I wasn't sure if it was real or bullshit."

He moved along the gully getting closer, trying to see what was going on. When he was about three hundred yards away, he crouched down and studied the train through the tall grass. Stacy followed, then lay on the ground beside him.

"Looks like they're pumping something out," he said, observing the huge rubber hoses that were attached to the top of the hopper cars and snaked down to coupling joints on the concrete pads in the ground. They could hear a distant electric pump-motor humming.

"We gotta go find Dexter DeMille's lab," Stacy said. "If Fannon and the Choir are here, that's where they're going to be. I remember it's in Building 1666. That's where Max said they developed the super-secret stuff. He was never allowed down there, but he told me it was where Dexter worked."

"You know where it is?"

"I was in a primate lab in that building a few days ago. I think I can find it."

"Lead the way."

Stacy moved in a low crouch along the gully, heading in the direction that Fannon and the Choir had gone. She and Cris moved into the treeline and shortly found the same natural path through the woods. Soon they got to the clearing where Fannon had waited for Randall and the Texas Madman to return. Cris looked down and saw something on the ground, then picked it up.

"What is it?" she said, unable to see what he had found.

"Cigarette butt." He looked at it carefully; it was hand-rolled. "They were here," he said.

"How can you tell?"

"Two reasons. No moisture on this butt yet. No night dew. This thing was thrown down a short time ago. Also, most hobos roll their own. Packaged cigarettes, called hardrolls, are too expensive. An F.T.R.A. dropped this. They were right here on this spot less than an hour ago," he said softly.

Chapter 46

THE DEVIL'S WORKSHOP

Dexter had finished arming the Pale Horse Prion. It took him less than thirty minutes. He had checked his protein mixtures with the pH meter, and everything looked good. Now he glanced at Fannon Kincaid, who was leaning against the counter in the lab, his gray eyes studying Dexter.

"I've finished," he finally said, trying to get that all-seeing, terrifying laser gaze off of him. Fear had dried his mouth to a sticky paste.

Fannon moved over and looked at the three new metal bio-containers that Dexter had prepared. They were labeled with his scribbled handwriting.

"This one targets African-Americans," Dexter explained, showing the container he had marked "Afr." with tape on top. "This one is Jews. I've targeted both Ashkenazi and Sephardic Jews. I divided them into two vials." He looked hopefully at Fannon, wanting to please him, but got no reaction.

"There ain't no such thing as African-Americans," Fannon said ruefully, still looking at the first vial. "There's Niggers and there's Americans."

"You're right," Dexter said softly, eyeing the metal catheter sticking out of Fannon's pocket.

Then, like a hanging judge in a forties western, Fannon glowered at him and pronounced sentence. "You wanna take yer pants off now, Mr. DeMille?"

Dexter's face felt flushed. Simultaneously he felt cold sweat on his skin. He shook his head, but he couldn't make his mouth work.

"Randall, help Mr. DeMille drop his trousers," the new Moses said softly.

Cris and Stacy were outside Building 1666. Cris had stopped about a hundred yards from the first-floor entrance and carefully studied the terrain. He tried to figure out how he would get into this building if he were Kincaid, with a complement of men. From everything he'd heard, the silver-haired minister would do it with military precision. If Fannon went by the book, it meant there was a rear guard set up outside to protect the exit line. The trick was to locate the rear guards, define their positions, then shut them down.

"Let's go. What're we waiting for?" Stacy said, in a too-loud voice.

Cris put a finger to his lips and waited until she nodded. They stood stone-still for almost two minutes until the night insects started up again.

"Listen," he whispered, his mouth right in her ear, so close no sound could escape. "No crickets up ahead. Something that doesn't live here quieted them." Then he made a palm-down motion, indicating that she should lie flat.

She did as she was instructed.

He held up three fingers, indicating three minutes, she assumed, then he was gone, disappearing like an actor into the wings of a darkened theater.

All of a sudden, Stacy was cold and felt very alone. She tried to imagine Max in this building, which loomed tall, dark, and forbidding in front of her. She knew that inside, in the lower basement, Dexter and his team had designed terrible threats to mankind. Moreover, something Cris said was echoing in her conscience, but she would not allow herself to even suppose Max's role in any part of it. That he had any complicity in what went on inside the Devil's Workshop was too insane to even contemplate. Then the moon suddenly slipped behind a heavy bank of dark clouds and Stacy found herself surrounded in blackness.

Cris moved slowly around the perimeter of Building 1666, staying as far away as he could. He breathed a sigh of relief as the moon disappeared, giving him greater protection in the inky darkness. He was using his ears now as much as his eyes. Then he heard a clink. It was metal on stone, maybe a clip on an automatic rifle hitting concrete, or perhaps it was a pistol belt. He located a spot in the bushes, picking the enemy position by instinct and knowledge of how sound travels. He started toward the spot he had chosen. It was in the heavy bushes south of the front door. He was on his stomach now, more in the open than he liked, using the darkness of the moonless night, snaking across the wet grass instead of going through the bushes because he didn't want to make any sound. But moving over the grass was a calculated risk. The moon could reappear suddenly from behind the clouds and he would be caught out in the open, an easy target. As Cris wormed his way nearer, he also edged closer to the hedge that grew along the base of Building 1666. Then he lay still, his eyes and ears straining in the dark silence. Then, just as he was about to edge forward, he heard a man cough. It was a soft cough, but it startled him because the man was so close, only a few feet away.

Now he lay very still, breathing only through his mouth. After a moment, he edged a few inches closer until he finally could make out the vague outline of the man. He was lying in the bushes, his automatic weapon in his hands. The man was proned out, on his stomach, sighting down the barrel of his weapon. If these men were well trained and deployed properly, they would be in a V formation from the exit point if there were two men, or in a W if there were four. Assuming a V, that would put the second guard at a forty-five-degree angle to the exit, perpendicular to the first guard's line of fire. This positioning would catch a closing force between them without causing the rear guards to fire on each other.

Cris tried to picture the shape of the man; to imagine him from what little he could see, and how much space he took up in the darkness. Once Cris thought he could see the shape of him, he tried to ascertain if the man was alone, or if there was another shape lying unobserved in the dirt beyond. It was possible that they had deployed incorrectly. He didn't take anything for granted. After searching the black shadows for several minutes, he detected no others.

Stacy was moving, trying to stay low and out of sight. She had decided on impulse to find the lab. She needed to see it with her own eyes. If Max had worked there she would know it. She would see something, some evidence. She needed to know. As Stacy moved closer she visualized the layout of the lobby of Building 1666. She had something close to a photographic memory, which had served her well all through college and grad school. She closed her eyes and tried to reconstruct the index board she had looked at in the lobby days before. She could easily see the listing for the primate lab she had eventually chosen. It was SB-16, in the sub-basement, and above it was . . . ? She saw a faint shadow in her memory. There were several labs down there, Biochemistry and something else. But, what? And then she knew. It was the neurotransmitter lab. She could see it now in her memory, plain as if she were looking right at it. Max's early specialty had been neurotransmission. He had written some groundbreaking papers on Alzheimer's and the use of neurotransmitters to stimulate failing memory. He had helped with the experiments that proved if you implant certain reconstructed DNA material in the brain, it stimulates the manufacture of acetylcholine, which in many cases retards memory loss.

She also knew that in order to test neurotransmission therapy on rats or chimps, it was necessary to have a full lab setup. The neurotransmitter lab would be a Class A facility, with a complete chemical closet. It was a good bet that was where Dexter's lab would be.

She closed her eyes again and tried to read the lab number off the memory board in her mind. She couldn't see it, but she had the strong impression that it was in the basement. So, she decided she would gamble and try going downstairs. She slowly crept along in the dark, trying not to step on leaves or rustle dry branches, and then she was at the edge of the building.

There was a door. It was slightly ajar, and the light was off inside the stairwell. She moved it slowly open and stepped onto the darkened landing. She looked up and saw that a light bulb had been removed above the inside of the doorway. She began to move down the concrete steps, her heart beating wildly as she descended. *What the hell am I doing?* she thought, as she crept toward the light at the foot of the stairs. When she got to the basement, she stopped. She thought she could hear voices, and ducked back into the stairwell. She listened for several seconds in silence. Then she heard men speaking again. She was sure she had found where Fannon and Dexter had gone, but she was trapped. If she waited where she was, they would find her when they left. The building went down one more floor to the sub-basement, where the primate lab was located. They would be going up when they exited, so she crept down the last flight of stairs to the small landing at the foot of the staircase. She pressed her back against the cold concrete and waited.

.   .   .

Cris had decided to disable the lookout. He got a good lungful of air, and with his right knee and left foot under him, he dug up a handful of dirt. Then, without giving himself any time for complicated moral debate, he sprang forward and landed on the man's back, simultaneously locking his right forearm across the guard's throat and slamming a handful of dirt into his open mouth just before he could cry out. Cris could feel the guard's teeth for an instant against his palm. Then Cris locked his left hand on his right forearm and squeezed hard with all his strength. He could feel the guard trembling and convulsing under him as the blood and oxygen were cut from his brain. The man struggled fiercely, and Cris bore down harder. No sound came out of the man's mud-packed mouth. His hands dropped the weapon and were now feebly clawing at his throat, trying to pry Cris's stranglehold loose. In less than twenty seconds, the guard was unconscious. Cris lay on top of him for thirty seconds to make sure there was no movement, wondering if the man was dead. Then he carefully untangled the sling from the weapon that was still wrapped around the guard's left forearm. He pulled the gun free. He instantly could recognize it by feel . . . a fully automatic Uzi assault rifle.

"Dale, you okay?" he heard another man whisper in the darkness.

"Yeah," Cris whispered, to disguise his voice. He placed two fingers on the carotid artery of the man beneath him. He could feel nothing.

Cris shook his head, then put the murderous act behind him. It was the way he'd been taught to do it in Special Forces Recon.

He moved away from the body with the newly acquired Uzi in his hand. The grip plate on the barrel was still warm with the heat from the dead man's hand. Cris estimated a spot forty-five degrees from the center point of the original line of fire. If guards were in either a V or W formation, that should be where the man who had just whispered would be hiding. Cris moved closer. . . .

"That you, Dale?" the man called out from almost the exact place in the bushes Cris had targeted.

"Please . . . oh God, oh God, don't stick that in me," Dexter pleaded. He was down to his underwear and shirt, seated in a chair in the lab, as Fannon plugged his homemade lie detector into a wall socket. Kincaid then adjusted the rheostat.

"Zero," he said, matter-of-factly. "Gotta start at zero, or it won't go in." Then he moved to Dexter DeMille. "Get 'em off, bub." Fannon pointed to DeMille's boxer shorts.

"Please, please, I'll do anything," Dexter whined.

Then there was a short burst of machine-gun fire outside, followed by another burst, which had a distinctly different pitch.

"Two weapons," Fannon said, reading the gun reports accurately. "Get everything loaded. We're pulling out," he ordered.

Randall Rader gathered up the three Prion vials, stuffed them into the foam-rubber carrying case, then jammed it into his backpack and headed to the door of the lab. "Get yer pants on," Fannon yelled.

Dexter jumped up and tried to get into his trousers. He was hopping around on one foot. He'd been saved the horrible experience of the prostate-cooking polygraph, but now with machine-gun fire outside he didn't know which to fear more.

"Let's go!" Fannon shouted.

Dexter got his pants on and was carrying his shoes as they pulled him out of the lab, running into the hall.

Outside the corridor, the three guards, including R.V. and the Texas Madman, were locked and loaded. They led the way. Fannon and Dexter followed, with Randall Rader bringing up the rear. They opened the door into the staircase and thundered up the metal stairs. None of them saw Stacy hiding down below.

Fannon held Dexter by the back of his shirt on the landing just inside the building. With his automatic pistol pressed against the scientist's shoulder blades, he whispered coarsely, "You go where I push, or I'm gonna drop yer sorry ass and move right over ya."

"Okay," Dexter squeaked.

Fannon pushed him out into the night, running behind him, using Dexter for a shield.

They ran across the grass to the right side of the building. Suddenly, a jeep came roaring up the street and turned into the yard. Inside the vehicle were two Torn Victor commandos.

Randall Rader and the Texas Madman opened up as soon as the jeep turned. Their deadly barrage of nine-millimeter automatic-weapon fire tore the commandos right out of their seats. The men flew backward, dead as they hit the ground. The last rounds sparked loudly against the jeep's metal, ricocheting with a rich whining tone as bullets tore off pieces of the still-moving vehicle.

The empty jeep, its headlights boring holes into the darkness, rattled on for almost twenty yards before it crashed into the monument sign announcing Science Building 1666, USAMRIID.

"Take the jeep!" Fannon screamed.

They all ran toward the vehicle. Then another machine gun ripped the darkness. Flame was shooting out of its barrel from about forty yards away.

It was Cris Cunningham, lying prone behind a low wall. He hit one member of the Christian Choir, who went down where he stood. The Texas Madman took the second burst. He stumbled as ten rounds blew his stomach wide open. He took two more uncertain steps, then fell into the back seat of the jeep. Robert Vail jumped in, and after one look, threw the Madman out onto the ground. Fannon got behind the wheel, dragging Dexter along with him and pushing him into the back seat with R.V. Randall Rader turned to where Cris was lying behind the wall and laid down a barrage of withering fire. . . . Bullets chipped off the low concrete-and-brick; masonry dust made a fan of unseen debris in the darkness.

Then the jeep was going, moving fast, the wheels throwing huge chunks of wet grass out behind it. Cris stood up and fired as it roared away. Fannon turned off the headlights, and then Cris was shooting only at the retreating sound. He didn't hear any of his rounds hit metal.

Stacy heard the gunfire and prayed that Cris was all right. She was moving up the one flight of stairs from the lower basement into the basement hallway. She found the lab where they had been working. The light was still on, the door open. She moved into the lab just as the sound of gunfire outside stopped. She glanced quickly around and saw the workbench. She moved over to it and looked down at the papers that Dexter had left behind. They were DNA charts, but she didn't have time to read them. Then she saw something that froze her heart. It was right in front of her on the glass beakers that contained the acids and bases used to alter pH factors. She reached out and picked up one of the beakers. The label was in Max's neat handwriting. It read: "A.C.12-16:C." She looked at the other beakers and saw that his handwriting was on all of them.

Max had worked in this lab. Worked on DNA samples, using acidosis to do what? *Was Max helping Dexter target these Prions?* she wondered. It was impossible for her to believe he had been working here in the basement of the Devil's Workshop.

Then she heard shouting out front, and more machine-gun fire. She ran up the stairs and out of the building.

She was standing outside in the moonless night wondering which way to run. She heard a jeep pull down the road and make a sharp turn, its tortured tires squealing on the pavement.

Cris had turned and gone back to where he had left Stacy. When he arrived, she wasn't there. "Stacy!" he called out.

"Here," she yelled from across the quad.

"Let's go!" he shouted.

Then the two of them started running out the way they'd come in, heading back toward the field and the narrow trail in the woods.

"What happened?" She was panting as she ran.

"Don't talk." And he moved even faster.

She could barely keep up with him. They were heading across the open field toward the hills when the moon suddenly reappeared, lighting their escape.

A siren went off behind them at the Fort. Then a bank of lights lit up the common area near Building 1666, but they were almost into the hills unseen and running for all they were worth.

They finally got to the temporary safety of the woods. Cris turned and looked back. Now they could see the headlights of twenty or so vehicles roaring on the campus streets a half mile away, converging on Building 1666.

"What happened? I was afraid you'd been shot," she said.

"I told you to stay put," he said, out of breath and angry.

"I heard shooting," she repeated.

He shook his head in dismay, then turned his attention to their escape route. "We can't stay here," he said. "In a few minutes they're going to find the guys I killed."

"You killed people?"

"Yeah, I think so," he croaked bitterly. "We've gotta get moving. This isn't safe. If those Fort commandos went to the same ground-ops school I did, they'll pick up our footprints in the wet grass. They'll make us in no time."

"There's a road I was on when I was here before. It runs along the fence on the east side of the property. I saw it when they brought me out to SATCOM Battalion HQ," she said.

"Let's go, show me," he said.

She took the lead and headed off around the side of the wooded hillside. They stayed in the trees, moving low and fast.

When Cris looked at the tracks where the ghostly four-car apparition had been an hour before, he was surprised to see that the White Train was gone.

They ran out from the trees, across the open field, in the direction of the fence on the eastern perimeter of the Fort that Stacy had mentioned. From behind them they heard the distant sound of a helicopter.

"Back into the trees," he yelled as he spun, pulling Stacy with him.

From the west, two Bell Jet Ranger gunships appeared, flying low over the moonlit meadow, their downdrafts swirling the long grass under them as they streaked toward the intruders. Simultaneously, both belly lights snapped on, and Cris and Stacy were quickly caught in a searing white light. The safety of the tree line was still fifty yards away.

"You're under arrest," a bullhorn in the lead chopper announced. "Stop running or you will be shot." And then, to make the point, one of the gunships let loose a stream of tracer rounds that tore up the grass ten feet from them, starting a small fire that quickly went out. "On your stomachs!" the bullhorn demanded.

Cris and Stacy stood motionless, their faces turned up to the blinding light.

One of the gunships was landing, and Cris knew escape was now hopeless. He nodded at Stacy, and they did as instructed.

Torn Victor commandos jumped out of the side door of the landing gunship and raced across the grass to Stacy and Cris, who were facedown in the dirt. The other hovering chopper was now directly over them. Their clothes rippled violently in the strong downdraft of the giant rotor. Then they could feel hands roughly grabbing and cuffing them. They were yanked to their feet, dragged to the idling gunship, and shoved through the door. The engine roared as the chopper lifted and they were whisked away into the night.

Chapter 47

DÉJÀ VU

They were in separate concrete-block rooms in Company A, First SATCOM Battalion Headquarters. Outside Cris's locked door, looking at him through a small window, were two stone-faced commandos. They suddenly entered the room and uncuffed him, and while one of the commandos held him at gunpoint, the other fingerprinted him. "Where's Stacy? What'd you do to her?" he asked, but they left without answering.

After two hours, Cris's door was opened again. He was pulled out into the corridor and led through double doors into a large windowless room labeled "Satellite Uplink Situation Room." His handcuffs were tight, and as he was jerked along he felt them cutting into his wrists. He was shoved roughly into a chair. Already in the room was a young Latin man, devoid of emotion, with Captain's bars on his collar.

"I want an attorney," Cris said. "Even in the Army you can't hold me without charging me."

"Shut up, don't talk. Don't say anything," Captain DeSilva said. A moment later the door opened, and another of the Torn

Victor commandos led Stacy into the room. Still cuffed, she was also thrown roughly into one of the wooden chairs. She realized this was where she had first met Admiral Zoll.

"You okay?" Cris asked, and DeSilva stepped forward and hit him hard in the face. Blood started to run out of Cris's mouth and down his chin.

"I said don't talk. That goes for you too, Miss," he said, glowering at Stacy.

They waited in anxious silence for almost half an hour, then the door opened and Admiral Zoll moved into the room with Colonel Chittick, followed by two more armed commandos.

Zoll approached the table and stood staring at Stacy for a long time. "Mrs. Richardson, whatever am I going to do with you?" he finally growled in his sandpapery voice.

She didn't answer as they traded hostile looks. Then Zoll looked over at Cris. "You turned out to be something of a surprise. Just got your print run back, Captain Cunningham. Silver Star, D.S.C. You're supposed to be one of the good guys."

"So are you," Cris said bitterly, reading the name "Zoll" off his nameplate under rows of battle decorations. This was the man he had targeted. This was the man responsible for Kennidi's horrible death. Suddenly, anger and suicidal disregard for his safety burned in Cris.

Admiral Zoll didn't change his expression as he sat down opposite them at the wooden table. It was exactly like before, only this time Stacy sensed she would not walk off the base alive. She now had a much better idea of what was going on at Fort Detrick. The stakes were too high for Zoll to let them survive.

"I understand that you and the rest of those scruffy bastards you brought in with you penetrated 1666, our neurotransmitter lab. You really don't give up, do you, Mrs. Richardson? Or are you just determined to fuck with me until I've completely lost my patience?"

"We know what you're doing," Stacy shot back. "We know

about the Prion experiments you performed on Troy Lee Williams and Sylvester Swift at the prison in Vanishing Lake. You ordered those experiments. Only you could have had them transferred up there.''

"My guess is you can't prove anything," he said softly. "You and Captain Cunningham are going to have to be dealt with. We're patriots here, serving this country's greatest needs."

"Hold me, Daddy. Please, it hurts so."

Cris stood up, and Nino DeSilva grabbed him and threw him back down in his chair.

"Let go of me, you piece of shit," Cris hissed, then turned to Zoll, anger spilling over him like flaming liquid. Vengeance was his higher power, but now that he was standing face to face with Zoll, he could do nothing. Cris's impotence quickly turned to rage. "You asshole! You've been fucking with genocide, creating a genetic bio-weapon. You're not a patriot . . . you're a fucking monster!"

"You don't know what you're talking about, Captain," Zoll said, rising to his feet. "This program will one day save the world from nuclear disaster. If people like me don't take huge personal risks to redesign military strategic thinking, the world is doomed to go up in a cloud of radioactive dust. Genetic bio-weapons are deadly, but unlike nuclear weapons, they won't indiscriminately end all life on earth."

"Daddy, I love you. It hurts so much. . . . Please make it stop."

"You son-of-a-bitch! That shit you were testing in Huntsville Prison back in the eighties got shipped to Iraq, and they used it against our troops. You designed Gulf War Syndrome right here, six years before Desert Storm. I've got it in me. I'm a carrier. You should've seen my four-year-old daughter die, you fucking asshole! Her head was swollen and discolored like rotting fruit. At the end, her eyes were so far down in the swelling she could barely see. You murdered her, you slimy bastard! Don't tell me these bio-weapons don't kill indiscriminately!''

Cris was out of his chair and out of control, raging at Zoll, who glowered back at him. The depth of Cris's hatred and passion was so acute that it froze everybody in the room. Nino DeSilva stared at Cris with his mouth agape. Then, in frustration, Cris lurched forward across the table and head-butted Zoll, catching the Admiral over the eye, opening a cut that immediately started bleeding onto his uniform. The Torn Victor commandos standing behind Zoll grabbed Cris and threw him onto the floor. Quickly, one of them was kneeling on his back. Only Nino DeSilva had remained frozen. He seemed to be in some kind of shock.

Zoll calmly removed a handkerchief from his pocket and held it to his eye to stop the bleeding. He looked down at Cris on the floor. "I'm sorry about the pyridostigmine bromide we designed. It was a mistake to ship it over there. But back then, Saddam Hussein was an ally. He was using it against Iran, which had some of our hostages. After that, our political fortunes in the Middle East changed. Maybe he turned it on us in the Gulf War, and some of our guys got hurt. We didn't see it coming," he said, the words spoken mechanically.

"The V.A. is still denying everything. Refusing to treat our vets who've got Gulf War Syndrome. Why don't you set them straight?" One of the commandos jammed Cris's head down to the floor and held it there roughly, but Cris continued, "You won't do it because it would expose everything you're doing here. It's easier to just throw those poor sick guys away," he said through clenched teeth.

"It must be nice to view the world from such a morally lofty position," Zoll said.

"The men who broke into your neurotransmitter lab are White power survivalists. They have samples of armed Pale Horse Prion, and they're going to use it against segments of the population. You're about to be exposed anyway," Stacy said.

"Are there any missing samples of that protein?" Zoll asked, looking at Chittick.

"All accounted for," Chittick responded.

"Dexter DeMille had two vials in marine depth containers at the bottom of Vanishing Lake. They took him back there after the fire and retrieved them," Stacy countered.

"Dexter DeMille is dead," Zoll answered, his demeanor changing slightly; some of his blustery command presence left him as the beginnings of doubt took hold.

"He's alive, and he's certainly not going to defend you or the Devil's Workshop after what you've told the media about him," Stacy said.

"That still doesn't change my responsibilities with respect to you and Captain Cunningham. You two are out of the equation." He looked at Nino DeSilva, who had once again regained his stoic expression. "You know what to do," Zoll told DeSilva, who nodded. Then the Admiral moved around the table to where Cris was being held down on the floor. "I'm sorry about your daughter," he said. "But the course we've chosen here is the right one. Your record says you were a brave soldier. Unfortunately, sometimes brave soldiers have to be left behind."

"Go fuck yourself," Cris growled. "Your apology and bullshit sentiment are not accepted."

They were in the back seat of the Provost Marshal's sedan being driven to their own executions. They watched in dismay as Nino DeSilva turned left off the rutted road and jounced out across the dark, uninhabited part of the Fort, where their graves would be lost forever.

DeSilva slowly brought the car to a halt, and sat behind the wheel with the engine idling. He rested his right hand on his nine-millimeter Beretta, which was bracketed in a gun rack next to the radio. The three of them sat in silence.

Nino DeSilva momentarily shifted his gaze to the rearview mirror and studied his prisoners. Cris and Stacy were forced to hunch over slightly because of the chains shackling their hands to the metal rings in the floor. "You got a good military package," Nino finally said to Cris.

"Yeah. Big deal. And the medal you're about to give me comes shaped like a bullet."

Again they sat in silence. Nino turned around and looked directly at Cris and Stacy through the metal grate. "That shit you were saying about Huntsville Prison and us making Gulf War sickness in the eighties—is that really true?"

"You didn't hear Zoll deny it, did you?"

They listened to the motor idling until DeSilva said suddenly, "I didn't join up to kill our own guys."

"None of us did," Cris said.

"My older brother was in Desert Storm. He got the sickness. He can't do shit anymore. Lays around, no energy, got rashes. Even his wife quit him. The V.A. tells him it's in his head, y'know, that he's got a psychosomatic illness like P.T.S., like he's fucked up in the brain, which is just plain shit, y'know?"

Stacy could see DeSilva hated what he was being asked to do.

"This bio-weapons program helped destroy your brother, Captain," she said. "Now it's in the hands of fanatic White supremacists who won't hesitate to use it."

But DeSilva didn't seem to be listening. He was reliving something else. When he next spoke, his voice was soft, almost a whisper. "I killed this Indian in Badwater, Texas . . . a deputy or something. He was just in the way. I had orders, so I killed him. Haven't slept good since." He was looking down now, at the front seat, his eyes fixed on nothing. "And I stole that kid's body. Now I gotta take you out, a Silver Star winner, a Marine like me, and a woman. It doesn't make sense I gotta do this."

"Let us go, man. Zoll won't know. He won't find out till it's too late."

"I'm in this up to my nose." Nino sat in silence. "Nothing's been the same since I killed that Indian. Nothing." He sat for another half minute, then turned off the engine and pulled the Beretta out of its bracket. He opened the driver's door, stepped out, and threw the keys to the handcuffs through the open window onto the back floor.

"What're you gonna do?" Cris asked.

"I let you go, I'm a dead man. Either that or I go to jail for life," DeSilva said. "I gotta do like I was ordered. Unhook yourselves and get out." Cris and Stacy exchanged looks in the back seat of the car. The glance told Stacy to be ready, that Cris was going to try something. She nodded subtly.

They unhooked the chain and got the cuffs off. Then DeSilva opened the rear door and motioned them out while aiming the gun at them.

As Cris stepped out, he tried to move as close to DeSilva as he could, but Nino was combat-trained and instantly backed off. "Stay where you are. Get down on your knees," he commanded. "I can do this so ya won't feel a thing." Cris and Stacy did as they were instructed.

"Like you did with Max Richardson?" Stacy said.

"I don't know nothing about that. Nick Zingo told me he committed suicide."

"He was murdered," she shot back.

"I didn't wanna kill the Indian," DeSilva said softly. "I can't stand it that I killed that guy."

Cris watched as Nino brought the gun up to his shoulder and sighted down the barrel. Cris had reached the end. He had nothing more to lose. He decided that he would lunge up off his knees, directly into the muzzle of the Beretta and almost certain death. He hoped Stacy would use his charge to get away into the night. But just as Cris was about to make his move, Nino DeSilva lowered his weapon.

"Can't," he said softly. "Can't do it again." He stood ten feet away, staring at them. "Get out of here," he finally said.

Cris nodded. He took Stacy's hand, pulled her up, and started to lead her away into the darkness. Then Cris turned and looked back at Nino DeSilva. He was standing with the gun at his side and his chin on his chest. "Sometimes men fall, but the good ones can stand again," Cris said.

Then he turned and moved away, holding Stacy's hand.

Nino DeSilva watched until he could no longer see them in the dark.

Chapter 48

HOW TO COOK A WEREWOLF

Y ou make movies about milking cows and picking flowers and I'll make movies about fucking and getting loaded and we'll see who puts more asses on theater seats,'' Buddy growled at Alicia Profit from the motor home's command chair.

She had been talking about a movie she loved, made by some fruity Italian director. The flick had died in the art houses, and Alicia's enthusiasm for it pissed Buddy off. He demanded a little more allegiance from a Brazil Nut. Still, Alicia, who Buddy thought was too pretty and too young to be as smart and self-assured as she was, didn't back down.

"Is it just about money, Buddy? You've *got* money. Is it just about seeing how high you can pile the greenbacks? How many Testarossas can you drive at once? I don't know why you never made *The Prospector*. That could have been a beautiful movie— a man's search for himself before death. It was full of pathos and humanity. You shoulda fought for it.''

"Pathos? What's that, a Mexican restaurant? That script was a boring piece of shit. An old guy who's dying? Who the fuck cares? What kinda rock 'n' roll score you gonna put under that snore?''

In fact, Buddy had loved the story, but had been talked out of it by the studio after he signed his new big deal. They wanted six high-budget kick-ass movies. The press release on the deal called it "The Buddy Brazil Action Pack." Buddy still pulled out the script of *The Prospector* and read it occasionally. Why the hell *hadn't* he fought for it?

"I think it would have made a difference in the way people perceive you," Alicia defended, "like after Spielberg did *Schindler's List*. He reinvented himself with that movie."

They were rolling through Gettysburg, Pennsylvania. John Little Bear was driving the big blue-and-white coach. Billy Seal was sitting with Alicia and Rayce at the fold-out table. Buddy could feel both a heavy weight on his shoulders and a tired weight on his eyes. He knew it was the beginning of a bout of depression. He had snorted a few more lines to try to stave it off, but his body was burning the coke like factory furnace fuel. He was going deeper and deeper into a funk, and it wasn't helped by this conversation with Alicia, and the fact that they were in Gettysburg.

The last time he'd been here he was only twenty-two years old, just out of film school and full of great ideas for redesigning the film business. He'd been in this historic town which had hosted the turning point of the Civil War, shooting a documentary, using five thousand dollars he'd saved up from summer jobs. It was every cent he had, but he had thrived on the challenge. The film was called *The Two Hawks of Gettysburg* and was about the Civil War, then and now, dealing with the socioeconomic and racial factors of American life one hundred years after the battle. He had tracked the lives of two people in the film: a black Union soldier named Evan Hawk, who died protecting a dream that was meager but filled with hope, and the black Union soldier's great-grandson, Reuben Hawk, a current Gettysburg factory worker. Reuben's life had fulfilled none of the hopes of his great-grandfather. "Seventeen minutes of pretty remarkable filmmaking," Sid Sheinberg had called it, comparing the work to *Amblin,* the film he'd seen by Steven Spielberg, which Sheinberg had loved and which had gotten Spielberg his first directing jobs in television. But Buddy had been afraid to ever direct again. It was his first bad Hollywood compromise, choosing instead to produce. Somehow, even at twenty-six, he had already started playing safe.

Producing a big studio hit was still a huge long shot, but Buddy found he liked not having to take the full responsibility for what he made. When you were a director, if a movie failed it was "on you." When you were a producer, there were plenty of people to put the blame on. The writer was always the best and easiest target. Buddy had fucked over more writers than *Kirkus Reviews.* Of course, the director was easy to pin it on, or the studio, although that was trickier politically. Sometimes on his flops, Buddy was so busy running around behind the scenes making shit fall on colleagues that he felt like the Wizard of Beverly Hills, pulling levers behind a big velvet curtain.

Slowly, over the years, he had slipped into the outlaw Buddy thing, with the black outfits and pimp accessories, his "McDaddy props," as Jack Nicholson called the hookers from Heidi's stable. There had been the endless stream of beautiful MAWs, who styled and profiled in his Malibu house. Munchable, long-stemmed wannabes: Models, Actresses, Whatevers, who perched on his sofa with their shoulders back, smiling, flirting, hoping for stardom. He had sampled these pleasures abundantly, but almost always felt horrible afterward, as if in all this luscious beauty there was also some hidden contamination, unrecognizable in its soul-destroying depravity.

All of these feelings confused him, so he did more lines and shot more drugs and tried to make any painful introspection go away in a haze of lost weekends. He had left the twenty-two-year-old filmmaker with a camera and a dream way back there on the side of the rocky Hollywood road.

Jack Nicholson, whom Buddy more or less idolized, called him "the Werewolf" because of Buddy's dark looks and nocturnal habits. In fact, Buddy was not much of a werewolf. Inside, he was more of a lost child, and in the moments before his depressions hit, he could see it all very clearly, could read his own uselessness like tea leaves in a Gypsy's cup. He knew that he was heading nowhere and accomplishing nothing. His mega-hits would not be watched by anybody when the cutting-edge sound-track music and trendy clothes were no longer popular. Like the Bee Gees and bell-bottom trousers, his material was caught in the moment in a way that defined him as temporary and unimportant.

"Alicia, crank me up," he shouted, and out came her little compact. The lines were chopped and Hoovered up by Buddy, then the little black plastic emergency kit was returned to Alicia Profit's purse. Buddy never carried his own drugs. He couldn't take another possession bust.

"Turn on the TV," he ordered, to change the subject and the memory. Buddy knew he was never going to make *The Prospector,* as much as he loved it, because he was afraid it wouldn't make any money. He couldn't stand the idea of producing a flop. Buddy was about flash, about winning. He was an end-zone dancer in a black shirt and vest, with three-inch-heeled ostrich cowboy boots. He was an outlaw.

"The bodies inside Fort Detrick have yet to be identified," a beautiful news anchor said, her dyed blond hair cut to helmet length. "But early reports say that the individuals who were shot apparently infiltrated the Army medical base by riding on a supply train. What they were doing in the lab of Building 1666 is still a mystery to the doctors there, but sources close to the investigation say that Army scientists are trying to reconstruct the reason from the chemicals and products used in the lab. The intruders killed two soldiers and left four accomplices dead before they stole a jeep and crashed out through the main gate of Fort Detrick. The Army still runs a medical facility at the Fort, but most of the property was decommissioned ten years ago . . .''

Buddy stared at the TV screen, and the depth of his depression grew. He felt like a man with a hundred-pound sack on his back. Were Cris and Stacy among the dead? Was the whole thing up to him now? He had made a promise to himself that he would not quit, and that promise was still driving him, but he had made a career out of shirking and ducking and claiming credit that was not his. Now he was pitted against a formidable enemy. Not just film critics with their angry, sarcastic jibes, but crazy fanatics with bio-weapons and automatic rifles. Buddy felt skewered by events, like a rotisserie chicken turning over a slow-burning fire, dripping fat and getting smaller by the moment.

''We're leaving Gettysburg. We'll be in Harrisburg in about half an hour,'' Rayce said softly.

Buddy wasn't listening.

''Where to then? You still want to go to the rail yards, like you said?'' Rayce persisted.

Buddy was thinking about Cris and Stacy: brave, committed, and maybe dead.

''How 'bout it?'' Rayce said.

''Huh?''

''I said, do you still want to go to the rail yard in Harrisburg?''

Buddy looked at the rugged stuntman, then around the motor home at the rest of his Brazil Nuts. Their faces showed a strange lack of commitment. He knew that most of them thought this was just another Buddy fantasy, a paintball fight that would make Buddy feel tough, but was not really dangerous. Their expressions told him they doubted they were ever going to find Kincaid, that Buddy didn't want any trouble, he only wanted to look tough . . . only wanted to be able to brag about it in Hollywood

afterward: " *'Member that time we were locked and loaded, goin'
after that crazy motherfucker? That gonzo preacher? He's lucky I
never got close enough to light him up, the fuck.*"

"Harrisburg switching yard, Mr. B.?" Alicia repeated, looking
at him and seeing a strange lost-child expression she had never
seen before.

"I guess so," Buddy answered weakly.

Rayce nodded at John Little Bear, who shifted into overdrive.
They passed out of Gettysburg, heading toward Harrisburg, and
Buddy's strange collision course with destiny.

Chapter 49

SWITCHING YARD

The blue-and-white motor home arrived in Harrisburg a few minutes past noon. They pulled into the parking lot next to the rail yard without taking any precautions whatsoever.

Buddy was still in the command chair, trying to find his old Captain Kirk persona that he used in his Malibu living room before a paintball fight. He would sit in his five-hundred-dollar custom cammies explaining the rules of engagement and dividing the participants, making sure he always had the best shooters on his team. Now, as he sat behind John Little Bear, who had just shut off the engine, he didn't know exactly what to do, how to even begin to instruct them. All he could think about was the terrifying sensation he had felt when the burst of nine-millimeter slugs tore into the rented Blazer up at Vanishing Lake. As he gazed out the front window of the motor home, Buddy could see hundreds of stainless-steel tanker cars that he assumed were full of gas or oil.

"Whatta you want to do, Mr. B.?" Alicia said brightly.

"I . . . I don't know." Buddy uttered the unfamiliar words and looked at Rayce for help.

"I'm gonna get out an' check around," Rayce said. "You wanna give me a better description of what I'm looking for?"

"I told you, the leader's got silver-gray hair and they're all dressed like bums with F.T.R.A. tattooed on their arms. You better take one of the weapons," Buddy said.

" 'At's okay, I'll just have a look," Rayce drawled. He got out of the motor home, and Buddy watched him stand in front of the vehicle before he moved off in the general direction of the lines of silver tanker cars.

"This guy Kincaid's a motherfucker," Buddy warned. "We take no chances. It's important that I run this operation from the motor home. It'll be our C.P. We'll be on radios and I'll call the plays from here."

"Good idea," Alicia said, rolling her eyes slightly as she looked over at John Little Bear.

They sat in the motor home and waited for Rayce to return. Almost half an hour passed as Buddy paced in his plush command post. He was looking at the Brazil Nuts. John Little Bear was characteristically stoic, sitting like Geronimo, the renegade chief, his flat features betraying nothing of what might be going on inside. Billy Seal, the black stunt captain he had used on ten pictures, was calmly playing solitaire at the small table. Alicia Profit was reading a magazine. Buddy was another story altogether. He was a collection of nervous jerks, twitches, and strained expressions.

"They got Rayce. I know it!" he suddenly blurted. "He was just gonna take a look around. A look! That takes a fucking half hour? He's gone. Okay, okay . . . all right, they got Rayce. We're down one man. We need to organize something. Personally, I think if Rayce got scragged, we've got a police situation here. Alicia, get on the cell and scare up somebody at the Harrisburg P.D."

Alicia picked up the telephone and was dialing Information when the door jerked open and Rayce appeared in the threshold, scaring Buddy shitless. He jumped back, terrified, and whacked his hip on the motor home's low counter.

"They're here, over thirty a' them. They're on the far side of the switching yard. I first saw a group of them over by the Yardmaster's office, going through the trash, getting some papers out. I followed 'em back and found the rest of the group in a gully, on the other side by the big water tower. A real scruffy buncha bohunks."

"They're carbon-sheet spotting," Buddy said, showing his knowledge of the rails gleaned during two days with Cris Cunningham.

"Carbon what?" Alicia said.

As he rubbed the sore spot on his hip, Buddy explained how the extra train line-up sheets thrown away by the Yardmaster could be used to select cars.

"One other thing, pard—you're right about these guys being armed. They got a pile of artillery. All of 'em are packin' side arms, and I must've counted at least six or seven fully automatic weapons: a couple Uzis, some B.A.R.s., a couple mini-fourteens . . ."

"You still want me to get the police on the phone?" Alicia said, holding up the cell.

Buddy nodded. "Tactically that's the right play," he whined with damn little command presence.

"Thing is, they looked like they're heading off. Soon as the guys showed up with the sheets they got from the trash, they started moving out."

"Away from the station? Away from us?" Buddy asked hopefully.

"I think so . . . they moved off that way." Rayce pointed out of the motor home's front window in the direction of the northeast section of the yard.

"Okay, Alicia, you get the cops on the phone. I'd better stay here and talk to 'em. John, Rayce, and Billy, you each take an automatic weapon and move out. Keep them in sight. Reconnoiter back here after we find out where they're heading.''

"Sir, not to disagree, but if you're calling in the law, I'd just as soon not be caught with an illegal fully automatic weapon in my hands," Rayce said.

"If you're gonna stand around acting like a pussy, then you joined the wrong team," Buddy said, finally getting some Captain Kirk into it.

"You're the one hiding in the motor home, asshole," Rayce said angrily, and suddenly the inside of the vehicle needed de-icing. Everybody was frozen in silence, waiting for Buddy to explode. A Brazil Nut never questioned the producer's testosterone level.

"Look, Rayce, I'm not fucking hiding," Buddy said in a less hostile voice, so everybody took a deep breath and relaxed slightly. "Somebody has to run this ground op, otherwise we got nothing but confusion. Don't worry about the automatic weapon. I have a gun dealer's license. I'll tell the cops we're doing pick-up shots on a film, or some fucking thing. . . . Movie work, everybody loves the movies.''

Buddy moved to the closet and broke out the Dominator, which was way too big to lug around, and neither John Little Bear, Rayce, nor Billy wanted the sniper's rifle. They had also brought an Uzi and two H&K Close Assault weapons. Rayce and Little Bear each took one of those; Billy grabbed the Uzi. They all tromboned the slides and checked the safeties. The motor home was filled with the sound of well-oiled weapons as they clicked and clacked inside the hot narrow space. Buddy handed each of them a headphone walkie-talkie that he always insisted his paintball team use to communicate.

"Okay, move out," Buddy ordered. "We're on Channel 18."

Rayce, Billy, and Little Bear exited the motor home and split up. The headphone units looked slightly ridiculous on them as they ran into the hot sunshine, miked up like a Japanese ski club.

"Get the cops on the phone," Buddy instructed.

Alicia, who had been listening to Buddy with the forgotten phone in her hand, started dialing again, and after going through half a dozen people, telling each one who Buddy was, she finally got a Public Affairs Officer and handed the telephone to Buddy.

"You're going to make a movie here?" the man said excitedly.

"We've got a situation at the switching yards," Buddy corrected. "There's armed hobos with weapons, and I think you need t'get some people out here fast."

"It's a movie about armed hobos?" the Public Affairs Officer said, still completely missing the point.

"Look, asshole, it's not a movie. Okay? This is real life. I have people on the ground right now, trying to contain the situation. We need police back-up."

Suddenly there was the sound of machine-gun fire and ricocheting bullets. The fusillade brought Buddy's heart up into his throat.

"What the fuck . . . ! Did you hear that?" he shrieked at the Public Affairs Officer.

"No, sir . . . what?" the man said.

Then there was more machine-gun fire. Through the front window of the motor home, Buddy could see Rayce Walker running for his life, alongside a string of flatcars. As Buddy watched, more automatic weapons barked out and Rayce went down, spinning wildly, hit and bloodied on his right side.

"Shit! They got Rayce," Buddy mumbled, dropping the phone by mistake, disconnecting it.

"Buddy, you've gotta get out there! They're killing Rayce!" Alicia screamed.

"Huh?" Buddy said.

There was more machine-gun fire, followed by the high-pitched scream of bullets ricocheting off metal.

"They're dying out there! You've gotta help 'em!" Alicia said, as she ran to the gun cabinet and started fumbling with the weapons, obviously about to go herself.

Buddy felt like a complete asshole. As she turned toward the door, he grabbed her, spun her around, and took the Browning automatic pistol with a twenty-shot clip out of her hand.

"Get the cops back on the phone!" he said. "Get 'em out here!" Then, without really knowing why or what he hoped to accomplish, he moved out of the motor home and onto the field of battle. "Shit, this is fucking nuts," he said to himself as he hit the ground at the foot of the motor home steps. He cowered next to the rear wheel.

"Go find out about Rayce!" Alicia shouted, leaning out of the door and glowering at him.

"Right, right," Buddy said, powered by her disdainful look and obvious disappointment in him. He moved across the tracks toward Rayce Walker, and finally found the stuntman lying in a pool of his own blood, struggling to get to his feet but too weak to pull it off.

"Stay where you are," Buddy ordered. He looked at Rayce's wound; the whole right side of his body was soaked in blood. "Shit, man, this looks awful," Buddy said, with no discernible bedside manner.

Rayce spoke in painful gasps. "They're two lines of cars over, 'bout a hundred and fifty yards up. John is moving in on the gully side. I don't know what happened to Billy. Kincaid's men are up on top of three tanker cars, trying to get 'em open."

"Get 'em open? Get what open?"

"The tanker cars. I think it's milk. The cars're refrigerated. Have that red cow symbol on 'em," Rayce said through gritted teeth. "Y'gotta get help. There's too many, an' that Indian's got no fucking reverse gear. He'll charge 'em and get killed."

"Gotta get you out of danger first," Buddy said. Then he took Rayce's weapon, and using the barrel, pried open the door of the boxcar they were next to. Inside were wooden crates. Buddy lifted

Rayce over his shoulder and dropped the wounded stuntman into the car. He took the walkie-talkie off Rayce's head and put it on. "Stay here," Buddy ordered stupidly, because Rayce wasn't going anywhere. Then Buddy picked up Rayce's automatic weapon and moved off in the direction of the tanker cars.

"Little Bear, it's Buddy . . . talk to me," he whispered into the wire-mike, but got nothing back. The damn units, which had cost Buddy a fortune at the Malibu Ranger Store, were now broadcasting nothing but static.

Then Buddy heard a blast of machine-gun fire, followed by four sharp pistol retorts.

"John, it's Buddy. Billy, come in," he said, trying to contact his two stuntmen, pulling the wire-mike closer to his mouth. Again, all he heard was static. He dialed the volume way down to cut the static so he could concentrate on the sounds of the switching yard.

Buddy didn't know what to do. His instinct was to just hide, to simply crawl under a car and wait until it was over. But a force he didn't understand, and couldn't control, now seemed to have hold of him. It willed him to stand, to start walking in the direction of the gunfire. *Why am I doing this?* some part of him kept asking, but still he moved on.

Holding Rayce's H&K Close Assault, he ran in a crouch, between cars. He heard muffled talking a short distance in front of him and slowed. Edging around a parked boxcar, he leaned out for a careful look. Directly in front of him was a line of refrigerated metal tanker cars, and as Rayce had said, each had a little red cow insignia indicating that they were milk cars. Then, while he was searching the area looking for the rest of the Choir, he felt the ground around him begin to shake. It took him a moment to realize that bullets hitting around him were causing the ground-shaking vibrations; the slower sound of gunfire came a heartbeat later.

"Shit!" Buddy screamed. "I'm being shot at!" He dove sideways, rolled up, and started blindly shooting the H&K. He wasn't even sure what he was aiming at. He was firing by instinct, aiming at something he saw moving on top of one of the cars. Then two bodies slid off the top of the tanker car. Hobos with tattoos on their biceps fell hard to the ground, ten feet in front of him. Milk started pouring out of a few holes he'd punched in the tanker.

"I got 'em! I got 'em!" Buddy yelled gleefully, then spun as he heard more gunfire slamming into the car he was standing by. He bolted, and without even thinking, was running low. He dove under a tanker car and came out the other side, then saw three more men on top of another milk car. They had the top off, and one of them was pouring something into the open hatch. Buddy raked the top of that car with the assault weapon until the bolt locked open, indicating that the smoking gun was empty. He didn't have a second magazine, so he dropped the H&K and pulled the Browning automatic pistol out of his belt.

When Buddy turned and aimed, he saw that the men on top of the car he had just fired at were already sliding off, leaving red streaks of blood on the polished aluminum.

"I got 'em," he said with real surprise. "I got the fuckers." He kept moving, this time crouching even lower as he ran, looking for cover.

He wasn't sure how long it took him to get to the northeast end of the yard. Time had become elastic. He was lost in the moment; his senses of sight, smell, touch, and intuition were all straining, adrenaline blotting out all notion of time.

Then Buddy saw Fannon Kincaid. He was standing at the bottom of the third milk car, looking up. Buddy took aim with the automatic pistol and fired at the crazy Reverend. The bullets missed, chinking into the tanker car behind. . . . Fannon spun and fired at Buddy. The first bullet hit him in the stomach and threw him back, blowing Buddy's intestines and stomach lining out through his spinal column. The second shot hit his right thigh. Buddy's legs collapsed; he went down and rolled. Then he saw that up on the top of the car where Fannon had been looking were three more men also pouring a vial into the open hatch.

Buddy was hit, but strangely he felt nothing. Although he knew that he was mortally wounded, he was determined to complete his mission. He raised his right arm weakly and fired at the men on top of the milk car, missing badly. He was way low, blowing several huge holes in the bottom of the tanker. Milk started to flow out of the ruptured hopper. Fannon aimed his nine-millimeter, then fired directly at Buddy, who was now watching his own death play out like a bad killing on TV. He saw flame shoot out of Fannon's weapon and felt a round hit his shoulder. It rolled him over, then he was riddled with several more shots. They punched deadly holes in his kidneys, lungs, and liver.

Buddy was back in the house suspended over the mile-high canyon. He and Mike were walking across the grids, and just like before, they were not falling through.

"Now we can finally do all the things we've always wanted to, Dad," Mike told his father. "We'll have long talks and share our feelings. We'll be father and son, but we'll also be best friends."

"I'd like that, son, I really would," Buddy said to his dead boy. "I've been longing for it. I always wanted to love you, but I didn't know how." And then, just like the character in his unshot movie *The Prospector,* he said, "I finally found myself. I think I finally know who I am."

The two of them walked out onto the pool deck, suspended thousands of feet above the fertile valley floor. They stood on the grates and looked out at the breathtaking view.

"Come on, Dad, I'll show you the way." Then Mike took Buddy's hand and led him off the deck. They floated there like angels, above the rich green valley, bathed in a soft white light.

Chapter 50

ROD OF IRON

annon had been preaching from Revelation. They were under
a bridge abutment near the rail track, about fifteen miles
south of the Harrisburg switching yard, where they had left
four men dead, including Randall Rader, the Angel in the Church
of Per-ga-mos. Now, Dexter sat licking an open cut on his hand
that he'd received from a flying piece of shrapnel.

" 'He shall rule them with a rod of iron. They shall be dashed
to pieces,' " Fannon recited from Revelation 2:27. He had been
ranting against the U.S. Government for almost an hour.

The members of the Choir sat in the dirt under the railroad
bridge and listened quietly, lost in their own thoughts.

Dexter had begun to accept his own death as inevitable. He was
seeing the end of his life in vivid images. With this acceptance
came a rush of pent-up anger and resentment; he was sucking on
his wounded knuckle and seething.

Finally, Fannon closed the Bible and put it back in his pack. He
removed the rimless glasses, then stowed them carefully in his
breast pocket. He looked up at his battered Choir.

"We have failed to poison the Niggers and Jews, but we are not without options. We have one final act of war to commit. We must now attack the Great Satan in Washington."

"I'm sorry . . . what?" Dexter asked, looking up from the open wound on his hand.

"You heard me, sinner," Fannon said sharply.

"Attack Washington, D.C.? Is that what you just said?" Dexter couldn't believe his ears.

"That's right, bub," Fannon said. "You have been my greatest instrument of failure, but our course is written down. We need only follow the map drawn by the Lord." Then, from Revelation: "'And out of his mouth comes a sharp sword, that with it he should smite the nations.'"

"I hate to bring up relevant information, but there are more police officers and armed military personnel in Washington, D.C., than in any other city in the world. I think, at last count, there were over nineteen police and military agencies, ranging from the U.S. Army and the FBI to the Park Police and everything in between."

"This victory has been promised to me in Revelation," Fannon ranted on.

"Revelation? That's the only chapter assholes like you and David Koresh ever read." Dexter was going over the edge now. His voice was shrill. He was losing it. "This whole plan to poison Jews and Blacks was insane. That guy with the machine gun back there in Harrisburg ruined it, thank God. All the Prions are either on the ground or leaking out of bullet holes from those milk cars. The cops and Admiral Zoll will surely figure out what you were up to. That guy, whoever he was, ended your revolution, *Mr.* Kincaid!"

"Reverend Kincaid!" Fannon shouted. He seemed very different, flapping badly, like the tattered remnants of a torn flag.

"If I'm not a doctor, you're not a reverend. I don't see any Certificate of Ordination."

It was as if they had both snapped. All consequences forgotten, insanity shone from both sets of eyes.

Now Fannon stood slowly and pulled out his gun, pointing it at Dexter.

"That's your answer to everything, isn't it?" Dexter raged. "Shoot, kill, destroy anything or anyone who disagrees with you." The members of the Choir watched in awestruck silence. "Revelation! Did you know that book was written three hundred years after the death of Christ? Did you know that?" Dexter was too far gone to stop. "Most theologians can't stand that book. It's insanity!"

Fannon was looking at Dexter with a pinpoint stare. His maniacal gray eyes contained the frightening madness of evil and intellectual corruption.

"Revelation isn't even part of the Bible. It's madness, written by madmen," Dexter screamed.

Fannon pulled back the hammer.

"Go ahead, do it!" Dexter dared. "Anything is better than this."

" 'And behold, I come quickly; and my reward is with me, to give every man according to his work.' " Fannon's eyes were burning. " 'I am Alpha and Omega, the beginning and the end, the first and the last.' "

Then, without another word, he pulled the trigger and the nine-millimeter Beretta in his hand kicked, throwing Fannon's fist up over his head.

Dexter flew backward, off the rock he was sitting on, and landed on his back in the dust, a huge hole in his right cheek where the bullet had hit him. The left side of his head appeared to be missing.

" 'And if any man shall take away from the words of the book of this prophecy, God shall take away his part out of the book of life.' Revelation Twenty-two, Nineteen." Fannon turned and faced the children of the Choir, violent men who were stunned by the violence they had just witnessed. Nobody moved or looked at the body of Dexter DeMille. "Pack up," Fannon said. "We're moving out. We have God's work to do."

Chapter 51

SPILT MILK

The motel was called the Blue Frog. It was on the outskirts of Frederick, Maryland, and was a bungalow-type motor lodge run by a middle-aged couple.

Cris and Stacy were in a one-bedroom unit at the end of the paved area next to a dry riverbed. The room was clean, but small. They had taken turns in the shower. Both had washed their clothes in the tub, with soap and water, and they were now in wet underwear, waiting for the rest of their things to dry under the heat lamps in the bathroom.

The TV was an old Yamaha with a sensitive vertical hold, which needed constant tuning. They were watching the news to get updates on the situation at Fort Detrick when another breaking story interrupted the network anchor:

"We're switching you to our affiliate station in Harrisburg, Pennsylvania," the anchor said, and then they were suddenly looking at a tall man with gray hair and a bloodhound's sagging expression. The name on the screen identified him as Harrisburg Police Chief Wilton Pierce. He cleared his throat, then started reading from a typed sheet: ''Hollywood producer Buddy Brazil has been shot to death in a gunfight that took place an hour ago at the Harrisburg switching yard. Apparently, he had traveled here with members of his production company in a reported attempt to stop a bio-weapons attack. Mr. Brazil died on the scene along with three unidentified men, who appear to be members of a vicious rail-riding cult known as 'Freight Train Riders of America.' A fourth member of the cult was pronounced dead at the Harrisburg County Hospital shortly thereafter. An associate of Mr. Brazil's, Rayce Walker, a movie stuntman, was badly wounded in the gun-fight, and was also taken to the Harrisburg Hospital. According to members of his staff, Mr. Brazil came here after the bizarre kid-napping of his dead son's body from the morgue in Santa Monica, California. The body was stolen during an autopsy to determine if Michael Brazil had been exposed to a deadly toxic bio-agent. It appears that Mr. Brazil was attempting to stop the F.T.R.A.s from putting this infectious bio-agent into milk container cars headed to Detroit and New York. Until members of the C.D.C. and the U.S. bio-weapons defense team from Fort Detrick, Maryland, can fully analyze the milk, it will not be known exactly what the toxic agent was. Before he died, the fourth member of the F.T.R.A. told police they were about to attack the Great Satan. From this point the FBI will be spearheading the investigation, and further questions should be directed to them. That's it,'' he said, and turned away.

Cris turned down the volume and stood there looking at the screen as the vertical hold began to roll. ''Jesus,'' he finally said. ''Poor Buddy. How did he even find out where they were?''

Stacy said nothing. They sat there in silence for a long time.

''I wonder if Kincaid was one of the dead,'' Cris said.

Stacy still didn't speak.

''Or Dexter. Where's Dexter DeMille?''

Still silent, Stacy had her head down looking at a spot on the floor a few feet in front of the TV.

"I can't believe Buddy actually shot it out with those guys. If he did, he saved a lot of people's lives. He died a hero," Cris said.

Suddenly, Stacy got up and moved to the phone on the cigarette-burned bedside table. She picked it up and dialed a number.

"Who're you calling?" Cris asked, but she wouldn't look at him.

Wendell Kinney answered the ringing phone in Los Angeles. "Yes," the old walrus of the Microbiology Department said softly. He was in his small apartment on the edge of the University grounds, half a block from the Science Building. He had also been watching the news report.

"Wendell, did you see the news?"

"Yes."

"Did you do a test on the canisters I sent you?" Her voice was clipped. She was holding herself in tight control.

"Yes . . . The foam rubber had some ink transfer. From what we could read, the canisters contained Prions, but they were not genetically targeted. They—"

"You still have them? You didn't turn the canisters over to the C.D.C.?" Stacy asked.

"I still have them," the old scientist said softly. "Stacy, where are you? I'm worried. You don't sound right."

Cris had moved closer. He was looking at her profile from over her shoulder, watching her strained expression, lit by dim light coming through the faded yellow lampshade.

"Was Max involved in this?" she asked bitterly.

When she said it, Wendell flinched, then took a deep breath, and waited too long to answer.

"So he was," she concluded. "He was helping Dr. DeMille design this stuff." Her voice was so tortured that Cris couldn't bear the sound of it, as if pieces of her were being torn away.

"Stacy, it's not an easy equation. You don't want to make judgments; it's way too complex."

"It's fucking genocide, Wendell! Genocide! These assholes at

Fort Detrick were arming Prions to attack genetic groups of people. Max was working at the Devil's Workshop! His handwriting was on the acid-base vials that altered the pH to arm the weapon. He was working down there with DeMille, targeting this stuff.'' Her voice was shaking.

"If that's true, then why would they kill him?'' Wendell asked calmly.

"I don't know. Maybe he got cold feet. Maybe he tried to pull out. How do I know why they killed him? But I was in that lab six hours ago. I saw his handwriting. He told me he was just doing work at the think tank, reading notes and creating hypotheses, but that was bullshit. He was in that lab helping to design it, to genetically target it. Why didn't you stop him?''

Again, Wendell was quiet. The two of them listened to each other breathing.

"God damn you, Wendell, you were in on it too, weren't you?'' She was stunned by his silence. "We're supposed to be curing people, not killing them!'' she shouted. "Science is supposed to discover and heal. You and Max perverted it all, destroyed everything we all believed in!''

"You don't understand,'' Wendell said softly. "To get funding we had to—''

Stacy didn't hear the rest, because she hung up on him. She sat on the bed and began to cry. She sobbed deeply, and Cris didn't know what to do or how to comfort her.

Finally, he sat on the bed and put a tentative hand on her shoulder.

She bucked at his touch, arching her back as if hit with a jolt of electricity. "Don't!'' she said sharply.

"I'm sorry,'' he whispered, and started to rise, but she reached out and stopped him. They sat side by side on the edge of the bed in their underwear.

"Oh God, Cris. Oh God . . . I loved him so much. How can this be happening?''

Cris said nothing, and she continued to sob. He wrapped his arms around her and pulled her close, trying to give her some measure of human warmth. He could feel the racking sobs undulating through her body, shaking her to the core. Each sob was followed by deep, painful breaths. They sat on the bed for a long time.

Stacy was crying, but she also could barely contain her rage, rage at the betrayal of everything she had loved about her dead husband. She was crying, but she was also remembering Max . . . remembering his soft touch and the way he would lovingly caress her, with gentle abandon.

As she cried, somewhere in her mind she was aware of Cris's hands on her back, rubbing her, trying to comfort her as Max had often done. Her rage flickered, like a candle guttering in the wind. She couldn't tell where her emotions were taking her. As Cris rubbed her back and talked soothingly in her ear, she could feel his rhythmic heartbeat. Then she sensed something else. It was unmistakable. She felt the heat of passion coming from him. It suddenly turned her anger into lust. She needed to smash everything that was left of Max, to set herself free from his corruption and dishonesty. Now, without questioning it, she felt herself responding to Cris's gentle caress, felt her own sexuality coming alive. She knew she was jumbled up inside, but something suddenly felt right about this. She tilted her mouth up to his face and brushed her lips against his cheek, then as he turned toward her, she found his mouth and kissed him softly.

Cris moved so fast it startled her. He pushed her back. "What are you doing?" he asked, a strained, anguished look on his face.

"I need something. I need you," she said, tears still brimming in her eyes.

"No . . ." he said, pulling away, disengaging himself.

"You find me attractive, I know you do," she said. There was defiance and displaced anger in the remark. It was a challenge, but sounded to him like a curse.

"I think you're one of the most attractive women I've ever met," he answered softly. "But this is wrong, Stacy. You can't get back at Max by using me. He's dead. I won't let it start this way. It would end up making you feel cheap. You'd hate yourself, and me afterward."

Her expression changed. Now she seemed small and dejected.

"He was human, Stacy. He made bad choices . . . just like me. Just like Captain DeSilva. People aren't perfect. . . . I tried to be perfect, and I fell way short. We all just have to do the best we can." In that moment, Cris suddenly felt a strange measure of peace inside. While trying to make her feel better about Max, he suddenly understood something about his own emotional sickness.

The moment between them had passed, so Cris slowly took her back into his arms. She laid her head against his shoulder, and he felt a deep shudder run through her. Then her muscles relaxed, and she quieted in his arms.

"I expected so much more," she whispered softly.

Chapter 52

DERAILMENT

Admiral Zoll's post living quarters were in the old Nallin Farmhouse. The property had been sold to the U.S. Army in 1952, but the house had originally been built in 1772. The farm had been part of a pre–Revolutionary War English land grant. The rectangular, two-story brick structure had eight rooms and two bathrooms. It stood like a dowager princess on the southeast edge of Fort Detrick; its double windows and large front porches were overhung by a pitched, gabled roof.

Admiral Zoll found the house architecturally pleasing, but hard to live in. His ambling gait and huge frame were ill suited to the small rooms. Still, the farmhouse had served as the Fort Detrick Commander's personal quarters for almost half a century, so, in keeping with tradition, Zoll had quartered himself there for over six years, ever since his wife died.

He was dead tired when he arrived home at nine P.M. After giving the order to eliminate Stacy Richardson and Cris Cunningham he had stopped by the base hospital to have his eyebrow stitched. Then he had personally gone to inspect the neurotransmitter lab. Nothing had been stolen that they could identify. Still, he worried about Mrs. Richardson's claim that DeMille had retrieved a sample of PHpr that had been hidden at the bottom of Vanishing Lake.

It had been a long harrowing day. Aside from dealing with Stacy Richardson and Captain Cunningham, he had supervised the removal of thousands of gallons of deadly bio-weapons that had been sucked from old leaking drums and casks up into the White Train's specially designed toxic waste hopper cars. Once loaded, the deadly cargo would travel through Maryland, over the Appalachian Mountains, and across the South to Texas, where it would eventually be pumped into the earth's core and be lost forever.

Earlier in the day, as the storage room was slowly emptied, Zoll had brought in a team of Torn Victor HAZMAT volunteers wearing canvas suits and HEPA filters, who recapped the empty barrels, then covered them with industrial waste vacuum bags. The air was then sucked out of the bags until the heavy plastic clung to the empty barrels and casks like latex skin. The empty containers were loaded onto trucks, then were driven to the east side of the Fort and dumped into a deep hole that had been dug in preparation two days before.

From his upstairs bedroom window, he could hear the distant rumbling of the John Deere bulldozer a mile off as the hole with the old barrels was bladed over and the bio-containers buried forever.

The bell at the front door bonged, and he moved across the upstairs hallway and down the narrow, curved staircase. The old pine floors creaked under his heavy footsteps. He opened the front door and found Colonel Chittick standing there in a fresh uniform, a tired smile on his recently shaved face.

"I just got the call. Investigating subcommittee is going to be here at oh nine hundred tomorrow morning. Two Senators and some cowboys from C.D.C. in Atlanta."

"Not our people, I assume."

"No sir. We're pretty much out of the Atlanta C.D.C. operation. That unit now functions strictly according to its mission statement."

"Let's pour a stiff one," Admiral Zoll said. "This has been a tough day." Chittick nodded. Neither of them wanted to discuss the lab break-in, or the disposal of Mrs. Richardson and Captain Cunningham. It was a defining moment in their relationship. They were now even more dangerous to one another.

Chittick followed Zoll off the slanting porch into the old farmhouse with its framed oil paintings of American farm scenes. Zoll walked across the sloping floor, dropped some ice into two chunky glasses, then poured a shot of Scotch for each of them. He crossed back to his Chief Medical Officer and handed him the heavy crystal glass, and they touched rims. The two men stood a few feet apart and exchanged hooded looks as they sipped the blended twenty-five-year-old Macallan Scotch.

"Whatta you think of that mess up in Harrisburg?" Chittick said, looking for neutral ground. "Four F.T.R.A.s died, so it had to be connected to what happened here."

Zoll set down his heavy tub glass on an Early American spindle-base table. The weighty silence in the room was sliced evenly by a tick-tocking grandfather clock.

"Depends on what our guys up in Harrisburg find in those milk tanker cars. Whatever happens, we're gonna stonewall through it."

Chittick put down his empty glass and smiled at Zoll. "I think we dodged a bullet today," he said hopefully.

Zoll grunted. Then he moved to the door and opened it. Colonel Chittick stepped outside, but then turned to face Zoll on the front porch. "We're shut down at Vanishing Lake. Now, more or less, we're shut down here. That means the Devil's Workshop is out of business."

"Not for long, Colonel. The political climate is changing. God bless that crazy bastard Saddam. The more he threatens us with bio-weapons, the more likely it is our government will reopen the front door to its research again. In the meantime, I've got a few university labs who wanna play ball, and a marine research facility on an island in the South Pacific that I think might make a good base of operations. This is too important for our nation's survival. These are the only tactical strategic weapons that make sense in the new millennium. We've got to man this operation until the fucking Congress and the President come to their senses."

"Yes sir," Chittick said. "I'm with you on that." But he was thinking it was time to request a transfer. He had a strange feeling that Zoll had run out of political highway. "Good night, sir," he smiled.

"Yeah," the Crazy Ace growled in his unfriendly sandpaper voice, and then he shut the door directly in Colonel Laurence Chittick's face.

The hundred-car manifest train was on the CSXT track, heading through the Appalachian Pass. The track was a two-way narrow switchback that climbed up the side of the mountain and then, after cresting the summit, made its long downhill run into Georgia, Arkansas, and East Oklahoma, finally ending in Texas. The engine was a full-width, high-nosed Canadian Bombardier HR616, which was fronting a three-diesel unit. The engineer was an old-timer named Calvin Hickman who had been working the Appalachian run for almost two years. He knew every bend in the track, and had a tendency to push the forty-eight-cylinder, three-hundred-ton power package a little too fast.

The hundred cars he was pulling were mostly farm produce, some pipe fittings and building supplies; all of it was heading to Atlanta. He had just finished the last switchback, cresting the pass onto the west side of the mountain, and was now heading downhill. He had his right hand on the dynamic brake control handle, and one eye on the train line-pressure gauge. He was looking down and missed the first red warning flasher, which indicated that the switch up ahead had just been opened. He didn't hear it either, because the warning bells from the cab signal system had been disconnected. Even if he had seen it, he might have been going too fast to stop. He had way too much weight behind him, all of it hurtling downhill.

A mile farther on he was jolted by the sight of the second warning light. He immediately threw the lever on the automatic brake valve; exhausting air underneath each car instantly operated the pneumatic brakes. The brake levers activated. The shoes slammed hard against the metal wheel tread. Tortured metal screamed as the brakes engaged.

"Son-of-a-bitch," Calvin said, as he anticipated going off the tracks. Out of the right side of the cab, he could see several men running on the graded bank. At first he thought they were hobos ill-advisedly still trying to board the doomed train. Then he realized they were running away, trying to get as far from the screeching train as possible. They knew the freight was about to derail.

The last man Calvin Hickman saw was a tall silver-haired hobo. He was standing on the grade beside the tracks. He was the only hobo who wasn't running, and it appeared as if he was reading aloud from an open Bible as the train cab flashed past.

Calvin knew that these men had thrown the switch open. The track supervisor had often warned that F.T.R.A.s would derail freights, then steal what they could from the wreckage before police or emergency crews arrived.

The cab passed by the last warning light, and Calvin could feel the wheels under the Bombardier jump the rails and begin rattling over open ties. Then the engine was completely off the tracks, still going fifty miles an hour. He felt the huge locomotive start to dig itself into the dirt. It slammed abruptly to a stop and Calvin was thrown out of his seat into the front of the comfort cab, smashing his head violently on the metal dash.

The cars behind began to slam into each other, piling up, breaking off the tracks, snapping couplers, and being flung off into the trees that lined the rails. The sounds of crashing cars and tortured metal filled the air. The fifty-foot sections of continuous welded rail snapped and speared upward, right through the floors of the first cars. The wrecked cars were immediately overrun by the cars behind, and as the energy dissipated from the in-train collisions, the cars jackknifed, spilling lading everywhere.

More than fifty cars derailed, throwing themselves all over the side of the mountain grade, before the whole smoking, ruptured mess finally came to a shuddering stop. Ash and dirt filled the air.

Fannon inhaled the smell of disaster, then said, " 'And I heard a voice from heaven saying unto me, "Blessed are the dead which die in the Lord henceforth, that they may rest from their labors, and their works do follow them." ' " Then he closed his Bible and folded up his glasses, returning them to his pocket.

Fannon Kincaid had been only five feet from the track, yet he was not hit by any of the wreckage. For some reason, known only to God or the Devil, the crazy Reverend had miraculously survived.

Chapter 53

RUSH TO JUDGMENT

They were on the Norfolk Southern track from Frederick, Maryland, heading southeast toward Baltimore on a unit train, which was only thirty cars long and making good time. Cris and Stacy were in a sleeper car buried in the middle of the train. They had heard about the huge derailment in the Appalachian Mountains, which had killed the engineer and the fireman, and injured several others. Talk of the wreck had spread down the rails like a burning trail of gas.

"You're worried about that derailment, aren't you?" Stacy said.

"Yeah. Something tells me it's Kincaid."

"Why? Why would he do it? Why derail a manifest train full of pipe and agriculture products?"

"To block the Appalachian Pass, maybe. I've gotta get my hands on a track map."

"Why?"

"He says he's gonna attack the Great Satan. Who's the Great Satan?"

"I don't know. I guess it's anything that Kincaid thinks is evil."

"F.T.R.A.s are a lot like survivalists. Kincaid is an ex-'Nam vet who got shut out by the system after the war, so who's the Great Satan?"

"Saddam Hussein says it's America."

"And that's Washington, D.C."

"So that's why you wanted to get on this train, heading east?"

"Believe me, this isn't over." And the ominous tone in his voice convinced Stacy he was right. Cris looked at her. "There's a Yardmaster station in Alexandria, just on the Maryland-Virginia border. I've never been through there, but I've heard it's a friendly yard. We look pretty clean—maybe I can get the Yardmaster there to let me take a look at the track map."

"Will he show it to you?"

"Maybe . . . if you smile at him and bat your eyelashes."

"That's a politically incorrect idea," she said mischievously.

"You wanna help, or you wanna march in a parade?" He grinned at her.

They moved into the switching area in Alexandria, skirting the edge of the yard to keep out of sight of the patrolling cinder bulls. Finally, Cris led her up to the Yardmaster's office. It was in a two-story brick building, with a tower on the far end that went up an additional story.

Cris knocked on the wooden door. A twenty-something, dark-haired girl, with a trim figure in tight jeans, opened the door. She had a wide, engaging smile.

"Hi," she said brightly.

"Hi," Cris replied. "I'm looking for the Yardmaster."

"You're looking at her," the girl said. On closer examination, Cris could see the collection of smile lines around her mouth and at the corners of her eyes. He revised his age estimate; she appeared to be in her early thirties. She smiled at Cris, who quickly smiled back.

"I'm working on an insurance claim for some missing truck air bags and radios," he said. "We lost 'em out of a hundred-unit shipment that was delivered to D.C. Motors about ten days ago; half the stereo components and almost all the air bags had been ripped out. We think F.T.R.A.s did it. I was wondering if I could take a look at a map of the local system. I'm trying to get an idea which way they went."

"You got a card?" she asked.

Cris dug into his wallet and pulled one out, handing it to her.

"You're Al Kleggman," she said. "Insurance Underwriter."

"In the flesh."

"You don't look like an Al Kleggman," she said with a smile.

Stacy could see that the girl found Cris attractive. She felt a flash of jealousy, which surprised her with its intensity.

Cris let out some more line. "I could call my office and get the map from them, but we were here and I thought it would just be easier and quicker to . . ."

"You know your office number?" she said, holding the business card like a winning poker hand, peeking over the edge at him.

"This is a test?" he smiled.

"If you wanna look at my system map it is," she answered.

"My office is 555-7890," he recited. "You want my fax and e-mail?"

She handed the card back. "Come on in, Al. I'm Sylvia." Then, looking at Stacy, she added, "Who's this?"

"I'm Lenore Kleggman," Stacy smiled sweetly. "We were going out for lunch and a nooner."

Sylvia looked at them speculatively, then turned and led them into a small, cluttered office with several radio and phone hookups, which kept the Yardmaster in touch with the trains on her section of track.

"You hear about the derailment up in the mountains?" Cris asked her.

"Kinda hard not t'hear about it. Got the whole system futzed," she said, as she led him to the map.

"Who do you think did it?"

"Damn F.T.R.A.s. Leastways, that's what the dispatcher's train delay report says." She pointed to a boxed section of the wall map. "This is us, here."

Cris studied the map, memorized the track configurations, and finally nodded. "Okay, that helps a lot. Thanks for everything," he said, and turned to Stacy. "Okay, dear, time to tie on the feed-bag and find a motel."

"Such a romantic," Stacy smiled, as they headed to the office door.

"By the way," Sylvia said, "you aren't fooling anyone."

Cris turned and faced her.

"You two aren't married, you're having an affair."

Cris smiled as he and Stacy stepped out the door of the office and began moving across the pavement.

Sylvia's eyes were burning holes in their backs.

"That was cute," Stacy said, "with the little card."

"A nooner?"

"She was about to jump on you and rape you. I had to do something."

He grinned. They turned the corner and were out of Sylvia's sight.

"Who the hell is Al Kleggman?" she asked.

"I don't remember. Probably some insurance guy I met back when Kennidi was sick. I had the card in my wallet, so I memorized the number as we were walking up there."

They arrived at a public park. Cris sat at a wooden picnic table and took a sheet of paper out of his wallet. "You got a pen or pencil?" he asked.

"Lipstick." She got it out of her backpack and offered it to him.

He took it and began to draw a map on the back of the piece of paper. "Okay, here's the CSXT Appalachian rail line. . . .

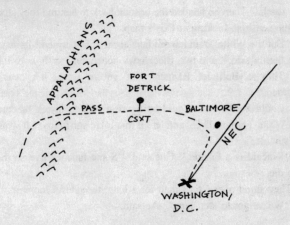

Here's the main pass heading through the Appalachian Mountains; any train going south from New York or Philadelphia or Baltimore has to go on that CSXT line. Unless you detour back up into New Jersey or Pennsylvania, which adds hundreds of miles, this track through the Appalachian Pass is the quickest shot south.''

"What're you getting at?"

"If Kincaid threw the switch and bounced that manifest train off the tracks up in the mountains, then he had to have a good reason, and it wasn't to steal some apples off an agriculture car."

"Then what was it?"

"I've been wondering where the White Train that left Fort Detrick was headed," Cris said. "When I was in the Rangers, I heard that a lot of the nuclear waste was pumped out in Texas. If it's going south, and the Appalachian Pass was blocked, then the only other way to get there is on this Northeast Corridor track here." He added that track to his drawing and labeled it ''NEC.'' Then he put the tip of the lipstick on a place on the NEC track, making an X.

"What's that?" she asked.

"Washington, D.C. The route the White Train will most likely take now is through the capital. It's the only other good way to get south." Then he handed the lipstick back to her and they stood in the sunshine looking at Cris's map.

"But the White Train has soldiers aboard. Ten armed Marines," she finally said, "and two Blackhawk helicopters to fly over it."

"They're Bell Jet Rangers, but you're right, it's heavily guarded."

"Could he do that? Could he figure a way to hijack or derail the White Train in D.C., and let all that toxic stuff loose? It would be suicide."

"Kincaid is a fanatic," Cris said. "Some fanatics live so they can die."

They stood over Cris's map for a long, thoughtful moment.

"We've got to stop him," she said.

Chapter 54

DETOUR

The White Train had been on its way up the east face of the Appalachian Pass when they had been radioed and informed of the wreck up ahead. Now they were parked on a siding two miles east of the accident, with the engine idling. The two Bell Jet Rangers had landed in a clearing next to the train, and the Marines had set up an armed perimeter around it.

Major Adrian Flynn now sat in the small communications office in the troop car, trying to make arrangements to get them on their way. His first call was to Admiral Zoll, who growled at him through the scrambled speakerphone.

"Get that load outta there, Major," he said. "I don't want you parked. Find a way around."

Major Flynn looked with dismay at the Marine Captain seated next to him. "Sir, there are only two ways out of here. Unless you want me to go all the way into Pennsylvania, I'm going to have to back this train down twenty miles of track through the mountains, then switch to the NEC track heading into Washington, D.C.

Because we're a toxic event, I'm going to need to get half a dozen district area track clearances.''

"Then do it. But that stuff has got to get lost. It's still possible that some nosy Senator's gonna hear that the White Train was on base and stop you before you can pump out in Texas. Time is critical here. This stuff can't be just hanging around, waiting for an accident!'' Zoll was glaring at the scrambled phone on the conference table in his huge office at Fort Detrick.

"Yessir,'' Major Flynn said, and then hung up. He quickly called the area Trainmaster for the Eastern Section and applied for the clearances to run the White Train backward down the mountain into the Brunswick, Maryland, switching yard. Then he began working on the clearances necessary to take the NEC track into Washington. Later, he would get the required clearances for Richmond, down to Atlanta, and on to Texas.

A little past two P.M. the clearance for Brunswick came through, allowing them to back down out of the mountains. Major Flynn ordered the perimeter guards back up onto the roof of the Train. He radioed the helicopter gunships, and they began to wind up their turbines. The whine of the Bell Jets' engines was drowned out by the locomotive's deep, throaty roar as the White Train's diesel engine powered up.

Then, in a matter of minutes, the Marines were in position up on the roof and the black gunships were hovering a hundred feet overhead.

"Ready to roll,'' the engineer's voice came to Major Flynn through the headset.

"Okay, let's go,'' the Major said. Then he felt the troop car lurch, and the White Train was again moving, backing off the siding onto the main track and down the long CSXT grade, descending into Maryland.

"I'll feel better when we get off this damn mountain,'' Major Flynn said to the Marine beside him.

· · ·

Fannon Kincaid did not have time to look for the perfect car on a spotting sheet. He divided up the twenty men he had left and told them to take sections of the Washington area track and move in pairs. He ordered them to send one man back to alert him when they found an acceptable car. Everybody would regroup in two hours to take stock of things. Then Fannon found a place to rest.

He chose an open boxcar on the northeast end of the Washington line, which ran directly through D.C., parallel to Interstate 395, and crossed the Potomac near the Pentagon. At that spot, at the intersection of 7th and C Streets, the rail line was only a block from the F.A.A. building. From there the railroad tracks ran south toward Richmond.

But Fannon was tired; he had gone without sleep for two days. Almost all of his energy had left him. His muscles felt weak, and yet he knew he must go on. He would find a way to strike this one blow for the Lord. Somewhere out of his ranks of unrewarded and discarded Christians would rise a successor. Certainly the successor would not be a man as holy or divine as Fannon, but he would be someone who could carry on in His glorious name.

His mind was cut loose from all logic, freewheeling above his dreams of glory. " 'The curse of the Lord is in the house of the wicked, but he blesseth the habitation of the just,' " he whispered.

With that prayer on his lips, Fannon fell into a deep sleep in the still heat of the open boxcar.

Robert Vail saw the gas tanker car parked on a siding about half a mile from him. He was with his new partner, Peter Kelly, who had been a Navy explosives expert in the Gulf and was known in the Choir as "Gas Can Man." His job was to rig the explosives.

They moved across the ties until they were next to the huge painted tanker with the Texaco star on the side.

"Looks good," R.V. said, as he glanced up at the mammoth tanker car. Then R.V. picked up a rock and banged the side of the tanker. He listened to the sound that rebounded back at him. " 'Bout half full," he said. "Whatta ya think?"

"I can rig it so it'll blow the fuckin' paint off that dome over there," Gas Can Man said, pointing off at the Capitol Dome rising from behind a line of trees about a half mile away. "I'll go back, tell Fannon, and get my ammonium nitrate and shaped charges. You wait here, see if you can get the tanker open." Then Gas Can Man moved away at a trot.

R.V. looked at the tanker car. He knew it was not uncommon for a gas tanker to be dropped inside city limits to wait until the correct delivery dates. What impressed him was that this tanker car was perfectly placed. It was as if God had ordained its location. The Reverend Kincaid would be rewarded at last, he thought. The Christian Choir and the Lord's Desire would make its final statement, and the world would be forced to take heed.

R.V. patted the side of the tanker, half full of gasoline. He looked at the red hazardous material sign on the end of the car that read: FLAMMABLE.

"Ain't you a beauty," he said in a whisper, almost as if the tanker possessed the spirit of the Lord. Then he climbed to the top of the hopper and, using a pocket wrench, began to undo the stubborn bolts of the hinged hatch at the top of the car. As he worked, he remembered Fannon's words preached in hushed tones a week before. *"Death will precede the armies of the Lord,"* the Reverend had prophesied.

Chapter 55

BRIGHT BURNING STAR

Behold, he cometh,' " Fannon said. He stood atop the Texaco
tanker car and watched as Gas Can Man poured two bags
of ammonium nitrate into the half-full gas tanker. " 'Every
eye shall see him, and all kindreds of the earth shall wail because
of him.' " After he finished reciting from Revelation he stood there
in silence, the wind blowing the treetops and his fine silver-gray
hair. Gas Can Man had promised that the mixture of ammonium
nitrate would magnify the explosion a hundredfold.

Several of the Choir helped Fannon down from his precarious
perch on the tanker car, back onto the ground. He had changed
radically in the last seventy-two hours. From gruff and menacing
he had become somewhat frail and uncertain. His fists no longer
seemed to be powerful weapons attached to lethal muscled arms,
but rather like fluttering appendages. It was hard to comprehend
so quick and devastating a change in someone who so recently
possessed such an inner strength and power that he held them
spellbound with his forcefulness.

Robert Vail and the Gas Can Man had crawled under the Texaco gas tanker and were attaching a radio-detonated shaped charge to the bottom of the car. The charge was pre-wrapped in a metal sheath, and R.V. was securing it to the belly of the tanker with one-inch metal screws. The shield around the charge was fashioned to direct the explosion up through the skin of the car. The concussion of the accelerated gasoline would magnify the impact, as in the blast in Oklahoma City. Gas Can Man said it would obliterate everything within two hundred yards.

"Is it done yet?" Fannon suddenly demanded, coming out of it and for the moment reclaiming himself from a stuporous haze.

"Almost," Gas Can Man said.

In ten minutes they had completed the job, but by then Fannon again seemed lost inside himself. They got out from underneath the tanker and moved across the clearing. R.V. and Gas Can Man had to help the dazed Reverend down the steep grade at the side of the tracks.

"He sent me. It was promised," Fannon muttered to his escorts. " 'I have sent mine angels to testify unto you.' He has instructed me in his works."

"We've got to get out of here, Reverend," R.V. said. "We've got to get to the roof of the F.A.A. building. We'll take a back stairway up. We can see it from there. We've rented a truck to get us out of town immediately after the explosion, before the winds shift."

"I'm His Bright, Burning Star," Fannon mumbled, not seeming to hear R.V. "His Apocalypse, His Messenger of the Ages."

R.V. nodded and pulled on Fannon's arm, trying to get him off the tracks. "Come on, Reverend, we gotta get to a place of safety before the White Train gets here."

Things are finally working out better, Major Flynn thought. He had just received special track clearances all the way to Richmond. He looked at his watch. They were moving at only twenty miles an hour, and were about to switch to the NEC track that would take the White Train through Washington, D.C. He triggered the headset mike that was hot-linked to the engine cab.

"How're we doing?" he asked the engineer.

"We're clear up ahead. I have the Capitol Dome in sight. We're about a minute from the NEC switching junction."

"Good," Major Flynn said, and flipped over to his "air mike," which connected him to the choppers overhead by ultrahigh frequency. "White Angel to Air One. We're a minute from the NEC switch. This is a previously unscouted line, so be sharp."

"Roger," the Air Commander said. "We have two tankers and two boxcars sighted up ahead of you. They look normal, but maybe you should call the District Trainmaster and double-check if they're supposed to be there."

"Roger that," Major Flynn said, then picked up his cellphone and with his other hand began flipping through his Eastern Section Trackmaster's book. He found the District of Columbia Trainmaster's number and called.

"This is the Military Waste Priority One White Train. We're diverting through your area on the NEC," he told the track warrant officer.

"Right, we've got you pegged. All clear."

"We want a siding report for the Northeast Corridor track through D.C., from South Capitol Street to the Potomac River," Major Flynn said.

"Right. Hang on a minute, I'm changing screens," the dispatcher said, and after a minute he came back on. "We've got one Texaco funnel flow tanker car at Seventh Street. She's about half loaded with petroleum. We have two sided boxcars with pipe fittings, and another tanker at the river full of powdered phosphate."

"Okay, thanks. We're on our way through. We'll notify you when we clear city limits."

"Thank you, sir. Standing by," the dispatcher said.

Major Flynn hung up his cellphone, and hit a button that hot-miked the entire White Train team. "Everything checks out. Be alert. Let's go."

The engine, which had been moving at quarter speed, accelerated and headed straight through the center of Washington, D.C., pulling two carloads of deadly chemical and biological weapons.

Before Cris and Stacy left Frederick, Maryland, they called the National Response Center (N.R.C.) and were transferred to the Coast Guard office at Buzzard's Point. The Coast Guard was the federal agency that handled all accident notifications and reportable emergency events for the inland waterways and the rail system on the East Coast. A Lieutenant Commander named Robert McKinley listened patiently as they explained what they thought was about to happen.

Lieutenant Commander McKinley turned on a tape recorder. "You have firsthand knowledge that a band of F.T.R.A.s are going to attack the White Train going through Washington, D.C.?"

"Yes," Cris said. Commander McKinley was already looking up the White Train's routing schedule on his HAZMAT computer. He found the Train's icon under "Nuclear Waste Transportation" and clicked "On," quickly accessing the track routing data, which listed the White Train's destination as Midland, Texas, by way of the Appalachian Pass. But the data had not been updated since the derailment in the mountains. Without saying so, McKinley now assumed that the caller on his phone was just another nuclear waste fanatic. The White Train drew a lot of crank calls from "No Nuke" special-interest groups.

"If you fail to respond, millions of people could die," Cris added, sensing that he had somehow lost the man.

"We'll investigate your complaint. Who am I speaking with?" the Lieutenant Commander asked, and Cris gave his name and address.

"Cris Cunningham? Wasn't that some famous West Coast college quarterback about ten years ago?" the Lieutenant Commander asked. Now he was pretty sure he was being jobbed.

"Look . . . You gotta get the National Guard to stop that train before it gets on the NEC track."

"Thanks for the call. We'll look into it," McKinley said, and disconnected, thinking that the fanatics who harassed the movement of the White Train would go to any lengths to detain it.

After he hung up, Lieutenant Commander McKinley stood in his office and tried to decide how to deal with the warning. He couldn't just ignore it, but he couldn't treat every call with the same level of concern, or he would be calling out the National Guard or FBI three times a day. He made a note to verify the Cunningham address in Pasadena, but concluded there was no need to stir up the "Big Noises" at the FBI or the Pentagon, since his computer indicated the Train wasn't even heading through D.C. To cover his ass, he decided he would add the call to the six-o'clock summary report and monitor the White Train until it arrived in Texas.

Cris and Stacy rented a car and drove to Washington. It was seventy miles, but it took them only forty-five minutes. On the way, Stacy used her cellphone and tried to get in touch with Wendell Kinney at USC, but he didn't answer. She left a message on his machine to call her immediately.

Just after two P.M., when they were inside the Beltway, they heard the sound of two helicopters beating the air overhead. Cris pulled to a stop in the middle of traffic, got out, and looked up. People in the cars behind him started shouting and honking. He ignored them as he spotted the two black Bell Jet Rangers, hovering and moving slowly west two blocks away. Then, while he was watching, the two choppers began to pick up speed. Cris assumed they were directly above the White Train, which now seemed to be heading right through Washington. He jumped back into the rental and accelerated away from the horn-honkers.

Stacy had the city map open, on her knees. "Turn right up ahead on C Street. It goes straight down to the rails and dead-ends," she instructed.

Cris hung a right at C Street, which was near the huge F.A.A. Building. He drove the Hertz rental down the narrow street, then stopped at the dead-end barricade where the rail line intersected. He jumped out of the car and ran toward the tracks, which were bordered by a low retaining wall. Cris vaulted the wall and came to a stop. The White Train was now visible two blocks away, moving slowly toward the spot where he was standing. The Train was a loud and spectacular sight. It approached slowly, its nose light flashing, its white cylindrical hopper cars glistening. Eight armed, white-helmeted guards were on the roof, and the two black helicopters hovered above it.

Cris scanned the track, and quickly spotted the Texaco tanker parked about two hundred yards east of them, five hundred yards from the approaching White Train.

"Gas car . . . gotta be the ignition package," he said out loud, then started running across the tracks toward the tanker. His feet stumbled on the gravel-filled, uneven surface. Suddenly, as he ran, he had a strong sense of Kennidi's presence. She was somehow with him, giving him strength, urging him on. He could see her courageous smile, and her swollen forehead; the memory of her painful death made him run even faster. He could now see the unnatural shape of something underneath the tanker car.

The remaining members of the Choir watched Cris running toward the Texaco tanker from the roof of the F.A.A. building. It had been easy to break the lock to the fire door and take the concrete stairs to the roof. Fannon Kincaid seemed to have lost all interest. He was sitting on a roof air-conditioning unit, its hot exhaust fluttering his pant cuffs.

"Blow the damn charge!" R.V. yelled from the edge of the roof as he watched the man run across the tracks and dive under the tanker. The man started to fiddle with the shaped charge.

"No, you can't blow it! Not yet!" Gas Can Man answered, grabbing the detonator from Robert Vail. "The Train's still too far away. It's gotta be inside two hundred yards."

They watched in silence as the White Train moved closer. Far away on the tracks below, the man underneath the gas tanker suddenly started kicking at the bracket that held the shaped charge to the bottom of the car.

The White Train was now four hundred yards from the tanker. Then it was only three hundred.

"White Angel, we've got a bogie," the Air One pilot said from his leading Bell Jet Ranger. "Some guy just ran under that sided gas tanker up ahead."

"Roger," Major Flynn said. He jumped up and looked out the side window of the troop car. His angle was too acute, and he couldn't see far enough forward to spot the tanker, or the man. "Slow to five miles an hour," Flynn said to the engineer over the headset mike. Then he instructed his air cover: "Air One, make a pass. Take a look at what he's doing. Air Two, hold position."

"Wilco," the chopper pilot said, and he peeled off. The White Train slowed, but still it crept closer. It was now only 250 yards away from the tanker.

Cris was desperately trying to kick loose the shaped charge from the bottom of the gas tanker. The one-inch metal screws that held the metal package to the bottom of car were wiggling, but they refused to break free. As he lunged several more times, trying to dislodge it, he looked up the tracks from under the car and saw the White Train moving slowly toward him. One of the black Bell Jet Rangers had passed the Train and was flying low along the track, directly at him.

Cris had been under chopper attack before, and knew that the gunship was not flying at attack angle. If any rounds were fired at him from its current attitude, they would go high. He continued to kick at the shaped charge as the White Train rumbled slowly toward him. It was now only two hundred yards away.

"Stay back, dammit!" he screamed helplessly into the rumbling of helicopter and train-engine noise enveloping him.

"He's gonna knock the charge off!" R.V. screamed.

"We can't do it yet," Gas Can Man said. "Gotta get a little closer. Wait till it's opposite that wall. Them casket cars is tough. Gotta shred 'em to put all that sarin and anthrax high into the air where the winds'll carry it."

R.V. was looking down at the man under the tanker car, still kicking futilely at the package.

"Just shoot the motherfucker," Fannon muttered, stating the obvious. They turned to see that the dazed Reverend had moved off the air-conditioner housing and was now standing beside them looking down at the section of track.

It surprised R.V. that in the heat of it, so simple a solution had not occurred to any of them. Three members of the Choir now aimed their automatic weapons at Cris and started firing.

R.V. watched as the bullets starred the ground all around the tanker. One of the bullets hit the man under the car, knocking him clear around. R.V. could see the man's small white face looking back up at them.

.   .   .

"Gunfire coming from the roof of the F.A.A. building," the pilot of the leading Bell Jet Ranger said. "Condition Red. Cover me, I'm going in." He peeled away from the tanker and flew toward the roof of the huge building.

Kincaid and the Christian Choir saw the chopper coming at them and pulled their aim off of Cris to target the approaching gunship. Ten automatic rifles opened up from the roof. The noise of rapid-fire weapons filled the air, mixed with the ringing jingle of hot brass ejecting out of their gunports and bouncing on the hard cement roof.

Cris was jolted by the nine-millimeter round as it tore into him and shattered the bone in his right shoulder. It blew him around, so he was suddenly looking up at the roof of the F.A.A. building. He could see Fannon's men up there firing at him. Bullets continued to spark off the metal rails and tear up the ground around him. Then their line of fire was blocked by the black helicopter, which had pulled off him and was streaking toward the roof.

Cris couldn't move his right shoulder or arm, but he finally got swiveled around again under the tanker; on his back, with his shoulder oozing heavy arterial blood, he once again took aim at the loosened shaped charge. He positioned himself for another try. He was getting weaker. He knew he had only one good kick left in him. Using every ounce of strength that remained, he launched his foot forward. . . .

The shaped charge flew off the belly of the tanker, but it landed ten feet away, right in the middle of the center rail that the White Train was heading down.

As the Bell Jet Ranger climbed toward the roof of the F.A.A. building, it began taking withering machine-gun fire from the

F.T.R.A.s. Suddenly its gas tank ignited, and the black chopper exploded, raining hot pieces of metal and plastic all over the men on the roof of the building. The main fuselage and rotor were blown forward, then fell in two fiery pieces on top of the adjoining four-story parking structure.

The engineer of the White Train saw his "security" gunship explode, and he panicked. He decided, without orders, to get the hell out of there and make a run for it. He pushed the throttle down, but didn't see the shaped charge that had just landed directly on the track, forty yards in front of him.

Cris saw the chopper crash, then heard the White Train speeding up. He got to his feet, with maddening slowness, and began to stumble toward the shaped charge lying on the track. His right arm was limp and his destroyed right shoulder was pouring out blood.

The White Train was gaining on him. Suddenly, his vision began swimming. He felt as if he were moving in a dream. His legs were like lead, and everything was happening in slow motion. "No!" he yelled at the closing train. He knew if the White Train ran over the charge, it was still close enough to explode the tanker and blow everything to bits. But he could not keep moving forward. He stumbled, then fell.

Somebody ran past him, moving so fast that he felt the rush of air against his face. He struggled to look up, and saw Stacy reach the track a few feet away and grab the shaped charge. She started running away from the rails, carrying the package in both her hands, moving as fast as she could. She was almost to the wall.

From the roof of the F.A.A. building, R.V. was holding the detonator, but he was not looking at the tracks. He had shifted his gaze to watch the burning helicopter, which had just crashed on the parking structure.

Fannon Kincaid grabbed the detonator out of R.V.'s hand as the woman scooped up the shaped charge and ran away from the tracks. Suddenly the second Bell Jet Ranger streaked toward the roof and attacked. As nine-millimeter shells from the nose cannon blew chunks of concrete out of the roof around him, Fannon pointed the radio detonator at the woman. The helicopter pilot adjusted his aim and fired again. A stream of armor-piercing bullets blew Fannon Kincaid's left leg off. He spun in anguish and pain, and pushed the button on the detonator as he went down in a hail of gunfire.

Stacy threw the detonation package as far away from the tanker car as she could. Her arm was outstretched, and her face turned away. She never saw the package explode, but she felt it.

The blast ripped part of her right hand off and threw her backward almost two hundred feet. Debris and smoke rained down around her. Her clothes and hair were on fire. She could feel searing heat and intense pain. Then she was on the hard gravel. She looked up and saw Cris falling toward her. He was screaming something, but she couldn't understand any of it. All she could feel was his weight on top of her and his breath on her neck as he smothered the flames with his own body.

She could feel herself in a new place, balancing somewhere between life and death. There was peace and no pain. Cris's voice was somewhere far away, whispering, ''Don't die, please . . . I love you.'' Then there was complete silence and a white light, clear and beautiful.

Chapter 56

THE BEGINNING

Clancy Black arrived in Washington, D.C., at five P.M. It was raining, and an electrical storm was flashing thunderbolts down on the Capitol.

Earlier that day, Cris had called Clancy from Walter Reed Hospital and asked him to come without telling him why. "The Black Attack" had gone directly upstairs at the mission to throw a few things in a bag. CNN was on in his small, cluttered room and the story was already breaking. There were pictures of Cris and Stacy.

"It appears from early reports that the nation's capital has narrowly escaped a horrendous biological weapons attack," the news anchor said.

Now, as Clancy walked through Dulles Airport in Washington, he could see the expanding story on every gift-shop TV screen. There were shots of the shootout on the rooftop of the F.A.A. building caught by a local news helicopter, and shots of the Bell Jet Ranger burning on the top level of the parking garage. The TV coverage of the government assault on the remaining F.T.R.A.s seemed to Clancy to be faintly reminiscent of Waco, as flak-vested FBI agents jumped out of choppers and rained death down on the members of the Choir. The news reports said all of the militant survivalists died on the rooftop.

There was a great deal of coverage on ex-UCLA quarterback and Silver Star winner Cris Cunningham, along with the USC microbiology post-grad Stacy Richardson. The story speculated that they had probably saved millions of lives by thwarting the White supremacists who were attempting to blow up a Pentagon train carrying biological and chemical weapons inside the Beltway.

Clancy moved on, stopping only once in the door of an airport gift shop to look at shots of the strange-looking White Train, and to listen to Major Adrian Flynn's vague on-the-scene statement.

Then he moved out of the airport terminal into the rain-wet night, where he hailed a waiting cab. "Walter Reed Hospital," he said to the Arab cab driver, who punched the meter and pulled away.

The hospital was a mob scene. There were satellite uplinks and news vans everywhere. Spectators and cops clogged the streets under a mushroom field of umbrellas. The sky had finally opened, and a heavy rain pelted the crowd. Clancy paid the driver, then picked his way through the throng. He was soaking wet when he got to the main door of the hospital, where he was stopped by security.

"Sorry, can't go in there without a pass," the cop said.

"I'm on your list, I hope. Clancy Black, Cris Cunningham's counselor."

The cop looked at the list, and found his name. "Go on up. It's the top floor," he said, and stepped aside, letting Clancy track rainwater into the huge marble-and-stone entry.

On the top floor of the hospital there was more confusion. Reporters crowded the corridor; TV lighting cables spaghettied on the linoleum floor.

Clancy picked his way through the news crews and stepped nimbly over the cables until he finally arrived at a door guarded by another cop.

"Clancy Black," he said. "I'm on the sheet."

"Yeah. Okay," the cop said, looking at a clipboard, then motioning him inside.

Cris was in the hospital bed at the far end of the VIP Room. Clancy could see that his whole right side was wrapped in tape. There were IV drips and drainage tubes hanging off him like river leeches.

The wall-bracketed TV was on low. Cris turned and waved weakly as Clancy moved toward him.

"From what I'm seein' on TV, you did good," Clancy said softly. "Not bad for one a' my ear-bang Nickel graduates."

"I wanna get outta here, Clancy. I wanna see Stacy. It says on the news she's in the Washington Burn Center. They say she's lost a hand, and that she's critical. She can't die, man . . . she's got to make it."

"Well, from what I'm seein', you ain't going nowhere. Not for a while, at least. You've got enough tubes on ya here to plumb a fuckin' duplex."

Now on TV were videotape shots of Cris playing quarterback in the Rose Bowl against Ohio State. Clancy paused to watch, as Cris faked a pitch on an option and went wide crossing the goal line. "You were pretty good, Hoss." There were also some still shots of him being awarded the Silver Star. The TV switched to his father, who was being interviewed by Peter Jennings.

"I understand that the President intends to award the Freedom Medal to your son. It's the highest civilian honor our country can bestow."

Richard Cunningham's voice was barely audible. "My son is a hero; he was always one, on the football field and in the Gulf. So it's no surprise to me that he would risk his life to save others."

Cris turned his head away from the screen, and Clancy could see that there were tears in his friend's eyes.

"What's wrong, man? Why you crying?"

"I can't do this again, Clance. I'll be back on the Nickel, drinking 49 out of a bag."

Clancy was no psychologist, but psychology was his beat. He knew how to read men in crisis, knew how to listen. Clancy had always suspected something wasn't right in Cris's relationship with his father. He knew that Cris's mother had died when he was young and that his father had been an All-American end at Michigan. Beyond that, Cris had said very little. When Cris had landed at the mission, he seemed to not want to talk about his father. He always got edgy and changed the subject whenever it came up. Clancy also suspected Cris's alcoholism was caused by something more deep-rooted than the tragic death of his daughter; that Kennidi's death had been just the trigger. Clancy hesitated for a moment, then went on.

" 'Member when you wandered in and puked on my floor in the lobby? I gave you a bed, and told you we cared what happened to you. You remember what you said?"

Cris didn't respond.

"You said nobody ever wanted you, nobody cared."

"I was drunk," Cris said, but the tears were still in his eyes. He found the TV control and angrily turned down the volume, cutting off his father's glowing memories of him. The conversation continued in silence on the screen. Under his father's talking head it said:

HERO'S FATHER

Clancy pushed ahead. "Back then, you said shit like that a lot. You said, 'I don't have anyone.' 'Member that?"

Cris still didn't answer; he was looking up at the screen, where his father talked with pride.

"So if you don't got nobody, then who the fuck is that jamoke up there, bustin' a gut braggin' on you?"

"He's my . . . my . . ." and Cris stopped, then said, "He agreed to . . ." He stopped again, and it now seemed as if Cris was off somewhere else, far away.

Clancy wondered if he should take a chance and make a guess. He had learned that people in Cris's state could be shattered easily, but he also knew that periods of extreme emotional crisis were the time when people were most susceptible to suggestion, most apt to deal with their real demons.

Clancy decided to take the shot.

"Are you adopted, man? Is that what this is all about? You tryin' t'get your daddy to accept you? So you become an over-achiever, an All-American like Dad, and a Gulf hero, so he'll finally love you and take you in. Did you feel like trash all your life, a throwaway baby nobody wanted?"

There was now a mixture of anger and self-contempt on Cris's face. Then it broke, and was replaced by a look of anguish. Clancy took a deep breath and pressed on.

"Okay, so this guy up here, this hero's father, he took you home, but he made you work to earn his love. You never felt good enough."

Cris's face turned red with embarrassment. He looked over at Clancy, but didn't answer. There was a plea for help in his eyes.

"Listen, man. You know why Kennidi died?" Cris was silent, so Clancy went on. "She died because those fucks at Fort Detrick were making poison. You went over there, you brought it back, and *it* killed her. Not you. It ain't yer fault, man. She didn't die because you failed her. Her death isn't proof of your worthlessness. You had nothing to do with it. If yer dad never made you feel like you belonged, then that's *his* fault. He wasn't smart enough to see what he had, or he was too selfish to care. But I'll tell you this, Cris—it's about time to come to grips with who you really are.

Until you find out, you'll never be at rest. Don't let this moment pass, man. You might not get so close again.''

When Cris looked over at Clancy, the Black Attack could see he'd hit a bull's-eye. His wounded friend was crying.

"I ain't a psychiatrist, I'm just a broken-down middleweight who hates ta see guys layin' on street grates, but I can get you the right help. . . . For what it's worth, I love you, and I care. I always did.''

"I can't be alone," Cris croaked.

Clancy reached out, took Cris's good hand, and held it in the darkened hospital room. "Who's goin' anywhere?" the Black Attack said. "Not me, I ain't goin' nowhere."

It was two weeks later, and Stacy had still refused to see Cris. He had asked the hospital staff repeatedly, then had gotten the word back that Stacy had been moved out of the Burn Center and was now recuperating somewhere else in Washington.

Cris refused to talk to the press, which just made him more desirable to them. They had camped out in front of the hospital, then after he'd moved to a hotel a week later they were staked out there.

He made his statement to the FBI and agreed to testify before the Senate investigating committee. The TV news said that Admiral Zoll had been put under house arrest at Fort Detrick, and that Colonel Laurence Chittick had agreed to testify against him in exchange for immunity from prosecution. Wendell Kinney had committed suicide, taking an overdose of prescribed Xanax.

There were a lot of questions from Congress and the White House about the contents of the White Train and, more important, what had really been going on at Fort Detrick. The whole situation at the Devil's Workshop was beginning to unravel in the national press.

Cris made repeated trips to the hospital to get the dressings changed; he'd become very adept at dodging the press. The nine-millimeter bullet that had hit him had almost obliterated his shoulder blade, and he was told by Walter Reed specialists that he would never have full use of his right arm again. They set up a physical therapy schedule, which he had not kept up with.

The days stretched into weeks. The monotony of his convalescence was disrupted once a day by a balding psychiatrist, also a recovering alcoholic, whom Clancy had recommended. The man came and sat in a chair in his room while Cris tried to unscramble his feelings about himself, his father, and the death of his daughter. After the second week, Cris could no longer stand to hear his own repeated complaints about his childhood, which now sounded to him like whining. But he felt he at least understood what had happened to him and why he had cracked up. He thought the healing could be accomplished over time, but he needed Stacy's help, and he wanted desperately to help her. But she would not see him. In fact, she was hiding. He longed to see her, but she had disappeared.

One afternoon he called Carl Brill, the FBI agent who had sat with him for hours, taking his statements. He left a message for the agent that something else had just occurred to him.

An hour later, there was a knock on his hotel-room door and Brill was standing in the threshold. He was bull-necked, with sloping shoulders. He'd been an offensive lineman at Mississippi State before joining the FBI.

"Y'all got somethin' else ta tell us?" Brill said, his huge trapezius muscles stretching a starched collar.

"Yeah. Come on in," Cris said, and stepped aside, allowing the oversized agent to enter. They sat down and looked at each other. Cris wasn't sure how to begin.

"How's the shoulder?" Brill asked, breaking the silence.

"I won't be throwing any more long outs or deep fades," Cris said.

"So what? Them days are over," Brill said. "What's up?"

"I think . . . I remember something. I need to talk to Stacy Richardson. It's kinda something nagging at my subconscious. I think she could help me jog it loose."

"So this is basically bullshit then," Brill said, busting Cris easily.

"I need to know where she is, Carl."

"Last time I looked at my badge, 'FBI' stood for 'Federal Bureau of Investigation,' not 'Find Babes for Invalids.' "

"I need to talk to her, Carl. You took her statement. You gotta tell me where she is."

"I'm through blocking for quarterbacks," he said. "All that ever got me was bad knees and a dirty jersey."

"I don't want anything except to know where she is. C'mon, you owe me. If we hadn't stopped that train from blowing, the Hoover Building mighta been full of dead Frisbees and you'd probably be taking a dirt nap."

Carl took a deep breath and finally let it out slowly. "She's at a private hospital on Rosemont. I don't have the address on me, but you can't miss it from the Beltway. It's got five buildings with a tower in the middle. Kinda looks like a giant sculpture of a hand giving this town the finger, which makes the place a favorite of mine. She's in Room 606, under the name Laura Kendel."

"Thanks."

Carl got to his feet, moved to the door, then stopped. "Hey, Cris, you ever heard the expression 'Be careful what you wish for . . .'?"

"What's that supposed to mean?"

"She don't look too good," he said, and moved out of the room.

Cris took a cab from the hotel and instructed the driver to get on the Beltway. They drove around the huge highway that encircled the capital until he saw the building, which did indeed look like it was flipping off the town. He pointed to it and told the driver to get him there.

Cris got out of the cab, paid, and moved into the lobby of the building, skirting the desk. He moved down the sterile linoleum hallway, up the elevator to the sixth floor, finally finding the right corridor, then Room 606.

His heart was beating wildly inside his chest as he pushed the door open and entered, unannounced.

She was sitting in a large armchair by the window, wrapped in a robe, watching TV. She spun toward him as he entered.

Her face had been horribly burned, and she had been undergoing skin grafts. Her right hand looked smaller and her forearm was heavily bandaged all the way to the elbow. Her hair had all been shaved off in order to treat the burns on her head.

"Go away," she pleaded. "Go away . . . please. Please, don't look at me."

Cris moved to her and kneeled beside her.

"No, please," she said, trying to hide her face from him.

Now he had his good arm around her and was gently pulling her to him.

"No," she said.

"Stacy . . . Stacy . . . please don't." His voice was a whisper, and despite the fact that the explosion had scarred her, the mere act of holding her took away the ache that had been living inside him since they'd been separated.

"No, please go," she said, with tears in her eyes.

"Never again," he said softly. "I can't let you go. I love you," he said.

She pushed him away. "How can you love this?" she said, turning toward him.

"Because real beauty is on the inside. I know how much I loved Kennidi, and in the end, her tumors were everywhere. And still she was the most beautiful person I ever knew . . . until you. Only one thing will make me go. Look at me and tell me you don't love me."

"Please, Cris."

"Then tell me."

She looked at him with tears in her eyes, and she shook her head. "I can't," she said, "but this will never work."

"I've already had my Golden Boy life. Guess what? *It* didn't work. This is what I want. I love you. I want to make my life with you."

She was laughing and crying all at once, then he held her close.

"They say after the grafts take and the hair grows back, and the—"

"Shhhh, none of that matters. I've come a long way," he said softly. "I still have a lot to learn and a long way to go. . . . But one thing I'm sure of: This is where it all starts. I've finally found the beginning."

*Please turn the page
for an early look at*

THE TIN COLLECTORS

by Stephen J. Cannell

Coming soon in hardcover

Dear Dad:

Chooch arrived this afternoon as planned (actually, I picked him up). This is already shaping up as one of my biggest boners. I pulled up at the fancy private school Sandy's got him enrolled in and I had to go to the principal's office to sign the pickup permission slip. The principal, John St. John, is a wheezing, hollow-chested geek who seems to honestly hate Chooch. The way he put it was "That child is from the ninth circle." I had to ask, too. It's from Dante's Inferno. *Apparently, the ninth circle is the circle closest to hell. Now that I've met Chooch, not an entirely inappropriate analogy. Then, this pale erection with ears hands me a packet of teacher evaluation slips. For a fifteen-year-old, his rap sheet is impressive . . . pulled fire alarms, and fights in the school cafeteria (food as well as fists). Mr. St. John informs me that they have notified Sandy that Chooch is not to return to Harvard West-lake School next semester and that I need to get him enrolled elsewhere (like this is all of a sudden supposed to be my problem). It's not as if this boy doesn't have a good reason to be angry. I*

*think I wrote you, he's a love child with one of Sandy's old clients.
Making it worse, Sandy doesn't want him to know how she makes
her living, so she's been shipping him off to boarding schools since
third grade.*

*Needless to say, I had no idea what I was getting into here.
Maybe I can last the month until Sandy takes him back or sends
him to the next sucker on her list. One way or another I'll work
it out.*

*I'm planning to get out to Florida again sometime next year. I
was thinking you and I could rent one of those fishing boats like
we did last time, drink some beer and cook what we catch over a
beach fire. Those memories are treasures in my life.*

*I know, I know, cut the mush, blah . . . blah . . . blah. I miss you,
Dad. That's all for now.*
Love.

Your son,
Shane

S hane was in deep REM black. Way down there, but still he
heard the telephone's electronic urgency. The sound hung
over him, a vague shimmer, way above, up on the surface.
Slowly he made his way to it, breaking consciousness, washed in
confusion and anger. His bedroom was dark. The digital clock
stung his eyeballs with a neon greeting: 2:16 A.M. He found the
receiver and pressed it against his ear.

"Yeah," he said, his voice a croak and a whisper.

"Shane, he's trying to kill me," a woman hissed urgently.

"What . . . who is this?"

"It's Barbara." She was whispering, but he could also hear a
loud banging coming over the receiver on her end, as if somebody
was trying to break down a door.

"He's trying to kill you?" he repeated, buying time so his mind
could focus.

Barbara Molar. He hadn't seen her in over two months, and then just for a moment at a police department ceremony, last year's Medal of Valor Awards. Her husband, Ray, had been one of three recipients.

A crash, then: "Jesus, get over here, Shane. Please. He'll listen to you. He's nuts, worse than ever."

Shane heard another crash. Barbara started screaming. He couldn't make out her next words, then "Don't, please . . ." She was whimpering, the phone was dropped on a hard floor, clattering, bouncing, getting kicked in some desperate struggle.

"Barbara? Barbara?" She didn't answer. He heard a distant, guttural grunting like a man sometimes makes during sex, or a fight.

Shane got out of bed and started gathering up clothes. He slipped into his pants and grabbed his faded LAPD sweatshirt. He snapped up his ankle gun, hesitated for a moment, then pulled it out, chambered it, and strapped it on. He ran out of his bedroom toward the garage without even looking for his shoes. He was already behind the wheel when he realized he had forgotten that Chooch Sandoval was asleep in the other bedroom. He wasn't used to having fifteen-year-old houseguests. He knew he shouldn't leave Chooch alone. The garage door was going up as he backed out his black Acura. Grabbing for his cell phone, he dialed a number from memory. He streaked down the back alley away from his Venice, California, canal house, as cold beach air slipstreamed past the side window onto his face.

Brian "Longboard" Kelly, his boned-out next-door neighbor, picked up the phone. "Whoever this is, fuck you" was the way he came on the line.

"Sorry, Brian, it's Shane. I got called out, and Chooch is still asleep in the guest bedroom."

"Chooch? Who the hell?"

"The kid I told you I was taking for the month. Sandy's kid. He came yesterday."

"Ohhh, man . . ."

"Look, Brian, just go over and sleep on my couch. The key is in the pot by the back door."

"Good place, dickbrain. Who would ever think to look there?"

"Just do it, will ya? I'll owe ya."

"Fuckin' A." Longboard slammed the phone down in Shane's ear.

Shane was now at Washington Boulevard. He hung a left and headed the short distance to the Molar house. When they'd still been partners, he'd made this trip at least once a day to pick up Ray; then across Washington to South Venice Boulevard, through Gangbang Circle, where, once it got dark, the V Thirteens and Shoreside Crips staged their useless, life-ending street actions, occasionally killing or wounding a tourist from Minnesota by mistake.

He shot across Abbot Kinney Boulevard and turned right onto California, finally coming to Shell Avenue. All the way there, he wondered why Barbara would call him. Why not dial 911? Of course, the answer was sort of obvious after he thought about it. Even though she was scared spitless, she still didn't want another domestic-violence beef in Ray's LAPD Internal Affairs jacket. He was a thirty-year veteran with a big pension, which another DV complaint would jeopardize. That pension was an asset that was half hers.

Still, Shane Scully was the last guy Ray Molar would want to see coming through his door, quoting departmental spousal-abuse regulations at two A.M. *So why Shane? Why not Ray's current partner?* He guessed he knew that answer, too. She called him because she thought she could control him, use him for protection, then keep him from talking. Also he was handy, only five miles away. . . . Just like before, he had turned up as the double zero on her slow-turning roulette wheel.

When he got to Ray's small, wood-sided house, he pulled into the driveway behind Ray's car and jumped out. The hood was warm on the dark blue Cadillac Brougham; the lights were on in the house. Then he heard muffled screaming.

"Shit, I hate this," he mumbled softly, feeling the cold grass on his bare feet. Then he moved toward the house. He tried the front door and, to his surprise, found it was open. Reluctantly, he stepped into his ex-partner's living room.

Ray's house always seemed delicate and overdecorated. Too much French fleur-de-lis upholstery, too many knickknacks and hanging lamps. It was Barbara's doing and definitely didn't seem like the lair of a street monster like Ray Molar. Ray should live in a cave, cooking over an open fire, throwing the gnawed bones over his shoulder.

Shane could hear Barbara's screams coming from the back of the house, so he moved in that direction. He came through the bedroom door just in time to see Ray Molar hit his slender, blond wife in the solar plexus with the butt end of his black metal street baton. Then, as she doubled over, he expertly swung the nightstick sideways, catching her in the side of the head with a "two from the ring" combat move. It was a baton-fighting tactic taught to every recruit at the Police Academy. Shane stood frozen, as Barbara, her head bleeding badly, slumped to the floor, almost unconscious.

"Ray." Shane's voice, a raspy whisper, cut the temporary silence like a sickle slashing dry wheat. "What's the story here, buddy?"

Ray Molar swung around. He was at least six four and weighed over two-forty, with huge shoulders and long arms. He had bristly blond hair and a corded, muscled neck. Adding to these Blutoesque dimensions was a huge jutting jaw and almost total lack of a forehead. "Get the fuck outta here, Scully. We don't need the Boy Scouts," Molar growled, his dilated pupils round points of focused hatred.

Shane had seen that look in the street many times before and had come to fear it. "Let's just back off, slow down, and give it a rest, Ray." Shane was moving slowly toward him, not wanting any part of the fury and craziness he saw on his ex-partner but feeling compelled to get close enough to protect Barbara if he swung on her again. When Ray lost control, he could turn instantly murderous. He spewed white rage without thought, violence without reason.

"You got anything to eat?" Shane said, trying to refocus the energy in the room. "I'm starved. Missed dinner. How 'bout I get us a beer and a sandwich, something. . . . We chill out a little . . . Cool out . . . Talk it down . . . Get solid . . ."

"You wanna eat somethin'? Eat shit, Scully!" He was halfway between Shane and Barbara, still brandishing the black metal police baton.

"Ray, I don't want trouble, but you can't go hitting Barbara with the nightstick, man. You're gonna fuck her up bad."

Then Ray started toward Shane, swinging the metal stick in a lose arc in front of him. "Yeah? Who's gonna stop me, dickwad?"

"Come on, let's stay frosty here, Ray. Let's . . . let's—" And he stopped talking because he had to duck.

Ray swung the nightstick. It zipped through the air an inch from Shane's ear. As he was coming back up, Ray swung a fist, hitting him with a left hook that landed on Shane's right temple, exploding like a pipe bomb, sending him to the floor, ears ringing. Then Ray yanked a small-caliber snubby out of his waistband. It looked to Shane like an off-brand piece, a European handgun of some kind, maybe a Titan Tiger or an Arminus .38, definitely not standard police issue. Ray always kept a "throw-down gun" on him to drop by a body if some street character got funky and had to take a seat on the big sky bus.

"Put it away, Ray."

"You fucking this bitch, too? You fucking her? 'Cause if you ain't, you should get in line—everybody else is."

"Come on, Ray, that's crazy. I never touched your wife; nobody's messin' with Barb, and you know it. Why're you doin' this?"

"She's been getting snaked by half the fuckin' department." He turned back and glowered at her. "Am I right, baby? Tell him 'bout all the wall jobs you been doin' in the division garage."

Barbara groaned. Ray, turning now, aimed the gun at Shane, pulling the hammer back. Shane watched the cylinder begin to rotate on the center post as Ray applied pressure on the trigger. He was strangely mesmerized by the hole in the barrel, a dark eye of damnation, freezing his stomach, dulling his reactions. He was seconds from death. . . . Almost without realizing it, his right hand slipped down to his ankle, fingers encircling the wood-checked grip of his 9mm automatic. He slid the weapon free.

Shane dove sideways just as Ray fired. The bullet thunked into the wooden doorframe behind him. Shane was operating on instinct now, with no control over what happened next, going with it, not questioning, rolling, coming up prone, his Beretta Mini-Cougar gripped in both hands.

As Ray turned to fire again, Shane squeezed the trigger. The bullet hit Ray Molar in the middle of his simian brow.

Huge head jerking back violently.

Brainpan exploding, catching the 9mm slug. Then Ray looked directly at Shane as the gun slipped from his meaty paw and thumped onto the carpet. Ray's pig eyes, bright in that instant, registered hatred and surprise, or maybe Shane was just looking for something human in all that animal ferocity.

Then Ray Molar took one uncertain step backward and sat on the edge of the bed. Even though his heart was probably still beating, Shane knew that his ex-partner was already dead. But the street monster sat down anyway, almost as if he needed a moment to consider what he should do next or where he should go, momentum and gravity making the decision for him, toppling him forward, thudding him hard, face first, onto the carpet.

Shane looked over at Barbara, who was staring at her dead husband, her mouth agape, her puffed lip split and bleeding.

"Whatta we do now, Shane?" she finally asked.

And don't miss out on Stephen J. Cannell's previous bestselling thrillers!

THE PLAN

From one of America's most popular storytellers comes a riveting and explosive tale of a terrifyingly possible tomorrow. For twenty years, the top forces of the Mafia have secretly plotted for power, using vast amounts of untraceable cash over the whole of America. Gaining control of a major television network is only the first step.

When TV producer Ryan Bolt stumbles over the organization's plan to run their own puppet candidate for President—and win—it seems like a story that could salvage his damaged life and career. But Bolt doesn't know whom he truly serves. By the time he finds out, it may already be too late to win this ruthless and deadly power game. With one unlikely ally—the beautiful Mafia princess Lucinda—he must fight to save himself, his new love, and his country.

FINAL VICTIM

Leonard Land is a seven-foot-tall, hairless computer genius—and a psychopath. He is a twisted multipersonality maniac. He is many people wired into the cyber-subculture of Santanism and Death Metal. When he is The Rat, he is smart and cunning; when he becomes the Wind Minstrel, he is God and the Devil. The Rat only covets women; the Wind Minstrel possesses them. Leonard is smart and cunning. He is quick, brutal, and deadly. He is systematically murdering women. And he is everywhere.

Hot on Land's trail is a formidable, if unlikely, trio of heroes: John Lockwood—a renegade U.S. Customs agent who never met a rule he didn't break or a regulation he didn't violate; Karen ''Awesome'' Dawson—a beautiful and brainy forensic psychologist who never met a challenge she couldn't overcome; and Malavida Chacone, a streetwise master hacker who never met a computer program he couldn't crack. The hunt leads the three across an imperiled nation . . . and deep into the darkest corridors of cyberspace.

But there is no system the maniac cannot infiltrate, no secrets he cannot access. He knows he is being hunted, and by whom. And he is determined to strike first—in ways too terrible to anticipate.

KING CON

Raised in a world of flimflams, come-ons and con jobs, Beano Bates has done so well he's earned a reputation as the finest con man of his generation—and a spot on the FBI's Ten Most Wanted List. But his lucky streak vanishes after a card game in which he scams a cool eighty grand from a notorious Mafia don who retaliates by having Beano nearly beaten to death.

For the first time in his legendary career, Beano wants more than a big score—he wants justice. Aided by a beautiful, no-nonsense female prosecutor and a legion of crafty cousins—all accomplished grifters—Beano, the king of the cons, puts together the ultimate swindle, a well-planned sting of strategy, skill, and deception. The targets are America's most powerful mob kingpin and his psychopathic brother. In this game, winner take all!

People Magazine described this fast-paced, action-packed tale of the ultimate con as "pure fun."

RIDING THE SNAKE

Wheeler Cassidy, black sheep of a wealthy Beverly Hills family, has spent most of his life drinking, playing golf, and seducing other men's wives. The golden boy's glow is fading as he parties his way on toward dissipation. Until his brother is found dead under mysterious circumstances.

Wheeler's need to investigate sends him on a perilous journey to find the Chinese gangsters who murdered the only member of his family he ever loved. Along the way, he teams up with Tanisha Williams, a stunning African-American detective raised in Watts and now assigned to the L.A.P.D. Asian Crimes Task Force. The two make an unlikely pair as together they face the violence and corruption stretching from Hong Kong's notorious criminal Trida to the highest reaches of the American government. It's an international conspiracy of huge proportions that will take Wheeler and Tanisha halfway around the world and into the most dangerous adventure of their lives . . .